Dangerous to Know

Endorsements

From page 1, Megan Whitson Lee's novel *Dangerous to Know* captured my attention. With her true-to-their-time characters and an intriguing plot, I found myself immersed in an Austen-like world and Bronte-like suspense. Miss Lee offers readers of Regency fiction a superior read. She brings the era to life, the hallmark of an outstanding writer, in *Dangerous to Know*.

—**Rita Gerlach**, author

Lee's novel, *Dangerous to Know*, is a fascinating take on Lord and Lady Byron's tumultuous relationship. It beautifully depicts the romance of the Regency Era while simultaneously delving into the darkness and depravity that comes with living a life of facades, idolatry, and self-indulgence. Its message is timeless. *Dangerous to Know* is a must read, but fair warning; it will haunt your thoughts for days.

—**Dana Romanin**, author of *Abby's Letters*.

Dangerous to Know

Megan Whitson Lee

Elk Lake
PUBLISHING, INC.
Plymouth, Massachusetts

Cover Design: Derinda Babcock
Interior Design: Derinda Babcock
Editors: René Holt, Deb Haggerty
Published in Association with the Steve Laube Agency

PUBLISHED BY: Elk Lake Publishing, Inc., 35 Dogwood Dr., Plymouth, MA 02360
Library Cataloging Data
Names: Lee, Megan Whitson (Megan Whitson Lee)
Dangerous to Know / Megan Whitson Lee
316 p. 23cm × 15cm (9in × 6 in.)
Description: Regency novel depicting in fiction the lives of Lord and Lady Byron. True-to-their-time characters and location is a hallmark of the novel.
Identifiers: ISBN-13: 978-1-946638-80-9 (trade) | 978-1-946638-81-6 (POD) | 978-1-946638-50-2 (e-book)
Key Words: regency period, romance, love story, Byron, England.

LCCN: 2018933355 Fiction

Dedication

To my grandmothers:

To Carol—even though you will never read this novel, I know you would have loved the story. Thank you for giving me quality books as a child and always encouraging me to read.

To Grandma MaryAnn   I hope you enjoy this story. You taught me the principles lying within.

Acknowledgments

There are many people to thank going all the way back to my graduate school days, when Susan Shreve, Richard Bausch, and Beverly Lowry encouraged me to write my version of Lord Byron's story.

I am thankful to all who have helped with the formation of this novel. Many people read various versions and offered their critique and suggestions on how to make it better. Alycia Morales, Donna Sweeney, Jacqueline Patterson, Deborah Harris, and Cheryl Rice. Your input was invaluable.

To everyone at Elk Lake Publishing—many, many thanks! Thank you, Deb Haggerty, Ralene Burke, and René Holt for your skillful edits.

To my family, for always supporting me and standing with me through this quest to write tough, gritty, sometimes dark topics. You guys have always been my biggest fans and my cheerleaders.

To my husband, Stephen, for always encouraging and motivating me. You've cheered with me in my victories and grieved with me in my losses. Your support and love means the world to me.

Finally, to my Lord and Savior, Jesus Christ. I write stories about and for those who need You in their lives. Thank You for allowing me the honor to serve You.

PART I

One

March 1812

"Don't look at him, dear. He's dangerous."

Isabella Bankmill glanced at Aunt Lydia before turning her gaze once more toward the subject of the older woman's warning. She had yet to have a proper look. The grand salon of Holand House was a whirling kaleidoscope of moving bodies. Ladies, arms encased past their elbows in white gloves, dressed in elegant billowing gowns, whirled with their partners as they moved through the paces of the waltz. The man in question was shielded from her view by the forty or more guests standing around the fringes of the dance floor—at least half of them clustered around the man himself.

"Pray tell, how is he dangerous, Aunt Lydia?"

Underneath the curls so carefully arranged against her forehead, Aunt Lydia's brow arched with impertinence. "I have read his poem."

"Do you mean 'Heralds of the Morning?' Oh, yes. I have only begun reading the poem, but I find his words quite illuminate a certain romantic way of thinking. Did you not enjoy the work, Aunt?"

Aunt Lydia's furrowed brow and pursed lips made apparent she did not. "The poem is a shocking journey through foreign lands—all too free thinking and questioning of moral decency. Why, one would think the poem was not written by an Englishman at all." Extending her fan, she fluttered it back and forth in front of her face as though she might faint at any moment. Small gusts brushed against Isabella's cheeks. "Have nothing to do with him. Your mother and father did not send you to London to fall under the spell of Lord Gregory Gordon Bromby."

Isabella tilted her head back and took in the high, domed ceiling with its gilded inlays and painted frescoes of cherubs and lovers. She had spent time in many ballrooms and salons during the last two seasons, but none quite as fine as this.

Finally, the waltz ended, and the crowds cleared just enough to allow Isabella a fleeting glimpse of the man, still surrounded by a flock of admirers. From her vantage point, he appeared harmless enough. The rumors about his good looks were true. He possessed a pleasing, youthful face as pale as the moon, framed by curling locks the color of a raven's feathers, and his large eyes seemed to penetrate the distance between them.

When Lord Bromby stood, his significant height became apparent, but his movements were slightly impaired by a limp—a defect of birth, she had been told. As to his character ... Of course, she could not make out his character from a few glances across a London morning room, but she'd heard the gossip about the throngs of women who hung upon him like clothing—a byproduct of his unrivaled talent.

Although this was not her first season, when amid a ballroom full of beautiful and eligible young girls, Isabella still felt a little out of her element. A country girl from Durham come to London.

"You'll find many fine prospects at the ball tomorrow evening. I doubt there is anyone worthy of tempting you here this morning," said Aunt Lydia.

Prospects or no prospects, the morning party was a welcome diversion. London offered a nonstop carousel of activities, parties, and balls—so many in fact, she had little time to read her favored books. She had, however, managed to begin reading Lord Bromby's acclaimed poem. Who was not reading the work? The poem had been an overnight sensation in its first printing and had sold out in three days. All five-hundred copies.

"Did you really find his poem offensive?" Isabella was eager to return to their original subject.

"Yes, indeed. I do not wish to pollute my mind with such trifles in the future."

Isabella laughed. "But his poem is the only thing anyone is talking about. That and the man himself."

Aunt Lydia placed her hand on her niece's forearm, tugging her to the side so as not to be heard by the other guests. "I would much prefer to talk about more important matters. And as for reading, my mind is more suitably engaged while reading from the Bible. Or if I must read poetry, I'll stick with the Shakespearean sonnets."

After an announcement, the crowd began to move from the grand salon into a rear drawing room where refreshments were served. Isabella and Aunt Lydia walked with them to take their assigned places at the tables.

As they walked, Aunt Lydia began in a low voice, "My dear, perhaps you may be able to talk some sense into your cousin's wife while you're here. Someone should apply the reins to her."

Isabella raised her chin to look over her shoulder and across the room where her cousin's wife, Lady Catherine Lyons, sat all too close to Lord Bromby, monopolizing every moment with him. The poet was surrounded by young women, some of them married, some of them single and hopeful, but none of them held vigil like Catherine. She appeared mesmerized by his every word and added at least twenty of her own for each of his.

Isabella compared her own appearance with that of her cousin-in-law. Lady Catherine was petite and impish with hair the color of gold silk, which she wore short and draped with various hair pieces and turbans. *If that is the sort of woman he wants, I shall never measure up.*

She pulled at a strand of her brown hair and tucked it behind her ear. *Plain but pleasant to look at. But I am no Lady Catherine.*

"That is shocking behavior." Aunt Lydia clucked. "Shameful. She does not even attempt to disguise her flirtations. She will be all the talk of the *town* tomorrow."

"She only married my cousin seven years ago," Isabella remarked.

"Yes, and poor Walter," Aunt Lydia sighed. "But he was warned. And with seven years more life experience than Catherine, he should have known better. There was talk of her propensity toward mad antics and histrionic tantrums even then."

Isabella had heard their marriage was fraught with tension and dramatic quarrels from the very beginning. Catherine was a wild, impetuous, and unbridled character with little regard for propriety or societal expectations, and her dear, gentle cousin suffered for his choice.

"Do you know," Aunt Lydia continued in whispered tones, "just last month she actually sent Lord Bromby a letter telling him she was desperate to meet him. She didn't sign her name, but everyone knew the missive was from her. She had harassed him with ridiculous letters about his poetry before. He recognized her handwriting, of course, and wasted no time in announcing to everyone that Lady Catherine Lyons had been writing to him." She continued gossiping as they took their places.

As Bromby stepped into the drawing rooms, Lady Catherine came with him, still clinging. Not staring was difficult. Although many of the ladies and gentlemen now seated around him consumed their food, Bromby did not eat and neither did Catherine. She continued to sit close to him, her mouth moving all the while, going so far as to touch Lord Bromby's hand. Isabella turned her gaze away.

Aunt Lydia grasped her arm. "Do you see? Oh, do you see? Shocking."

Isabella nodded, her heart racing. "Yes, I do see, Aunt Lydia." She attempted to turn her attention back to her plate and the conversation at their table between Mr. Scott and Lord Peterson, who animatedly debated the frame-breaking bill.

"I beg your pardon, Mr. Scott, we simply cannot allow unbridled rioting in the streets. There must be order. Cooler heads must prevail." Lord Peterson, a grand figure of a middle-aged man, tall of stature with thick, silver hair, lifted a thin slice of meat from his plate and rolled it into a tubular configuration before popping the entire piece into his mouth.

"But the stocking weavers' very livelihoods are being threatened. What would you have them do?"

Lord Peterson finished chewing before he responded. "I would not have them destroy perfectly good pieces of equipment. Vandalism is never the answer. Neither is rioting."

"I am afraid I do not understand," said Aunt Lydia, attempting to enter the conversation. "Who are these rioters? And what are they protesting?"

"They are fabric weavers from Nottingham, Lady Liddens," said Mr. Scott. "Because of the creation of large, mechanical frames that hold many bolts of fabric at once, the workers themselves are being made redundant."

"Oh, I see." Aunt Lydia sat back in her chair.

Bored with the conversation, Isabella couldn't help but admire the artistry of the painted chairs in which they sat. Painted chairs were all the fashion these days. Her attention to the conversation was minimal as she examined the perfectly straight painted lines and dots upon the chairs' legs and back. She was drawn to symmetry in all things.

"Technology, and the furtherance of it, is inevitable," said Lord Peterson flatly. "And these people are destroying property that does not belong to them. A huge problem in these industrial places—weavers breaking and smashing machines, thinking that will somehow solve their problem. Disgraceful."

"And what would this bill propose?" Aunt Lydia dabbed at the corners of her mouth.

"It would make destruction of the equipment illegal—as it should be."

"It would make it a capital offense. Punishable by death," said Mr. Scott soberly.

"That does seem harsh," said Aunt Lydia. "Two wrongs do not a right make."

Mr. Scott nodded in the direction of Lord Bromby. "The poet over there—just last month he gave a fair speech in the House of Lords in opposition of the bill. Reminded the members that these people are starving, their livelihoods being stolen from them."

Lord Bromby was interested in such things? Isabella, immediately intrigued, turned her attention from chairs to conversation. She had imagined he was a man concerned with no one other than himself—certainly not philanthropically inclined.

"Another bleeding heart." Lord Peterson swirled the drink in his glass.

Mr. Scott continued. "Lord Bromby stated there should be a better way of handling the situation. 'Will we sacrifice the men of our nation to mechanization?' said he. A good point, indeed. He said that these unemployed workers are an injured lot, much in need of leniency and understanding rather than hanging. It was a well-intentioned speech, meant for the good of the nation, I felt. No matter what they may say about him, or how eccentric the man might be, I think him a very fine individual with a heart for the human condition, not just full of pretty words."

Isabella pondered the conflicting accounts regarding Lord Bromby. She and her aunt sat several tables away from him and his entourage—where women and men alike leaned in to hear his every word. And even as she was ashamed at her own contribution to the voyeurism, she could not tear her eyes away. Indeed, Lord Bromby was very handsome. She decided she had to finesse an introduction to the compelling Lord Bromby despite her aunt's warnings.

Two

David Beringer's heart broke into pieces.

Kneeling on a powder-blue Axminster carpet in the overheated and stuffy drawing room of the Robertson's Mayfair home, he wasn't sure he'd heard Amelia correctly. Had she just rejected his marriage proposal?

He looked up into her steel-blue eyes.

She shook her head again. "I'm afraid I cannot accept."

David stood, his face downcast and burning with embarrassment. He hoped for mistaken hearing or her explanation as his gaze traced the billowing and frenetic pattern of the designs on the carpet beneath his feet.

"We are friends, Mr. Beringer. I care very much for you as I might my own brother. But I do not love you ... not in *that* way. You are too ... well, you are too affable, too kind, and far too steady for my tastes."

"I see."

How had he missed such differences between them? When he had made the decision to ask for Miss Amelia Robertson's hand in marriage, he'd had every confidence his proposal would be acceptable.

"We have known each other a long time," she said. "We used to play together as children, did we not?"

"Yes."

"And I have always esteemed you, Mr. Beringer, and I'm sorry to be the cause of pain to anyone ... but I cannot marry you. I shall marry a more adventurous man. A poet or a painter. Someone of noble birth who also possesses the desire for artistic pursuits. It is not that I do not like you, it is only that we are too dissimilar."

David frowned in puzzlement. In all the years he had known Amelia Robertson, he had never been aware of her interest in art and poetry. Had something changed? Perhaps he had not asked her enough questions. Certainly, he had misread her regard for him.

He did not wish to draw out this painful encounter. "I wish you good morning, Miss Robertson. I regret I am not the man you seek. I wish you well." As he exited the room, he caught a glimpse of a book sitting on the gilded table by the door. "Heralds of the Morning." He recognized the title, but he could not be sure from where. More evidence of his ignorance of the literary world. Although his parents were lovers of poetry, he was not. He much preferred to read history books or doctrinal writings.

Lifting first one, then the other leaden foot, David climbed into the carriage. "Drive on," he called out to the driver before collapsing against the seat. *If I were a man of a more indulgent nature, I could drown my sorrows in a strong drink.* He rarely took spirits of any kind—the occasional glass of port on social occasions, a spot of wine for medicinal purposes. But no, I must bear the full weight of this sorrow.

Just an hour ago, my heart was pounding and my palms were damp with anticipation. Surely Amelia's answer would be, "Yes! I will marry you!"

Amelia's rejection echoed in his mind along with the staccato beat of the carriage horses' hooves upon the cobblestones. *You are far too steady for my tastes. Steady. Steady. Steady.* She'd spoken the word as though being steady were a moral failing. As a gentleman in society, David tried to be a solid person—someone who did not invite ridicule or undue scrutiny. He liked to think he lived by God's leading. *Am I too staid? Dull, even?*

As the carriage slowed for a corner, they passed a group of people standing around an attractive man dressed in green coat and trousers, an impeccably tied cravat at his neck. His wavy, black hair w*as long and wild. That's Lord Bromby. The poet everyone is talking about.*

Bromby's passionate and unconventional poetry had set a new standard for London's literary world. His good looks and exotic tales of his travels abroad caused women to swoon. Even so, David perceived a darkness about him that extended beyond his black hair and smoldering eyes, although he could not pinpoint the derivation.

One thing was clear: *this* was the sort of man all the women in society desired. Including his Amelia.

Three

Isabella had planned only to indulge in a few pages of Lord Bromby's epic poem the next morning while her aunt visited a sick friend. Aunt Lydia stayed away longer than expected, and by midmorning, she was reading through the poem a second time.

Should she be reading these words at all? Her face heated at some of the inappropriate suggestions within, but at the same time, she could scarce move her eyes from the page. Could any of the unchivalrous antics described in the poem reflect the poet himself? Surely not. Lord Bromby's forehead had been too noble, his eyes too full of intelligence and potential for goodness.

The speaker in the poem confessed to an ungodliness, having given himself over to evil and wicked practices. Lord Bromby was most certainly a gentleman, not capable of such misconduct.

"Mr. David Beringer and his sister, Miss Rebecca Beringer."

Isabella jumped at the servant's announcement of arriving visitors, and the quarto fell to the ground, its pages splayed fold-side up. Grabbing the pamphlet, she stuffed it under a pillow and quickly smoothed her hair. Who were Mr. and Miss Beringer? She felt unsettled and anxious about receiving visitors with whom she was not acquainted. Especially when her aunt was not at home.

Patting down the front of her skirt, Isabella stood with the morning sun at her back, assuming her best pose as she awaited the approaching guests. Their laughter echoed in the hallway.

A young man and woman entered the drawing room, their faces shining with the flush of the cool, early spring. They were both young. The lady was most likely no older than Isabella, but a little taller with curly, reddish-brown hair and a pretty face. The man was tall and well-formed with clear blue eyes and light brown hair that looked as though it might go blond in the summer.

"Do pardon us, Miss Bankmill. I hope we are not intruding," said the young man. "We were in the neighborhood and took the liberty of calling upon you."

"We are acquainted with your aunt," said the lady a little breathlessly, "Lady Melwood."

"You are not intruding. I am at home alone this morning and was just reading." Isabella motioned to the peach-colored settee behind her. "Won't you sit down?"

David and Rebecca Beringer situated themselves on the settee, smiles affixed to their faces. Isabella lowered herself onto an armchair covered in the same peach fabric.

Rebecca began, her bright blue eyes shining. "Your aunt has told us so much about you."

"Has she?" Isabella laughed. "I cannot imagine what she has told you. Lady Melwood is my mother's sister, but I've spent very little time in her company."

"Yes. She speaks very highly of you," David said. "She says you are an intellectual—quite the mathematician."

Isabella's cheeks heated at their compliments. "Well. I wouldn't wish you to have any grand expectations about my intellectual abilities. I'm exceedingly flattered at my aunt's praise, but I can assure you I am average at best."

Rebecca smiled. "She also says you are a skilled equestrian."

Isabella covered the smirk spreading over her lips with the tips of her fingers. "My aunt has been overly generous, I'm afraid. But I won't deny I am a fairly accomplished rider. I adore horses." She glanced at David, meeting his gaze. She liked the look of him. Despite the droop and sadness of his eyes, his nose was perfectly straight—an asset to the face of any man.

She suspected her slight attraction to a man she had known less than five minutes had something to do with the fact that this was her second season. Time to find a suitable husband grew short. All eligible men were in the running—at least until she found fault with them.

"Miss Bankmill," Mr. Beringer cut in, "My father and mother, Lord and Lady Beringer, are also friends of Lady Melwood's. The purpose of our visit this morning is to make your acquaintance prior to tonight's ball. Rebecca and I are both attending. We thought you might wish to have a few more acquaintances at your disposal."

"Yes," Rebecca added. "We know how daunting London society can be for those newly introduced to it."

A surge of excitement flowed through Isabella. David would be at the ball. And now that he had formally made her acquaintance, he could, if he so desired, ask her for a dance. "Thank you both so very much. This is my second season in London, and I have been made to feel at home here—and even more so now."

"It is my first season," said Rebecca.

"How are you finding it?" asked Isabella.

"A bit daunting. I am not sure I'm suited for the rush of parties and balls every night. I think I am suited for a quieter life."

"That is certainly what I am used to," said Isabella. "My family lives in Seaham, in the county of Durham. A small village and nothing at all like London."

Mr. and Miss Beringer smiled simultaneously. Mr. Beringer spoke. "Our family lives in Mayfair, but we also have a country home in Kent, and that is where Rebecca and I prefer to spend our time, do we not?"

"Yes, indeed. There we ride horses and walk the open land all day long."

"It sounds wonderful."

Mr. Beringer stood. "We will take our leave of you now, Miss Bankmill. And I hope I may be so bold as to ask for a place on your dance card."

Exactly as she had hoped. "Yes, sir. Of course, you may."

From the window, Isabella watched the brother and sister depart in their carriage. Yes, indeed. She liked the brother and sister pair very much.

And I shall dance with Mr. Beringer at the ball.

———————⟨✵⟩———————

Isabella had never attended one of her Aunt Ophelia's balls before, but from the moment she arrived at Melwood House, located in the most illustrious part of Mayfair, she was completely swept away by the decorations, the food, and the home's grandeur. Every table was strewn with lush, floral bouquets in muted shades of rose and cream. *And I thought Holland House had the most beautiful ballroom I'd ever seen.* Ladies in all their finery twirled about the floor, their silk and sateen gowns swishing around them as they circled and moved in tandem with the gentlemen.

Isabella had worn one of the many new gowns she'd purchased for this season, a light rose-colored frock. Her Aunt Lydia, moving in a dignified, matronly pace beside her, wore a blue one. They were received by Lady Melwood herself, who met them in the hallway just outside the ballroom.

"Thank you for inviting us, Aunt." Isabella curtsied to the tall, slender woman with the impressive face and form. Lady Ophelia Melwood was one of the most well-known women in all of London and not wholly because of her positive attributes.

"It is a pleasure to see you both." Lady Melwood nodded to Aunt Lydia.

Isabella scanned the ballroom, immediately drawn to an alcove just off the main dance floor, an area covered with fog-like shadows, untouched by the direct light. There were the figures of Catherine and Lord Bromby. Her cousin had already claimed a spot by him. Determined not to spend her evening staring, Isabella turned away.

"Are you enjoying your season, Isabella?" Lady Melwood asked.

She smiled. "Yes. There are many more dances and parties than last season."

"Well, let this one be your last. There are plenty of eligible young men to choose from. The Duke of Welford is in attendance this evening, along with Lord Hartley. Lord Hartley has just returned from India, and he's full of wonderful stories. Oh, and Mr. George Eden is in attendance tonight."

"Mr. Eden. He has a seat in Parliament, does he not?" Aunt Lydia's eyes widened with interest.

Lady Melwood smiled, probably plotting a match. A woman of a certain age—at least sixty—she was known to London Society as "The Spider" for her tendencies to lie in wait for an opportunity to influence, scheme, or control either a family member or those she held in her far-reaching sphere of power. "He does, indeed. He is a well-respected member of the Whig Party, and his father, Sir William Eden, is the first baron of Auckland."

"Fascinating." Aunt Lydia cast her gaze intently upon Isabella's face, no doubt searching for signs of interest in this news.

Perhaps this was a good time to proclaim the qualities she often rehearsed in her mind. "To find a husband who is committed to all that is good, moral, and true—someone devout in his faith—that is my most fervent desire," said Isabella resolutely. "I seek a companion, a confidant, a man with whom I may have long and interesting conversations about religion, politics, and all things mathematical and literary. A calm and benevolent spirit is most important."

"And have you come across such a person?" Lady Melwood laughed.

"I have found parts of the whole in many men, but I am still searching for the man who carries all of the qualities within one body."

"It is a tall order." Lady Melwood's tone almost sounded like a scold. "Perhaps you must settle for one of these virtues. A man possessing all of them is a rarity, indeed."

"With God, all things are possible." Isabella did not think her requirements were too much to ask. A marriage was forever, after all. If she did not show discrimination in this—the most important decision of her life—she would prove her character to be reckless and imprudent.

Lady Melwood scanned the crowds, changing the subject. "You may have heard that Lord Bromby is in attendance as well." She glanced toward the alcove. "Although he has refused to dance."

"He has a foot defect, I understand." Isabella was curious to know more about this deformity. It added a sort of mystery to him.

Lady Melwood's mouth twisted. "Yes. A clubbed foot. A pity. He is a fascinating man. Have you been introduced?"

Isabella shook her head. The thought of meeting him made her palms perspire.

"You must meet him. He's a bit eccentric, to be sure—he eats practically nothing, prefers the skeletal physique. Apparently, his mother was obese, and he was a plump child. So, he errs on the side of vanity, I fear—but his talent, his genius, soothes that flaw somewhat."

Despite her attempts not to stare, Isabella's gaze returned to the darkened alcove and scene of her cousin and the poet.

"Perhaps you might ask your cousin for an introduction," Lady Melwood suggested, a wry expression flattening her mouth. "He brought her a rose one day, and she has been a devoted follower ever since." She arched her left eyebrow and allowed what seemed to be a long and intentional conversational pause before continuing. "I trust you ladies will enjoy yourselves this evening." Lady Melwood departed at the curtsies of Isabella and Aunt Lydia.

"Well! What do you make of that?" Aunt Lydia whispered. "Even Lady Melwood is aware of her daughter-in-law's dalliance. I have heard Lady Melwood herself was rumored to have once been a mistress of the Prince of Wales."

Isabella waved away Aunt Lydia's gossip. "I do not know, Aunt. But I'll prefer not to think of my mother's sister in such an unpleasant light."

Aunt Lydia went on, unfazed. "Well, regardless of whether it's true or not, one would be hard pressed to find a person in London who would decline an invitation to her dinners and balls. You know she entertains some of the most interesting people in Whig society. Poets, actors, politicians, and princes alike have been guests here."

"Yes, so I've heard."

Eager to distract her from further gossip, Isabella grasped her aunt's arm and stepped forward into the ballroom.

I will only look at him once more. I shan't stare all night.

In the alcove, Catherine sat close to Lord Bromby, her mouth moving, and her eyes riveted upon him as he swilled his wine and reclined on his chair, looking out over the sea of people with an expression of barely veiled boredom. For a fleeting moment, his bright eyes gazed upon Isabella, and at the sharp thump of her heart, she promptly looked away.

"Miss Bankmill." Isabella's drift interrupted, she snapped to attention and turned toward the voice of David Beringer. Her heart fluttered a little. David bowed , and she curtsied.

They stood side-by-side for a few moments, staring out on the ballroom laden with deep, rich hues of red, gold, and green. It was as though they were inside a French palace awaiting the arrival of an emperor. The marble columns flanking the sides of the room were the largest Isabella had ever seen, and the oil paintings that lined the walls were some of the finest.

Behind her, two ladies spoke of Lord Bromby, praising his poetry reading from the night before and referencing the sonorous and lilting tones of his voice.

"You know his mother's family was Scottish," one of them tittered. "From Aberdeen."

"Yes, and his father was that mad man who ran off with some baroness. He was drowned at sea, I believe."

"But he is very handsome, don't you think?"

Mr. Beringer finally spoke, interrupting her eavesdropping. "How long are you in town, Miss Bankmill? Will you stay until the end of the season?"

"Yes, sir. I believe so. I hope so. Unless my parents need me urgently, of course. I am their only child, and if they were to call me home to Seaham, I should return at once."

"Naturally, of course." He turned to her. "I was in the north just last month on some business with my father. We often stop in to see a lumber dealer in York."

"Oh? Is your family involved with the lumber industry?"

"No, not at all. But we hold a keen interest in doing what we can to help the local parishes with orphan care. Often that involves building for such purposes."

"How wonderful. That is a noble undertaking, Mr. Beringer. There are so many orphans in need."

He colored, seemingly embarrassed by her compliments. Humble as well as handsome. "There are. We do what we can. What do you do when you are at home in Durham, Miss Bankmill?"

Isabella smiled. "Well, I am passionate about mathematics. And as you know, I adore horses, so I spend much time riding."

"Yes, I remember you speaking of that this morning. Well, how fortunate we should both treasure that activity."

"Yes, I love a fast ride on an open meadow."

"Well, we have plenty of open meadows at Holly Bridge. My sister and I spend hours riding through them, jumping old fences and streams. There's no other feeling." He smiled, revealing fine, straight, white teeth. Isabella was particular about teeth. She took great pains to clean and care for hers.

A shrill cackle from the other side of the room turned Isabella's head. Lady Catherine rocked with laughter at something Lord Bromby had said.

The musical strains of violins marked the beginning of the next song, and dancers began to gather on the floor.

"Miss Bankmill, if you are not engaged, may I ask for this dance?"

Isabella nodded, anticipation swelling within her chest. "Yes, of course."

Mr. Beringer gently took her hand in his and led her to join a dozen other couples. As the dance commenced, Isabella moved through the skipping steps without fault, grasping hands with alternating gentlemen partners as they circulated down the line and then moved back into formation to kick out their feet in a shuffle.

"Auretti's Dutch Skipper" was a lively dance affording her little time to speak with Mr. Beringer. When there was a second for them to converse, Isabella inquired, "Is Miss Beringer here tonight? I have not seen her."

"Yes. She is currently speaking with Sir Malcolm Meade and his party, I believe. But I know she is anxious to converse with you again."

Their conversation was temporarily halted as they wove their way in and out of the other couples, finally joining up again some minutes later.

"I very much enjoyed meeting your sister," Isabella continued.

Mr. Beringer smiled. "Thank you. She said the same about you."

Isabella smiled a little as they parted again. Perhaps she was thinking too far ahead, but she could imagine Rebecca as her sister-in-law.

David Beringer was a fine dancer. She scrutinized his well-executed turns and graceful movements. Once, she had been paired with a man who had no grace, no musical sway, and his clunky, awkward movements embarrassed her and other attendees around them. It was wrong, of course, to judge a man on his ability to dance, but the effort a man used in his dancing mirrored the effort with which he pursued the important things in life. After all, pursuing a wife should be taken seriously and an ability to dance was part of that pursuit. Both should be undertaken in an enthusiastic manner.

As the music drew to a close, the dancers returned to their respective lines and bowed to their partners. The final note of the song ended with a prolonged strain of the violin. Mr. Beringer bowed and smiled, his bright eyes still dancing. Isabella curtsied to him. He took her hand and led her off to the side of the dance floor, allowing them time to catch their breaths.

"Will they have the waltz, do you think?" he asked, a little out of breath. I hear it has begun to appear in private ballrooms all over the country, even though it's still strictly banned in many other places in Europe."

The ban was due to the close physical contact required by the dance figures. Isabella's face grew hot. "Even so, it is becoming quite fashionable in London," David continued.

"I understand it is nearly the only thing they dance at Almack's,"

"Have you been to Almack's?" he asked.

"I have not. But I should be pleased to go. I hear it is diverting. Have you attended, Mr. Beringer?"

He shook his head. "Oh, no. Not at all my scene, I assure you. I understand Lord Bromby detests the waltz. Finds it scandalous."

"Indeed?" To think the poet should find anything scandalous surprised her.

"What do you make of Lord Bromby?" Mr. Beringer glanced in the poet's direction.

"I know not what to make of him. I have not met him."

"You have not been introduced?"

"No."

He arched an eyebrow. "He is a member of my club. I see him nearly every week. I thought everyone in London Society—especially every female—had been introduced to the enigmatical Lord Bromby."

Isabella laughed. "Well, not I. Nor do I have any special interest in the introduction." That wasn't entirely true, but at least while she was in David Beringer's pleasant company, her curiosity in Lord Bromby was not as strong.

He grinned. "Then you are singular, indeed, Miss Bankmill."

Did his smile indicate some pleasure at her indifference? "I marvel at everyone's obsession with Lord Bromby."

"He is a poet—always a draw. He is intelligent, cold, and aloof enough to create mystery about his person, and his face is pleasing."

"I suppose he is attractive enough, but does that warrant such fawning over him?"

Mr. Beringer stared down at her. "Come. I shall introduce you."

The prospect of meeting Lord Bromby brought on an attack of nerves. But why? She would not be one of his admirers—his *worshippers* more like. Her insides tensed. "Oh, no. Truly. It is not necessary, I assure you." But Mr. Beringer was already moving in that direction, and she had no choice but to follow him. Involuntarily, Isabella's eyes traveled to the alcove. "It matters little to me. I see no reason to worship at his shrine."

Mr. Beringer laughed heartily. "What an excellent comparison, Miss Bankmill."

"Only God deserves such attentions. Anyway, I believe Lord Bromby has plenty of admiration and does not need mine."

"Your heart is in the right. I am glad to hear you say this."

Isabella's face grew hot as they approached the man, and she fisted her gloved hands.

Lady Catherine Lyons looked up from her vigil by Lord Bromby's side. "Isabella!" she exclaimed, holding out her hand to her cousin. "Have you met Lord Bromby?"

Lord Bromby turned his gaze upon her slowly, purposefully. Isabella detested the involuntary stomach lurch and contracted muscles under her shift as she peered into his dark green eyes.

Mr. Beringer's voice sounded faraway as he spoke the introduction. "Lord Bromby, may I present Miss Isabella Bankmill."

Lord Bromby stood and bowed.

Mr. Beringer continued. "Miss Bankmill is the niece of Lady Melwood."

"It is a pleasure, Miss Bankmill." His voice was deep and resonant. "Your aunt is one of my favorite people in the world. She has shown immense kindness and generosity toward me."

"I am glad to hear it, Lord Bromby."

Yes, up close, he was extraordinarily handsome. But not in the way to which she was accustomed. Even now, handsome men were all around her—including Mr. Beringer. But these men all looked the same—they wore their stability and respectability as they wore their clothing—just so, just as expectations dictated. Lord Bromby wore his with the top button undone that might have been considered an oversight were it not for his wild, unruly black hair. As a writer and a poet, however, Lord Bromby could pass in society even with these foibles.

He arched a well-formed black eyebrow. "If there were but fewer years between us, then perhaps Lady Melwood and I might make an excellent match."

Everyone standing around him laughed loudly at his remark. Lady Catherine was the loudest of them all. "What nonsense!"

Lord Bromby smiled. "And why not, dear Lady Catherine? Your mother-in-law is extraordinary."

"She's an outright thorn!" Catherine exclaimed. "She's the most diabolical person. I tell you, if she had the chance, she'd have me murdered in my sleep. And she'd do it with such successful secretiveness that no one would suspect it was her. For that matter, they'd probably never discover my body."

"Surely you jest, Lady Catherine," said David Beringer. "Your mother-in-law seems a most generous person."

"You are correct in that assessment, Mr. Beringer." Lord Bromby smiled. "With her I can be completely honest, and there are precious few others to whom I may tell all my secrets."

"Oh, speak of the devil herself," Catherine said in a whispery hiss. "Here comes the thorn now." She backed away as though she thought to hide behind Lord Bromby.

With purpose and precision, Lady Melwood moved toward their gathering, her gaze fixed upon Catherine. Her approaching presence pierced the conversation, and her words were sharp and to the point. "Please excuse me. Catherine, Walter is looking for you." She reached out and grasped Catherine's arm, forcibly pulling her away as Catherine cast longing glances over her shoulder at Lord Bromby.

Once she was gone, Lord Bromby stepped closer to Isabella. Too close. Perspiration was beginning to form underneath her shift. She stepped back a little.

"From where do you hail, Miss Bankmill?"

"I am stopping with my aunt, Lady Liddens, but I live in Seaham— in Durham."

Bromby nodded, an amused and interested smile tugging at his lips. "Durham. Lovely place. I've visited there myself."

"Have you?"

"Yes, about a year ago on my way up to Scotland. I wrote part of Heralds of the Morning there, in fact."

"I have read your poem."

"Oh? And how did you find it?"

"I found it quite compelling. But … is it … did you write about your own experiences?"

Lord Bromby's gaze was steady. "There are some elements of my life experience contained within, but I would like to think Master Harry bears little resemblance to me."

"Do you mean you believe in a heaven and a hell, whereas he does not?" Isabella leaned forward to hear his answer as strains of the next dance began.

Lord Bromby took his time in responding, his eyes turned toward the ceiling as he considered. "It is difficult for me to allow for any world which supposedly follows death, Miss Bankmill. Have we not enough trouble in this life without having to begin thinking about another one?"

She stifled a gasp. Surely, he did not really believe his words.

"But you believe in God, Lord Bromby?" asked David Beringer, his brow wrinkled.

He sighed. "Of course. But God does not believe in me, you see … for I am a Bromby, and therefore, cursed."

Cursed? What on earth could he mean by that?

The strains of a lively tune cut through her thoughts, and David Beringer turned suddenly to her. "Miss Bankmill, would you honor me with another dance?"

She was both relieved and disappointed to have her conversation with Lord Bromby cut short. She curtsied to him and moved away.

David led her toward the floor where couples prepared to dance a reel. This would have to be her last dance of the evening with Mr. Beringer. Two dances were all she could afford with one man. Otherwise people would begin to talk. They would think she was pledged to him. And she had not set her cap for him yet. Not when there were other interesting men to consider.

As they lined up alongside the other couples, Lord Bromby's perplexing words regarding his cursed state returned to her. She glanced over her shoulder where he now engaged in a serious discussion with another gentleman.

Perhaps Lord Bromby needed only to be informed of God's great love and mercy. And perhaps she would have the opportunity to be the bearer of this wonderful news.

Four

"You must despise me, cousin. You have been in London for over a week and I've not come to call until today." Catherine's dark eyes flashed with impishness.

Isabella and Lady Catherine sat opposite one another in Lady Liddens' drawing room. Isabella tried not to stare at her cousin's attire—a blue silk pageboy's outfit. It was an odd idiosyncrasy of Catherine's that she wore what she pleased without any thought for propriety or season. She was known to dress in flamboyant costumes and even clothing inappropriate for her class.

"Indeed, I do not despise you, Cousin. I know you have been otherwise engaged."

Catherine rested her bare hands upon her breeches. "And have you yet heard from your parents? They must miss you frightfully."

"I believe they do." Isabella smiled, thinking of her mother and father alone in Seaham. As their only child, and considered a miracle at that, her parents doted on her. "And Walter looked well enough when I saw him four days ago."

Catherine's face drooped at the mention of her husband. "He is well enough, I suppose. We fight with the most ferocious intensity. He bellows, I throw a teacup or two at him—or perhaps a fire iron—and then, we both settle in for a game of spillikins."

There had been plenty of talk about Catherine's temper tantrums over the years. Apparently, on one occasion, doctors had to be called in to sedate her wild state.

"I do hope to see little Gus while I'm in town," said Isabella.

"You shall. He's such a happy boy. Poor Gus. Much of his time is spent above stairs with his governess. As you know, my mother-in-law cannot bear that he be exposed to polite society," she sneered. "He does not speak much, and sometimes he is given to fits, but ... well, he draws and paints all day long. Beautiful, colorful paintings." Randomly, Catherine ran her hand over the surface of the table positioned at her side. Did she admire the wood or was she checking for dust?

"What does he paint?"

"Mostly shapes—ellipses, quadrangles, that sort of thing. You of all people would appreciate his art, Isabella. You with your love of mathematics and geometry."

Isabella smiled. Catherine's devotion to her son was endearing. "I'm sure I should like his drawings no matter the case. I love art of all kinds."

Catherine's gaze roamed over the walls, the paintings. "Your aunt must have little regard for art. There is so little life or passion in these paintings. Flowers, a bowl of fruit. Very dull. Lord Bromby says he will not allow any painting to hang upon his wall that does not tell a story or elicit an emotion." Catherine's eyes sparkled. "What did you think of Lord Bromby?"

Isabella remembered his wide, green eyes—like moss just under the surface of the ocean waters. "Our meeting was so brief. We hardly spoke fifteen words to one another."

"Have you read his poem?" Catherine asked. "Oh, but I believe I asked you that the other night and you said you had."

"I have."

"Is it not delicious? I have read it three times. Is it not the most passionate, most brilliant masterpiece you've ever read?" Catherine's voice spilled over with admiration.

Isabella restrained her response. "Yes. Well, it was certainly not a dull or conventional read." Catherine mustn't know how many times she had read his poem.

Catherine's dark eyes were like those of a school girl's, cast heavenward, swimming in ecstatic pools of emotion. "Once I had read his words, I knew I must become acquainted with him. I'd no idea at all what his appearance would be, but even if he were as ugly as an ogre, I longed to meet him."

Isabella stared at her. She had never seen her cousin-in-law so overwrought. "Good heavens. You speak of his poetry as though it were Holy Scripture."

"Oh, but it is like that to me."

Isabella cringed. "Catherine, he is only a man."

"He is unlike any man I've ever met, Isabella. The way he speaks, his deportment ... the way he looks at me."

Isabella was both aghast and fascinated by her cousin's passionate, worshipful way of speaking about Lord Bromby. She was a twenty-seven-year-old married woman and mother, after all.

"Catherine," Isabella began gently. "Are you not concerned with London's gossip about you and Lord Bromby? I've already heard a great many rumors about your relationship with him. And what of Walter?"

Catherine's face clouded. "Walter doesn't care a whit about what I do. He is far too engaged with his political pursuits to worry about anything else."

Isabella knew better. "Walter is very kind. He is intelligent, successful, and he is not selfish and harsh like some others."

Catherine waved her hand. "Yes, yes. And I realize he's your cousin. But you do not know who he is in private, Isabella." She would not meet Isabella's eyes, her face pinched and drawn. She glanced around the room, her fingers drumming against the reticule in her lap.

"I hate to point out the obvious, Catherine, but you were advantageously married. Your husband is well-known and respected as a Whig parliamentarian, and one day he will ascend to his position as Viscount Melwood. I might add that your mother-in-law is greatly esteemed by society and wields much power within it."

Catherine sighed. "Oh, that woman! She makes my blood boil."

"Catherine!" It was as though she were speaking with a spoiled, obstinate child who had been told they might not have another sweet.

Catherine's lower lip jutted out, and her eyes flashed with venom. "This is very tedious, Isabella. I do not wish to talk about my husband or my mother-in-law."

Isabella pressed her lips together—the only way she could keep from speaking more about the subject.

When Catherine's gaze met Isabella's again, her expression was hard, tinged with anger. "I know you are exceedingly moral and religious, Isabella. I know you believe in blind fidelity and the inescapable bonds of marriage, but you do not live in my sphere. My world is quite different from yours, I assure you."

Catherine's words stung, and Isabella fought the urge to defend herself. "I beg your pardon. Let us say no more on the matter."

She was relieved when Hilda interrupted their conversation.

"Excuse me, ma'am. But there's a Miss Beringer here to see you."

Catherine stood abruptly. "I must go."

"Oh, no, Catherine. You need not leave. Miss Beringer—"

"No, I must," Catherine said coldly, sliding the strap of the reticule over her arm. "We'll no doubt see each other often while you're in town." But her tone suggested the opposite. Catherine would likely avoid her if it meant her behavior would be called into question.

Rebecca Beringer and Catherine Lyons crossed the threshold simultaneously. Rebecca paused to curtsy. "Good day, Lady Catherine."

Catherine nodded and mumbled a brief greeting in reply.

Rebecca appeared to look over Catherine's attire before returning to meet her gaze. With her chin raised, Catherine disappeared around the corner in a shuffle of silk with blue ribbons trailing out behind her.

Isabella's mind reeled from her conversation with her cousin as she ushered in the fresh, freckled Rebecca Beringer. The tendrils of the young woman's curly, reddish-brown hair sprang out in various directions. As if self-conscious, she patted and smoothed at the stray wisps, only making them more wayward.

Relieved to be in easier company, Isabella exhaled. "I apologize, Miss Beringer, but my aunt is calling on a sick friend this afternoon. Otherwise, she would join us." Isabella smiled. "I trust you enjoyed the ball last evening. I was sorry to have missed conversing with you."

"I was sorry too. Anyway, you were engaged with much dancing. I know my brother enjoyed your company."

An image of David Beringer's sad, blue eyes flashed through her mind. "Yes, indeed. Were it not for him, I would have had no dancing partners at all."

Rebecca laughed. Her cheeks dimpled as her eyes crinkled. "Miss Bankmill, I happen to have it on good authority that there were many men there who enjoyed dancing with you. Although, I scarce think they could have relished your company more than my brother."

Isabella's face grew hot. "Won't you sit down?"

Rebecca sat in the same chair Catherine had recently vacated, her pale, thin fingertips pulling at each of the five points of the gloves on either hand until she had them both off and in her lap.

"Shall I order tea?" Isabella prepared to signal for Hilda.

Rebecca shook her head. "Oh, no, please, Miss Bankmill. Do not trouble yourself. I cannot stay. Mainly, I come bearing an invitation. My parents, my brother, and I would be delighted if you and your aunt would join us for the week at Holly Bridge—our country home in Kent.

I know it is a bit out of season, and there will be no pheasant shooting for the men this time of year, but there will be parties and balls and—"

"Oh, yes, how lovely!" Isabella exclaimed. "I do not believe my aunt or I have any fixed engagements. I would be delighted and very honored." Her heart swelled. She would have more opportunity to get to know David Beringer in his own home. House parties were often known to turn out good marriage matches.

Rebecca's cheeks raised with a smile. "We are the ones who are honored. This will be a small party, and we may not have an even number of single ladies and gentlemen, but I know you are a great lover of horses and riding, and we have plenty of that. My father is a great lover of poetry too, and he has invited the poet Lord Bromby. I believe you met him last night."

Isabella's heart jolted uncomfortably. "Why, yes. In fact, I did. Your brother introduced us."

"An invitation was sent 'round to Lord Bromby this morning, and he has happily accepted. So, I'm sure we are all to be entertained with readings and poetry," Rebecca laughed.

"Yes. To be sure." A lightning-like charge struck Isabella's core at the notion of a week in Lord Bromby's company.

Rebecca Beringer's smile faded suddenly, and she looked down at her gloved hands as if embarrassed. "I'm sorry to say, although we did extend an invitation to your cousin Walter Lyons and Lady Catherine, Mr. Lyons has said they cannot come."

A glance of understanding passed between the two women, and Isabella nodded gravely. "Of course." Catherine had said nothing about it during her visit. Likely Walter had not shared the invitation with her.

Best for all if Walter and Catherine did not attend Mr. Beringer's party. Nothing good could come of it with Lord Bromby in attendance as well. Catherine's present course was set upon self-destruction. As for Isabella, and despite her own attempts at restraining the sensation, she was eager for a closer acquaintance with Lord Bromby.

Five

"I realize it is not my place to decide such things, David, but it is my opinion you and Miss Isabella Bankmill would make an excellent match." Rebecca grinned in a very unladylike fashion as she spoke the words.

David turned away from his sister. Not this again. He had just recovered from Amelia Robertson's rejection. He didn't think he could contemplate another match so soon after ... as much as he liked Miss Bankmill.

Shaking his head, he ignored her comment and busied himself with a letter to a local clergyman. The parish needed immediate funds, or they would not be able to support the orphans, and the children would be sent off to workhouses or who knew where. He meant to help them and wrote to tell them so.

Rebecca was not to be put off. "David, I'm serious. Did you not like Miss Bankmill? You danced with her twice at the ball."

The muscle in David's jaw tensed involuntarily. "Yes, of course I liked her. I liked her very much. But it does not necessarily follow that she liked me."

"Oh, she liked you. I could tell that she liked you."

David glanced up at his sister. Her face was a mischievous mask of plotting and scheming—arched brows, wide eyes, and that infernal grin. "How could you tell that Miss Bankmill liked me?"

Rebecca shrugged. "She danced with you twice. And she accepted the invitation to come to our house party—even though I suggested there might not be an even number of single ladies and gentlemen. I'd say that's a good indication."

David sat back in his chair and let his hands drop from the desktop to hang at his sides. Admittedly, the idea of Isabella Bankmill as a potential match had not completely escaped him. He found her very attractive, and she seemed to have a sweet disposition. She was also intelligent and well-read. But his heart was still tender to the touch after Amelia …

As though she had read his mind, Rebecca's voice was gentle. "I know Amelia's rejection was painful, David, but I, for one, never saw her as a good match for you. She was too conceited. Even Mamma saw that."

David hung his head and compressed his mouth. He didn't want to think about Amelia. He wished he were not so sensitive to these matters of the heart. Other men he knew pressed on as though love meant nothing to them. He didn't know why God had seen fit to make him so eager for marriage. And not just any marriage—as much as his parents were eager for him to marry and produce an heir—he wished for a union arranged by God to a woman who wanted to marry him for reasons other than income and status.

Rebecca sighed. "At least consider her. I like her very much, and I hope to know her better."

David passed his hand over his face. Turning, he faced Rebecca with a wistful smile. "She likes poetry."

"And you see that as an impediment?" Rebecca's brow furrowed.

"Perhaps."

"In what way?"

"Well, Lord Bromby will be in attendance at Holly Bridge as well. Miss Bankmill may, as did Miss Robertson, prefer the company of a poet with wild eyes and wild ways and a heart like a stone."

Rebecca scoffed. "Oh, nonsense. What woman in her right mind would ever desire to marry such a creature? Women may like to look at Lord Bromby, read his words, and pontificate about the idea of him, but the reality of a man like that is very different."

David rose from the desk and walked to where Rebecca sat by the window. He glanced down at the people moving on the street below. "I have no doubt you will choose wisely. You know what traits are important in a husband."

Rebecca placed her hand over his and squeezed. "That is because I have a wise and good brother to whom I look as an example. If I find a man half as good as you, I shall be blessed, indeed."

Six

The initial sight of the Beringer's country home, Holly Bridge, could not help but impress. The house was positioned at a perfect angle overlooking the surrounding hills with their puffs of white—the neighboring sheep—and trees of varying colors of green, olive, and moss.

Stepping out of the carriage, Aunt Lydia and Isabella were greeted by several footmen and the housekeeper—a Mrs. Farrell—who led them swiftly and silently out of the wind and into the house where they were welcomed by Lord and Lady Beringer as well as David and Rebecca Beringer.

"It's wonderful to see you," David Beringer said with a radiant smile. "I trust your journey wasn't too long and arduous."

Aunt Lydia untied her bonnet. "On the contrary, Mr. Beringer. We had the wind at our backs, as they say, and the carriage sailed along quite nicely."

Standing in the foyer, Isabella's gaze traveled over the painted green walls. Fine paintings hung all in a line, family portraits in gilded frames. Somber-faced men and women—relatives, probably—all with that same perfectly symmetrical aquiline nose.

"We are so pleased to meet you," Lord Beringer said to Isabella. "David and Rebecca have told us so much about you."

Lord Beringer possessed a ruddy face graced with an expression of cheerfulness. He was a tall but portly man, with the same twinkling blue eyes reflected in both his son and daughter. But David's eyes had a sad droop to them, one that somehow lent an extra charm.

Isabella glanced reservedly at David and was met by his fixed stare. Warmth flooded over her and into her face. He quickly looked away.

A few minutes later, the servants led Isabella and Aunt Lydia to their rooms. As the maid helped Isabella unpack, Aunt Lydia sat on the edge of the bed, smirking. "I do believe Mr. Beringer has taken a fancy to you, Izzy."

Isabella cast a glance over her shoulder at the maid. Of course, the young woman heard her aunt's words. Now she would probably tell the other servants and rumors would spread. "Shh. Please, Aunt. Do not speak of such things."

Turning to the maid, Aunt Lydia said, "That will do for now. Thank you."

Relieved, Isabella held out her arms to receive the dress the maid had been unfolding. With a curtsy and a shy smile, the girl exited the room.

Once she was gone, Aunt Lydia continued. "Well, don't you agree? Have you not noticed the way he looks at you?"

Isabella shook out her favorite turquoise-blue tea gown, releasing the fabric from its folds. "I had not noticed." Although she had.

Aunt Lydia's smirk widened and twisted into a sidewise smile. "Oh, come now. You can't be serious. It is perfectly obvious."

"Mr. Beringer and his sister are lovely hosts, and I should like to know them both better. That is all I will say on the matter at present."

Aunt Lydia sank into a chair, her light blue eyes sparkling happily. "Well. I hope you will allow him some of your attentions, Izzy, and favor him with your smiles and intelligent conversation. I believe Mr. Beringer is the sort of man who will appreciate your education, your love of mathematics, and your sincere Christian convictions. He seems to be a good sort of man."

"I'm sure he is."

Despite David Beringer's appearance of goodness, he didn't possess that extra je ne sais quoi that Isabella longed for in a man. Dare she say it? He was almost too polite—if such a quality was to be criticized. Even so, she would not exclude him from her considerations. Looking around her bedroom—the expensive, handcrafted Spanish wood, the costly satin bedspread—Isabella knew that to live as David Beringer's wife would be to live very comfortably, indeed. If she were to fall in love with Mr. Beringer, it would not be the worst thing.

Lord Bromby and Mr. John Hobby arrived just before dinner, while everyone was assembled at whist tables or hovering by the fireplace. As the tardy guests arrived, everyone stood for the customary rituals of greeting.

Lord Bromby regaled them with tales of a faulty carriage wheel and Mr. Hobby's compunction to walk back to a tavern he'd seen as they passed.

"I do believe that was your idea, dear fellow," Mr. Hobby said with a playful, scolding expression.

Everyone quickly resettled into their chairs. John Hobby moved across the room to sit quietly in the corner.

"And how was the wheel mended?" Rebecca asked.

Lord Bromby slipped into an empty chair beside Isabella, and her eyes met his. Her skin tingled with pinpricking pulses.

"I haven't the vaguest notion how the man repaired it. Hobby and I sauntered down to the tavern for a drink, and when we returned, the wheel was magically mended."

"We are so happy that you have joined us, despite your misfortune, Lord Bromby," said Lady Beringer.

Lord Bromby's command of the room was mesmerizing. Moments before, everyone's attention had been on playing their best card, but now the focus seemed to rest on one man.

Miss Anna Tickney, Rebecca's childhood friend, had also come to stay for the week. She might have completed the single ladies-to-gentlemen ratio, except she was engaged to a soldier stationed in the Iberian Peninsula. Even so, her gaze fixed upon Lord Bromby's bright eyes and alabaster skin.

"And that reminds me of our time in Greece. Hobby, do you recall the time we were stuck behind a processional of Turks?"

Hobby nodded, his facial expression grave. "I have tried to forget, but yes, I do remember all too well."

Lord Bromby shook his head and peered down at his hands. "Chilling business. A wagon stopped at a sheep crossing right in front of us, carrying a burlap sack which writhed and screamed—quite obviously containing a person."

"A person?" gasped Lady Beringer. "In a burlap sack?"

"Yes," continued Lord Bromby. "A burlap sack tied shut with a rope."

"Why would anyone do that?" Anna Tickney's hand fluttered to her neckline where a cross charm hung, which she grasped and tugged back and forth across the chain.

"She was a woman convicted of immoral behavior," said Lord Bromby. "In the Turkish tradition, women are to be stoned or drowned for such offenses. They were on their way to the ocean to drown her."

"Shocking!" exclaimed Lady Beringer. "Savage people."

"In some ways yes, and in other ways, no. In this case, I felt I had no choice but to intervene. I drew my pistol and demanded that they unhand her."

Isabella's heart sped. The suspense of the tale was nearly unbearable.

"And did they?" whispered Rebecca as she leaned forward in her seat.

"Not at first," Lord Bromby continued. "I forced them all to follow me as we went before the governor."

"Weren't you frightened?" asked Isabella.

"A little, yes. But I was more anxious to have the unfortunate affair all over and done with. And with some persuading and a bit more bribery, I finally convinced them that exile was a much more appropriate punishment. Hobby and I took her to a nearby monastery where she slept for a time, and by cloak of nightfall, we delivered her safely to the town of Thebes."

"Indeed," sighed Lady Beringer. "You are a veritable hero, Lord Bromby."

John Hobby snorted.

"I can bear to see no one punished so cruelly, Lady Beringer."

This was the second time Isabella had heard of Lord Bromby coming to the aid of those in need. Perhaps he was a hero—much like Master Harry of his poem. She studied the side of his face—the slightly prominent but straight bridge of his nose and the firm, pronounced chin. Bromby turned and looked directly into her eyes.

"Miss Bankmill. Quite lovely to see you again."

The heat shot up her neck, causing her face to flush prettily. "And you, Lord Bromby. That is quite an amazing story."

With one arm casually slung over the back of the chair, he motioned to the table and its players with his other arm. "I appear to have interrupted a game."

"You have." She nodded with a smile and a slanted glance. "But that's not to say you were an unwelcome interruption. I was losing badly to Mr. Beringer."

"Not at all," David said. "As a matter of fact, we were just ending the game and preparing to move into the dining room. You're just in time."

He stood and extended his arm to Isabella. "Miss Bankmill, would you do me the honor of accompanying me?"

Isabella rose from her seat. "Of course, Mr. Beringer."

The other men at the table stood, including Lord Bromby, who seemed to take an extra couple of seconds to push himself to his feet. As they filed into the dining room, David Beringer's light conversation bounced off her like rain. Lord Bromby seemed truly heroic. He defended the poor before Parliament and saved damsels in distress. Could the rakish stories about him really be true, then?

Despite her attempts to focus on David's voice, her attention drifted to the conversation behind her between Lord Bromby and Mr. Hobby.

"I think you will find most ladies would be highly offended by your words, Bromby."

"I find that most *ladies*, as you say, are offended only because they are unused to such coarseness of tongue and behavior. As you familiarize them with the language, by sheer repetitive exposure, they become less offended and more tolerant."

"Good heavens, man," Mr. Hobby said, following with a short, staccato laugh. "You are incorrigible—I daresay a veritable monster."

"Monster? Perhaps that is why you, my good fellow, are my only friend in the world."

His only friend in the world? What could he mean by that? Isabella was instantly sympathetic to his self-pronounced, friendless state. Although her conversations with Lord Bromby had been brief, she saw no monster. He was merely misunderstood. She would befriend Lord Bromby, if only to show him that he was not so unworthy as he proclaimed.

Seven

Mr. Beringer had not over-exaggerated his fine horses. The Beringers' stable, a short walk from the house and tended by several grooms, contained four chestnuts, two whites, one black, a bay mare, and a yellow pony.

With Aunt Lydia opting to stay behind, the riding party was complete with David and Rebecca Beringer, Lord Bromby and John Hobby, and Anna Tickney.

"May I ride one of the white ones?" Isabella motioned to a smallish horse with an especially long mane and tail.

David walked to her side, smiling. "Yes, of course. This is Thaddeus. He is one of my personal favorites. I was going to suggest him for you."

Isabella ran her fingers down the horse's long, taut neck as small, white hairs knitted themselves into the fabric of her coat sleeve and clung to the leather of her gloves. The horse exhaled and nodded its head up and down several times, shaking the dust from his mane. "He is beautiful," she breathed.

"There's a wonderful stream just over the next hill," David informed the riding party. Shielding his eyes from the morning sun with one hand, he pointed off in the distance with the other. "And just beyond that, there's another one. But do be watchful when you come to the woods. My sister and I usually go around. There are some ... unsavory sorts in those forests."

"Unsavory sorts?" Miss Tickney wrinkled her nose and eyebrows simultaneously.

"Yes, I'm afraid so, Miss Tickney. Gypsies they tell me," David explained. "But fear not. You have three able-bodied men to defend you."

Out of the corner of her eye, Isabella glimpsed a groom standing behind Lord Bromby and assisting him to mount as another held his horse. *His lame leg must no doubt present an impediment in this instance.*

She noted that once astride, Bromby appeared as capable a rider as any of them, nimbly steering his horse with a tug on the reins.

Urging their horses forward, the group started out at a slow trot as they made their way down the hill toward a line of trees. Isabella longed to challenge her mount. She imagined gliding over the hill just beyond, the wind in her hair and ears, stinging her eyes with brisk, spring dew. Instead, she was trapped in conversation with Miss Tickney who struggled to hold the reins properly, barely controlling the bay mare.

"She wants to eat the grass," she complained with a little cry, nearly toppling over as her mount lowered her head.

"Bring her head up, Miss Tickney. Don't let her pull you," Isabella called out.

Anna's blonde curls bounced as she tugged at the reins of the obstinate mare that insisted on stopping every few paces to rip grass from the ground. Finally moving alongside, Isabella grasped Anna's reins and yanked back with a decisive, "No!"

The horse thrust its head back with annoyance, but as long as Isabella walked or trotted her horse closely alongside, there were no additional cheeky attempts from the mare. Isabella was disappointed to restrain her horse at a much slower pace.

"I've always been a little afraid of horses." The sheen of perspiration on Anna's forehead indicated as much. "But I can see you're an experienced rider, Miss Bankmill."

Isabella smiled, glimpsing the hill beyond as the other riders broke into a canter and disappeared just beyond the apex. "There is no reason to be afraid of horses once you understand how they think."

"The ones I ride always think how they can frighten me." Anna's voice shook.

"Horses do sense fear," Isabella confirmed. "And it's best if you immediately exert your control and demonstrate the upper hand. If you do not, they may take advantage—like this lady here." Isabella motioned to the mare. "But if you take the time to form a friendship with them, they will trust you. Then, they will want to do as you ask them."

Isabella could no longer see the other members of the riding party. They had gone ahead, and she only hoped they would wait by the stream. As Isabella and Anna reached the rise of the hill, Anna appeared more at ease, having acquired some ability with the reins. She sat in the saddle looking very pretty, her two legs cast to the left side of the saddle, and her deep, rose-colored skirts covering her boots and ankle in a graceful flow.

"Are you much acquainted with Lord Bromby?" Anna asked as they caught sight of their lost party at the bottom of the hill.

"Not much acquainted," Isabella said. "I've met him thrice—this being the third encounter."

"He is handsome, isn't he? I'd heard he was, but I hadn't expected to find him so …" Anna's voice trailed off.

Isabella was quick to answer. "Yes, he is quite handsome. I met him while in London, and I can tell you there were many young ladies who flocked about him."

"Oh, well, I'm engaged, so it matters little," breathed Anna. "And I hear he is a supporter of Napoleon, of all people, which is impossible to imagine—especially since my fiancé is currently stationed in the Iberian Peninsula fighting against that monster."

Bromby supports Napoleon? Could that really be true? Isabella had not heard so before. She knew no one who supported the French military leader and his ambitions.

"You must be quite anxious for your fiancé's return."

Anna nodded and smiled. "Yes. Especially since news from the Peninsula suggests so many casualties. We're to be married as soon as he returns."

Isabella was thankful never to have loved a man in regimentals. Too much heartache threatened such an attachment.

A sudden movement in the brush nearby—perhaps a rabbit scampering away—created an odd rushing sound. Miss Tickney's horse lurched and bolted toward the woods. Anna was unseated and her foot loosened from the stirrup. She screamed as she reached for the ground, tumbling headlong.

Isabella prompted her horse forward and stopped near Anna's crumpled form. Unhooking her right and left leg simultaneously, she slid from the saddle to the ground and rushed to the girl's side.

"Are you hurt, Miss Tickney?"

The girl appeared disoriented as she put a hand to her head, and then her face wrinkled with pain and realization. "I—I'm afraid she headed for the woods … with the gypsies," she cried.

Isabella cradled her head and looked up. The hillside was empty. Where were the others? She would never be able to lift Miss Tickney on her own. Just then, the faint outlines of Rebecca and David reappeared over the crest of the hill. Apparently glimpsing the accident, they urged their horses on, stopping just short of where Anna sprawled.

"We heard a scream." Rebecca's voice was shrill with worry. "What happened? Is she hurt?"

"She fell."

David Beringer sprang from his horse at the girl's side. Rebecca slid from her mount and rushed to grasp her friend's hand.

"I'm fine," Anna assured them. "It's only my head."

At that moment a trickle of blood, like a small, red stream, wound over Anna's temple and slid down her cheek.

Mr. Beringer pulled a handkerchief from his pocket and pressed the cloth against the side of her face. "Oh, dear," he said softly. "I think we should get you back to the house. Rebecca, please ride ahead and fetch the doctor."

"Of course," Rebecca said breathlessly. She rushed to mount her large, chestnut mare and galloped off.

Isabella hurried to Anna's other side, grasping her left arm as David held her right.

"Where are Lord Bromby and Mr. Hobby?" Isabella glanced over her shoulder to the empty hillside.

"I don't know," David said. "We did not see them when we turned back toward the sound of Miss Tickney's cry."

"Perhaps I should wait for them," Isabella suggested.

Hoisting Anna onto her horse, he replied sternly. "Absolutely not, Miss Bankmill. I shall require your assistance. I will walk Miss Tickney back to the house, and if you will be so kind as to ride Thaddeus and lead my horse, I would be much obliged."

With David's assistance, Isabella remounted Thaddeus, taking hold of the reins of David's gelding. The threesome made their way back until they were safely upon the path leading to the stables.

David appeared greatly concerned for Anna. His hand rested upon her foot and he constantly glanced up at her, checking to see if she was still conscious. "Are you quite all right, Miss Tickney? We shall be at the stables in no time at all."

Once they had arrived back at the stables, Mr. Beringer lifted Anna from her horse and carried her toward the house.

Rebecca flew from the front door like a bird released from a cage, speaking in fast, flustered phrases. "The doctor has been sent for."

Hanging back, Isabella stood in front of the grand house, staring up at the many windows above her. *What a disappointing ride.* At the pattering of horses' hooves behind her, she turned. Lord Bromby and John Hobby were riding toward her.

"Miss Bankmill!" Lord Bromby called out, waving his black-gloved hand.

Isabella waved in return as the two men brought their horses to a stop in front of her. "We thought you might have been lost," she said. "We had to turn back, for Miss Tickney took a spill and injured herself."

"Oh, dear," said John Hobby. "Not too seriously, I hope."

"She did hurt her head, I'm afraid."

Lord Bromby slumped a little. "Hardly got to ride at all. I'd hoped to at least make the haunted forest Mr. Beringer spoke of."

John rolled his eyes. "Good heavens, Bromby. The poor girl has taken a tumble. We should offer our assistance."

"I believe a doctor has been summoned," said Isabella.

Lord Bromby stared down at her from his black stallion. His glossy black curls blew freely in the wind, much like the horse's mane. His eyes, large and dilated with interest, focused upon hers with intensity.

She looked away. The man was very hard to look at with his penetrating stare.

"What say you, Miss Bankmill?" he said in a low voice. "Shall we have another go at that ride?"

Isabella's voice cracked. "I thank you, Lord Bromby. But I must decline your offer. As you well know, riding now would not be at all fitting."

With a wide grin, he turned to John Hobby, who shook his head with a look of incredulity.

"That is precisely the point, Miss Bankmill." One of his side teeth looked like a fang.

Mr. Hobby spoke quickly. "You'll have to excuse my friend, Miss Bankmill. He bears no resemblance to a gentleman, I'm afraid."

"On the contrary, Mr. Hobby. Lord Bromby bears every resemblance to a gentleman. Until he opens his mouth." She smiled.

Lord Bromby did not move his gaze from hers.

John Hobby laughed. "A very astute observation! You'll excuse me, Miss Bankmill. I'll return this mare to the stables. It looks as though it might rain. Come on, Bromby." Mr. Hobby reeled his horse away from them. When Lord Bromby did not follow, Mr. Hobby headed for the stables alone.

"I should go inside, Lord Bromby. Miss Beringer might need my help." She began to walk away.

"Miss Bankmill."

She stopped and turned, hoping no one was looking out of the windows watching them.

"Perhaps we might take that ride tomorrow." His eyes bore into hers. "With a chaperone, of course."

"We'll have to see about that, Lord Bromby." Heat rose into her face, but she curtsied and turned to ascend the stairs.

Later that afternoon, Isabella carried a book to the gardens in hopes of finding a few moments to herself. Everyone else was indoors. Most of the guests played cards. Rebecca tended to Anna, who had merely bumped her head and was not seriously hurt. "Wounds to the head always bleed profusely," the doctor told them. "Often they look worse than they are."

The clouds bunched together and hung heavy in gray billows—a water-filled canopy just above her head. Within moments of her finding a stone bench under a thick cover of trees, rain started to fall.

"Hello."

Startled by the soft, deep voice behind her, Isabella spun around. Lord Bromby stood under a tree, his hand against its trunk.

"Lord Bromby, you frightened me."

He stepped closer, his eyes very green. "You are not the first to say that."

Isabella looked around in the hopes of seeing someone else—Rebecca, her aunt, a gardener. There was no one. She was alone with him. "Oh, come now, Lord Bromby. You will not convince me you truly frighten women. I was merely startled. I happen to know women flock to you as I witnessed myself in London."

He laughed. "Ah, Miss Bankmill, what you do not see are the ladies who run screaming from me upon closer acquaintance. I'm afraid the charm wears off once my true character is discovered."

Isabella stood rigidly. She had two choices: excuse herself to go inside and not risk scandalous speculation of being alone with a man, or stay and hope that no one had seen them together. Shakily, she lowered herself onto the stone bench, thankful for the thick coverage of leafy tree limbs over their heads as the rain began to fall in earnest. "And what, pray tell, do they find so offensive in your character as to drive them away screaming?"

Bromby stood just to the left of her, looking down at her perched form. "Most likely they discover a depraved individual with a blackened soul. If you've heard less than commendable stories about me, Miss Bankmill, you should believe them."

Isabella tensed and stared out at the puddles beginning to form. This situation was growing worse by the moment. She risked her reputation with every second she was alone with him. Even so, she could not will herself to move from the bench. "I simply don't believe them, Lord Bromby. You are too harsh upon your own character, I'm sure. And we are told all of us possess blackened souls. That is why we need a Savior to redeem us."

Lord Bromby looked out over the gardens. "You are religious, then?"

"Religious? Yes, I suppose so. If you wish to call it that."

"You believe absolutely in what the Holy Scriptures say about life, salvation, death, damnation."

"Yes. What do you believe?"

Bromby sat beside her. "I believe that from birth I was doomed. Damned. It is the lot of my family name, Miss Bankmill. Part of my inheritance as it were." The twist of his mouth suggested sarcasm, but his eyes appeared deeply grieved.

"But you will not find that in the Scriptures, Lord Bromby. The Lord's forgiveness is for all—regardless of our parentage or what sins we may have committed."

He dropped his gaze to his hands. "I'm sure, Miss Bankmill, you would be shocked by some of my sins."

Eager to lighten the mood and calm the nervous bubbling in her stomach at his elbow rubbing against hers, Isabella waved her hand. "Lord Bromby, God knows all our sins. He knows them, and He forgives them."

He laughed. "You would not say that if you knew my sins. I am predestined for hell."

A chill ran through her, probably due to the cold rain. Change the subject. "Well, I'd hoped I might take a turn in the garden, but it looks as if that plan is spoiled."

"I see no reason we shouldn't walk now. What is a little rain?"

"Oh, you must be joking. You would catch a cold, and I would catch a fever, and everyone would think us insane for such outlandish behavior. As it is, I risk my reputation simply by sitting out here alone with you."

He looked at her, and his pupils swelled.

He is perfectly serious.

"I do not consider that sort of behavior outlandish at all, Miss Bankmill. You are young, strong, and healthy. And if you were to catch a fever and die, by your own account you would find yourself at the gates of heaven. There is nothing to be lost in such a courageous action."

Isabella raised her eyebrows. What was she to make of this man and his strange philosophies? "And what of you? It would not do for you to catch a cold and die."

"You would not plead for my soul at the gates of heaven?"

"It does not work that way, Lord Bromby. If you do not make the decision to believe for yourself, there is little I, or anyone else, can do for you."

"But does not it say in the Bible that Jesus himself intercedes for us? If he does, why could not one of his own?"

A smile stretched across her lips. Perhaps there was hope for this man after all. "So, you have read the Bible."

"Yes, of course. I am schooled in its contents. As are most boys with an English education, I daresay. As a child, I had a careful nurse who beat it into me. You will find I know much scripture by heart, Miss Bankmill."

"You do not mean that she actually beat you? Surely!"

His expression drooped, his mouth relaxing into a grave line. "But I do. Nurse Green beat me most severely if I did not recite scripture to her satisfaction."

What nurse could do that to a child in her charge? "That is terrible. That is wrong. As wrong a wrong if ever there was one."

He nodded. "Yes. It is why, I suppose, I have never had any great love for the faith you speak of, nor have I drawn comfort from it. Only fear."

Her heart weighed heavy. How could she not feel sympathy for this man? If what Lord Bromby said was true, who could blame his skepticism and abhorrence for something which had given him such pain as a child?

Perhaps his heart could be changed from this ridiculous belief that he was inherently cursed. Or perhaps his words were said simply to shock her, to make her believe he was as black-hearted as he claimed.

"Lord Bromby, I have read your poem, and I believe it reveals the soul of a man who possesses much goodness—a man who needs spiritual tending for his heart to develop and bloom."

He smiled. "What better place to use such a metaphor than here, in Holly Bridge's gardens."

"Yes." She turned her gaze to the flowers, their heads bowing with the steady onslaught of rain. "I had not meant to do so."

"There is a poet in you as well, I do believe."

Isabella blushed. "As a child I wrote a bit of poetry, I confess."

"I am not surprised. You must allow me to read it some time."

Lord Bromby read her amateurish poetry? Never. "Oh no. I beg you, do not ask me. I was very young and wrote it for my own amusement and nothing more. I have no talent. My talent is in mathematics. I adore the challenge of equations and puzzles."

Lord Bromby shifted closer so that his knee touched her dress. Through the fabric, the heat radiated from his leg. A funny fluttering assailed Isabella's stomach, and cold chills formed at her back.

"Do you know, Miss Bankmill, when I first met you at Lady Melwood's ball, I found you most puzzling."

I am astonished he has any recollection of our first meeting. I cannot have made a good impression. "How so, sir?"

"You appeared kind and generous, yet reserved and restricted."

"We spoke little more than ten words to one another. I wonder that you could make out any part of my character with such a brief meeting."

He angled his gaze and smirked. "Miss Bankmill, I will divulge a secret to you—one I do not tell many people. Among the many other strange things surrounding my childhood, I was born with a caul over my face."

"A caul?"

"Yes. The membrane that holds the unborn child. Ancient superstition suggests that this is good luck and a preventative against drowning. But I believe it may account for the fact that I am somewhat clairvoyant. I know and sense things about people with great ease."

Oh, no. Not that. Isabella turned away. "I am not superstitious, Lord Bromby."

"You do not believe in special foresight?"

"I believe that foresight is for God alone and not to be mishandled by humans."

She jolted as he suddenly took her left hand in his. Shifting his eyes back and forth between hers and the palm of her hand, he ran his fingers over it. *Pull away!* She should slap his face for being so forward. She wasn't even wearing her gloves! What would people say? *Oh, please let no one see us.*

"Even now, Miss Bankmill, I can see your future."

"What nonsense." She jerked at her hand, trying to pull it from his.

He held her hand tight and continued to draw lines over the grooves of her palm. "You are a woman with a large, kind heart. You are practical and reserved to a fault. Your love of propriety and morality will bring judgment upon others, but you will also be tested in this area."

Isabella stopped trying to pull away. His fingers traced lines over her hand; his touch, nearly hypnotizing. What was happening to her?

"When you love, Miss Bankmill, you will love with passionate intensity." He looked up, his eyes concentrated and peering deep into her own. His voice dropped to a whisper—a melodic sound amongst the rhythm of the rain. "And you will love more than once. In at least one of the matches, you will be greatly disappointed. Devastated, even," he concluded with an arched eyebrow.

Isabella's heart thumped wildly. With an insistent tug, she freed her hand.

"I've never been wrong."

"'Tis not right. We are not meant to know the future," she scolded. "We are told not to meddle in such things."

"Do you always do what you're told, Miss Bankmill?"

What was it about his expression that was so unsettling? She could not escape the sultry look in his eyes, and suddenly the entire meeting felt wrong. *If you're not careful, people will begin to think of you as they do Lady Catherine.*

"I should go back." She rose from the bench.

"I've offended you."

"Perhaps. I must see to my aunt."

As if to prevent her premature departure, Lord Bromby spoke quickly. "You are fortunate to have so many aunts who care so deeply for you."

Run away. Do not listen to him. He is trying to snare you.

"Lady Melwood also speaks highly of you." He met her gaze. "Lady Melwood has been very kind to me. She is like a mother to me, or an elder sister. I do not know how I should exist in London were it not for her."

Despite the voice in her head telling her to go, Isabella's feet remained anchored to the ground. "I am glad she has been kind to you, Lord Bromby. I daresay you deserve every kindness imaginable."

He met her stare with his own. She looked away. Her heart was heavy, yet it pounded with involuntary attraction for this man. How she wanted to lighten his heart, assure him of life beyond the grave, and beg him to be a part of it.

"I see her kindness and wisdom in you, Miss Bankmill."

Her heart clenched. She looked down at her hands. "I thank you."

"In this dark world there are few rays of light. But you are certainly one of them. I hope I may count you as a friend. I have so few."

"Of course, you may, Lord Bromby. I desire very much to be your friend."

He bowed his head. "I am grateful."

"Now, if you please," she said, standing, "I really must beg you excuse me."

Lord Bromby stood and bowed deeply.

She hurried away, unwelcome tears springing to her eyes. She could feel his gaze following her, burning into her back.

Eight

Rain plagued Holly Bridge for the next three days, and the party was relegated to the inside for the duration of the weather. Lord Bromby kept to his rooms during much of the three days, and David was relieved. It pained him to watch the man send out his sultry stares upon the ladies—especially his sister … and Isabella.

Why had his father invited him?

Perhaps his father had viewed Bromby as an interesting fellow—man of the hour—who would entertain his guests and add an element of intrigue to the small party.

Isabella Bankmill paid a great deal of attention to the poet—just as he'd feared. Even so, she appeared to be a lady regulated by sound mind and principles. The thought of her ending up with a man like Bromby galled him. Under different circumstances, he would entertain the thought of pursuing her. But it was clear she had no special interest in him.

As he passed through the foyer on his way from the library, she was there, making her way up the staircase, trailing her fingers along the cast iron balusters. She wore a simple muslin dress, the color of milk. Brown tendrils curled around her face.

"What do you think of our country home, Miss Bankmill?"

She turned. In contrast with the gray morning light offered by the large windows off to the side, her eyes glowed with life "It is very grand, Mr. Beringer. I wonder that your family spends so little time here. Your mother tells me you do not frequent it." Isabella descended the stairs to meet him.

"Our land steward, Bingham, handles the place as well as any could, I daresay. But I do come as often as I am able, although at present we are much engaged in London." He took a step back from her. She might think him impertinent by standing too close. Even so, he caught the faintest scent of roses.

What sort of man was Isabella Bankmill seeking? Of course. She wanted a man like Lord Bromby—not staid and dull like him. *I must think of her only as an acquaintance—a friend of my sister's—a friend of mine at most.* "Perhaps, when I am married … if my wife should like to come here, then we may travel into Kent more often." The words tumbled from his lips, and he froze, wishing he could retract them.

Isabella shifted her weight and turned her attention back to the cast iron gryphons on each of the balusters, running her fingers over the eagle's head and across the lion's body.

God, is there no way You could stop my tongue from saying such things?

David cleared his throat. "Are you finding your accommodations comfortable? Do you have everything you need—you and your aunt?"

"Yes, sir. We are more than comfortable, I thank you. 'Tis a shame about the rain."

"Yes."

She looked around, seemingly uncomfortable. Oh dear. Now he'd produced a terribly awkward moment between them.

"I'm looking forward to the party tomorrow night," she said.

David's shoulders relaxed with the change of subject. "Oh, yes. So am I. My father's friend, General Russet, will be in attendance, along with several neighboring families."

"That will be lovely. I have grown so accustomed to parties that a day without one feels as though something is missing."

David smiled. Perhaps the damage was not irreparable. "Yes, and I do hope, Miss Bankmill, that you will honor me with a dance or two—as you so graciously did in London."

"Of course, Mr. Beringer."

She might only agree to dance with him out of politeness, but at least he had done no further damage to their friendship.

The following night, Isabella stood alongside Rebecca, as women in fine silks and men in their coattails and well-polished shoes paraded through the doors, each arrival announced with grand fanfare by the butler. .

"Mr. and Mrs. Barlowe!"

After their names were announced, the guests swept into the room.

"Lord and Lady Paillard and their grand-niece, Miss Exley."

Miss Exley wore a sea-blue dress with an embroidered hem of black, looping design.

"Isn't her dress wonderful?" Rebecca sighed.

Isabella smiled. "Yes, very smart."

Rebecca touched Isabella's arm, directing her attention toward the next arriving couple. "Oh, and look! General Russet and his wife. How handsome he looks in his uniform."

"Yes, very handsome."

"Could you ever marry a man in a regiment—as Anna plans to do?"

Isabella considered. "I suppose if I fell in love with one. Could you?"

"Yes. If he loved God. I should like to fall in love with a man whose heart belongs to God first. What sort of man should you wish to marry, Isabella?" Rebecca's eyes squinted with genuine curiosity.

"The same as you have mentioned."

The room buzzed with activity. People laughed and talked. A group of young ladies stood around the pianoforte, trailing their fingers over the polished wood and waiting for an appropriate moment to sit at its bench.

"I'm sure you've noticed that my brother is also devout in his faith," Rebecca said.

Isabella nodded. "Your brother seems very sincere."

Rebecca rushed on. "Not only does he believe sincerely, but charity is one of his highest priorities. My brother is not a braggart, and so he would never speak of this, but he regularly hand-delivers money to the Foundling Hospital in London. He spends time there, visits with the children. He says it brings him great joy."

Yes, this was impressive. Many people made charitable contributions, but few hand-delivered them to the orphanages.

Rebecca's lids lowered. "I know my brother likes you, Isabella. I shouldn't say this, but ... I know he likes you very much."

Isabella tried to ignore the glint in her friend's eye. Of course, Rebecca wished her brother to be happily married. It did her credit. Isabella could not begrudge her that. She looked across the room at David Beringer as he stood talking to General Russet. Yes, he was a nice-looking man—tall and lean. His light brown hair was tousled rather than overly coiffed like so many other men who tried to appear as Beau Brummell sorts.

"Your brother is a fine gentleman. I like him very much." The words felt like stale bread in her mouth. Despite all of David's goodness, she did not experience tingles of excitement in his company.

She scanned the room, stopping and doubling back. There was the familiar, dark-clad man standing in the corner. His arms crossed, his brow furrowed as he listened to an older woman dressed in an impressive lavender gown.

Just then, Lord Beringer arrived with a tall, thin man whose nose was red and blotchy as if he suffered a cold.

"Sir Malcom Meade, I believe you have already met my daughter, Rebecca Beringer, and this is her friend, Miss Isabella Bankmill." Sir Malcolm Meade appeared well into his thirties. Although his face was no paler than Lord Bromby's, there was a grayish tinge to his pallor that hinted at prolonged illness.

Isabella curtsied to his bow. "I remember you, Sir Malcolm. I believe you attended Lady Melwood's ball in Mayfair. I recall seeing you dancing with Miss Beringer."

"It is wonderful to see you again, Miss Beringer." His smile widened as he glanced at Rebecca. Suddenly, he collapsed into a fit of coughing. He pulled a handkerchief from his pocket and clapped it over his mouth.

"Are you unwell, Sir Malcolm?" Rebecca's face collapsed with concern. "I believe you had a cough last week at Melwood House as well."

He cleared his throat and shook his head, but his eyes watered. "I do apologize," he finally sputtered. "A chronic malady, I'm afraid. Nothing contagious, I assure you. An infernal cough that comes and goes with the weather."

"May I have one of the servants fetch you some tea with lemon or honey?" asked Lord Beringer.

Sir Malcolm shook his head. "Thank you, sir, the company of such lovely ladies will suffice for now."

Over the course of the evening, Isabella danced nearly every dance—two with David Beringer, one with Mr. Hobby, even one with Sir Malcolm. By that time, the poor man seemed drained by his own coughing, and he'd had to leave the floor before the reel was done.

It wasn't until the last dance of the evening, when Isabella felt a light touch upon her arm and turned to look into moss-green eyes.

"Miss Bankmill, if you are not engaged, would you do me the honor of dancing the next dance with me?"

If he had proclaimed to her a complete heart change and a sudden, fervent desire to become a monk, Isabella would not have been more astonished. "But—I … I thought…I would be honored, Lord Bromby." She curtsied to him, and her heart soared. He would risk ridicule and humiliation to dance with her?

Lord Bromby took her hand and led her out to where the couples lined up. A thin sheen of perspiration coated his forehead as the violins began to play and couples waited to make their first step of the dance. Whispered words reached her ears.

"Do you see? Lord Bromby is dancing."

"What? He never dances. He simply does not dance … his foot, you know."

"I only thought he did not waltz."

"No, he never dances at all. Who is the girl?"

"The Bankmill girl. Her father is Sir Ralph Bankmill … of Durham."

Isabella smiled at Lord Bromby, her heart pounding—not only for Lord Bromby's sacrificial gesture, but for her own potential embarrassment if he did not know the steps. Everyone knew what disaster befell those who muddled the dance steps and spun left when they were meant to spin right, or stepped when they were to remain standing.

But as the dance commenced, it appeared that Lord Bromby did know the steps and how to execute them. He was in no way graceful, but he performed the steps admirably, his brow furrowed as he clumped along. This must be costly for him—both in physicality and pride.

As he led her off the floor, Lord Bromby was silent.

"You performed the steps exceedingly well, Lord Bromby"

His face was flushed, his skin blooming with pink color, and his forehead beaded with sweat. "I could not pass up the one and only opportunity I might have to be your partner," he stated. "It was an honor and a privilege to dance with you, Miss Bankmill. Thank you for granting me the final dance of the evening." Bromby abruptly bowed and limped off in the direction of the foyer. Isabella had never been so honored to dance with anyone in her life.

It was very early the next morning when Isabella joined arms with her aunt and they ascended the stairs. They walked silently to the door of Aunt Lydia's room. "Good night, Aunt Lydia."

"Izzy," her aunt whispered, gently grasping her niece's wrist. "Come inside a moment."

Isabella followed her into the room. Aunt Lydia sat on the edge of the bed, her face drawn as the candlelight cast shadows over her eyes and mouth, aging her. "I'm concerned, Izzy. Lord Bromby—well, he's not the sort of man I would wish for you. And I think your parents would not approve."

Isabella perched on the bed beside Aunt Lydia and ran her hand over the green silk of the bedcovering. *It was only one dance...*

"Tell me. Are you in love with him?"

Isabella laughed. "In love with him? Aunt Lydia, I hardly know him." That much was true.

Aunt Lydia's voice was a sharp, frantic whisper, her eyes wide and bulging with concern. "It is my feeling that he's not a good sort of man."

"He's misunderstood. I think he is a good sort of man, but he's caught in the net of society's conventions and expectations. He's different from most, to be sure, but—"

"Izzy. I have suspicions that he is not like-minded in the area of faith."

Isabella agonized over how to respond. By telling her aunt that Lord Bromby did not believe in God's saving grace, she admitted that he was not a good match. But she could not lie. Perhaps her explanation of offering Bromby friendship and an example of someone committed to their principles might suffice.

"He says he does not know what he believes. He has read the scriptures, but he is uncertain as to his own salvation ... or the manner by which he may be saved."

Aunt Lydia's mouth pursed with disapproval. "Well. That is certain enough, then. Isabella, you should discourage his advances. The Bible speaks clearly against inequality in marriage when it comes to one's faith."

Isabella took a deep breath. She longed to end this conversation. "I am well aware of what the Bible says. It is my hope and fervent prayer that our friendship might do him some good. That upon closer acquaintance I might lend some understanding and credence to what he neither understands nor believes."

Aunt Lydia's blue eyes shimmered in the candlelight as she took her niece's hands in her own. "Take care, Isabella. It is much more common for an ill-mannered child to adversely influence a well-mannered one ... rather than the reverse."

Isabella swallowed. "I understand, ma'am."

"Remember that the heart is deceitful above all things. Love between two parties is borne of like-mindedness, mutual respect, and self-sacrifice. Do not allow yourself to be drawn in by Lord Bromby's good looks and melodious voice. You'd much better look to Mr. Beringer for—"

"I understand your meaning," Isabella said, her stomach twisting. What had previously been rivulets of perspiration upon her back were now damp spots soaking into the material of her dress.

"Pray on it, my dear. Do not make rash decisions. Choosing well will chart the course of the rest of your life."

Isabella rose from the bed and bestowed a kiss upon her aunt's forehead. "I will pray. Thank you for your good advice."

Aunt Lydia managed a smile and patted her hand. "Your uncle and I were very happy, Isabella. I only desire the same for you."

———————

The next morning was their day of departure. Isabella came downstairs rather late, having only gone to bed a few hours before. As she made her way along the hall toward the dining room for breakfast, she paused to admire a painting—probably a portrait of one of the Beringers' ancestors.

Bumps and shuffles drew her attention to the alcove just beyond where she stood.

"Did you hear?" It was one of the servants, her voice barely above a whisper.

"Hear what?" A second servant asked.

Isabella did not move and strained to listen.

The first servant sounded out of breath. "It is about Lord Bromby."

"What is it?" whispered the other.

Isabella moved further down the hallway and closer to the voices, still pretending to admire the hanging portraits.

"Last night, there were a series of express posts received by Smith. The first arrived at eleven o'clock. The second at one. He said the final one arrived at three this morning. All of them for Lord Bromby."

"Who were they from?"

"They were all from Lady Catherine Lyons."

"Who's she?"

"Are you daft? She's married to the cousin of Miss Bankmill. Anyway, they say she's mad, and she's mad in love for Lord Bromby. She sends him all sorts of correspondence around the clock when he's in London too."

Isabella's chest tightened. Catherine sent messages to him during the night? For what purpose?

The voices continued. "Well, you know what I heard? I overheard Sir Malcolm Meade say that Lord Bromby is attached to the Countess of Oxford."

"Who's she?"

"She is married to the Earl of Oxford, Edward Harley, and she is a radical. She has many children of dubious origins, and no good society will receive her."

First Lady Catherine, now the Countess of Oxford. Could this be true? If so, she had been deceived about Lord Bromby.

"Apparently everyone knows it. Lord Bromby himself confided to Mr. Beringer that once he leaves Holly Bridge, he is off to Herefordshire to see her. And Lady Oxford is thirteen years older. Apparently, the Earl of Oxford has many political connections in Parliament, and Lord Bromby has political aspirations."

Isabella's spirits sank like a stone in a river. A wave of dizziness swept over her. She stepped forward and a creak resounded beneath her foot.

"Shh," one of the servants whispered. "Someone's coming."

It wasn't her own footfall that had stopped the servants' gossip, but the echo of footsteps in the hallway behind her as they approached. Dread rose in Isabella's throat, forming a hard knot. *Clump, slide, clump, slide, clump, slide.* The first step staccato, the second a slithering sound.

She turned and came face-to-face with Lord Bromby. He bowed to her. "Good morning, Miss Bankmill."

Isabella curtsied. "Lord Bromby."

Perhaps he sensed the tension radiating from her like steam from a lake. He made no other conversation but passed by her. She stared at his retreating back, her insides twisting with deep disappointment. The night before she had danced with him—thought him generous and good and even a potential match. Had she really deceived herself that he might have feelings for her? Now she did not know how she should sit at the same breakfast table with such a man or how she would force down so much as a bite of her breakfast.

Oh, what did it matter? In a few hours' time, they would depart for London, and she need not see Lord Bromby for some time—or ever again, if God permitted.

Part II

Nine

July 1812
St. James's Street, London

Boom! Boom! Boom! The knocking at the door sounded like thunder rolling in the distance. Who could be calling at this hour? Bromby was ready to leave his rooms for a reunion with some friends at a nearby tavern when the pounding began. He looked over at John Hobby, who sat in an armchair.

Hobby's eyes widened. "What in the world is that noise?"

"I have no idea." It was far beyond the hour for social calls. Why was no one answering the infernal knocking?

"Fletcher!" Bromby called into the corridor. "The door, Fletcher!" His valet appeared from an antechamber. "Yes, milord." Fletcher moved sluggishly, his eyes drooping with fatigue, but Bromby couldn't help that. They were all tired, after all. It came with the territory of being a celebrity and a celebrity's valet. The poor man's wife had passed away within the year, and Bromby had tried to be appropriately regretful for Fletcher's loss, but life and all its duties continued around them.

Bromby rubbed at his forehead as he sensed a sudden headache coming on.

The pounding stopped, and voices echoed from the corridor. Within a few moments, Susan, the maid, appeared in the doorway. "Pardon me, milord, but there is a … person … here to see you."

"Well, who is it?" asked Bromby.

Susan stammered. "Sh—*He* said his name is Carl Lamb." She leaned in a little closer and whispered, "And he's dressed in a page boy's clothing beneath a black cloak."

Bromby cringed. *Oh, dear.* A black cloak. Page boy's clothing. Carl Lamb. Lamb—the antithesis of the lion. There was only one person it could be.

"Leave us!" Bromby shouted just as the person in question shoved Susan out of the way and entered the room.

Susan curtsied quickly and departed.

The cloaked figure stood before them. Bromby caught a glimpse of Hobby's face—eyes wide and mouth slack—as the petite page boy threw off the concealing cape to reveal livery beneath, including a blue silk cap. Then, whisking away the cap, revealed a tumble of blonde curls.

"Catherine!" Bromby exclaimed, his heart pounding. Had she really appeared at his house alone, dressed in a costume? She was mad.

"I am here. Prepared to leave with you tonight," she panted. Her eyes were wild, darkened by dilated pupils.

"What?" gasped Hobby. "No. Lady Catherine, you must leave at once."

With a shriek that rattled Bromby's brain, Catherine threw herself at Bromby's knees. "You promised! You said we could run away together!"

His blood froze. Had she truly taken him seriously? He'd been joking. He'd had no intention of eloping with this hysterical woman. Even so, when he'd spoken the words, there had been a part of him that suspected she might have believed him. She was lunatic enough for anything.

Bromby met Hobby's eyes—all chastisement and derision. The strained set of his mouth confirmed the emotion.

"You must go, Lady Catherine," Hobby insisted.

"No!" she screamed at him, knotting her fists at her side.

"You must!"

"There will be blood!" she shrieked.

Hobby approached her forcefully, jutting out his chest and asserting his lawyerly intimidation. "Yes, there will ... if you do not go immediately."

Bromby nodded in agreement. What else could he do? The servants would be talking, spreading the news in no time.

Catherine turned her head to look at him, her eyes pleading. "Do you really wish for me to leave?"

"Yes, you must, Catherine. What will people say?" Many already thought he was a rake, and he did not disagree with that summation in total, but he would not risk his reputation in London's literary society—one he had worked hard to acquire—for a brief dalliance that had gone awry.

Balling her fists and closing her eyes, Catherine let out an animalistic wail. "Then the blood shall be mine!"

Bromby followed her eyes with his own as they moved toward the sofa where his dress sword lay encased in its sheath. In a sudden rush of fabric and stomping feet, all of them moved toward the sword at once, grasping for it, resulting in a tangle of arms. Catherine grabbed his little finger as she attempted to wrench the sword from his hold.

Then Hobby had it in his clutches. Holding it high above his head, he stepped backward and away from the flailing couple.

A few more moments of struggle, and Bromby had subdued Catherine while standing behind her, wrapping his arms tightly around her midsection and forcing her hands to her sides, both panting wildly. Bromby wondered what charms he had ever seen in this woman. She was little more than a wild animal.

"Do be sensible, Cat," he wheezed.

Her voice echoed off the rafters in the room. "You said we could elope!"

"In a moment of madness," explained Bromby, glancing up to see Hobby scolding him with his eyes. "I thought you knew I was only being fanciful. We could not possibly elope. What would everyone say?"

"I don't care what they say! I only care about you—about us."

"There is no us, Cat. That cannot be. Look, you must go. If you do not, the whole neighborhood will be spinning tales and spreading them throughout Mayfair."

Underneath his hold, the fight ebbed out of her. Her muscles softened and finally went slack. Although he was loath to release her lest she attempt to harm herself or him, he was anxious to pack her into a carriage and be done with this madness. How he hated scenes.

"I will only go," she puffed, "if Bromby consents to go with me."

Hobby held up his hands. "Look, I cannot allow you to be left alone with Bromby. Sanity must prevail here, Lady Catherine. I know your mother, and it would not do for me to allow even a hint of impropriety here at this juncture. We will send you back to Mayfair in a hackney coach."

"Then I shan't go." Her eyes flashed flames of defiance. "Not of my own volition. Not unless Bromby accompanies me."

This struggle was useless, and more and more time was passing. At this rate, his servants and the merchant whose store was just below would no doubt be spreading this news far and wide. He released her.

Catherine stumbled away and then turned to face him, her eyes blazing. "You lied to me!"

What have I done? He could not ever have fathomed this sort of ending to a harmless tryst … with a woman who knew the stakes. What was so unusual about this? The aristocracy engaged in such behavior behind closed doors every day. Everyone knew it, and no one batted an eye. But never had Bromby witnessed such a scene conducted in his presence. It shook him to the core, rattled his conscience—which was not easily rattled—and embarrassed him. The sooner he could be done with Lady Catherine Lyons, the better.

"Lady Catherine," Hobby entreated, "I really must insist you leave." His expression, usually calm and unruffled, was tense—a muscle in his jaw throbbed and a line formed between his eyebrows.

"I will go with you as far as Westminster." The words were out of Bromby's mouth before he could think better of it.

Hobby held up his hands. "No, Bromby, you cannot—"

"Hobby, you will hasten to your own house to receive me. Once we reach Westminster, I shall climb down from the carriage, leave Lady Catherine, and walk through your front door. Easy as you please."

Hobby shook his head. "This is madness. It is too dangerous."

Bromby insisted. "We have no time to stand here discussing any other plans. Even now the merchant in the store below is probably running to tell his friends of this scandal."

With a shaky breath, Hobby nodded. "All right. I will make my way down St. James's Street and cut across the park. I'll meet you in Westminster."

It took some doing for Bromby and Hobby to entreat Catherine to resume her cape and make her way to the awaiting coach, but the plan went off as Bromby suggested.

As the coach went along, Catherine sobbed.

"I love you. Do you not understand that I love you?"

"I do understand that you think you love me, Cat. But there are to be no more of these absurd games. Let us spend some time apart for now." He could not bring himself to say that he would be forever quitting her. The ramifications of such words would surely end in more histrionics. *I cannot take anymore this night.*

As they approached Hobby's house, the coach paused. Bromby cranked open the door and leapt out even as he disentangled his arm from Catherine's. He did not look back at her as the carriage moved on. Hobby's front door was already open and awaiting his entrance.

Once inside, he stood with his hands on his hips, puffing as though he'd run all the way.

Hobby stared at him and shook his head. "Idiot," he mumbled under his breath.

He deserved it, but he held up his hands. "What could I do? She's mad."

"You're mad. Whether you know it or not, you are encouraging her bad behavior. You must end all correspondence with her."

Bromby shook his head. Women came and went. Why should this one continue to hang on with such tenacity?

Recovering his breath, he checked his appearance in the hall mirror. His black hair was wilder than usual, his pale skin flushed. A smudge of dirt accented the side of his face. He wetted the edge of a handkerchief with his tongue and rubbed until the blemish disappeared. "I confess, dear Hobby, that I do find it difficult to cast off anyone who has become so attached to me. Poor soul. She is more doomed than I."

Hobby's sigh echoed in the foyer. "It is already a quarter to the hour. We are late. Shall we go?"

Satisfied with his appearance, Bromby nodded. "Yes. Let us go eat."

Hobby laughed as he picked up his gloves from the table. "Eat? You never eat. What? Some hard biscuits and vinegar?"

They made their way out the door. Stepping onto the street, Bromby experienced a twinge of paranoia. He looked to the left and the right, making certain no flailing Catherine Lyonses were coming his way with sharp objects raised overhead. But the street was empty and there were only the sounds of passing carriages and polite greetings in the darkness.

Ten

Bromby sipped at cold tea while reading the *Morning Post*. According to the paper, Lady Catherine was often seen at Almack's and other parties around town, waltzing masterfully. He sighed, shaking his head. At least she did something well. The paper went on to say, *Lady Catherine Lyons has been spotted with the poet Lord Bromby at several recent functions. The pair has also been seen at morning parties ...*

"Oh, this will not do," Lord Bromby spoke aloud. The only thing needed to completely destroy his reputation was news that they were seen exiting his rooms at St. James's Place just the other night under cloak of darkness.

His maid, Susan, appeared in the doorway, holding a letter. "Someone brought this, sir."

Bromby took the letter from her. Breaking the seal, he scanned the words on the page. It was from Catherine's mother, Lady Chatworth.

Catherine has disappeared without word or indication of her whereabouts. Last night, Lord Melwood harshly scolded his daughter-in-law's behavior. In response, Catherine dashed from the house, and none of the servants running after her were able to apprehend her.

Walter and I have spent all morning riding up and down the neighboring streets in my carriage. She is nowhere to be found.

Lord Bromby, I beg that if she is with you, or if you have seen her, please return her to Melwood House or alert us at once, and we shall send a carriage for her.

Bromby sighed and raised his fingers to his mouth. More drama. No matter, he would go at once to Melwood House and assure them Catherine was not with him.

Another knock at the door sent him pushing past Susan to answer it himself. Standing upon the stoop was a coachman, dressed in his full livery, holding out a stack of letters tied with a ribbon.

"I have been asked to deliver these from Lady Catherine Lyons." His hand jutted forward, holding out the letters.

Bromby hesitated. "Where is she?"

"I am not at liberty to say." He waved the letters up and down. "Please take these, sir."

Bromby shook his head. He could play this game as well. "Not until you tell me where she is."

"I can't, sir. I promised."

Bromby straightened to his full height. "I demand that you tell me."

The man bobbed the letters in his hand.

The coachman had obviously been paid to deliver the letters, so why not do the same to discover her whereabouts? "Whatever you have been paid, I shall add to it."

The man's beady brown eyes widened from the size of hazelnuts to that of walnuts as Bromby pulled notes from his pocket and held them out. Gingerly, he pulled the letters from the man's hand at the same time the coachman grasped the notes with his other hand. "She's in Kensington. She's staying at a surgeon's house there."

"A surgeon's house? Why?"

"I don't know, sir. And I should say no more. I promised."

With a clenched jaw, Bromby stepped out into the street, throwing a penetrating gaze toward the heavy-set coachman, forcing him to take three steps backwards. "You are in great danger, my good man. I am well connected and have many friends—several of whom are of the legal variety."

The man's lower lip jutted out in a defiant pout. Even so, a glimmer of fear lingered in his eyes.

"You are in danger of legal ramifications for helping to harbor an endangered member of the nobility. So, I advise that you tell me where she is."

The coachman's lower lip trembled. A moment of silence passed as did people on the street who looked at them with curiosity. Finally, the man took a deep breath. "Lady Catherine told me she ran away with no money on her person. I told her I wouldn't do her deliveries for free, so she sold one of her rings to hire me to take her somewhere."

"And you took her to Kensington?"

"That's where she said she wanted to go, so I took her there. I accompanied her to the door of the surgeon's house. She told him—like she told me—that she was fleeing from friends and family who meant to kill her."

"What?" Bromby scratched his head. But then he supposed he shouldn't be surprised. Catherine was mad enough to fabricate such a story.

"It's not true, is it, sir?"

"Of course, it's not true. Lady Catherine is not well. You have done a great service by revealing this information."

"She gave the surgeon strict instructions not to let anyone in who might ask for her." The man's face looked a little uncertain as he shrank away from Bromby and moved back to his carriage. "You won't tell her I told you this, will you, sir?"

Bromby shook his head. "No, of course not." What an idiot this man was. Of course, she would know. Everyone would know. "Certainly not. Your secret is safe."

Lord Bromby sifted through the letters during the carriage ride to Melwood house. Catherine had penned a letter for her husband, another for her mother, and one for him.

Breaking the familiar *L* symbol of the seal, he unfolded the parchment and read: *No doubt you broke the seal on this letter just as easily as you have broken my heart. You have drained the life from my body like a vampire drains blood from his victim. I cannot go on living in Melwood House pretending that all is well. It is not well and will never be well unless I can live somewhere far away from you. I must not be threatened with seeing you at parties or dinners.*

Bromby groaned, flinging his head backward against the seat of the coach. What was the point in continuing to read such a letter? Catherine's words gave him indigestion.

He entered Lady Melwood's drawing room, bowing to her before advancing to place a kiss upon her hand. "Lady Melwood."

As he straightened, he eyed her sixty-year-old face, coated in powder. Yes, she looked quite well for a woman of her age. Her hair, barely streaked with gray, had maintained its deep, rich hues of chocolate brown, and despite a few trailing creases around the eyes, the lines were minimal.

"Bromby. You have heard of our misfortunes."

Lord Bromby sighed heavily, throwing his coattails out behind him before perching at the edge of one of Lady Melwood's green velvet chairs. "I am just as astonished as you are. And since I am a main player in this sad drama, I have come to act out my next part."

Lady Melwood sat in a chair across from him. "She has contacted you?"

From the inside of his coat, Bromby produced the stack of correspondence from Catherine bound together with a light-blue ribbon. "I received these just today. A coachman brought them to my house. There is a letter addressed to you, another to Walter, and another to her mother. There was one addressed to me as well, which, of course, I have exempted from this collection."

"Of course." Lady Melwood took the letters as he held them out and tore open the one addressed to her. She scanned the words on the page. He cringed as he imagined the thoughts going through her head. Yes, he was partially to blame for all of this, and he was sorry for the part he'd played—even if his regret extended only to the inconvenience it caused him.

Lady Melwood read a few of the lines aloud. "I cannot return to Melwood House ... am a terrible wife and mother ... little Gus will receive better care in my mother's house ... my love for Bromby is too great..." She looked up at him with scolding eyes. A heavy, trembling sigh escaped her throat. "She is mad for love of you."

He cleared his throat and looked at her with a slanted glance. "Well. The feeling is not mutual. Nevertheless, I do care for Catherine and her welfare. And my esteem for you, Lady Melwood, is even greater. When the coachman delivered the letters, I managed to convince him—through a bit of monetary coercion—to reveal Catherine's whereabouts."

Lady Melwood leaned forward in her seat. "Where is she?"

"She is in Kensington. She is lodged in the home of a surgeon."

"Good heavens. We will send for her at once."

"It's not so simple. She has told them that she is being pursued by friends and family who wish to kill her."

"What?" Lady Melwood shrieked. "This has gone too far, Bromby. She is completely out of control. This must be stopped. We cannot have this sort of scandal at our feet."

Bromby laughed. "Do you think I wish to have it? I have not a moment's peace. For months now, I've endured an onslaught of most inconvenient charades. She turns up all over town—following me to the places where I dine, places I gather with friends. She has the audacity to turn up at my abode dressed in an outrageous costume, horrifying my friend Mr. Hobby, who was with me at the time."

"Oh dear."

"There is not a day that goes by I am not buried in a proliferation of her letters or drowning in her tear-stained ink. I've written and told her I no longer care for her. She will not hear it."

Lady Melwood's arched eyebrows knitted together. "I wonder if such a letter has precipitated these wild antics. *Are* you done with her?"

His raised his hands in the air. "Yes, yes! Over and over yes. Heaven protect me from this insanity."

Lady Melwood's gaze chastened him, even as a smirk pulled at the corner of her mouth. "It is all very well when the pursuit is new and challenging—a fox rushing headlong down a hill chasing a rabbit—but once the conquest is over, those moments of exhilaration are quickly forgotten."

Bromby pulled a handkerchief from his coat pocket and blotted at his brow. Yes, yes. It was always about the chase. He knew that well enough. "Nevertheless, I believe it is my duty to collect her from this surgeon's house in Kensington. I believe if she will see no one else, she will see me. Let me go and fetch her."

Lady Melwood rose from her seat and walked to stand beside the window, looking out on the street below. Placing a finger to her lips, she appeared to consider the situation. "That may be best. Perhaps she will allow you to bring her home."

Lord Bromby frowned. "Forgive me. I realize this is a delicate matter."

Lady Melwood waved her hand. "You will find me quite tough in these matters, Bromby. I am by no means a delicate woman. I'm not as much concerned with Catherine's choices as I am with her determination to openly flaunt them. If these things are to occur, they must be conducted using one's head. Something Catherine is obviously incapable of doing.

Bring her to Melwood House, and that should be the last time you are to meet for the foreseeable future."

Bromby grimaced. He could only hope.

Eleven

Bromby stood on the stoop of the surgeon's home on Kensington Terrace and knocked loudly. Within moments the door opened, and a tall, thin man loomed in the doorway with a gaunt, expressionless face.

"Yes?"

"I wish to see Lady Catherine Lyons," Bromby demanded sternly.

"She is not receiving visitors at present." The servant spoke with a flat, unwavering voice.

Bromby straightened, staring directly into the man's eyes. "I know she is stopping here. I *will* see her. I am her brother." It was the only thing he could think to say that would allow him more clout than his own name. She had no brother. But if he knew her as he thought he did, she would appear for this false relation. She was just dramatic enough to want to explore this curious claim.

"Wait here." The servant promptly closed the door.

The afternoon heat, combined with his own nerves, brought sweat to his brow, and he pulled a handkerchief from his pocket to wipe at his forehead. A few moments later, the servant returned and opened the door wide for Bromby to step inside.

He was shown up the stairs and into the room where Catherine stood like a frightened child. Her dark eyes widened. She held her clasped hands to her neck. "Bromby," she breathed. "I thought it might be you."

"Good heavens, Cat. What is all of this about?"

"Have you come for me?"

"I've come to fetch and bring you home."

Her face fell. "I'm not going back there."

"You must."

"I will not. I'm never going back."

As though approaching a wounded animal he didn't wish to frighten, he held out his hand, careful to block the doorway from her exit. "You cannot stay here."

"They said I could stay as long as I wish."

He looked around him. Although the home was draped in a modest respectability, it in no way compared with Melwood House and the niceties to which Catherine was accustomed. "Catherine, this is madness. You cannot stay. What would you do here?"

She raised her chin defiantly. "I do not plan to stay here. I have already booked a stagecoach. I will leave for Portsmouth in three days' time."

"Portsmouth! You know no person in Portsmouth. What will you do there?"

"I plan to sail on the first boat that leaves port. No matter where it is bound, there I shall go."

He moved toward her. "Catherine, this is absurd! You will do no such thing. You will leave with me at once."

"And go where?" The defiance in her face crumbled, a sliver of hope returning. "With you? Cannot we run away somewhere together, Bromby? Let us go to Scotland or Wales … or to your home at Broadwell Abbey. We could live there quite happily, I'm certain."

Oh, dear. Not this again. "We can do nothing of the sort. I am taking you straight back to Melwood House where you will reunite with your husband."

She turned away and clenched her fists at her side. Dread filled him. These were all-too-familiar signs of a tantrum building.

"I will never go back there. Never!"

Bromby nervously chewed at his fingernails—a habit he indulged in moments of tension. He would have to take charge of this situation, or he would never lure her away. Turning to the hallway, he called out to the servants. "Hello, there!"

The tall man fairly floated out of the shadows. "Sir?"

"Please have someone fetch Lady Catherine's things. She shall be departing as soon as possible."

Without warning, an agonized shriek tore from Catherine's throat.

———— ⟡ ————

Less than an hour later, Catherine and a sack full of meager items she had procured in her two days' run were packed into the carriage where they met Dalton, an obliging servant brought along from Melwood House. He had been asked to wait in the carriage to serve as chaperone, as well as insurance against Lady Catherine bolting.

Inside, Catherine was sullen, refusing to look at or talk to him. All for the best. He'd rather her silent in her anger than carrying on with hysterics as before. It was best if as few words as possible passed between them, especially with Dalton present.

He exhaled as the carriage arrived in front of Melwood House. They were met by several servants, one of whom flew up the stairs to alert the rest of the household of Lady Catherine's return. Bromby disembarked from the carriage and stood outside. He stared at the ground, shoving at a loose stone with his shoe. *Let this all be over and done with quickly.*

"Come now, Cat. You must come inside."

She turned away from him, facing the window on the other side of the carriage.

She would make a scene, wouldn't she? It was the only power she had left. The one thing she could do was refuse to leave the carriage. Bromby rubbed his forehead. When this was all over, he'd go home and pour himself a stiff brandy.

Lady Melwood and Walter Lyons descended the stairs. Bromby locked eyes with Walter, and the two men nodded tersely at one another. Bromby chewed at his fingernails while they all stood by waiting for Catherine's next move. This was absolutely the last time he involved himself in such a muddle. It was hardly worth all this to-do.

"Thank you for returning Catherine to us, Lord Bromby," Walter said in a low voice as he stepped forward to approach the carriage.

Bromby exchanged a nervous glance with Lady Melwood.

It was strangely fascinating to witness Walter speaking to his wife. "Come now, darling. Come inside. Let us forget all of this and start afresh."

Although Bromby could not see Catherine's expression within the carriage, she must have been crying. Walter pulled a handkerchief from his pocket and handed it inside the carriage. "Little Gus is waiting for you inside. He's missed his mother terribly. The servants have prepared the best meal imaginable. All of your favorites. There's pudding as well."

Poor, longsuffering Walter. What tortures he must suffer. To be married to such a creature ... well, Bromby could only imagine, and he thanked his lucky stars it was not his fate.

Walter's groveling was sufficient to coax Catherine's thin, ragged form from her carriage cocoon. She really did look shocking—her eyes all wild and sunken. He was not to blame, however. She had brought herself to this low point.

Walter handed her down from the carriage, and she looked around as though she were seeing the world for the first time. Her eyes grazed his before darting away, and without a word, she glided into the house on the arm of her husband.

Bromby departed and made his way home to St. James's Street, relief and heaviness simultaneously tipping his heart this way and that. He would wait a few days, and then he would compose his farewell letter to Catherine once and for all. Of one thing he was certain. He would never again allow himself to be alone with her.

Twelve

It was a warm afternoon when Bromby next visited Melwood house. Despite recent occurrences, Lady Melwood appeared happy to see him as she greeted him in the garden, where they were soon seated in the gazebo.

"Dalton," she called out to her servant. "Please bring tea out to the gazebo." Dalton nodded and rushed off toward the house.

Lady Melwood turned to Bromby. Her cheeks were flushed with heat, and she unfurled a yellow fan and flittered it back and forth before her face.

"You see my flowering currant is producing fruit." She pointed to the nearby shrub with its blue-black fruit and white flowers. "We will soon have currant jam served with our tea."

Bromby smiled. "I will look forward to my next visit when I may enjoy it."

Lady Melwood sat back in her chair, her gray eyes fixed upon him as a slight smile graced her lips. "I'm sure you've heard that Napoleon has been successfully defeating the Russians. You must be pleased. I know how you admire him."

Bromby nodded. "I admire his bravery, his tenacity. I constantly marvel at his choices and wonder what he will do next."

Lady Melwood's eyes narrowed. "You are obviously attracted to all things exhilarating, unconventional, and dogged." Dalton arrived with the tea, and she prepared their cups. "And have you been writing more poetry?"

"I began writing a new poem, *The Pilgrimage*. It is reminiscent of my time in Greece—inspired by some of my more ... colorful adventures there. My publisher is eager for the finished product, so I am busily polishing the rough sections. He wants nothing that is not equal to *Herald of the Morning*."

"Of course. And London is eager for more. We know the effect your words have on those who read them." She shot him a wry smile.

He would have to bring up the problematic topic sooner or later. He took a deep breath. "How fares Lady Catherine?"

"She is in Ireland with Walter and her mother and little Gus. The best place for her. Your farewell letter to her was not quite as effectual as you might have intended."

"Was it?" He squinted against the sun as it shifted overhead. "I scarcely remember what I said." He reached for his tea cup and lifted it to his lips.

"She had a sort of letter-burning party one night not long after she received it. It seems she feels quite certain you still love her and would live with her if she were free."

He shifted in his seat, slightly amused by this image of Catherine burning letters while others looked on. "A letter-burning party? How droll! Oh, dear Cat. She is mad, isn't she?"

Lady Melwood nodded. "Completely. She will stay in Ireland for the foreseeable future, but I would not be surprised if she does not attempt to contact you again."

She grew pensive for a few moments and appeared to be studying him as a smile drifted over her lips and her eyes twinkled. "Bromby, I've been thinking. Why don't you marry?"

He looked up, his brow knitting as his amusement transformed into surprise. "What?"

"Yes. I think that's the very thing. You should marry."

He stood abruptly, vigorously rubbing at his mouth and chin. "That's the last thing I expected you to say." Was Lady Melwood in need of some new hugger-mugger to occupy her time. Marrying him off must seem like a good ploy.

"Why? Haven't you ever considered it?"

A sudden bout of edginess joggled him. He looked to the right where flowers grew in the garden and then to the left where a hedgerow blocked his exit. "I suppose I've considered it in theory, but—"

"It makes perfect sense, Bromby. You shall marry, thereby cutting off all of Catherine's continued pursuit. If she believes you love another …"

He chewed on his thumbnail as he began to pace the length of a patch of grass. His head churned. In fact, he had not considered it, but now that she suggested it, marriage might be the very thing to curtail Catherine's advances and repair Society's opinion of him. "The idea is intriguing, I must admit. But who on earth would I marry?"

Lady Melwood waggled her head. "I've been pondering this for a few weeks now. I can think of several young ladies who would match quite nicely." She ran through the list of names. "Miss Cordelia Noble, Rose Pryor, Tabitha Leighton, or … my niece, Isabella Bankmill. She's the right age and rank. She would be a perfect match."

Smiling slowly, he began to laugh. Isabella Bankmill. The religious one. Very pretty and intelligent. He had liked her very much in Kent. But when he truly considered the prospects of being married to her, he could not envision it. "Oh, no. Not her."

"Why not?"

"She is *too* perfect. And I am doomed. I would corrupt her. I can't have that on my conscience."

Lady Melwood laughed. "Oh, nonsense. She would be a good match for you. And she is to inherit a healthy sum from her uncle, who is childless. You've told me more than once that you're in debt and must sell your childhood home. Perhaps this could be an answer for you."

He chewed harder at the edge of his thumb, unearthing a hangnail. "Intriguing. But I thought Miss Bankmill was already engaged to Sir Malcolm Meade."

"Goodness, no. Sir Malcolm has been very ill of late. He can hardly get out of bed, much less marry. Whatever gave you that idea?"

"I believe Lady Catherine told me as much." But then, of course Catherine would say such a thing—anything to throw him off course of a potential match.

"Catherine was mistaken. Isabella is unattached."

He shook his head and dropped his fingers from his mouth. "At any rate, I'm quite certain she'd not be happy as my bride. She is devoted to her religious beliefs and principles."

"Well, that should keep you in check, Bromby. Christian principles certainly would not hurt you. Anyway, I know she admires you."

He shook his head. "Heaven only knows what Catherine has told her about me."

Lady Melwood smiled and nodded as though she had already decided the matter in full. "You must renew your acquaintance with Isabella Bankmill."

At least Isabella was pretty enough to be appealing but not so attractive as to invite trouble. Her inheritance was enticing as well. "I see what you are saying. It could be a good plan, I suppose."

"It's an excellent plan."

"But Miss Bankmill has returned to Seaham, I believe?"

"Yes. You should write to her father. Ask his permission to correspond with her. Then write to Isabella. Tell her you've thought of her continually since your last meeting. Send her some of your finest poetry. Woo her, Bromby. You know how it's done," she said with an arched eyebrow. "You've proven to be quite effective in this area."

An image of Catherine's desperate face passed through his mind. He scratched his chin. Perhaps it was not the worst idea.

Thirteen

13 October 1812
London

Dear Miss Bankmill,

It has been sometime since we last met or spoke, and I pray you will not take offense to my letter as it aims to renew our friendship, now somewhat stalled by our separation.

Lady Melwood graciously allowed me to see some poetry you bestowed upon her last summer, and I hope you do not mind that I took the liberty of reading your verse, the purpose for my writing now. I was greatly interested in your poems, Miss Bankmill, and I found them full of feeling and promise. With practice and guidance, if you take the time to concentrate on the feeling budding inside the words you've employed, your future poems will bloom with vitality. I would never have known that underneath your somber countenance, such depth of feeling existed.

Miss Bankmill, please permit me to tell you how I admire your strength of character. Your dedication to faith add to your many virtues. I realize our conversations in Kent were not altogether satisfactory to you—especially in spiritual matters. Please do not think me insincere— my own beliefs are unchanged. A great many opinions within a person alter with the ebb and flow of life, so it goes without saying that perhaps one day I may share your sentiments. For now, however, I consider myself far beneath you, morally and spiritually. If you were less of an angelic being, I should probably find myself soliciting more of your friendship and company.

Yours, B

31 October 1812
Seaham, Durham

Dear Lord Bromby,

I am in receipt of your letter with its undeserved praise. I must admit surprise that my aunt shared verse intended only for her eyes. My words were written a great many years ago as a gift to her, which I had not intended to be shown to you or anyone else. Although humbled your unwarranted praise, I shudder to think you might have assumed I asked her for your good opinion on my amateurish endeavors.

As for your comment regarding my goodness, I must also refuse these compliments. No one is good but God himself. Any virtues you see in me are dispensed from above. As for your spiritual state, Lord Bromby, I am pleased that you are not completely averse to the possibility of change. It is difficult to advise someone who desires no immediate aid, but as I look upon you as a friend, I feel it is my duty to do what I can. Ephesians 1:7 tells us that in God we have *redemption through his blood, the forgiveness of sins, according to the riches of his grace.* God's forgiveness is offered to us through the death and resurrection of his son, our savior, Jesus Christ. You only need believe and call upon his name, and he is faithful and just to forgive. But perhaps this is enough said on the subject for now.

I wonder at your feelings regarding Napoleon's retreat from Moscow, as I know you are one of his ardent admirers.

For the present, I wish you much health. Please give my love to my aunt and cousins.

Fondly,
Isabella

12 November 1812
London

Dear Miss Bankmill,

I assure you my praise of your poetry was in no way unwarranted or insincere, and I hope you will continue to press forward. The seeds of this emotional crop grow within your mind. Once harvested, you will have words that taste sweeter than the best of wines, and future vintages will be all the sweeter.

I am perfectly willing to further discuss spiritual matters with you. You will be pleased to hear that I attended a church service this past

Wednesday. It was a funeral, mind you, but I found myself greatly uplifted by the vicar's reading of Psalm 56, verses 6 and 7.

Every day they wrest my words: all their thoughts are against me for evil.

They gather themselves together, they hide themselves, they mark my steps, when they wait for my soul.

Shall they escape by iniquity? In thine anger cast down the people, O God.

It was an odd choice for a funeral, but the deceased man asked that it be read, so we may only assume this reflects the state of his mind—his fears, his vexations. I could relate to the verses, finding myself in a similar state.

As you may know, Miss Bankmill, there has been much talk of and about me here in London and beyond. I do not wish to deceive you. These unflattering portraits of me may be exaggerated, but they are probably accurate. I would wish that you consider my desire to improve and mend some of these sins of which I am accused.

Yours,

B

20 November 1812
Seaham, Durham

Dear Lord Bromby,

Regardless of any gossip surrounding your character, I am inclined to think you are a man misjudged. We are all sinners, and all of us have committed acts for which we later repent. I do not think ill of you, nor shall I.

It pleases me immensely that you are pursuing a life of more worthwhile living and considering scripture as part of your present course. Funerals are not a bad place to contemplate this, as they remind us of our own mortality. We shall all die, and we must know our fitness for eternity. I'm sure you will not be surprised, Lord Bromby, when I tell you that I pray daily for your heart, mind, and your soul. It is my sincerest wish to see you in God's grace.

And I hope you know I consider you a friend, Lord Bromby.

Fondly,

Isabella

28 November 1812
London

Dear Catherine,

I hope this letter finds you well in Ireland.

Coming straight to the point, here is my purpose for writing. You have forced me into a corner so that I must be harsh. Your behavior—so unladylike and rash, bordering on lunatic—induces me to state my intentions clearly. I have done everything I can to disengage from you, yet you persist on flooding my doorstep with letters and trinkets—even from Ireland.

I thank you for the kind preference you have shown me over the past few months, but my heart is now quite engaged with another. I will not mention names, nor will any further persecution induce me to reveal them.

If you so desire, we may remain friends. As your friend, I offer you this morsel of truth: your behavior is unguarded at best, reckless at median, and atrocious at worst. Spawned by your own self-importance and narcissism, you make yourself ridiculous with your costumes and mad scenes. I advise you to alter your behavior and immediately cease your determined pursuit of me. It is hopeless.

Sincerely,

B

12 December 1812
Broadwell Abbey

Dear Lady Melwood,

Once again, I find myself soliciting your good opinion and assistance. The clutches of mad-cat Catherine are still upon me, and I must once and for all be free of her. I have also been in correspondence with her mother in Brighton, and she agrees that we must do something to end this insanity. At this very moment, I am in receipt of yet another express from Ireland. Will this drama never end?

I have written to Catherine, unconditionally severing our relationship. The letter she sent me, delivered via John Hobby (as I would not divulge my location to her) made it clear that she will not quit her suit. She seems to think that I am insincere in my words. My only hope now lies in the remedy which we discussed when I was last in your company.

If I must marry, I would prefer your niece to anyone else of my acquaintance. She is kind and intelligent, with good breeding and correct family titles, and she is of the same Norman and Scottish descent as I. However, if she will not have me, I shall consider a marriage to the next suitable woman who does not loathe the sight of me. I am not at all concerned with love and romance, as that is easily acquired in a week's time as long as the lady's fortune is substantial.

I would now ask if you would be so kind as to write a letter to your niece inquiring if she is in the least bit disposed to enter into an engagement with me. Although I assure you that I possess full capabilities of domestic tranquility, I have never in my life ventured a proposal, and I will not impose a formal offer upon your niece lest she indicate that her affections tend toward that end. As you might conclude, there is some urgency in my request.

Yours most affectionately,

B

27 December 1812
Melwood House
London
Dear Isabella,

I hope this letter finds you and your parents in the best of health and trust your Christmas was a festive and fruitful time.

Niece, I write to you on behalf of Lord Bromby. As you may be aware, Lord Bromby is most fond of you. He admires your intelligence, your clever speech, and the vivacity you possess. More than once he has spoken to me of your moral superiority and spiritual sincerity. He feels you are a kind, good person who would make a proper wife. It is for this purpose I now write and inquire on his behalf. Would you consider a marriage proposal from Lord Bromby? He has made it clear that he will not advance in this suit unless given your permission.

I await your reply.

Affectionately,

Aunt Ophelia Melwood

10 January 1813

Seaham, Durham
> Dearest Aunt,

I was greatly astonished by the contents of your letter. Although Lord Bromby did write to my father to ask permission to correspond with me, there has been little indication that he looks upon me in a romantic way. I am flattered by Lord Bromby's regard for me, but I find myself unable to accept an offer of marriage from him.

Lord Bromby lacks attributes which I desire most in a husband. Although he has expressed some interest in pursuing a deeper understanding of God, I do not detect a sincere commitment, nor have I seen any evidence of conversion. Before I could consider any such proposal, these characteristics would need be present.

As I had some opportunity to judge his behavior during my stay at the Beringer's estate last spring, I observed a man ruled by passion and folly—not a person in whom a regulated, moral value system reigns. I hope you will pardon my stark words, but there is the truth as I see it.

It is with regret that I reject this offer, but I remain his devoted friend and pray this will not hinder my acquaintanceship with Lord Bromby. I continue to think of him fondly.

> Lovingly,
> Isabella

28 January 1813
London
Melwood House
> Dear Bromby,

My niece has refused your offer. Upon her high horse she speaks of your moral failings but hopes her rejection will not hinder your friendship.

We will devise another remedy for your situation.

> Sincerely,
> Lady M

9 February 1813
Eywood, Herefordshire
> Dear Lady Melwood,

Fear not. I'm not in the least troubled by the rejection, nor am I offended by Miss Bankmill's reference to my moral failings. She is right in this assessment, of course, and as I've said many times before, she is too good for my blackened soul. I say, all the better for her. As for her concerns regarding our friendship, this rejection in no way affects my regard or friendly feelings towards her. If anything, my admiration of her is improved.

You should not be so angered by her rejection of me, Lady M. In the words of Lord Foppington, "I have lost a thousand women in my time but never had the ill manners to quarrel with them for such a trifle."

On a happier note, *The Pilgrimage* is published and flying off the shelves faster than it may be stocked. The Edinburgh Review has called the poem bold, unique, and rhythmically superior to anything of its kind. I am already receiving letters—invitations—from Samuel Rogers and William Wordsworth to join them for literary lunches upon my return. I suppose I am still very much in demand. If I were to receive monetary rewards for my poetry, I might be fairly flush in the pockets. Of course, as a gentleman I shan't consider it.

All is well for now. I have met a very dear friend in Herefordshire— Lady Oxford. Her husband is a political figure who may help me with pursuit of political oratory opportunities. At any rate, I shall travel with her and into the country for a few weeks. You know how the story goes from there...

Your friend,

B

Part III

Fourteen

August 1813

Six months had passed since she'd rejected Lord Bromby's marriage proposal. Had she made a mistake? Perhaps God was calling her to be Bromby's reform. This would be her last season in London. Everyone knew that if a young lady came through three London seasons without a husband, she should assume it was not to be. She'd encountered many promising suitors, but none of them fulfilled all the qualities from her carefully constructed list. In fact, the man who had come closest to fulfilling all of them—save the first on her list regarding devotion to God—was Lord Bromby.

In fact, as of late, she'd lain awake at night, remembering Lord Bromby's face—his luminescent beauty and astonishing philosophical musings that had so challenged her prayer time. His letters—his words— had nestled into a shelf of her heart. Perhaps he was just a misunderstood, sensitive soul who needed the acceptance and guidance of a woman to introduce him to God's love. Why else had she been put into this world if not to spread the word of the Lord to those in need?

The weather had been terrible for the past few days. Rain and wind kept her indoors at her Aunt Lydia's, and despite herself, Isabella missed the parties, dances, and social gatherings that had marked this season. On the afternoon of her fourth day indoors, while sitting in the morning room reading a novel, Rebecca and David Beringer came to call.

"It is so good to see you both!" Isabella said, rushing to grasp Rebecca's hands. "But you are the last people I expected to see. Your last letter stated you were still in the country."

"We were," Rebecca said. "But we'd had enough of it. The weather turned bad, so we thought we'd return to town—except all we've had here is more bad weather. Anyway, we thought to pay you a visit when we first arrived, but the rain!"

"Yes, I know. I've been indoors for days. But I am so glad you came."

David was very quiet, his sad eyes more melancholy than usual.

"Won't you both sit down?"

David and Rebecca settled into chairs.

David suddenly sat a little straighter and met her gaze. "Miss Bankmill, it has been much too long. A year, I think?"

"Longer, Mr. Beringer. Since last spring at Holly Bridge."

"Have you been enjoying yourself?"

"Yes, the celebrations in London have been nonstop. Despite the weather, everyone is in a good mood. The victory of Wellington's armies in the Peninsula has been on everyone's tongue."

"Yes, yes," he agreed, punctuating each word. "I daresay things are looking up in terms of preserving England against the French. Napoleon looks as though he will be defeated eventually. Defeating Napoleon and holding him at bay has been first on the prime minister's list."

Isabella's mind flashed to Lord Bromby's last letters filled with excitement about Napoleon and his armies. He must be lamenting this news.

"Other than balls and parties, my stay has been very uneventful indeed," Isabella said. "I regret I have no humorous or interesting stories with which to entertain you."

"No entertaining stories required at all, Miss Bankmill. We are simply glad to be in your company," said David.

Staring into his eyes, which lingered just a little too long on hers, she recognized the same emotion from a year earlier when she had suspected that David might have formed a romantic attachment to her.

As though he read her thoughts, David's face colored, and he dropped his gaze, swallowing hard before he next spoke. "When will you return to Seaham?"

"Next week," said Isabella. "The season will be over, and my parents will expect me home."

Rebecca's eyes brightened as she sat forward in her seat. "Our real purpose for coming was to ask if you would accompany us to the theater tomorrow night. Macbeth will play at The Theatre Royal. I am sorry 'tis not a comedy, but I have not been to the Drury Lane Theatre since it burned down a few years ago. It recently reopened last year, and I've been eager to go."

Isabella grimaced. She was not opposed to attending the theater, but it was not one of her favorite pastimes. She did not like the pretend aspect of acting and watching players upon the stage move through scenes as though they were in a different place or time. She especially did not like those violent plays in which murder and mayhem were simulated. But she didn't want to disappoint the Beringers.

"I'm not a lover of theater myself," said David. "But Rebecca does enjoy it."

Isabella forced a gracious smile to her lips. "Of course. I shall be honored to attend."

When the Beringers were ready to leave, David went in search of the servants to bring the carriage around. Rebecca leaned close to Isabella, checking over her shoulder to make certain he had left the room. Then her face and shoulders sank. "My poor, poor brother."

"Whatever is the matter?"

Rebecca shook her head and looked down at her gloved hands. "I suppose I will tell you, Izzy, because you are my closest friend. But please do not breathe a word of this to David. He would be so angry with me if he knew I had confided in you. But I am worried about him."

What could be so terrible and so private? "Of course, I will not say anything."

Rebecca inhaled sharply. "I know I have said it before, but my brother is the kindest, most well-meaning, and good-hearted man I know. It grieves me that he has been so abused in matters of the heart."

She looked over her shoulder again and turned back to Isabella, whispering. "He has again been rejected."

"Rejected?"

Rebecca nodded. "Yes. Last year he proposed to a young lady—none of us liked her—but it was someone with whom he'd had a long friendship. When she did not accept him, he was devastated. That was last spring—just before we met you in London. This past week, he made an offer to a Miss Felicity Bowden. Her father's estates are very near ours in Kent. David spent the whole of the summer in Kent so that he might call upon and visit her frequently. He felt so certain that she was to be his wife." Rebecca's gaze dropped again, and she shook her head. "But she will not have him."

"I'm so sorry." Isabella really was sorry for him. Two rejections of a man who seemed in every way desirable … well, it was almost unheard of. "Did she give an account as to her reasons?"

"That's the rub, you see. She rejected him for nearly the same reason as the first young lady. She claimed that although she had great respect for him, she did not love him. Apparently, her affections lay elsewhere. My father says that ladies these days read too many novels, and from them have received very strange notions about love."

Isabella glanced at the novel splayed on the divan where she had earlier left it.

Rebecca continued. "That is why we have returned to London. David needed to put distance between himself and Kent … and the Bowdens. He may wear a brave mask, Izzy, but he is truly heartbroken. He feels perhaps God does not intend for him to marry. But I know this is not true. Many women have said that he is handsome, and one has only to look at him to see that he is."

She looked up at Isabella, her brows bent, a question in her gaze. "Do you find my brother handsome, Izzy?"

A flush of heat shot up Isabella's neck and into her face. Oh, no. This was a predicament, indeed. She did not wish to hurt her friend, but she also did not want to offer her false hope. Yes, David Beringer was handsome, but her feelings for him did not extend beyond friendship either. "Yes, your brother is handsome, Rebecca. But you need not enlist my good opinion for this."

"Oh, but I think he greatly admires your good opinion." Rebecca's eyes twinkled.

Isabella tensed as imaginary stone masons began to erect walls inside of her. She was only too thankful when David reappeared and announced that the carriage was being brought around.

The following night, Isabella and the Beringers arrived at the Theatre Royal. It was alight with an incandescent glow that spilled over into the carriage-lined street where ladies were handed down. The ground was wet and soft from days of rain. Isabella frowned at a squelching sound as she stepped out of the carriage. She looked down and lifted her foot. The bottoms of her new shoes were caked with mud.

She moved alongside David Beringer, her arm tucked in his—as was his sister's on his right side—and they moved into the overly warm foyer which teemed with people. The noise and movement overwhelmed Isabella. Ladies in all their finery spun as though they were at a ball. In stark contrast, a group of drunken, lower-class men pushed and shoved one another just through the inner doors of the gallery. A woman screamed. Glass broke nearby. Isabella turned as another pair of men were ushered from the theatre and thrown into the street.

David escorted Isabella and Rebecca into the safety of the theatre box, which allowed a clear view of not only the stage, but the pit below. There, more working men and women crowded into the gallery, sufficiently removed from those who could afford the seats Isabella and the Beringers currently enjoyed.

A handful of peanuts flew through the air, followed swiftly by a half-filled container of ale, its contents splashing over the heads of the people below. All of this and the performance had not yet started.

"Lord Bromby!" cried Rebecca.

At the sound of the name, Isabella whipped her head around. Indeed, it was the man himself—dressed in a fashion that Beau Brummell himself might have worn, a deep green coat over top of his gold waistcoat and a white cravat. His hair was not nearly so wild and unruly as she remembered it.

Her heart jolted into a hammering rhythm. It had been over a year since they'd last seen one another during that fateful week at Holly Bridge, which ended with such misgivings and disappointment.

"Miss Bankmill, Mr. and Miss Beringer. What a happy surprise."

Isabella then noticed the lady clutching his arm.

"Allow me to introduce my sister, Mrs. Agatha Morley."

"Stepsister," Agatha Morley corrected.

"Yes," confirmed Lord Bromby. "It is a long, sordid story, but we have just been reacquainted with one another after—how long's it been?"

"Thirteen years," she responded.

"Thirteen years?" Bromby's eyebrows rose. "Has it really been that long?"

"Yes. You were eleven. I was eighteen when I left Broadwell Abbey. Thirteen years ago."

Isabella's gaze traveled over the form of the tall, thin woman whom Bromby had termed as his "sister, but not really his sister." There was no question as to whether Agatha Morley was his sister, as they looked nothing alike. Agatha's head was topped with a mass of white-blonde, perfectly formed curls resembling palest moonlight. Her eyes were large, almost overly so, their color practically nonexistent. Isabella supposed they could be termed a pale blue, but they were clear like water. Her dark-gray dress emphasized the paleness of her skin.

"It is so nice to meet you, Miss Bankmill. Gregory has told me so much about you." She looked up at Bromby, her expression alight with admiration.

David Beringer appeared to be watching the pair closely. "I hope you will not find that I'm being remarkably obtuse, but I'm intrigued. So … the two of you were raised together as brother and sister? I confess, I'm a bit confused. Please forgive my rudeness, Mrs. Morley."

"Mrs. Morley's mother married my father," Bromby offered. "When she died, he married my mother."

"Yes, but we never met until you were around eight," Agatha added.

He nodded. "When you came to live with me and my mother at Broadwell Abbey."

Agatha laughed cheerfully and grasped Bromby's arm once more. "Yes, 'tis a strange, fascinating history we share."

Isabella was relieved at the sound of the bells signaling the performance. "Shall we all sit?"

Lord Bromby and Mrs. Morley moved into the front seats while Isabella and the Beringers seated themselves behind them.

Lord Bromby turned and addressed Isabella. "I'm amazed that you would attend a theatrical performance, Miss Bankmill." His left eyebrow raised mischievously.

"The Beringers invited me, Lord Bromby. I do not care for the theater myself."

"That is a shame. I adore the theater and go whenever I can." He paused a moment before continuing. "But I daresay you find it vulgar and violent."

"Yes, Lord Bromby, I do."

Bromby paused, apparently considering her words. "But then life is vulgar and violent, Miss Bankmill. Don't you agree? Perhaps the theater merely reflects this fact."

Agatha Morley turned in her seat to join the conversation. "I, for one, am excited to see the performance. This is the first time I've been to the theater since my husband died."

"Oh, I'm so sorry," said Isabella. "When did he pass?"

"About eight months ago," said Agatha without a hint of sadness in her eyes. "Have you enjoyed a fine season, Miss Bankmill?"

"Yes. Although now it is drawing to a close."

Agatha smiled as though remembering it for herself. "A rush of dinners and balls and morning waltzing parties ..."

Bromby groaned. "The infernal waltz. Let me hear no more about it."

"You do not care for the waltz, Gregory?"

"Not at all. It is—" he glanced at Isabella with an arched eyebrow "too vulgar for my tastes. Why not turn off the lights and have it over with?"

Agatha smacked his arm with a little shriek. "Oh, you are a bad man. You do not even dance, Bromby."

"I have been known to dance once or twice—when the partner was especially worthy." He maintained his gaze upon Isabella.

She blushed to the roots of her hairline and looked away. "I believe the play is starting," she said quickly, pointing her fan at the stage. They all turned toward the sound of the music and the parting curtains.

The play began, but Isabella could not concentrate on any of it. She stared at Bromby's back, the shape of his shoulders, the way the waves of his hair touched the sharp point of his collar.

He once asked me to be his wife, and I refused him. Perhaps I was wrong...

Two days later, Isabella and Rebecca met once more at Lady Heatherton's morning waltzing party.

Lady Heatherton's party was Isabella's final engagement of the London season. At the end of the week, she would return home to Seaham with no great prospects. In addition, at the end of her trip, with nothing to hope for, she had once again encountered Lord Bromby. And since seeing him at the theater, her fascination with him had returned. One glimpse of his handsome face had awakened that sleeping giant in her heart. *I might already have been his wife ...*

But then, ashamed, Isabella shook her head, expelling the thoughts from her mind, repeating assurances to herself like a mantra. No, she was not like the others—she would not allow her imagination and her emotions to run wild. She had refused him for good reason.

Lady Heatherton lived in Mayfair, not far from Melwood House. A frequenter of Almack's, Lady Heatherton was well-known as a lover of the waltz and anything new and fashionable. Her gatherings were frequent, and invitations were much sought after.

Isabella looked for Lord Bromby when she arrived at Lady Heatherton's that morning. No one had mentioned his name, so perhaps he would not come.

As Isabella moved into the room where the other partygoers congregated, she breathed a little sigh. It was probably all for the best. Of course, he wouldn't be here. Lord Bromby did not like the waltz.

"Lord Bromby is here," Rebecca whispered in her ear some minutes later.

"Where?" Turning to the right and the left, Isabella scanned the room.

Rebecca nodded. "Over there."

He stood against the teal-colored wall, alongside his stepsister, Agatha Morley.

"I did not think he would come," Isabella breathed.

"He is still very much in demand in London, especially now that his newest poem, *The Pilgrimage*, has been published—and reprinted at least once."

With his brow sitting heavy over his eyes and his lips pursed, Bromby scanned the room, pausing on Isabella. With a nod of his head, he advanced in her direction.

"They are coming over," Isabella whispered, straightening her posture.

Lord Bromby and Mrs. Morley stopped before them and bowed. "We meet again, Miss Bankmill, Miss Beringer."

Agatha Morley wore a mauve dress, a matching ribbon woven into her platinum tresses. "Will you waltz, Miss Beringer? Or are you opposed to it as well?"

Isabella met Bromby's eyes and quickly looked away. "I am not opposed."

"Good. Neither am I." She joggled her stepbrother's arm. "I would waltz if someone would ask me."

Bromby smiled a little, staring up and into the air as though he watched a bird's flight.

"Do you live in London, Mrs. Morley?" Rebecca asked.

"I live in Newmarket."

Rebecca seemed to consider the location. "Newmarket. I believe that is horse-racing country, is it not?"

"Oh, yes. We have a well-stocked stable. When he was living, my husband—Colonel George Morley—was obsessed with the sport ... or at least the money that was to be won with it."

Was that a flash of regret flickering over her face like the shadow of a flame? Perhaps the colonel had been imprudent in his obsession with the sport.

"We are fond of horses as well," Rebecca continued. "We have several on our property in Kent."

"Very fine horses, I might add," Bromby said. "I had the pleasure of stopping with the Beringers at Holly Bridge last spring."

"And you rode?" Agatha asked, turning her pale eyes upon him.

"Yes, I did," he answered in a smug tone. "And quite well. Miss Bankmill can vouch for me."

Isabella arched an eyebrow. "I can only vouch that he managed to stay astride his horse, Mrs. Morley. Remember, Lord Bromby, you and Mr. Hobby rode ahead. I only glimpsed your return to the house when Miss Tickney took a spill."

Agatha seemed to enjoy this very much and clasped Bromby's arm as she laughed. "Oh, how very droll! I'm glad you are not afraid to tease him, Miss Bankmill. He can be far too serious and intense, but I'm sure you know that."

"I believe I did see some of that behavior in Kent," Isabella said.

"Like a moody, broody bear at times?" Agatha hugged Bromby closer, looking up at him.

"Yes. Very like."

Bromby smirked and turned his gaze back to Isabella.

A streak of pain coursed through Isabella's palms—probably because she was clenching her fists so tightly.

Suddenly, Bromby's attentions were drawn away, his brows lifting as his eyes widened and his lips parted. "There is Madam de Staël. She came after all."

Isabella turned to catch a glimpse of the woman she'd heard so much about this season. The French intellectual and writer had captivated London. Stories abounded regarding her forced flight from Napoleon's reach. Middle-aged, with dark hair and large, inviting eyes, she wore an amber frock and a matching tied turban about her head.

"I like her turban," observed Agatha Morley. "I appear so little in society these days, I feared a tied turban had gone out of fashion."

"Oh, no," said Rebecca. "The turbans are still terribly fashionable. A fine turban may be worn with nearly anything."

"Yes, I have one or two myself," said Lord Bromby. "I prefer to wear them with my Albanian costume. The turban renders it very authentic."

Isabella stifled a laugh as she tried to imagine him wearing such apparel.

"Why was it again that Madame de Staël had to go into exile?" Rebecca asked.

"Her politics were anathema to Napoleon. She wanted a moderate republic, and her writings reflected such leanings. Napoleon feared her influence," explained Lord Bromby.

"But I thought you liked Napoleon," said Isabella.

"I admire him, yes, but I also admire her. Any woman who fights with Napoleon and wins—at least to some degree, as she managed to escape his sphere in secret—is admirable in my book." He turned his gaze upon Agatha. "Come. Let us speak with her." He bowed to Isabella and Rebecca. "Please excuse me, ladies. I promise not to leave you for long."

As soon as Bromby and Agatha were out of earshot, Rebecca turned to Isabella and pulled her just out of the crowd.

"Izzy, I know you are soon to be leaving London … and, well, I have not yet spoken to my brother about any of this, but …"

Unpleasant tightness gripped Isabella's insides. *Oh, please. Not this topic again.* She was not ready to talk about David Beringer. She did not know that she ever would be. Her heart was irreversibly decided on this matter. He was not for her.

Rebecca paused and then rushed on. "Do you think there would ever be a chance you could consider my brother? I'm so anxious to see him happy, and I know he admires you so …"

Rebecca's voice drained away as Isabella scanned the room, her gaze resting upon Bromby. He sat very close to Mrs. Morley on a red sofa across from Madame de Stael. His leg touched the fabric of Agatha's dress, much the same as it had touched the fabric of hers when he sat with her in the garden at Holly Bridge. He leaned over and whispered into Agatha's ear.

Low voices mumbled and whispered all around her. Lord Bromby's name tipped every conversation.

"But are they not related?"

"They are not blood relation."

"Mrs. Morley's not been widowed a year."

"I hear he is considering half a dozen young ladies to play the role of his bride."

The music began, strains of violins drowning out all discernible side conversations.

Rebecca's voice faded back into her consciousness. "I would not even suggest to him anything of the sort unless I knew you might harbor some affection. I would not want to risk his heart again."

Silently, Isabella turned away from her friend and focused instead on the waltzing couples. They stood in a circle, each with a partner, the women's light muslin dresses of lavender, white, and pale yellow, the men in their tightly affixed cravats and dark coats, revolving around one another—their hands clutched and held high as they circled and moved to the music. Her mind spun. Bromby, Agatha Morley, David Beringer … it was all too much to think about.

A flash of blue moved through the room—someone, a woman, pushed past people. Gasps erupted from the crowd. Was that … could it be?

"Good heavens, is that your cousin?" Rebecca asked.

Isabella didn't need to answer, for the whisperings had begun.

"That is Lady Catherine!"

"Was she invited?"

"Yes, she's been here for an hour, lurking in the corners, watching Lord Bromby."

"Look at how she crosses the room to him."

Frozen to the spot, Isabella covered her mouth with her gloved hand. This was a terrible scene to behold. How shocking. How mortifying.

Catherine stood and faced Bromby as he sat. He did not immediately rise.

Catherine's words were inaudible and her face was not visible from this angle, but the wild state of her hair was apparent—as though she'd been tugging at it in fury. Her dress was crumpled, and some silvery object glittered in her gloved hand. As Catherine turned the thing in her hand, the tool's sharp point appeared. Bromby and Agatha both stood.

With a gasp, Isabella grabbed her friend's forearm. "Rebecca, help me. Please. I must somehow prevent this."

The music ended, and couples bowed and backed away from each other. With Rebecca beside her, Isabella hurried through the couples as they prepared for the next dance. She arrived at her cousin's side just as she pressed her hand against Bromby's and muttered, "Do not think I won't use this on myself." He pulled his hand away quickly.

"Lady Catherine," Isabella panted. "It is good to see you."

Catherine spun toward Isabella, her eyes dark and enraged. She turned back to Bromby. His mouth turned downward in a deep frown as he shifted to stand in front of Agatha. *I must get her out of this room.*

"Shall we take some air, Lady Catherine?" Isabella asked.

With a scream of agony that stopped musicians, dancers, and nearly Isabella's heart, Catherine shot off like a scared deer, performing wild turns as she moved and crashed against startled guests. Then she rushed up the stairs toward the room where food and refreshments were laid out.

Isabella shifted her eyes to Bromby. How could this be happening?

"Leave her," Bromby said. "It is merely her usual drama. Do not take her threat with any seriousness."

But she could not leave Catherine to do something rash. If possible, they would bundle her into a carriage and take her home at once.

"Play on!" Lady Heatherton instructed the musicians, and they clumsily resumed their strains.

Trying to move with as little fanfare as possible, Isabella and Rebecca made their way through the crowd where eyes and tongues feasted on the antics of mad Lady Catherine. Isabella's cheeks felt hot with embarrassment—for Bromby, for Catherine, but mainly that she was in any way connected with this situation.

"Do you think she would actually harm herself?" Rebecca asked.

"I hope not." But she no longer knew what her cousin-in-law might do.

Isabella arrived on the landing just as Catherine disappeared behind the double doors at the top of the stairs and flung them shut. The click of the lock sounded. Isabella grasped a doorknob and Rebecca grasped the doorknob on the second door. But the entry was locked and wouldn't open no matter how violently they shook the knobs.

Inside the room, breaking glass and screams—some from Catherine, others from the ladies locked inside the room with her.

"I will end it all!" Catherine's shriek reverberated through the door.

Would she really use the knife on herself or someone else? Isabella shook the knob harder. "Catherine! Stop. Open the door. Please let me in."

Silence.

Isabella pressed her ear against the door.

"Heaven defend us!" One woman within the room called out.

Catherine's words were barely intelligible. "He told me I should stab myself in the heart if I were to use this, because that is what I have done to him!"

"My dear Lady Catherine, please do not harm yourself. There is no—" More screams and breaking of glass ensued.

Suddenly, the door jerked and gave way, and a gray-haired dowager rushed past her and down the steps, screaming.

Inside the room, Catherine held the broken shard of a jelly bowl against her neck, a knife against her side. Five elderly women pressed themselves against the wall on the opposite end of the room, trembling as though she held the sharp objects to their throats. They glanced over at Isabella, standing in the open doorway, and fled the room all at once, in various states of running, limping, and shuffling.

Without her previous audience, Catherine turned slowly toward Isabella and Rebecca. "Leave me to my death!"

"Catherine, please," Isabella approached her, holding out her hand. "You must drop the knife. Do not do this! Think of your husband ... and little Gus."

Catherine's eyes were feral. She poised the knife in her grasped fist, the sharp end pointed toward her torso. "They do not care for me! No one cares for me. And what does it matter now that I have lost Bromby?"

Catherine's arm jerked, and Isabella covered her eyes and screamed in unison with Rebecca as her cousin-in-law plunged the knife into her side.

Catherine shrieked as she sank to the ground, dropping the jelly bowl shard and the knife before collapsing into a fit of sobs.

Isabella rushed to Catherine's side. A small circle of blood slowly formed in the blue material of her dress.

"At least she is not dead, nor anyone else," breathed Rebecca.

"How could he do this to me?" Catherine wailed. "I wish he'd stabbed me in the heart rather than to break it and leave me in such misery."

A servant appeared in the doorway. "Can I help at all, milady?" His face was pale and slack.

Isabella exhaled. "Yes, could you please send for a doctor?"

"I will not see a doctor! Not here!" Catherine shrieked. "I wish to see my own physician."

Isabella attempted to inspect Catherine's self-inflicted wound. Fortunately, there was only the stain on her dress and no gushing blood.

Isabella nodded to the servant. "Could you please have Lady Catherine's carriage brought 'round? We must leave at once." Isabella breathed in ragged breaths. She must remain calm. Her hands shook violently as she held her own handkerchief to Catherine's wound.

"Let us not take her down until we can move her straight to the carriage. The guests must not see this," Rebecca suggested.

Isabella lifted one of Catherine's arms, and Rebecca took the other. Together, they raised the sobbing Catherine to her feet, holding her aloft as they waited.

"Let Bromby see me! Let him see what he has done to me!" Catherine howled. "I should tell the world about him."

"No, Catherine," Isabella reasoned, her heart racing. "Calm down now. This is nonsense. You must stop this." *Oh, please. Let the carriage hurry.*

Even now voices from downstairs reached her ears with their questions, accusations, and speculations.

It seemed an eternity before the carriage arrived, but finally Isabella and Rebecca half-carried, half-walked Catherine down the stairs and outside. Isabella did not look at any of the guests directly. They were surely watching them.

Once all three women were in the carriage, Catherine slumped against the side, her previously untamed cries now quiet, hiccupping sobs.

Too exhausted and disturbed to think or say anything, Isabella sat beside Catherine and held her shaking hand. Weak and tremulous, she was parched with thirst. She stared blankly out the carriage window, watching the morning sun disappear behind early afternoon clouds that blew in, threatening a summer rain. Her head swirled.

Was Catherine as mad as she seemed, or was Lord Bromby really such a blackguard that he had driven her to insanity?

Fifteen

How did she even begin to relay the events from Lady Heatherton's morning party to her aunt? Somehow, she managed to do so—at least what she remembered from the chaotic scene.

Upon hearing the details of Catherine's antics, Lady Melwood's brow furrowed. "Dalton, please fetch Dr. Coaxley at once." She then turned to Isabella. "Doctor Coaxley has been called in several times before. He knows and understands Catherine's high-strung nature."

A short time later, Doctor Coaxley arrived and examined the stab wound to her side.

"It is only a wound to the flesh. Nothing serious. Hardly any blood at all. The knife only punctured the skin, the force of the stab buffered by the stays of her dress."

Isabella released her shoulders, and her sigh mingled with Lady Melwood's and Rebecca's.

Lady Melwood rolled her eyes to the ceiling. "I am at a loss."

Dr. Coaxley took Catherine's pulse and pronounced, "It is very fast. I shall leech and bleed her. That may calm her and relieve some of the anxiety she feels." He went to his bag and pulled out a jar containing the black, slimy, sucking instruments so commonly used for treating fevers or other disorders caused by having too much blood in one's system. At the appearance of the leeches, Isabella's stomach turned over.

"We shall leave you, Doctor." Lady Melwood motioned to Isabella and Rebecca.

Isabella followed her aunt and Rebecca from the room and closed the door.

"They do say it helps," Rebecca said as they descended the staircase. "The bleeding."

"Perhaps it may, Miss Beringer, but I think my daughter-in-law's illness goes far beyond the help of the common leech."

Soon after Doctor Coaxley departed, Rebecca suggested a need to return to her home. Lady Melwood insisted that she be transported in the barouche to her parent's house in Piccadilly.

After Rebecca had gone, Lady Melwood turned to Isabella. "I hope you will stay and take tea with me, Isabella."

What could she do? She desperately wanted to return to Aunt Lydia's and forget this morning had ever taken place, but her aunt was surely distraught over her daughter-in-law. The least she could do was take tea with her. "Yes, of course."

Lady Melwood nodded and called for a servant. "Dalton, would you have tea brought to the drawing room? You will find us there momentarily," she instructed.

"Yes, milady."

"And please send Mrs. Wallace or Mary to sit with Lady Catherine."

"At once, your ladyship."

"Come dear, let us have a talk in the drawing room over some tea. I believe we have a few things to discuss."

Isabella rose and followed Lady Melwood into the drawing room. Shaky and a little hungry since she'd had to leave the party prior to eating, she looked forward to the arrival of the tea.

The afternoon sun streamed through the windows casting stripes of light across the Oriental rug as Isabella seated herself across from her aunt.

"You look tired, Isabella," her aunt observed. "You are pale, and there are dark smudges under your eyes. Are you quite well?"

"Yes, ma'am. I just have a slight headache. This was a trying day."

Lady Melwood nodded. "I know. And I'm sorry to hear it. I hope taking some tea will help."

"Perhaps it shall."

"I want to talk to you about what happened this morning at Lady Heatherton's—"

"You'll forgive me, but I would prefer to forget the incident altogether." She would be thankful if she could ever put aside the image of Catherine plunging the knife into her side.

Lady Melwood's mouth compressed. "I can certainly understand why. And of course, there will be plenty of talk. Unfortunately, talk with which your name will be associated."

Isabella's eyes flew open. "My name? Why should my name be mentioned?"

"Well, you were there. You witnessed much of the incident, and some may say you were partially the cause."

"I? In what way?"

The tea arrived. *Finally.* Isabella's mouth watered at the sight of the plate full of crumpets, marmalade, and lavender shortbread.

Lady Melwood began to pour the tea. "Well, the fact that Lord Bromby is very fond of you could not have escaped Catherine's notice. And I'll be very frank—there is talk that Lord Bromby may shortly renew his offer to you."

Isabella's breath caught in her throat, and a mixture of hurt and confusion swept over her. Her heart raced. *What? How could this be?*

Lady Melwood smiled and passed Isabella a cup of tea. She sipped at her own and seemed to wait for a reaction.

Isabella swallowed. "I have not received any special attention from him." Her voice emerged as little more than a whisper. "I did not accept his first offer. And my understanding was that he would not renew it."

"You are mistaken, Isabella," Lady Melwood said. "I know Bromby holds you in the highest esteem. I think he may feel that you are too good for him, in fact."

Heat rushed into her face. *Could this really be true?* Lady Melwood was not above manipulation for her own benefit. "I have had no correspondence from him, and I only saw him for the first time in over a year while attending the theater with Mr. and Miss Beringer. He paid me no special attention."

Lady Melwood remained silent and continued to sip her tea.

Isabella continued. "In fact, the other night, when we happened upon Lord Bromby, he was with Mrs. Morley, Colonel George Morley's widow. And Lord Bromby brought her again today to Mrs. Heatherton's."

She replaced her teacup in its saucer. "So, you have met Mrs. Morley. She is a charming woman. I met her and her late husband in the autumn before he fell ill. Her husband's patron was the Prince of Wales himself, you know."

"No, I did not know that."

Lady Melwood put down her tea cup. "You do not think ... I daresay, you are not suspicious of Bromby's relationship with Mrs. Morley, are you?"

Hadn't people whispered about them at the morning party? She took a sip of her tea, avoiding eye contact with Lady Melwood.

Lady Melwood laughed. "Oh, no, my dear. Agatha Morley is his stepsister, and she was very happily married to her husband. He simply adored her. They had four children together. So, do not allow yourself to be taken in by idle chatter of dowagers with nothing better to do than eyeball everyone in the room and assign stories to them. If Lord Bromby paid her the slightest bit of attention, it would have been enough to set them all talking. That's how those parties are, my dear. They are like a parliamentary session for gossips."

Isabella pressed her lips into a line. "I must say, Aunt. I do not know how I am to feel. Catherine's reaction was so violent and severe, and Lord Bromby sat there with a guilty look upon his face, knowing he was the cause of her pain."

Lady Melwood waved her hand in the air. "Never mind that. Suffice it to say, Catherine alone is to blame for her state. You mustn't blame Lord Bromby. I certainly do not."

Isabella considered this. "It seems to me that as a gentleman, Lord Bromby should have rejected Catherine's advances. A man of character certainly would have done so."

Lady Melwood laughed. "Don't be naïve. Are you so ill acquainted with men, dear Isabella? Lord Bromby has legions of women throwing themselves at him. He is a celebrity. He cannot be expected to reject them all. He made an imprudent error with Catherine to be sure, but you must know he is still a man."

Isabella's gaze dropped to her clasped hands resting in her lap. Was it true that all men participated in illicit relationships with women? Her own excellent father would never think of it. She did not think David Beringer would ever behave in such a manner either.

"I still desire that my husband be a man who loves God, rather than someone who is a lover of women."

Her aunt's face hardened as her nostrils flared. "Bromby told me once he thought never to marry. Therefore, imagine my great surprise when he told me the only woman he could ever marry ... was you, my dear."

Isabella raised her head slowly, her eyes wide. Who could not be flattered by such words? Every female desired admiration from a man. And Lord Bromby ... well, never had she felt such a strong attachment to any other man.

Lady Melwood continued. "I know he cares deeply for you. He's often spoken of you as the 'Little Mathematician,' praising your wit and intelligence. Regardless of what you may think, he respects your religious fervor. Lord Bromby himself is a man concerned with the plight of the poor and the maligned. So, in many ways, I believe he reflects those qualities that would qualify him as Christian."

"But he professes no belief in them," Isabella argued, meeting her aunt's gaze with a serious expression.

"Upon my word, he's a good soul, Isabella. He simply needs a woman like you to guide his moral compass to the North—or at least Northeast. In other ways, you would be equals—in intellect and your love of literature and poetry. You are a perfect match of noble rank and breeding."

Tears leaked into Isabella's eyes, and she turned to stare off into the corridor. Her mind was a vortex of whirling feelings. "I do not know, Aunt. I will have to think—pray on this."

For the moment Lady Melwood appeared satisfied. She sat back in her chair, a contented smile stretching her lips. "You should do both, but, by all means, do not cut him because of any trifling gossip about Agatha Morley. There is not a word of truth to it."

Part IV

Sixteen

January 1814

You will be married at twenty-six, and dead by...

While attending a street fair with his mother in Nottingham as a child, Bromby encountered a fortune teller. She had beckoned him with gnarled knuckles and clouded eyes.

"Would you like your fortune told, Greggy?" His mother had asked, squeezing his hand. "I think I'd like to know mine. Shall we find out if we're going to be rich?"

But it was not his mother the old woman called forth. Instead, grasping his nine-year-old hand with her bony fingers, the woman moved her mouth, as though chewing something sour. Unbidden and before payment had been offered her, she growled her prophetic words: "You will be married at the age of twenty-six ... and you will be dead by the age of thirty-seven."

Horrified, his mother had grabbed his shoulders and wrenched him from the old woman's grasp. They could still hear her cackling as they moved away from her and into the crowds. He had never forgotten her words. Or the terror that welled within him as he heard them.

Bromby spent his twenty-sixth birthday with Agatha at Broadwell Abbey, where the snow piled against the windows in great white mountains. With the roads completely impassable, the two were happily imprisoned within the crumbling walls.

Agatha stood at the window, looking out over the idyllic scene—a front lawn swaddled in white—a blue gleam rising from the top of the snow as it skittered along, scattered like dust with each billow of the wind.

"Is the orchard still there?"

"Yes," Bromby said. "And our tree is there as well. You know the one I speak of, don't you?"

Agatha smiled. "The one upon which you carved our initials?"

He nodded. The house rattled slightly as a gust blasted the north side.

"Are you going to repair this place before you sell it? You know, it's falling into ruin."

Bromby reclined his head against the top of the sofa and sighed. Repairs would require funds—money he counted on from the sale of the place. "My hope is someone will buy it lock, stock, and barrel as is. I've invested more money than I can ever repay on the furnishings and the trinkets you see all around us."

Agatha turned from the window and cast a smile in his direction. "Adornments. Decorations." She lifted her eyes to the ceiling. "Your roof is leaking. There is a tree growing in the middle of the entrance hall."

Bromby smiled. "I think it lends a sort of Gothic romance to the place, don't you?"

Agatha arched her eyebrow. "Do be serious, Gregory."

"I am. I rather like the tree in the foyer."

"The person who buys this place might not like it."

"Then they can remove it."

She cocked her head and looked at him askance.

The morning light cast a glow against the white of her dress, making her form visible beneath the fabric. She nearly blended with the snow outside—his snow angel. He patted the seat next to him. "Agatha, come sit beside me. I hate it when you're so far away."

She returned to Bromby's side and seated herself on the sofa next to him, running her hand over his dark, unruly curls. "I've been sitting next to you all day, Gregory. My knees hurt from lounging."

He wrapped his arm around her waist, pulling her toward him. "Sit a little longer. You were the one who asked me to write this letter. Now I'm going to read it to you. I want your good opinion. If you approve, I shall send it tomorrow, and then we shall see what comes of all of this."

Bromby stood and moved across the room to the table that held his decanter. He poured himself a glass and lifted it to his lips, downing it in one swallow.

"What is that you're drinking?"

He swiped at his mouth with the back of his hand. The rear of his throat stung with an acidic tang. "Acid. Lemon acid." He hated the bellyache that always followed. Whether it was the bellyache keeping him from having an appetite or the acids themselves keeping him thin, he cared not. "To sustain my figure."

Agatha sighed and shook her head. "That is a silly notion, indeed."

He rattled the letter in his hand. "Shall I read the letter or not?"

Her eyes were earnest as she considered his. "Read it to me, then."

"There's a lot of uninteresting drivel at the beginning, where I'm asking after her parents and the weather, etcetera."

"Yes, yes, get to the second course."

"'I now come to my point in writing. Am I to conclude once and for all from your past correspondence that there is nothing I could say or do to alter your rejection of my offer? I do not expect a commitment of any kind from you, only whether your feelings remain unchanged.'"

He lowered the papers and eyed Agatha over the top of them. "What do you think?"

Her eyes filled with tears, and she inhaled sharply. "It's lovely."

"Shall I sign and seal it?"

"I would change one thing, though. To the line in which you profess your admiration for her, I would write 'I believe you are aware of my admiration and *love* for you.'"

His heart dropped. "You think I should write the *word* in the letter?"

"Absolutely. Gregory, you're asking the lady to marry you. She will want to know that you love her. She's not looking for money in this arrangement—you've already told me her family is amply funded. She wants to know you are marrying her because you truly want to be with her."

Now his heart groaned. He reached up and swept a lock of platinum hair from Agatha's face. "How can I write that, when you know the true nature of my feelings?"

Agatha clasped his hand with her own. "You know that cannot be. You must marry. And it cannot be me. Like you, I have nothing but debt.

If it were not for the Prince of Wales and Princess Charlotte, I and my children would be out on the streets."

"I would never allow that to happen—"

"But we will always be like brother and sister." She squeezed his hand.

Bromby pulled away. The sting of tears pressed against the backs of his eyes, and he squinted hard to clear them. "You alone know of my childhood—my mother's neglect, the abuse from my nurse. The way she used to beat me until my bones ached."

"*Shh.*" Agatha placed the tip of her finger over his lips. "Do not think of that now. You must concentrate on this most important letter. And I must think about going home. Once the roads are passable, I must get back to the children. And we do not want any more talk …"

With a sense of heaviness, Bromby tore himself away from the sofa and stalked to the table where a red candle threatened to extinguish itself even as its vermillion wax pooled beneath the candleholder. Pulling a clean sheet of parchment from the drawer of the desk, Bromby set to rewriting the last page, although he could not bring himself to add the word "love" to the phrase in question. He looked over his shoulder at Agatha, perched like a dove on a windowsill, preparing to fly away at any moment. Bromby sighed and turned back to the letter. With one bereft stroke of his hand, he signed his name. "Yours, most affectionately, B."

Seventeen

September 1814

"This letter writing has gone on for nine months now. Is he simply going to trade letters with you about the weather, Isabella, or will he finally ask for your hand?"

Isabella stared at her mother. "I don't know, Mamma."

Isabella had read aloud every letter she had received from Bromby since the beginning of the year—all of them full of admiration and promises of attempting to understand her beliefs, but none of them with a specific marriage proposal or date of arrival in Durham.

In the meantime, her mother's patience grew thin.

Isabella sighed. "Mamma, my understanding is that he has been much engaged in London at present. His latest poem, *The Privateer*, sold 10,000 copies on the very first day it was published. According to Lady Melwood, the sales are unprecedented. There is not a person in the whole of London who has not devoured the poem ten times over. Princess Charlotte has been rumored to have read it twice daily."

Lady Judith Bankmill rolled her eyes. "Your aunt exaggerates greatly, I'm sure."

"And he still will not take payment for his poems." Isabella was proud of Bromby's humility in refusing money for what he termed his "meager talents."

Lady Bankmill pursed her lips. "Isabella, have you not yet reflected on the reasons why you refused him to begin with? I do not understand this change of heart when you were so resolute before."

How could she explain it to her mother in a way she would understand? She was doubtful that Lady Bankmill would be moved by all that she had given up in refusing Bromby.

It was hard to overlook his public acclaim and adoration. "Brombymania" consumed the country, and perhaps she had fallen victim to it herself. Sitting at home in Seaham for the better part of a year had given her perspective. She was another year older, still husbandless, and still unable to shake her attachment to this man.

"He is not Christian, Isabella. You have said so yourself."

"I believe he possesses Christian generosity and kindness, Mamma. According to Lady Melwood, he is a philanthropist, concerned with others' well-being." Surely Lord Bromby merely needed spiritual and moral guidance, and with such things he would be a changed man.

From his seat in the corner where he had been reading his newspaper and eavesdropping on his wife and daughter's conversation, Sir Ralph Bankmill chuckled. "Well, Judith, if your sister deems him worthy, then he must have a great deal to recommend him. She never recklessly bestows her praise."

If Isabella and Bromby married, her good-natured father would no doubt overlook any spiritual failings, although he, himself, was as devout as any. His compassion and good will allowed him to think the best of everyone, asserting that a nonbeliever could find redemption and salvation around the next corner.

Her mother was quick to assess a lingering doubt in her daughter's halting words. "That my sister assigns him a benevolent character is all very well and good, but you hardly know him, Isabella. An exchange of letters only allows so much information about a person."

"I hardly knew *you* when I married you," Sir Ralph called out over the top of his paper. "And look how well that turned out."

Lady Bankmill frowned at her husband. "You are hardly helpful."

"I think I understand him, despite our brief acquaintance. He does not share my faith absolutely, Mamma, but I feel certain ... I feel ... he could be swayed with time, patience, and love."

Sir Ralph rattled his newspaper. "Dear Judith, let's leave our daughter some room to breathe, shall we? Lord Bromby has yet to make any binding promises. Let us wait to cross that burning bridge when the moment arrives."

Isabella sat indoors, staring out of an upstairs window at the garden below. The gardener was moving among the autumn flowers—a small shovel in one hand, a pair of gardening shears in the other. The grounds were especially green this time of year, but there was also an early chill in the air.

Millie grew fat spending her days in the fields, but in the past week Isabella had no energy to ride. She had not received a letter from Bromby in at least that time. Was her mother right? Perhaps he only toyed with her emotions and had no intention of renewing his offer. Or perhaps he was unsure—certainly he had many other options at his disposal.

The whirl and bustle of London now seemed like a dream. Had she danced at those balls? Had she actually danced with Lord Bromby? It had been so long since she'd felt the weight of his eyes and the thrill of his presence. Every day she went without a letter from him seemed interminable. Only reading and re-reading his newest poem, *The Privateer,* until the pages were wrinkled and smudged, helped her feel connected with him.

Sitting yet another evening at home, staring absently at another book as though reading it and making conversation with her father about Napoleon or listening to her mother tell about her whist match with Lady Stanton, seemed an insurmountable task. As of late, her prayer life was stale, and her mind wandered far too much to focus on the study of her Bible.

Oh, she had made a grave mistake in refusing Lord Bromby the first time.

She envisioned the years stretching out before her as a spinster—perhaps hearing of him marrying someone else. The thought was insupportable.

"I believe this is for you, Izzy." Her father dropped a letter into her lap.

A wax seal of a B was affixed to the back. Her heart raced.

"By the way, I have just seen Mr. Beringer."

She looked up at him. "Mr. Beringer?"

"Yes, while I was in town at the coffeehouse. We were introduced through Sir John Brownwood. Mr. Beringer had just arrived. He's staying at the Seaham Inn."

She looked down at the letter in her lap. Her fingers itched. "What does he do in Seaham?"

Her father moved behind his desk and placed the rest of the letters and post upon it. Sitting down, he secured his spectacles over his ears. "He is stopping for a day on a return journey from a visit to his aunt in Scotland. Some business about procuring funds for an orphanage he is hoping to build. He will journey from here to York, I believe. Seems a fine gentleman. Very good of him to think of the orphans."

"Oh." Isabella could hardly bear another minute. She was desperate to tear into the letter. She would take it to her room and read it there. She rose from her chair. "You'll excuse me, Papa—"

"Mr. Beringer is anxious to see you. I told him to pay us a call. He should be here presently."

"Mr. Beringer? Is coming here?" Any other time she would not have minded seeing Mr. Beringer, but now … the letter.

Sir Ralph eyed her over the top of his spectacles. "Well, yes, Bell. He is far from home. It was the mannerly thing to do. Don't you think?"

She rose from her chair. "Yes, I suppose."

"Perhaps a visit from a friendly face will brighten your pallor a bit."

Isabella nodded. "Yes, perhaps." Sighing, she scanned the letter. "Please excuse me, Papa, so that I may read my letter."

"Yes, yes. As you wish." He shooed her away.

She turned from her father and rushed up the stairs to her room. With an anticipation bordering on physical pain, she broke the seal and threw herself across her bed, already devouring the words on the page before her belly sank into the bedding. "Dearest Isabella…" She read the opening words in a whisper.

Her hands trembled as her fingers trailed over Bromby's writing. *I believe you are aware of my admiration and love for you, and there is little I would not do to procure your affections. If renewing my offer of marriage is acceptable to you, I will come to Durham.* "Oh, he loves me!" The words exploded from her lips. After many months of letters from him—here was the word she longed to read. "He loves me. He loves me," she panted, barely able to read the remainder of the letter as tears pooled in her eyes and blurred her vision. Propelling herself from her bed, she rushed down the stairs calling out, "Mamma! Papa! He loves me! Lord Bromby loves me. And he has proposed."

Her parents, both perched on their usual chairs in the drawing room, their eyes wide and mouths hanging. She could laugh. They looked a little frightened. Perhaps it was her unprecedented show of emotion, or the fact that she rushed at them like a young colt, flailing the letter in the air. "Look, Papa!" Darting to his chair first, she tripped over his footrest and would have fallen to the floor if he hadn't caught her arm and upheld her.

"Daughter, calm yourself. What is all of this running about and screaming? We will hear your news, but calmly if you please."

"Forgive me." Isabella swallowed, her hand flying to her chest. "But the letter is from Lord Bromby, and he has formally proposed."

"All right." Sir Ralph's bushy gray eyebrows twitched a little as he sat forward. "Calmly."

Isabella looked back and forth between her mother and father.

"Well, well," her mother said, her voice dripping with resignation. "You've never shown interest in any other young man."

Sir Ralph stood. "Yes, well, pray tell, Isabella, when is the young man to arrive?"

"As soon as I've written to him to accept his offer." Isabella's voice broke with something between a laugh and a sob.

"And may I assume from your frenzied state that you will be inclined to accept him?"

How could he even ask? "Yes, sir."

He nodded. "I see. Well, then. I will look forward to meeting him when he arrives." He squeezed her arm before once more taking up his paper. Her mother said nothing, taking up her embroidery and weaving the needle through the material once more.

Isabella hurried to her room where she read his letter again. Breathless, she penned a letter of acceptance, restraining herself from using the words of undignified adoration that swirled in her mind. She settled for a tame and generic reply—one which would assure him of her regard without reminding him in any way of Lady Catherine. *I am pleased at your offer and wholeheartedly accept.*

Later, as she read over her letter and the copy of it she addressed to Broadwell Abbey—just in case he left London before receiving her reply—she added, *My parents and I anxiously await your arrival at Seacrest Hall.*

Eighteen

As she sat with her mother in the drawing room that afternoon, Isabella pretended to read a book. What else could she do? In truth, she could not focus on one word of the text. Oh, if only she could fly her letters to Bromby herself.

May the horses run fast, and the weather from Durham to London be perfect. How would Bromby's countenance appear when he read her letter? Would his eyes register surprise at her willingness to concede her earlier reasons for refusing him?

Mrs. Cummings's announcement cut through her fantasies. "Mr. David Beringer is here ma'am."

Caught completely off guard, Isabella stood so abruptly as to upset the book from her lap. Oh, yes. She had almost forgotten that he was to come.

"Show him in, Mrs. Cummings," Lady Bankmill instructed.

David Beringer entered the room and bowed. "Lady Bankmill. Miss Bankmill. I do hope I am not interrupting anything."

"Not at all," Isabella said stiffly. "Mamma, this is Mr. Beringer. Mr. Beringer, this is my mother, Lady Judith Bankmill."

Mr. Beringer stood perfectly straight before them. He looked elegant in a black coat, buckskin breeches, and boots.

"Mr. Beringer." Lady Bankmill rushed forward, offering her hand to David. "What a pleasure to meet you. My sister, Lady Melwood, spoke so highly of you and your sister when she had the good fortune to meet both of you in London."

David smiled. "The pleasure was and is all mine, I assure you, ma'am." He turned his gaze to Isabella. "I hope you will forgive my impromptu visit, Miss Bankmill. When I met your father in town today, he extended an invitation to me. I made a last-minute decision to stop off in Seaham on my travels from Scotland. I've been longing to see you."

Now it was Isabella's turn to blush. Her eyes flicked to her mother's face, whose expression changed from polite interest to curious wonderment. "Do you hear that, Isabella? Mr. Beringer has longed to see you. What a lovely thing to say, Mr. Beringer."

She couldn't possibly clutch her palms together any more tightly. The pain of her fingernails was nearly enough to make her scream. Was this some scheme of Rebecca's? That she might spend time alone with her brother? If so, she would indeed be disappointed with the news Isabella had to relay.

"Won't you sit down?" Lady Bankmill straightened her skirt and lowered herself into a pink-striped velvet armchair near the window.

David Beringer threw back the tails of his coat and positioned himself on the sofa directly across from the ladies.

"How do you find the inn, Mr. Beringer?" Was that really her own voice? The tone was so icy and distant.

"Yes. It is a comfortable place." David's eyes shifted to Isabella and back to Lady Bankmill.

"Next time, Mr. Beringer, consider yourself invited to Seacrest Hall to stop your journey from Scotland." Lady Bankmill positioned her embroidery in her lap and threaded her needle.

David smiled and nodded. "I thank you, ma'am."

"What do you do in Scotland?"

"My favorite aunt lives there, ma'am. We used to visit often as children, but it has been some time since we've visited. The Beringers have an ancestral home there."

"Indeed?" Lady Bankmill's eyebrow arched, and she dabbed under her nose with a lace handkerchief. "An ancestral home?"

"Yes, ma'am. My aunt is contributing funds to a project I am endeavoring. An orphanage."

"An orphanage?" Lady Bankmill, pulled her needle through the fabric. "Where?"

"Somewhere in the country. I am already involved with several parish orphanages in London and the Foundling Hospital, but it seems to me that there are many orphans in the country as well. I am currently in search of a location, but it is my dearest wish to build a home for them, one in which they might receive shelter, clothing, and an education."

"That is very good of you, Mr. Beringer. Very unusual for a gentleman to take a keen interest in such matters, isn't it, Izzy?"

Isabella nodded. Yes, of course it was. No one could fault David Beringer's philanthropy and outward offerings of true religion.

"I shall stop off in York to meet with an attorney regarding real estate."

"Might you establish the orphanage here in Durham?"

"Perhaps, Lady Bankmill. I do hold a special place in my heart for Durham." His eyes grazed Isabella's, and a smile touched his lips. "I confess I could have traveled directly to York, but I preferred the idea of seeing Miss Bankmill again." Now he looked directly at her and smiled.

She must divert the subject from herself. "Is Miss Beringer well?"

"Oh, yes. Rebecca is quite well—she sends her regards and her regrets that she could not come with me."

Oh, why couldn't Rebecca have come with him? It was awkward sitting with Mr. Beringer as his light blue eyes focused on her. An uncomfortable silence fell over the room, and Isabella stared down at her fingers and flipped absently through the pages of her novel.

Small, insignificant chatter continued between the three of them about the weather, the British naval attack on the Americas, and which roads in the north were the best and safest to travel upon.

Another bout of silence settled. "Well, Mr. Beringer," Lady Bankmill finally said, "we've had quite a bit of excitement here." Placing the needle in her mouth as she pulled at the thread, she cast a sidelong glance toward Isabella.

David Beringer's eyes turned toward Isabella as well. "Oh. Yes?"

"Lady Bankmill?" Mrs. Cummings, the housekeeper, entered the room.

"Yes, Mrs. Cummings?"

"I beg your pardon, ma'am. But it's about the new cook. She seems to be having a bit of difficulty with the menu you provided, milady. She says she's never cooked mutton."

Lady Bankmill's expression sank. "What? Never cooked mutton? Well, she must not be from Durham, then." She stood and placed her embroidery on her chair.

David Beringer stood.

"Mr. Beringer, I do apologize. I hope this shan't take long."

He bowed to her as she hurried outside with Mrs. Cummings.

Mr. Beringer's pale skin flushed as he lowered himself onto the sofa once more, and Isabella's heart caught in her throat. Suddenly, she feared this was not just a friendly call.

As if he had mustered a rush of courage, Mr. Beringer stood and towered above Isabella's still-seated form. "Miss Bankmill, let me confess to you at once that this visit is not wholly for social purposes."

Oh, no. It was as she feared. Isabella flinched involuntarily, her fingers rounding themselves into fists against her skirt. Her mouth dry, she glanced behind her, hoping her mother would return or another servant would interrupt them. "Oh?"

David Beringer stood straight as a rod, his eyes fixed upon her face. "No. In fact, I came to speak with you—to seek out your disposition regarding … well, marriage. That is, marriage … to me," he stammered, dropping to his knee in front of her. "I do love you, Miss Bankmill, and it is my most fervent desire to marry you—to make you as happy as one man can. And if you would do me the honor of blessing me with your hand in marriage, I shall do all I can never to give you a moment's embarrassment or regret."

How could this be happening? She didn't dare breathe. Had David Beringer offered this proposal to her before she met Bromby, she might have considered it. But hadn't she discouraged him sufficiently? Now her heart was heavy. *The poor man has already been rejected twice … and now a third time…*

"You have only to say the words, and I mean to talk to your father this very day …"

Isabella stood abruptly to spare him from any more stammering or discomfort. "Mr. Beringer, I must stop you, sir."

His flow of words ceased. He rose slowly from his knee and brushed the wrinkles from his breeches.

"I am sincerely flattered by your attentions and this—wholly unexpected—proposal. You are a kind and good man, and I have no wish to allow you to continue down this path when I cannot accept you."

Don't look at his face. Oh, but I must, lest I be rude.

His expression relaxed into disappointment, the edges of his mouth sliding into a frown and his left eye drooping tiredly.

She raised her hand to her temple. "I am already engaged. To Lord Bromby."

He drew back as though she had struck him. "I see." He whispered the words, his lips barely moving. "I see. Of course."

Isabella's heart tightened, and her chest hurt as she stared at his pained face. "I'm so sorry, Mr. Beringer."

"I see," he said again. The redness that had flushed his cheeks only moments before settled into a blotchy and mottled coloring. Suddenly straightening his coat, he inhaled sharply, and a strained smile appeared upon his lips. "Well, Miss Bankmill, I wish you … all the happiness in the world—you and Lord Bromby." He turned and awkwardly squeezed past the maid to retrieve his hat from the table at the back of the room. Once he had it in hand, he turned back to Isabella. "Please do give your mother my best regards, and …" His hat fell to the ground and he quickly stooped to retrieve it. "… to your father as well. I should return to the inn. I'm … please give them my apologies for such a hasty departure. Well, I must go."

He bowed before he swept past her, and she instinctively reached out to him. "Mr. Beringer—"

"Yes?" He turned in the doorway. His smile was forced, but his eyes did not quite meet hers.

"I'm so sorry. I did not know—"

"Please do not trouble yourself, Miss Bankmill." He croaked. And with a short bow, he was gone.

Isabella collapsed into a chair, her head pounding. It had never been her wish to bring any pain to David Beringer. She hadn't sought his affections. Why had it happened that her friendly treatment of him had been misunderstood as something more? The image of him kneeling before her, his face full of admiration, burned into her brain and her heaviness of heart extended beyond having injured his. Had she also damaged her friendship with Rebecca?

For now, let Bromby come, and soon, so that she might replace that image of David Beringer's face with his sultry smile and eyes. It was galling that her first spoken proposal should have been from David Beringer and not Gregory Bromby. *Please let that be remedied as soon as possible.*

Nineteen

"She has accepted."

In his rooms at St. James's Place, Lord Bromby 's voice shook as he read Isabella's letter to Agatha. If Agatha were now to ask him how he felt, he would respond that he felt nothing. His hand flew to his mouth, and he bit down hard on his already worn nails.

"Splendid." Agatha straightened her dress and secured a tress of platinum hair that had come loose. "I knew she would not refuse."

Bromby grew quiet. Unlike Agatha, he had suspected that Isabella might refuse—after all, she had done so once before. Staring down at the letter in his hand was like looking at the death certificate of his bachelorhood. Was he supposed to experience a sense of elation? Relief? What? His heart beat in exactly the same rhythm as it had moments before; his breathing was unchanged.

"There!" Agatha exclaimed. She stood and walked from the chaise across the room to the mirror where she again fiddled with her hair. "That's all settled, then. You are to be married to Isabella Bankmill, and you shall live happily ever after."

A long, shaky breath seeped from Bromby's lungs. Suddenly, something in Agatha's face reminded him of himself. The shift of her eyes, the hard set of her mouth. She was pretending every bit as much as he was. "I don't think you believe that for a second."

"Why would I not?"

Bromby eyed her tall, thin form—like a willow in the fields—so fragile and yet so resilient. She was altogether different from Isabella's petite figure. Could it be that he would never sit like this again with Agatha after his marriage? Nausea crept over him ... like tar spilling and overtaking a path, seeping around the edges of a shoe.

"I feel ill." His hand moved across his stomach.

"You're not still taking the acid, are you? Because I've read—"

"No, I've had to stop. My stomach was giving me fits. My doctor instructed me."

"Good. I'm glad. You have no need for it."

He smiled, remembering an adventure he'd been meaning to tell her about. "Last week I had my head examined by a phrenologist."

"A what?"

"Yes. You know. One of those physicians who studies the skull and its shape and slope. The brain is an organ and all that. It was Dr. Spurzheim himself. Yes, he felt the bumps and lumps on my head and pronounced a diagnosis of my character."

"Which was?"

"That I am a study of opposites. Where one trait exists stolidly within me, another is warring against it. Good and evil are forever battling inside my brain, apparently." And the evil was winning.

"Well, I could have told you that. You need not have called in some fren—what do you call it?"

"Phrenologist."

She strode over to stand behind him and placed her fingers on his scalp, massaging it in such a way that sent tingles through his body. "Yes. What a bunch of nonsense." She tipped his head back so quickly that his neck cracked and stared into his face from an upside-down position. "I could have pronounced your character simply by staring into your lovely green eyes."

"Because you know me too well."

She released his head, and Bromby let out a long, audible sigh. "I do not want to be separated from you again. I've always loved you. When I was a boy, I worshiped you."

"Gregory, you mustn't—"

"But then you married the colonel and disappeared from my life for thirteen years."

If only things were different. If only she had money, or he had more money, or she did not have so many children. But there were too many obstacles between them.

"Gregory," she began with a tone that bordered on scolding, "you must make a concerted effort with Miss Bankmill. If you try, if you treat her well, she will bring happiness to your days. She will love you just as I do. Perhaps more."

Bromby took her long, thin fingers into his and squeezed them, pulling her down to sit next to him. A white-blonde curl quivered at her temple, and he reached up to touch it with his forefinger. "Perhaps she will love me even more than you do. But it doesn't follow that I shall love her more than you."

"You must."

"Why must I?"

"Your salvation depends upon it, Gregory."

Something in him recoiled at her words. He turned his face away and reclined on the couch, resting the heel of his boot upon his knee. "Why do women worry so about salvation? Why that word all the time—salvation, salvation, salvation …"

Agatha appeared undaunted by his sudden, surly mood. She seated herself beside him. "You will not live forever."

"Perhaps not." A slow smile crept over his lips. Perhaps Agatha and Isabella might even become friends—true sisters. The thought of such a relationship made him want to laugh. "You must promise me to visit us, to stay with us, as often as you can."

"What might your wife think if I did that?"

"I don't give a farthing what she thinks. Why must things be one way or another?" He started from the divan, clomping across the room to stand before the great mirror. He glimpsed his image, dressed only in his unbuttoned shirt and waistcoat; his hair a tousled mess; his face a darkened and drawn expression of sorrow. Behind his own reflection, the figure dressed in white, still sitting on the divan, already seemed to be disappearing before his very eyes—like an apparition or a beautiful dream.

Soon he would be in Durham, politely performing for his new in-laws and fiancée. Soon his life would be irreversibly tied to another. "Are we not to have guests in our home? What more important guests might there be but family?"

She laughed. "Soon I will be Isabella's family too."

He nodded and returned his gaze to the mirror, staring into his own eyes—eyes that assured him of his own damnation. And yet, Isabella would have him.

"True," he spoke to his likeness. "And won't that be a fine joke."

Rosebourne Inn, Cambridgeshire
20 October 1814

Dearest Lady M,

I am finally en route to Durham to meet my new mother and father. I am accompanied by Hobby, who will secure all the details of the arrangement and ensure that no one is unfairly compensated for the hand of our most illustrious Queen of the Quadrilaterals. According to news I have gathered from business acquaintances and a previous conversation with the Queen of Quads herself, Sir Ralph's fiduciary state may not be quite as solid as expected due to some bad investments. It seems that his daughter received her mathematical talents elsewhere and my future father-in-law cannot keep his numbers straight when it comes to money he has and money he has not. But as I am the pot, I shall not comment on the kettle.

Our travels are slowed only by a week's stopover at Broadwell Abbey where I have employed a housekeeper and an army of maidservants to clean and prepare the house for my new bride. I anticipate stopping off there for several weeks following our marriage. After that, I mean to promptly sell the place, and we shall make our home in London. Please do inform me if you hear of any available and suitable places. I trust your judgment completely.

With some amusement, just this week I read the contradiction of my engagement to Miss Bankmill in the newspaper. This was, indeed, news to me, but since I have received no letter from Isabella suggesting a change of heart, I must assume this piece of fiction was written by none other than my dearest Catherine. I did not write to her to announce my engagement, knowing the degree of theatrical emotion to which that might expose you, dear friend. I do recall Catherine once telling me that if I were ever to marry, she would draw her pistol (or was it her dagger?) and shoot (or stab) herself. Since she's already done the latter, I would not doubt her sincerity in this threat. My hope is that Isabella's familial relation to Catherine might assuage that urge. What is your take on her state of mind at present?

Please inform me if my marriage is to be cut short by murderous interludes.

Yours, B

Twenty

November 1814

Isabella awakened with a gasp and covered in sweat. Another nightmare. Lady Catherine was trying to kill her again..

Isabella sat up. She was in her room. Lady Catherine was nowhere close by. And Isabella was still engaged to Lord Bromby. All was well.

She dressed and prepared to go down to breakfast. Her Uncle Worthington had stopped with the family for a fortnight, anxious to meet her fiancé—the celebrity he'd heard praised to the heavens for his remarkable talent.

As she reached the bottom of the stairs, she nearly tripped over her uncle's suitcases. *Oh no, he can't leave yet. He hasn't even met Bromby.*

At breakfast, Uncle Worthington announced that he was leaving.

"Can you not delay for one more day, Uncle?"

"Dearest Isabella, I regret that I cannot. Business awaits me in London. I am only sorry that I can give neither my stamp of approval nor disapproval. I'd hoped to meet your intended, but I can stay no longer."

Isabella was sorry, terribly sorry … and so embarrassed. She cringed as Uncle Worthington donned his cap and stepped out into frosty November air to his awaiting carriage.

Uncle Worthington would make her a financially comfortable heiress when he died, and she had been eager for him to meet her fiancé for this reason, if for no other. Now, this would give her mother another reason not to like Bromby. *Oh, please Lord. Help him to hurry. This is a terrible way to start off a marriage.*

Just as Isabella feared, as soon as the door closed behind his coattails, Lady Bankmill, her eyes red-rimmed with exasperation, turned and rasped, "He is over two weeks late, Isabella! It is indefensible."

Isabella reached out a hand to her mother even as her own eyes filled with tears of anxiety. How would she make this right? "I'm so sorry, Mamma. I know he will arrive any day."

But her words were spoken to Lady Bankmill's back as her mother climbed the stairs, her sobs audible and echoing through the stairwell. "I am mortified," she called out in a muffled voice. "And so should you be."

Isabella sank into a submissive puddle on the bottom step. "God, help me," she cried aloud, her shoulders shaking with released tension from weeks of waiting, wringing her hands, and shielding her beloved's reputation from her parents' considerations. She could not continue to do this. She was running out of excuses. "Please let him come. I cannot bear the wait." She mourned the self-possessed girl with her emotions in check—the girl she used to be before meeting Bromby. Would she ever see her again?

It wasn't until later that evening that Lady Bankmill once again showed her face. She descended the stairs in a calm manner, with her hand gliding along the banister and her chin held high.

Isabella alternated between restlessly pacing the drawing room and sitting by the hearth, staring into its flames, thankful for the heat upon her face. Even if it burned her eyes, it dried her tears.

Lady Bankmill did not look at her daughter but swept past her seated form and perched upon a chair in front of her embroidery screen. She began to pass the needle through the material, and Isabella listened to the sounds in the room: the clock ticking, the crackle of the fire, and her own uneven breaths.

An hour later, one of the maids swept past the room on her daily errand to deliver the post to Sir Ralph in his office, where he no doubt hid from the tension of the house.

Within a few minutes, Sir Ralph emerged from his office and held out a letter. "Izzy, I believe this is for you."

Isabella stared at the letter. The postscript was unfamiliar to her. Breaking the seal and unfolding the parchment, she began to read the back-to-back pages of very fine hand.

———— ⚬✸⚬ ————

Dearest Isabella,

I hope you will not think me impudent for writing, nor do I wish you to blame your most excellent fiancé for sharing your concerns with me. I have wanted to write for ever so long for no other reason than to call you my sister—as I know you soon shall be. Certainly, I already love you as such.

I am so thankful for your adoration of my stepbrother. I consider him the luckiest of all human beings to have secured your heart, and I know he considers himself more than fortunate. Indeed, he sees you as a superior—nay, angelic—creature whom he does not deserve.

Next, I would like to apologize for my dear stepbrother's detainment, first in town and then at Broadwell Abbey. In town, there was unexpected business regarding our childhood home and its imminent sale. Mr. John Hobby, whom I believe you know, assisted in the acquisition of staff with excellent references. This delayed our travels out of London.

Therefore, dear sister, please do not blame our beloved Gregory. He is in quite low spirits at having to delay his meeting with you and your family. If you must blame anyone at all, let it be Mr. Hobby and his sluggishness. Or, if you choose, you may blame me …

The letter went on from there, all apologies and endearments and visions into the future when the two women would be the closest of friends.

Isabella finished reading it and looked up at her mother. Lady Bankmill stabbed at her embroidery and cried out as she accidentally pierced her forefinger. "Ow!" Bringing it her mouth, she grimaced but did not look up.

It is from the Honorable Mrs. Morley," she said at last. "Bromby's stepsister."

Her mother inhaled sharply, released the air, and resumed her embroidery.

"Would you like me to read the letter to you, Mamma?"

"Not particularly."

Isabella licked her lips. They felt dry from sitting so close to the fire. "She writes that Bromby is not to blame for his delay. They were detained in London on business that pertained to Broadwell Abbey."

"Why did he not write to you himself?"

Isabella wondered the same thing but would never confess it. "I'm sure he will, Mamma. And I'm sure he has very good reason for such a delayed arrival."

Lady Bankmill was quiet for some time. Finally, she nodded her head over her embroidery and once again commenced the rhythmic stab and pull of the needle. "We shall see. Seek ye first the Kingdom of God, Isabella."

But it was hard to think upon the kingdom of God when she was consumed with the kingdom of Bromby and what life there would be like.

On Wednesday afternoon of the third week of waiting for Bromby's arrival, Isabella sat in an alcove off the foyer where she worked and reworked a mathematical equation. To pass the time, she sometimes reduced fractions. Other times she measured geometrical shapes. It occupied her mind and allowed her to mold her thoughts into a logical, productive frame.

Today she was on her third line of square roots when their maid, Charity, tripped and fell through the front door as she called out for the family. Her fall was a hard one, flat on her belly, and it had apparently knocked the wind from the girl's lungs. For a few seconds, Charity gasped and remained prone.

Isabella shot from her chair and rushed to the tiny maid's side. "Charity! Are you all right?" Grabbing her right forearm and placing a helping hand under her other arm to lift the girl to her feet, Isabella glimpsed Charity's reddened face. "What is the matter?"

"I'm sorry, Miss Bankmill," Charity finally gasped, partially recovering her air. "I tripped over me own feet, I'm 'fraid." The young girl pawed at her skirts, attempting to straighten them, followed by the adjustment of her cap, which had pulled askew and to the side with her fall.

"It's all right, Charity. Are you sure you're well?"

"Yes, ma'am. It's just that I came to tell you the news. Lord Bromby and Mr. Hobby have arrived. They're coming even now—right down the road."

Isabella's heart jolted. Forcing air into her lungs, she called out, "Papa! Mamma!"

Her mind raced and so did she—back and forth across the tile floor and to the mirror to check her reflection. Was she presentable? Clara had done her hair earlier in the day, but should she fix it again? Oh, never mind. There was no time for that.

Next, she rushed into the drawing room, where both her parents were seated and employed with afternoon activities.

"He is come! He is come. Lord Bromby has come."

Lady Bankmill rose slowly to her feet. Her embroidery fell from her lap as she took to patting at her hair and rubbing at her front teeth.

Quite the opposite of his wife, Sir Ralph stood abruptly and tugged at his waistcoat, securing the gold watch and chain into its pocket. "Well, then. Let us go and meet the tardy gentleman." With a wink, he reached out to take his daughter's arm in his, and they followed her mother into the foyer. "Calmly, I might add."

Isabella wondered how much calmer they should appear, as she could barely restrain herself behind her mother's snail-like pace. "Mamma, we shall run into the back of you as slow as you are walking," she whispered sharply.

"Why should I hurry?" Lady Bankmill responded smugly with a turn of her head. "Lord Bromby certainly has not favored us with any haste."

God, please do not let Mamma be rude to Lord Bromby and threaten gray clouds over my first encounter with him in ever so long.

A blast of cold air nearly pilfered what was left of Isabella's breath as they stepped outside. Her father took her fingers in his and squeezed reassuringly.

The Bankmills descended the steps and stood before the carriages. Isabella clung to her father's right arm, and her mother took his left. To compensate for her inner turmoil and nerves, Isabella tried doubly hard to maintain an outward posture of composure. She would not faint. She would smile politely, shake hands with Lord Bromby, and they would all go inside and greet one another as civilized people.

The carriage door opened.

Isabella held her breath.

A black boot dropped to the ground. And then a second one.

It was not Bromby, but Mr. Hobby who waved and smiled at them. She tensed anew. The anticipation was nearly too much.

And then Bromby stepped out of the carriage.

Her arm dropped from her father's as he moved forward to greet the men. Frozen to the spot, she stared.

Dressed in a long, black coat, from which peeked a plum-colored waistcoat, Bromby made a figure to rival even the rakish scoundrel of his own poem. His eyes glimmered like the pond waters at dusk. His complexion paled against the November chill, and his black hair—longer and less kempt than when she had last seen him—blew back and forth across his forehead in the light breeze that tousled all their locks.

"Lord Bromby," her father called out. "I am pleased to make your acquaintance."

Once done with greetings, Bromby turned his gaze upon Isabella. She looked away. And then, with great trepidation, turned her gaze back to him again. The weight of his stare forced her to step back even as he stepped toward her.

"Isabella." As he spoke her name, her insides threatened to bubble away or evaporate from her body like summer steam off a lake.

He stopped just before her and extended his hand. That was where she concentrated her eyes—upon the strong bones in his wrist as it jutted out of his black sleeve. Placing her hand in his, she felt the warmth of his palm. He raised her hand and pressed his lips against it.

Sir Ralph motioned them toward the house. "Let us all go inside where it is warm."

* * *

The mood at dinner amongst the men was easy and celebratory.

Her mother remained silent and dour, but Sir Ralph, his spirits high, asked many questions of both Bromby and John Hobby.

Dear Papa. His love for all sorts of people did him credit. And his friendly verbosity left little room for Isabella to talk or be addressed. For this she was thankful. It allowed her to choke down a little food—a difficult task in her emotional state. Surely she was dreaming. Was this marriage really to occur? Would she actually be joined in matrimony to this man?

After dinner, Isabella asked her father to allow her some time alone with Bromby, and it was arranged for the engaged couple to meet in the drawing room.

Bromby was already in the room when Isabella arrived. He stood just to the side of the fire as it blazed and crackled and tossed tiny, glowing cinders from its flames onto the dark rug, already speckled with previous, miniscule burn marks.

He held out his hand to her, beckoning her forth, and Isabella's heart soared. What should she say to him? What did lovers say to one another on occasions such as these? Although she had never been particularly shy before, as she approached him, his form illuminated with firelight, an intense bashfulness overtook her.

She stood at the other end of the mantel and stared into his eyes, which reflected darkness and flame. He motioned her closer.

She took three steps forward. Now she stood near enough to feel the warmth emanating from his body ... or was that because he stood so close to the fire?

Grasping her right hand within his, he raised it to his lips and pressed them firmly against her bare skin.

A kiss to a bare hand was forbidden ... but they were engaged now. That allowed them more freedom for touch and time alone. Her face flamed, and she placed her free hand over her heart as it wildly battered her ribs.

"It has been ever so long since we've met," Bromby said in a low voice that sent shivers through her.

"Yes ... I—I daresay it has ..." Her voice quivered and trailed off, swallowed in a barely audible sound.

What was wrong with her? Why could she not speak? For that matter, why would he not speak more?

He released her hand. Should they continue to stand, or should they sit? Should she clasp her hands behind her back or hold them in front of her? Where should she place her gaze? Upon him or her hands? Oh, she felt like an imbecile.

And all the while the abominable silence.

Swallowing hard, she curtsied suddenly. "Please excuse me. I think ... perhaps I should invite my parents to join us."

With an inscrutable expression, he bowed.

Isabella could not leave the room fast enough. Tears pressed at the back of her eyes as she summoned her parents and Mr. Hobby. With confused expressions, they followed her into the drawing room.

She wanted to sob aloud. Is this how she would conduct herself as a wife? Shy, insipid, and completely overpowered by emotion? She felt dwarfed in Lord Bromby's presence, as though she were unworthy of his attentions. Why had he chosen her over all the other women in London? He could have had another just as easily.

"Shall we have some port?" Sir Ralph asked as an inauspicious silence settled over the room.

Once the glasses had been poured and several sips occurred amongst stilted, but polite chatter, her good-humored and jovial father threw out the first real conversational item.

"So, tell me, Bromby. Living in London—and a literary type like yourself—you must go to the theater a fair bit."

Bromby nodded. "Indeed, I do, sir. I love the theater."

"And what have you seen lately?"

As though ignited from within by a fanned flame, Bromby's eyes glowed. He shot a glance in Mr. Hobby's direction. "The actor, Edmund Kean. Have you heard of him?"

Her father nodded. "Well, yes, of course. The papers printed a great deal about him earlier in the year. Fine actor, I believe?"

His tone elevated. "I had the good fortune to witness his debut performance in January of this year. At the Theatre Royal, Drury Lane. He played Shylock."

"Oh, yes, of course. That's the one I read about. Theatre was on its end—ready to dissolve. Kean saved them from bankruptcy."

"Yes. In fact, he was their last hope. But in truth, I've never seen a performance to rival his upon that night. The man was brilliant. His portrayal of Shylock left us all speechless. Did it not, Hobby?"

John Hobby nodded. "It did, indeed. Very fine performance."

Bromby continued, animated. "Afterwards, we all clamored into the streets, howling with rave reviews of what brave humanity he brought to the character."

"Yes, I'd heard the crowds were quite demonstrative," said Sir Ralph, sitting forward in his chair. He lifted the decanter of port and helped himself to another glass.

Isabella looked down at her hands. They trembled. Her mouth was as dry as if she held a swath of muslin under her tongue.

"The crowds were uncontrollable." Bromby joined Sir Ralph in his forward-sitting motion. "They were all praising Kean's talents to the sky. I'll tell you, Sir Ralph, we were all moved. I attend Drury Lane and Covent Garden regularly, but I have never been privy to such a hallowed portrayal of a character."

She had never seen this side of Bromby—wildly animated. If only she knew more about theatrical performances so she might join him in his enthusiasm. Other than the time she had run into Lord Bromby at the theatre, she had nothing to add to the conversation.

It was only her nerves, her agitated spirits that made this meeting so difficult. That and the fact that it had been too long since she and Bromby last met. From here on out, it would be easier between them. They only needed to find their bearings with one another.

The room grew quiet again. Surely, they should all retire now. A good night's rest would do them all good.

"What time shall I rise in the morning to meet the rest of the household?" Bromby asked.

Isabella glanced over at her mother. Her eyes were closed, and her head bobbed backwards as she fought sleep. With a snort and a jerk of her eyes, she righted herself.

"Usually around ten," Sir Ralph said.

Bromby nodded, and placing his hands upon his thighs, he propelled himself from his chair. "Very well. I shall see you all at ten o'clock tomorrow morning."

And with that, they parted and retired for the evening. Isabella made her way down the cold, dark hallway, half-hoping Bromby planned to meet her there, swoop her up, and kiss her wildly.

But the corridor was empty.

Twenty-One

The next morning, Isabella rose early and dressed in her newest frock—a cream-colored muslin with an embroidered trellis up the back and sides. She asked Clara to re-pin her hair, so that it looked fresh after a night of tossing and turning. She'd been much too agitated to sleep.

She descended the staircase and moved toward the library, determined to keep her composure and offer better company today. She would be light and conversational and …

The library was empty. She had hoped that Bromby would rise early in anticipation of seeing her. Perhaps she'd succumbed to the romantic notion that he had lain awake all night thinking of her as she had done. But it was only a quarter to nine, so she pulled a book from the shelf and did her best to focus on the text as she awaited Bromby's appearance.

After a fitful and fruitless hour and a half, Isabella trailed into the dining room where her parents and Mr. Hobby were chatting. Her mother's demeanor had changed, and she laughed at something funny Mr. Hobby had said.

"Oh, Isabella. Please come and join us," her mother trilled, motioning her daughter into the room. "We assumed you still slept."

"No, ma'am. I've been up for hours." She walked past Mr. Hobby, who pushed back his chair and stood, wiping at his mouth with a serviette.

"Good morning, Miss Bankmill. I trust you are well this morning."

She nodded and sat, but a lump swelled in her throat. Why wasn't Bromby seated at the table?

Appearing to sense her displeasure regarding the missing person, he added, "I'm afraid my friend has slept in this morning. I think he must have been very tired from the journey."

"But you are here, Mr. Hobby." Lady Bankmill raised her teacup to her lips. "And you must have been every bit as tired as Lord Bromby."

"Aye, madam. I was tired after our journey. But as you know, I retired early last night, and I had not a beautiful fiancé awaiting my arrival after the long journey."

"Well said, Hobby." Sir Ralph chuckled. "Well said."

Isabella wished she could rest easy and laugh with the others, but she could not stop counting the passing seconds and staring at the empty place setting. Her mother was no doubt building a mental arsenal of offenses against Lord Bromby.

"I understand a great deal more had to be done to Broadwell Abbey than anticipated." Lady Bankmill popped a morsel of bread into her mouth.

"Yes, ma'am. The house had fallen into rack and ruin, I'm afraid. Bromby spent untold amounts of money repairing the place."

"Lord Bromby never let the place to tenants?"

John Hobby hesitated. "He did. I believe his tenants were partially to blame for its condition." Mr. Hobby's eyes touched Isabella's. "But now he means to sell the place. A wife and family of his own offers an incentive to let it go."

"And were the repairs successful?" Lady Bankmill asked.

"Yes, ma'am. By the time we departed yesterday morning, the house was well on its way to improvement."

"I'm glad I shall have a chance to see it before it's sold," Isabella said. "I've often heard it touted as the most beautiful property in all of Nottinghamshire."

Mr. Hobby nodded. "In its day, I imagine that was true. In its ancient state it was a monastery, as reflected in some of the original architecture. It is beautifully situated on a lake and flanked by trees and forest."

"I only hope it shall not be too painful for Bromby to part with his childhood home," said Isabella.

Mr. Hobby smiled at her. "I am sure you are worth any discomfort it may cause him, Miss Bankmill."

Another hour and a half passed, and noon was upon them. There was no sign of Bromby.

A pulsing pain blossomed just behind Isabella's eyes. "Mamma, I have a headache. I shall walk a little to relieve it."

"It is far too cold for you to walk outside, Izzy," said her mother. "Why do you not lie down for a spell and ask Clara to bring a warm compress for your eyes?"

"Thank you, Mamma, but I'd much rather go out of doors, breathe in some fresh air."

Her motivation for such a solitary excursion must be obvious to all of them, but a walk, regardless of the outdoor temperatures, could only do her head and heart good.

Isabella kept to the meadows and the trails just on the outskirts of the property. She breathed deeply from the damp air and tried to quiet her racing mind. Why had Bromby not yet come down? Did he despise her company? After all this time, it seemed he should wish to know her better.

She prayed aloud, but her words sounded hollow. Her obsession with Bromby's every move, thought, and feeling had completely eclipsed her desire to spend time with God. Once they were married, she would settle back into a routine of reading and prayer. If they ever got married …

Did he truly wish to marry her, or was this all convenience to him? Perhaps she was being silly and overly sensitive to Bromby's lack of urgency. They'd had very little time together, and it had been so long since they'd last met. But did he not know that her heart's every beat resounded for him alone? These were all feelings she'd never before experienced, and they frightened her. Would she be completely consumed by Lord Bromby once she married him? Would there be anything left of her then?

The sky spat out a cold mist, and the front of Isabella's carefully coiffed hair began to frizz and puff. Anxiety over what her hair would look like after a good dousing drove her back to the house. A carriage awaited. Her father's lawyer had arrived.

Isabella broke into a run and rushed headlong into the house. Once she stood inside, the front of her hair dripping with moisture and her boots soggy with mud, voices echoing from the drawing room reached her. Clara brought her a towel and did her best to help dry Isabella's dampened hair.

"They're all in the drawing room, Miss—oh, look at the state of your hair!"

"Who is *they*, Clara?"

"Your parents, Lord Bromby, Mr. Hobby, and Mr. Milton—your father's lawyer."

Isabella fell onto a bench and ripped at the lacings on her boots, her fingers sliding in the mud upon the sole. "Help me, Clara. Help me remove these. I must be presentable to go before them."

A rush of maids and servants rallied behind her as she moved upstairs to her room. One brought her a change of shoes, another brought her a fresh frock, another redressed her hair. A quarter of an hour later, as she entered the drawing room, Isabella was the picture of propriety and a well-groomed young lady.

As the gentlemen stood for her arrival, she smiled, her gaze falling heavily upon Bromby. He appeared well rested. He bowed as she entered the room.

"Well," said Sir Ralph, rocking back and forth on his heels. "Here we all are, then. Mr. Milton, you know my daughter."

It had been some time—perhaps two or three years—since Isabella had seen Mr. Milton. Her previous experiences with him had nothing to do with her, and now she felt self-conscious and anxious in his presence.

"Well, gentlemen," said Sir Ralph. "Shall we let the ladies read their books and embroider their pillows?"

There were general murmurings amongst the four men that they should remove themselves to the study and let the business negotiations begin.

As he passed by, Bromby touched his hand to hers, and a shiver shot along her forearm, elbow, and into her shoulder. All her angst from the morning hours disappeared. It was really happening. Soon, she would be his. Lady Bromby.

Twenty-Two

2 November 1814
Seacrest Hall

Dear Lady M,

Soon, I shall be Lord Isabella.

I have only just arrived here yesterday, and I am already anxious regarding my decision, but never mind. It is too late for second thoughts—all is in motion, and more importantly, the lawyers are here. As I write, they are scribbling away, putting all my life and worldly goods down to parchment.

I have not a clue as to whether Isabella and I shall be happy or not.

Oh, it has been pleasant enough, I daresay. I get on well with my new father, Sir Ralph. He is a likable fellow—jovial, polite—with a witty sort of humor. He is a fair cello player, well-read, and rather fancies himself a poet—a talent I cannot assign to him, I'm afraid. However, after puzzling over the amount of money that shall be settled at the end of all of this, Sir Ralph has quite a few debts to his name—from playing a tad too much at the tables, it would seem. Even so, I am assured there will still be plenty to accompany Isabella into her new arrangement. She is heir to his estates in North Yorkshire and her mother's in Leicestershire—worth around £5,000 a year. Of course, there is always a chance that Lady Bankmill will die, Sir Ralph will remarry and produce an heir to nullify Isabella's inheritance, but that is a roll of the die I will have to take. Nevertheless, her Uncle Worthington has bequeathed her £20,000 once he leaves this earth.

As for my part, Hobby has procured a loan for me in the sum of £60,000, which will be contingent upon the sale of Broadwell Abbey, of course—but if all goeth well—and I pray to that God Isabella loves so much that it does—then we shall receive £3,000 a year for any spawn we might conceive, or, of course, if Isabella should outlive me (and my clairvoyant spirits tell me I should count upon that). In the meantime,

I must find some means by which to pay my debts on the restoration of Broadwell Abbey. The merchants have already begun beating down my door, demanding payment and sending threatening letters.

I must also procure a special license from the Archbishop of Canterbury so that we may marry here upon my next visit.

As for my beloved, I cannot make her out, although I believe she is fond of me. Her eyes and mannerisms all bear that shy innocence I saw in her from the beginning. But she does not talk. Since being here, we have spoken almost no words to one another while alone, and she has only addressed me a very few times in the presence of her parents. I hope this does not set the precedent for our marriage. As you know, I like for women to open their mouths and speak—much and often—for when they are speaking, they are not thinking as much. A thinking woman will never work in my favor.

Isabella displays her quietude affectionately, whereas her mother is certainly the opposite. It is obvious she detests me—her every glance in my direction suggests it. I finally gave up in my attempt to win her favor, as she has made it quite clear that she will not bestow it. I know she is your sister, but the two of you bear little resemblance to one another, my dear friend.

The setting here is quite beautiful. As we rode up to the estate yesterday, I was impressed with the cliff-side views. Isabella tells me we shall walk there today.

Yours,

B

Even if it was November, and the skies gray with a rain that threatened but did not fall, Bromby was happy to mount the little mare from the Bankmill stable and ride out on the cliffs with Isabella. An obliging groom followed a good pace behind, making a fair attempt at pretending to ignore them.

They rode so close together at moments that their horses' sides touched.

"There's nothing else in the world I love to do more than ride Millie," Isabella offered somewhat awkwardly.

Bromby smiled. At least she was finally talking. "You love it more than solving your word puzzles and calculating the angles of a parallelogram?"

"Well, there is pleasure in both. In one, I have the opportunity to use my brain. In the other, I get exercise, spend time with my good friend here," she patted the horse's neck, "and clear my head of all that ails me."

Ah. The Queen of Quadrilaterals experienced perturbation? He was intrigued. "And what should ail you?"

She turned, and her eyes softened. "Nothing much until late."

"And what has troubled you as of late? I hope our engagement has not troubled you."

She looked at him with a pained expression, bent eyebrows and a drawn mouth. "I must confess that it has."

"How so?" What on earth should bother her this early on? They had not even shared a house yet.

Isabella looked out at the landscape before them, breathing in and out deeply. Little puffs materialized in the cool air in front of her face. "In the past, I've been accustomed to spending a great deal more time feeling a sense of peace. Much of my life, I've found my happiness in prayer and in spending time with God."

Oh, here we are again. More talk of religion.

She continued. "Since your letter of proposal to me … I … I have been able to think of nothing else. But you."

Was that all? Well, well. He was flattered. He had made an impression upon her. He straightened his shoulders. A small smile occupied the corners of his mouth. "That cannot be a bad thing."

"It can. If it overshadows my prayer time."

He was pleased that he overshadowed her religious fervor—even if only temporarily. It could not last. Once they lived together, some of that ardor would surely fade. But in the meantime, her inexperience leant itself to the thrill of all things new.

He spied a gathering of trees just ahead of them. There were three large oaks that stood alone, forming a covering of sorts. Bromby motioned to it. "Let us stop here for a moment. The groom can mind the horses."

Just under the trees, they dismounted and turned the reins over to the groom.

"Let us walk a little."

Taking Isabella's hand in his, Bromby led her along. As they ambled beyond the trees, their conjoined movement was lopsided—her gait smooth and his limping. They made their way toward another patch of trees several paces ahead.

Once the groom was out of eyeshot, Bromby held Isabella's shoulders in his gloved hands and turned her to face him. Her body shivered as he walked her backward and pressed her against a tree. Just before his lips met hers, he glimpsed her expression—a mixture of fear and longing. She fought him at first, pressing the heel of her hands against his chest. Little chirping sounds coincided with her light attempt to push him away, but within moments, her hands relaxed, moving up the lapels of his coat and coming to rest just below his shoulders.

He possessed many talents in his bag of tricks. In this case, he employed a kiss of insistence and confidence, urging her for more. With a gasp, she pushed away from him. Her cheeks were flushed, and her dark blue eyes shimmered with … dare he call it passion? He was delighted at having produced such an effect.

She stumbled backward, turned, and walked away from him. Intrigued by her reaction, he followed her. Her arms swung wildly at her sides as she moved faster. Ah yes, the chase. This was his favorite part. Oh, how he loved a good cat and mouse game. She was nearly too quick for him, the little minx!

When her right arm swung back a little too far, he was able to catch her hand and spin her around to face him again. He pressed himself to her and repeated the same kiss he had initiated at the tree. This time, she did not fight him. She melted into him. Her arms flew around his neck. He caught her face between his hands, moving his lips to her cheeks, her chin, and down her neck.

Again, she gasped and pushed away. A bit too much perhaps? He would try again next time. She would become accustomed to the physicality of love little by little. He had never known a woman not to eventually desensitize to the shock of touch even if attempted in an improper manner. When administered repeatedly, it became commonplace.

While her face was red as an apple, her eyes were wide and dilated—a fire burning behind each iris. Her gloved hand flew to her throat, and her mouth hung open as if she were attempting to speak but could not produce the words.

For a third and final time he approached. Slowly. One did not move quickly toward a frightened doe. With his eyes firmly attached to hers, he ripped his glove away from his fingers and took her hand in his own, gently removing each finger of her glove before pulling the entire restrictive covering from her pale, cold hand. Holding her hand in his, he raked her fingers across his cheek, stopping as they reached his mouth, at which time he kissed the tip of each finger, then the palm.

And now for the *pièce de resistance*. He unbuttoned the top two buttons of his coat and moved her hand inside against his shirt. She shook her head, and yanked away a little, but he held her hand fast, finally placing it just over his heart.

"This," he said, drowning out her feeble attempt at protests, "belongs to you now, Isabella. My heart is yours."

For a moment, he thought she might swoon. In fact, her legs dipped ever so slightly as her eyes threatened to flutter shut. He allowed the moment to linger. If she fainted, he would catch her. But he had no desire to dull his romantic assault. This was the moment he'd been waiting for—to discover just how much his bride-to-be desired him. Now that he knew, he was pleased. Yes, perhaps this union would go along nicely after all.

With a sudden jerk, she freed her fingers and turned on her heel. "I must go back," she gasped.

He nearly laughed as he watched her moving toward the horses as fast as her feet would carry her, her hand attempting to tuck stray tendrils back into her hair arrangement. "Just you wait," he chuckled to himself.

Twenty-Three

Isabella could not sleep.

Her head reeled as she replayed Bromby's kisses. Lying in her bed and staring at the ceiling as the burning candle flickered and shadows waltzed across the tiny cracks and miniscule chips of peeling paint, Isabella touched her fingertips to her lips, shivering with the memory of his mouth pressed so tenderly, then so violently against hers. The memory, indeed, the entire recollection of those five minutes left her breathless.

Her mind turned with emotions that volleyed back and forth between fear that she was engaged to a man whose appetites were too overwhelming, and the soaring anticipation of what was yet to come. His persistence, his fiery pursuit of her on the cliff side—even with a groom hovering nearby—unsettled her. He was not some farmhand, and she was not an obliging milkmaid. There were rules ... there was propriety to think of.

I shall not let myself be alone with him until we are married. But then, turning over in a fitful reconsideration, she whispered words aloud. "And yet I cannot wait for the next time I am alone with him."

The next morning, Bromby was already in the morning room when she came down. He looked as though he'd been up for some time.

He sat talking with her father and Mr. Hobby. Mr. Hobby was set to depart, headed for Cambridge where he would await Bromby's arrival in a week or so.

"I mean to be in Cambridge by the nineteenth in time to cast my vote for Mr. William Clarke, who is running for the Chair of Medicine," said Bromby.

"I see," said Sir Ralph. "I know very little of him."

"He is my good friend ... a brilliant and good man. He will do credit to the position."

"To be sure. And from there you will return to London?"

"Yes," said Bromby. "Yes, to London."

He was already planning to leave? Her heart plummeted. He had just arrived. She had hoped he would spend some time in Durham. She had hoped perhaps he might not depart before their marriage. But it seemed the wedding would not happen during this visit after all.

———————— ✦ ————————

Later that afternoon, after Mr. Hobby departed for Cambridge, Bromby asked Isabella to join him again on a walk. This time no one was to accompany them, and no one who saw them preparing to leave asked any questions as to their unchaperoned state.

Isabella shook violently as she donned her coat. Her thoughts raced. Would their previous encounter be repeated? Oh, how she longed for his kiss again. She wanted to be alone with him, yet her desire for their privacy scared her.

As they walked out of doors and down the path, Bromby reached for Isabella's hand.

"Take me where you will, Bell. Where shall we walk? Lead me."

Isabella looked beyond their little park and out into the gray afternoon haze, which seemed daily to cover the land since Bromby's arrival. "I do enjoy walking along the water's edge, if the tide has not come in too high."

"I will follow you." He squeezed her hand in his.

They made their way out of the park and down the hill where crashing waves battered the rocks and pushed at the shiny sand, plowing it into mounds of charcoal-colored, fauna-ridden debris just outside the water's edge.

Always a little concerned about Bromby's limp and that he might be in some pain, Isabella suggested they sit on a crag, just beyond the sand where the water rolled in.

Bromby hoisted himself onto the rock and patted the space beside him. "Come. Sit."

With some difficulty, Isabella climbed up beside him. She nestled against him for warmth from the cold rock beneath her and the wind blowing off the ocean..

Bromby scarcely hesitated before wrapping his right arm about her waist and twisting his upper body toward her. Isabella turned in response, and immediately his mouth pressed hers. At first, she was eager and allowed her hand to slide behind his neck, feeling the curls of his hair upon the top of her hand, the warmth of his face against hers, his breath puffing from his nostrils and warming her cheek.

Lady Catherine had referred to Lord Bromby as a vampire, and now Isabella thought the description fit. His mouth seemed hungry ... he devoured her lips, her face, her neck. She worried that someone might see them. With a gasp like someone coming up from the water for air, she pulled away.

"What is it?" he asked, panting. His breath solidified in puffs of smoke-like condensation.

She shook her head and looked out over the ocean. The white-capped waves rolled in, one on top of the other. "We are not yet wed."

"'Tis only a kiss."

Her face burned. "Yes, but ... there is so much more behind your kisses."

He turned his face to look out at the water too. The wind ruffled his hair, blowing it across his eyes. Breathing in the salty winds, she hoped to never forget this moment.

"I am used to showing ... more ... to women in my company."

A strange sensation crept over her, much like a fever in its early stages. She knew there had been other women, of course. Her own cousin had been one of them, and that had not been a chaste relationship. But she was willing to put those indiscretions out of her mind's ledger of wrongs. She would never chastise or even mention such things to him. Therefore, it was both surprising and disheartening when he began to speak about it an open, unashamed fashion.

"And you know, dear Isabella, there have been many women before you. I feel we should acknowledge this fact. I do not wish there to be any misunderstandings."

Isabella swallowed. "I am well aware of what happened with Catherine. I know she enticed and seduced you into an entanglement that was not—"

"She did not entice or seduce me as you think." His eyes blazed. "Rather it was I who seduced her—mistaken as I was that she was at least a sane woman. I suppose I was drawn in by her playful, free spirit. Often that which is improper by society's standards holds the most attraction. So perhaps I was lured by her love of danger."

Isabella stared hard at his face, watching the expression change from a dreamy, amorous expression to something hard and hot.

Playful. Free. Improper. Danger. None of these words described her. If these qualities drew the man who called himself her fiancé, how was it that he could ever consider her as his match?

She shook her head and stared down at her hands. "And yet you did the proper thing. You ended the affair."

"I grew tired of her antics," he answered simply. "I saw her folly for what it was … theatrics. That is all. Whereas once, her costumes were intriguing and thrilling, they soon wore thin."

Isabella bit at her lower lip. She hated the matter-of-fact way he spoke about such things. "I forgive you for Catherine," she said stiffly.

He turned his head sharply. The darkness in his gaze was inscrutable. A flash of a smile graced his lips and his eyebrow arched. "I have been a man with great passions, Isabella. You are innocent in your knowledge of love, and I would not have you any other way. But you must understand that my desires have taken me many places—some places so dark that if you knew about them, perhaps you would be unable to forgive me."

Her mouth was dry, and her stomach roiled with bitterness. "Please do not say any more."

"You see? Perhaps if you really knew me—who I was, who I am—you would not love me as you say you do."

She shook her head. "No. I do not want to hear about your past. The others."

"There have been many."

Why did he insist upon discussing this? "Please stop." She propelled herself from the rock, and her feet sank into the soft sand. Turning to her right, she spotted a grassy hillside and longed to be on top of it—away from him. Walking briskly, she headed for higher ground. The tide was rushing in even as she turned her back on it.

Bromby called out, his voice muffled in the wind. He struggled to keep up with her. "Isabella!"

A part of her wanted to turn and face him, but her heart hurt too much. *You should not marry him.*

"Isabella." He panted her name. He must have been running to keep up with her.

At the top of the grassy hill, she stopped short. Tears met her eyes just as he reached out and grasped her arm.

"Isabella, please. Stop." He breathed hard. "*You* are the woman I love now."

A hiccupping cry escaped her throat. "I long to return to the house. Please let me go."

It was unlike her to create a dramatic scene. Even so, she could not control her emotions. He tried to take her hand, but she pulled away and wiped at her tears. They began to walk again.

In silence, they returned to Seacrest Hall.

When they reached the house, they were greeted in the foyer by servants eager to take their coats and gloves and offer them hot drinks or towels to dry their damp faces and hair. Isabella lingered only a moment. She pushed past the servants and walked up the stairs. Once in her bedroom, she threw herself onto her bed, buried her face into the pillow, and cried bitterly.

Why did he wish to talk about such things? Did he mean to hurt her? To make her jealous of his past conquests? He need not smother her with his admissions. It was unseemly.

She must have fallen asleep briefly, for when she was again conscious, albeit groggy and disoriented, it was dark outside. She sat on the side of the bed and rubbed at her eyes. Then the memory returned to her. The walk with Bromby. The ocean. His confession.

No. She did not want to remember. It was too horrible. But she must face him. She must break off the engagement. The thought brought fresh tears to her eyes.

Breathing deeply, she splashed water on her face and then dried it with a fresh towel. Checking her reflection in the dressing table mirror, Isabella tucked her hair back into place and straightened her rumpled frock. A knock at the door was followed by a timid voice.

"Miss Bankmill? 'Tis me, Clara. Are you all right?"

"Yes, thank you, Clara. I'm quite well," she called through the door.

"Lord Bromby is waiting for you in the drawing room."

A twinge pulled at her heart.

"Thank you, Clara. You may tell him that I shall be down presently."

"Yes, miss. I'll tell him straight away."

Inhaling deeply, Isabella rose from her dressing table and made her way down the stairs—her heart pounding painfully, her hands shaky and sweating. Could she break off the engagement? Should she do it? Even though she loved him so very much.

You should not marry him. That voice again. Was it God? Her conscience? Her fears? It was driving her mad.

The drawing room door was open, and Bromby stood by the fireplace. His back was turned to her. She paused in the hallway, wondering what his face would look like once he turned around. Would he be angry? Sad? Repentant?

When he did turn and she looked into his wide eyes, limpid with apology, her nerve faltered.

"Thank you, Clara," she said. "You may leave us."

Behind her, the doors creaked shut, and Clara's quick, light step retreated.

Isabella's gaze locked with his.

"Come." He beckoned her with his left hand even as his right remained perched on the mantel and clasped a small glass of what looked like sherry.

As if she had no choice in the matter, Isabella moved toward him. His bare hand clasped hers and a sensation rushed along the length of her arm and straight down into the pit of her stomach. An image of his mouth upon hers assaulted her mind.

Oh, but she loved him. How could she sever this relationship when she truly wanted him?

He led her to the loveseat and they sat, Bromby still holding Isabella's fingers in his. "Bell," he began softly, "I regret my words from this afternoon. In an effort to be honest with you, to save you the trouble of curious questions, really, I hurt you. That was not my intention."

He sipped a little from his sherry. She was touched that he had called her Bell. No one but her father had ever calle her that. A term of endearment.

"Bromby," she said, her voice hoarse from a day in the wind, "I wonder if we have not made a mistake. I wonder if I've made a mistake in accepting you. Perhaps I am not the right woman—"

"Blast!" He shot from his seat, returning to the place before the mantel, his back to her once more. "Do you really think to cry off? I cannot believe this," he rasped.

She flinched in reaction to his violent outburst. "I—I do not know what to think. I am trying to think what is best for both of us."

He turned, and the flames of the fire reflected in his eyes. "How do you foresee that breaking our engagement would be best for both of us?

Is it best for me? I shall return to London, broken and disgraced, with everyone pointing fingers at me—surely, they will say, surely he is the one who cried off."

"No, I—"

"Or would it be best for you? You can continue your solitary life here in Seaham, sitting with your mother and father, reading your books and solving your mathematical equations, hoping that someone with your high standards comes along."

His words stabbed at her heart. Despite her best attempts at preventing them, tears sprang to her eyes. No. That was not what she wanted. And now she feared her words may have forever ruined what could have been between them.

"Indeed, Bromby, you do me wrong in assuming that it is my desire to break it off. I simply wonder if we are truly suited. Will we be companions? Your experience is so much greater than my own, and you speak of your past conquests so freely and with a sort of pride. It causes me to consider whether a marriage will produce happiness in you, or will you only feel confined? Will I be … enough for you?"

His face softened, and his shoulders lowered. He downed the rest of his sherry in one gulp and placed the glass on the mantel. As he moved toward her seat in the shadows, the flames of the fireplace behind him silhouetted his form. He sat beside her, pulling her against him.

She allowed herself to be held by him. Resting her head under his chin, she breathed in the scent of him—salty wind from their time by the ocean, burning wood and warm embers—she wanted to melt into him. She felt small and childlike, eager to please him. I hate this confusion.

"Do you love me, Isabella?" he breathed against her hair. "That is what I need to know."

"Yes," she whimpered. "I love you. I do love you so desperately." A stream of tears ran from her eyes, as though finally confessing her emotion galvanized a painful, final link of the tether binding her to him forever. Her mind was so addled, so muddied with love and desire for this man, that she could no longer hear any other voices in the fray. If God was the one nudging her to break off the relationship, his words were lost in the roaring waves of her feelings.

"Then that is enough for me." He ran his fingers over her hair, sending pinpricks of sensation throughout her body. Grasping her shoulders, he moved her away from him, looking into her eyes. "No matter who has come before you, Bell, you must know that I am wholly committed and devoted to you."

Bromby spoke his mind freely and did not attempt to shield his true nature from her. This was a mark in his favor. He was different from many gentlemen in this way. After all, many women were completely unaware of their husband's true nature until after marriage—after they'd lived with them for a time. At least in this, she was not to be deceived.

He kissed her then and her original purpose was forgotten. She would marry Lord Bromby. She could not turn him away. She did not wish to.

His hand moved around her waist and pulled her tightly against him.

Of course, she should push him away, but she wanted to show him she could be passionate. Squeezing her eyes shut, she endured the dangerously pleasurable sensations that coursed through every limb. This was not proper. This was not how young ladies—even engaged young ladies—conducted themselves when left alone with a man. This was why they were not to be left alone with a man. Heat radiated from his hand as it moved over the folds of her dress.

In one swift movement, she tore herself away from him, the fabric of her dress rustling as she scuttled to the other side of the room. "I do not wish to be ruined before our wedding night," she exhorted.

He wore a surprised, if not amused, expression as he slumped on the loveseat. "Dearest Bell," he said in a low voice.

She placed a shaking hand to her forehead. Perspiration formed there, and without even looking in a mirror, she knew her face was the color of the sherry in Bromby's glass. As her wits returned to her, frustration and propriety replaced the passion from moments before.

"If we cannot be immediately married, and it seems from your conversation with my father earlier today we cannot, then I think it best if you leave … until we can. I think you should go tomorrow."

His countenance fell. "Tomorrow? But I had not intended to depart for some days."

Resolved, she stated the words firmly. "I think it would be best. We should not spend more time alone until we are safely married."

His eyes rolled up in his head, and he fell against the cushions behind him. Had he fainted? But then he raised his right arm and placed it over his eyes as if shielding out some annoying sunlight.

"Very well." He pushed himself to his feet. "If that is your wish, then I shall depart in the morn."

She exhaled deeply. No, of course it was not her wish. Stay. Let's elope this very day. "Yes, that is my wish."

Straightening his waistcoat, Bromby approached her. Although his expression was cool, the eternal, passionate flame continued to burn underneath the green waters of his eyes. He lifted her hand, touched his lips against it, then pressed her open palm to his cheek.

Then he was gone. Air rushed into the room through the open drawing room doors. Isabella stood still. Her legs were weak and her breath ragged. How should she feel? What should she do?

Her mother's form appeared in the open doorway. "Isabella? Is everything all right? I heard raised voices."

"Yes, Mamma. Everything is fine. I'm sorry if we disturbed you."

Isabella had spoken very little to her mother since Bromby's arrival a few days prior. Lady Bankmill would only confuse and frustrate her with questions and unwelcome commentary. Even now, she longed to make her way upstairs and climb into bed to allow her mind to rest from the turmoil of emotions.

Instead, her mother closed the drawing room doors and moved across the room to sit beside the waning fire. Several silent moments passed between mother and daughter, until she finally spoke.

"Your father was not the first man I ever loved."

What? She glimpsed her mother's face illuminated by the glow of the fireplace. Isabella lowered herself onto a chair.

"There was a young man before him—a Mr. Whitdale."

"Mr. Whitdale?" She'd never heard of a Mr. Whitdale before.

"Yes. I met him my first season in London. He was of high noble birth, and like your Lord Bromby—well, not *exactly* like your Lord Bromby—he was much sought after by eligible young ladies of Society. I was flattered to find that I had miraculously caught his eye." Lady Bankmill smirked a little at the memory. "I was once thought to be quite a beauty, you know."

Isabella smiled at her mother's reminiscence of a younger, thinner, less-weathered version of herself. She still possessed the same dark hair of her youth without so much as one gray hair. Her dark eyes and pale complexion were probably once considered attractive. But now her mother's neck sloped without definition from her chin to her collarbones, and her eyes were seated above pouches of heavily wrinkled skin.

"Mr. Whitdale made an offer for my hand, and I thought to accept him, but ..." she trailed off, and her eyes took on a faraway gaze. "In the end I could not."

"Why not?"

Lady Bankmill drew in a slow, thoughtful breath. "I could not accept him because he had once told me that he did not know if he believed in God. For a couple of weeks when he first came to call upon me, I thought perhaps I could overlook this. Perhaps it did not matter so much to a marriage. I could still have my faith, and he could believe what he liked. But as we began to exchange letters, I realized that could never be. The very fabric of our beings was different. It affected everything that we thought about life and death and what was important. What was most important to me could never be shared with him. He would never understand that part of my life."

Again, a heaviness settled within Isabella's chest. "Mamma, I know why you are telling me this. But I cannot ... nay, I *will not* give him up. I love him."

Lady Bankmill's facial features tensed—an inner pain pushed at her eyes, her forehead, her mouth. "Take care, Isabella, that you do not love Lord Bromby more than you love God."

The pang of conviction in her chest was a physical pain. Of course, her mother was right. And if truth be told, her love for Bromby had eclipsed everything else in her life. And she felt guilt for it.

Isabella rushed on. She would not dwell on such thoughts. "Mamma, I know Lord Bromby is not the man you would have chosen for me, and you are right in thinking that he does not share my faith, but this may change."

"*You* may change, Isabella," Lady Bankmill said gravely.

Isabella shook off the words. "I am committed to making him happy. Is that not what God wishes us to do for others?"

Lady Bankmill stood and embraced her daughter. "I can see that you are in love with him. And I pray that you will experience all the happiness in the world, but please do not deceive yourself by thinking you will make that man happy ... or that you will make him love God. If you continue with that delusion, you will be the unhappiest woman alive within a year of marriage."

Lady Bankmill left her then, and Isabella stood for some time before the fireplace, thinking about what her mother had said. Her mother had never been wrong before. Could her warning in any way be prophetic? Would she find herself unhappy and disillusioned in her marriage to Bromby? Would he be happy with her?

Exhausted in mind and body, Isabella closed her eyes and tried to pray. But the words would not come. After a while, the crackling logs in the fireplace drowned out her attempts.

Part V

Twenty-Four

November 1814

David sat in the tavern on Albemarle Street where he always met with the members of his gentlemen's club. He stared at the remnants of his dinner. Some gravy from mutton pie, a smattering of peas. He pushed at a crust of bread but did not eat it. Instead, he watched the door. Would Lord Bromby make an appearance at the club this evening? He prayed not. The anticipation of possibly running into the man had ruined his appetite.

After the hour had grown late, all the members dispersed. Lord Bromby had not come. *Thank you, God.*

All around him the men swilled their ale and spirits. It was enough to make him wish he were so disposed. But then he remembered that prayer was his comfort, not liquor—an early lesson his excellent father had taught him.

Pulling his gold watch from his pocket, David checked the time. He should return home. Anyway, the noise in the tavern soared. He could barely think as the two men beside him shouted. Just as they raised their fists at one another, the tavern owner and his rather husky bar maid stepped up and escorted them out.

Two more men entered the tavern and quickly took their place.

One of the men reminded him of his father except that he was slightly more rotund around the middle and he possessed a ruddier, more weathered complexion. His graying hair swept forward, covering his forehead. He spoke in a booming voice, allowing David to overhear their conversation.

"I prefer the Lombard Tavern in Tackett Street," said the man who looked like his father. "You get less riffraff in there."

"But their venison stew is appalling, and last week they ran out of ale by eight." The man sitting with him was younger and well dressed. His dark eyes scanned the room with amusement.

"Still, at the Lombard you would be loath to find a better place to conduct business. Quiet tables in the back—none of this shouting and ducking nonsense."

David soon learned that the man who looked like his father was named Crane, and the younger man's name was Wigg. Mr. Crane apparently owned an upholstery business. Mr. Wigg was renovating his house and in need of an upholsterer.

"There's another reason I came here tonight," said Mr. Crane.

"The barmaids?" Mr. Wigg laughed at his own joke.

"No. Lord Bromby's gentlemen's club meets here on certain nights. This was to be one of them. I'd hoped he'd be here."

The mention of the poet's name twisted something inside of David. A hard knot formed just under his heart, and he shifted with a pain like indigestion.

It had been a fortnight since Isabella had refused him, but his heart still weighed upon him as heavily as if it had been yesterday. He could not have borne seeing the face of the man who had crushed his hopes with Isabella. And if, by chance, Isabella had breathed aught of the proposal to Bromby, David would have been exceedingly embarrassed in his presence.

"What business do you have with Lord Bromby?" asked Mr. Wigg.

"He owes me money. A lot of it," said Mr. Crane, his tone dripping with venom. "And I've had enough of his pitching the gammon."

"Really?" Mr. Wigg leaned forward, his eyes bright with a desire to hear more. "Lord Bromby isn't good for it?"

Mr. Crane's face reddened. "Oh, well, he comes across as though he is full of juice, but my men worked for weeks to bring all the furniture and drapery up to snuff on his Broadwell Abbey, and then ... too smoky by half ... he shoots the crow and decamps before the work is finished. Leaves word with one of the servants that he'll pay in due course. Well, I haven't seen a shilling of what he owes me. Turns out he finds himself on the rocks. He owes half of London."

"Indeed?" Mr. Wigg appeared to be enjoying this gossip. The corners of his mouth slid into a half moon, and he sat back against the bench in apparent satisfaction. "So, he's been drawing the bustle a bit too freely, then? I have heard he has spent untold amounts of money on clothes, interior decorations, and the like."

"It would seem so. Well, from what I saw, he spends all his money on incognitas and getting jug-bitten ... at any rate, he comes across as a neck-or-nothing blood of the fancy, but from what I know now, he hasn't a feather to fly with."

"I hear he is soon to be married." Mr. Wigg quipped smugly.

"Hence the repairs to Broadwell Abbey, or so he told me. Wanted it to be his honeymoon palace. Now I hear that he means to sell the place. But if he thinks he's waiting 'til then to pay me the blunt he owes me, well ... he'll find himself in a scrape with me. Wife or no wife."

David covered his mouth with his hand. Was this true, then? Lord Bromby was in deep debt? How could he ask for Isabella's hand if he knew that he was in financial straits? Perhaps he depended on the money from her family? Poor Isabella. Had she known? David shuddered to think of her life shackled to a man who could not govern his finances, but it was none of his affair. She was not his responsibility.

What had he been thinking? He had known her feelings were not as they should have been—his own sister had told him as much. Why had he not listened? Why had he insisted upon attempting a proposal with no chance of succeeding? It was as though he set his course on proving that he was unworthy of her or any other woman. Three proposals rejected! What other gentleman had such a record. He knew of none.

"I should have my men remove the curtains and strip the upholstery chair by chair until he pays me. Let him sit on a hard floor and throw sheets over the windows for all I care."

Mr. Wigg laughed. "Yes, indeed."

"I beg your pardon ..." David leaned toward Mr. Crane so that he might be better heard. Perhaps later he would regret this interference, but a still, small voice in his head was telling him to act. "I beg your pardon, gentlemen."

Mr. Crane and Mr. Wigg stopped talking and turned toward him.

His mouth went dry. Perhaps he should have ordered an ale after all. "I couldn't help but overhear your conversation." He took a deep breath. "I am well acquainted with both Lord Bromby and his fiancée—especially with his fiancée and her family. I can attest that no matter what Lord Bromby's failings, his fiancée deserves no such repercussions which would come from the humiliation of discovering that her husband owes money on the repairs of a house where they will spend their honeymoon."

Mr. Crane and Mr. Wigg were silent, staring at him as though they witnessed something strange emerging from the floorboards. From his pocket, David pulled a handful of notes. "I would like to offer my services in this matter … and clear Lord Bromby's debt with you."

Mr. Wigg's eyes stretched open and his mouth drooped into an expression of incredulity. "That is quite generous of you, sir. Pray, what is your name?"

"David Beringer."

"This is wondrous strange, Mr. Beringer," said Mr. Crane. "Why should you dispel Lord Bromby's debts? Is he a relation of yours?"

"No, not at all. I am a member of his gentlemen's club, and his fiancée is my sister's dearest friend. She is a good and kind lady, and I do not wish to see her harmed by any poor decision so wholly unconnected with her."

Mr. Crane's eyebrows raised. "Well, there are a great many poor decisions made by Lord Bromby, not just the one owed to me."

"I understand that, sir, but I will do what I can. And in this circumstance, I can be of assistance." He handed Mr. Crane several monetary notes. "Here is a hundred pounds. That should suffice in securing my intentions to pay the remainder. Tomorrow morning, I shall send any remaining balance owed."

With hardly a moment's hesitation, Mr. Crane took the money, and on a piece of parchment torn from an invoice, he scribbled his name and address and gave it to David. "He owes me £1,500."

Fifteen hundred pounds! David fought against allowing his mouth to drop open. "Well, sir. Now he owes you £1,400. Upon my word, you shall have the remainder by morning."

As he left the tavern that evening, his heart was heavier than before. Yes, he was thankful to have had the fortuitous encounter with Mr. Crane, allowing him to clear at least one of Bromby's debts, but what of the other debtors? He could not clear them all. And just how much did Bromby owe and to whom?

How could Isabella live happily with a man who overspent and could not pay? Now the heaviness came not from his rejected offer of marriage, but from the knowledge that the woman he loved would marry a man who was not worthy of her.

December 1814

It was late one afternoon when Bromby paid a call to Lady Melwood.

She was entertaining a young friend and protégé, Miss Lucy Rowe, but seemed happy to see him

"How nice, Bromby, that you would choose this day and time to visit." Lady Melwood nodded toward the young woman, who sat quivering. "Miss Rowe, you will have an opportunity to pick Lord Bromby's brains regarding poetic arrangement and conventions."

The girl stared at him, wide-eyed and silent.

Usually, female displays of awestruck adoration were mildly amusing, but on this day, he was too tired to care. "I did not realize you were entertaining," he said somberly.

"Miss Rowe is a young friend of mine. She is also a poet, Lord Bromby, and I think her poetry quite good. She is a huge admirer of yours, are you not, Miss Rowe?"

"Why, yes." The girl sounded out of breath.

Bromby smiled a little and Lucy turned away, blushing. Not another budding poet. He couldn't bear to hear or read any more drivel from novices who thought they could string words together.

"Perhaps you'll have an opportunity to show Lord Bromby some of your poetry," Lady Melwood said.

Oh, please no.

Miss Rowe looked stricken at the idea. "Oh, I couldn't possibly—"

"I should be glad to see it sometime." Bromby fought the urge to yawn.

"Would you? Would you, really?" she breathed.

"Yes, of course," he lied. He predicted the girl's pretty face and figure was more interesting than her poetry.

Several moments passed in which he was forced to listen to Miss Rowe's sudden profusion of adoration for his poetry, in which her eyes never left his face and her mouth never stopped flapping.

Finally, Lady Melwood cleared her throat. "Well, Miss Rowe, it has been lovely to see you. I do have some business I need to discuss with Lord Bromby. Please give my kindest regards to your father."

Once she was safely out of doors, Lady Melwood turned to him. "Sweet girl. A bit too eager."

"Aren't they all?"

Lady Melwood sat back in her chair. "How long have you been in London, Bromby?"

"Two days."

"Good. I want to hear all the news. You must stay for dinner."

His brow wrinkled slightly. "Lady Catherine is not at home?" He could not risk another scene. He had not the stomach nor the energy for it.

"Catherine is not at home. She is visiting friends in the country."

"What a relief." Then perhaps he would stay for dinner.

The mushroom soup contained cream, so he would not eat that. And, of course, he would not touch the duck. Instead, Bromby settled for potatoes, peas, and a little bread.

He cleared his throat. "Might I have some vinegar?" he asked the servant. The servant bowed and scurried away in search of his requested condiment.

"Why do you not take some duck?" asked Lady Melwood.

"'Tis all fat." Bromby sniffed with disgust. "Do you not think me as thin as you have ever seen me?"

Lady Melwood's slow moving, lead-colored eyes moved over his form. "Yes. You are looking a little thin for my tastes, Bromby. I like my men to have a little more flesh on their bones."

The servant brought the vinegar, and Bromby liberally doused his potatoes and peas. "The vinegar, you see, helps stave off my appetite."

Lady Melwood frowned. "I hardly think starving yourself to look like a skeleton is fashionable."

Bromby mashed his potatoes as he doused them with vinegar.

"You've always been concerned with your appearance," said Lady Melwood. "Your clothes are always of the best, most expensive quality.

That's how you've put yourself in such a financial predicament." She ate a forkful of duck.

"Speaking of debts, the bailiffs have ceased their pursuit of me. At least for the moment."

She stopped chewing. "Bailiffs? I do hope you are joking."

"I wish I were. Until a week ago, they were knocking at my door day and night. I can only hope Broadwell Abbey will sell the minute Isabella and I have honeymooned there. The money from the sale should be sufficient for my debts."

Lady Melwood sighed and dabbed at her mouth. "Now. Tell me. How is my niece?"

He paused from pulverizing his potatoes and looked at her. "When I last left your niece she was quite well, I believe."

Lady Melwood nodded. "I have written to her. She should not delay this marriage any longer. People are beginning to talk—to question why you are back in London and not already married to her. So tell me … when is the wedding to be?"

"Sometime in January, I think."

"You seem less pleased than I would expect. That is not the face of a bridegroom only weeks away from a felicitous union. I daresay that's the face of a man condemned to the gallows."

Bromby sighed and put down his fork. What did people expect him to say or do to show his anticipation of marriage? "It is difficult to know how one should feel when life as they know it is about to end."

Lady Melwood laughed. "You are a dramatic beast. Oh, Bromby. Come, come. Marriage is not the end of things. It is the beginning. You may look forward to a new life with Isabella, one that need not be drudgery. Marriage can be very fulfilling. And then there is the prospect of children—"

"I detest children." Ugh. The very image of a shiny-faced piglet gave him a headache. "After spending a few days in my stepsister's company and with her many offspring, I am assured that children are the very last thing I want or need in my life. Noisy, messy, mewling nuisances…"

"Does this sudden dark look and mood have anything to do with Agatha Morley?" Lady Melwood squinted. "I had hoped you would release this childhood fantasy and settle into a domestic life like everyone else."

Bromby cringed at her words. He adored Lady Melwood, but he did not wish to receive a lecture from her. He sat back in his chair and chewed at his thumbnail.

"Oh, this won't do at all, Bromby." Lady Melwood reached out across the corner of the table toward him. "You must quit her. You cannot continue with this relationship."

He looked up at her. "Oh, well, that is sage advice coming from you."

She pulled her hand away. "There are certain rules of decorum—"

"Yes, yes. So you've told me." Bromby sat motionless, staring at his plate. The peas bobbed on a little lake of vinegar. Perhaps he had used too much. They looked unappealing now. He was angry and displeased with the world around him. The more people talked about propriety and Society's expectations, the less he wanted to adhere to them.

"I am worried," she continued. "For you and Isabella. This is an advantageous match, to be sure, but only if you are willing to give up your folly. You cannot afford scandal, Bromby." She resumed her eating. After swallowing another bite, she added, "I'm not sure you can even afford another coat like the one you're wearing."

His plumb-colored velvet coat. He had just purchased it this week. It made him happy to buy new clothing. He should be happy now, but instead he felt an insurmountable emptiness. He wondered just what he could buy, drink, or enjoy that might fill it.

"What does Mrs. Morley say?" Lady Melwood lifted her crystal goblet and sipped from it.

"She says I should marry," he mumbled.

"Well, there you are. She speaks sense as well."

He grew tired of this conversation and wanted to be by himself. "I thank you for dinner, Lady M. I think it is time for me to return home."

"But you have eaten nothing." She motioned to his plate full of mashed up potatoes and peas.

He pushed away from the table and stood. "I am not hungry. I thank you."

Food would not fill the void within him.

Bromby set down his pen and looked out the window of his study. Poetic words would not come to him today.

Fletcher entered, carrying a small, silver tray with two letters. Bromby swiped them from the tray and turned the first over. The handwriting was Isabella's. On the second letter, the return address read *Mr. Daniel Crane.* A long sigh seeped from his lungs. Just when he'd thought all was well.

He passed a hand over his face. When would Agatha write to him again? Every day he awaited a letter from her, but none ever came. He broke open the seal of Isabella's letter and skimmed over the formal portions—salutations and inquiries as to his health. Then:

I hope you will forgive me for my bad behavior on the last night of your stay. I do not know what came over me, but I assure you that it was not my intention to offend you in any way. You know how I love and admire you. I would never dream of reproaching you for those behaviors which took place long before I knew you. Please forgive me and let us proceed with the marriage as soon as possible.

But, if this letter finds you less disposed to the idea, or if you are in some way wavering in your affection for me, then I beg you will write as soon as possible. In the meantime,

I am yours,

Bell

He sighed. These women. One day it was all desperation for love, and the next found them in a state of resignation. What was a man to do? How was he to manage a wife who constantly attempted to solve him like one of her mathematical equations? As he'd stated previously to Lady M, he did not like it when women thought too much.

Now for the second letter. No doubt Crane wrote concerning the debt. A week before he had sent Crane twenty pounds to show good faith.

"I *will* pay you back, you badger." Gritting his teeth and bracing for the scathing words within, he unfolded the parchment. Out of it fell the banknote he had sent the week before. Holding the note in his hand, he perused the letter within.

As your account is now paid in full, I herewith return your banknote for twenty pounds.

His account was paid in full? How was that possible? Who had paid his account? Lady Melwood? Or perhaps his future father-in-law? Perhaps Lady Melwood wished Broadwell Abbey to be free and clear before he endeavored to sell it—on behalf of her niece? Or perhaps Sir

Ralph had caught wind of the unpaid debt? Bromby shook his head. It made no sense at all.

Fletcher appeared again in the doorway. "Milord. There is a Miss Lucy Rowe here to see you."

Dropping the parchment and the banknote to his desk, Bromby turned. "What?"

But there she was. Dressed in a tan coat and a matching bonnet with a blue ribbon. And she had brought along her lady's maid.

He stood. "Miss Rowe. What a surprise."

She waited for Fletcher to move away from the door before turning to Bromby, her face a aglow with girlish brazenness. "You told me to come, sir." She thrust a sheaf of papers towards him. "You said you would look at my poetry."

A prickling sensation worked its way up his neck, much as it had when Catherine had shown up unannounced in her less restrained moments. Even so, the girl was here, and she was quite attractive in a bright-eyed, impish sort of way.

They stood with a desk separating them, and she threw off her coat revealing a light blue frock underneath. His favorite color. Coincidence? He thought not.

Her eyes never left his as she smiled from ear-to-ear.

He sank down in his seat. "Well, let's look at your poetry, then. Shall we?"

He shuffled through some of the pages, perusing a multitude of short, trite poems with titles like "Phrenzy" and "Orange Sun" and "Engagement of the Soul." One short poem caught his eye if only for the small, tight handwriting that characterized it. "Isle of Mornings," he read aloud. "Interesting title."

The curls peeking out from Lucy Rowe's bonnet trembled as her smile widened. Suddenly, something in the girl reminded him of Agatha. Perhaps it was her pale eyes or the way a few curls escaped from their pins.

He carried the poem around the other side of the desk and stood beside her, allowing his shoulder to touch hers as he read.

"The morning breaks upon the isle,
The wait for it was but awhile
The sun shakes the clouds from shoulders of gray;
'Tis but the heralding mark of day.

170

Crowding out the clinging night,
The stars shrink back and hide in fright
But offer they no light for morn
In judgment they sit and cast their scorn."

Overwritten. Melodramatic. His own poetry had been her inspiration. She had copied his form. But it wasn't bad. He turned to her. "I like it very much."

"Do you?" her pale eyes danced.

"It reminds me ... of my own poetry." He smiled and put the parchment aside.

Lucy looked over her shoulder at the lingering maid. "Leave us," she instructed. The maid hesitated, looked back and forth between Bromby and her mistress, and with a quick curtsy, she scurried from the room.

A smile tugged at the corner of his mouth. This was an all-too-familiar turn of events.

Lucy turned back to him and exhaled. "Oh, I am astonished you would compare my poetry with yours—well, I have read *Herald of the Morning* through four times complete. It's only fitting that some of it must rub off on me."

As he stood before her, his gaze fixed, he reached out to tuck an escaping curl into her bonnet. "You know, Miss Rowe, it is not fitting for a young, genteel lady to be in the presence of a man alone."

Her eyes widened. He suspected she thought herself brave and rebellious by sending her maid out. She knew what could happen—a story she could tell her friends or perhaps she would whisper it to her cousin in a dark corner at their Christmas gathering.

"If people knew that you were in my company without a chaperone, they would think the worst." He lowered himself into an armchair just behind him, and with one arm he grasped her around the waist and pulled her into a sitting position on his knee. She gasped and stood at once, whirling to move away from him. The blue ribbons on her bonnet hung loose. It was obvious Miss Rowe had not fully understood the implications of her decision.

She looked into his eyes, breathing hard. "You—you will not tell anyone?" she panted.

He stood and approached her slowly, his eyes fastened to hers. He ran a finger down the side of her face, over her chin, and down her neck until he reached the untied blue ribbons of her bonnet. He tied the ribbons into a bow that fitted under her chin. "Do you not know about me, Miss Rowe? Have you not heard what people say about me?"

She nodded, making some barely audible sound.

Oh, why not? This might be his last, free moment before he was shackled to a wife. Then he changed his mind again. Oh, blast it all. What was he thinking? He was to be married within weeks.

Staring at her wide eyes and open mouth, he thought to say something to her. But what? An apology? A mockery. Instead, he took two steps backward and bowed. "You should go. Please. Quickly."

Lucy staggered backwards to the leather-topped desk. With shaking hands, she gathered her scattered poetry. Stashing her papers under her arm, she reached up and adjusted her bonnet. She started to leave but paused in the doorway, her blue eyes watering.

"Lord Bromby, you are a truly noble man." With a gasp, she bolted from the doorway. The staccato beat of her shoes resounded as she retreated down the steps.

Noble? It was almost laughable. He stood with his hands braced against the desk, breathing heavily. What had come over him? Why did he feel the need to seduce every woman who entered his presence? He supposed it was something to do with the curse that hung over his family. All the men had been doomed from the start. What was to render his fate any different from theirs?

No matter what Isabella said, he saw no way out of his own damnation. Unless, by marrying her, he was in some way sanctified.

Twenty-Five

15 December 1814
London

Dearest Bell,

You are incorrigible! What is all this nonsense about being "less disposed" or "in some way wavering"? If you had allowed me to linger in Seaham two weeks ago, we could have been man and wife by now. When we next meet, let it be to have the whole matter over and done with. I will depart at the end of this week. With any luck, I shall spend Christmas at your family's home, and we shall be married immediately thereafter. Let us not unnecessarily spend any unmarried nights under the same roof. I believe we saw last time the sort of discord to which that leads.

Hobby will join me on my travels. If for whatever reason you choose not to marry me, I would wish for a traveling partner for my return.

All my love,

B

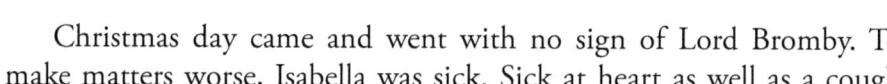

Christmas day came and went with no sign of Lord Bromby. To make matters worse, Isabella was sick. Sick at heart as well as a cough and stomach malady.

Although Sir Ralph maintained his usual joviality, playing his cello, drinking his port, and even joining some friends for a game of cards, Lady Bankmill had stopped speaking of Bromby and a marriage altogether, yet cake and honeymoon arrangements went forth.

Around eight o'clock that evening, Isabella went to her room. Perhaps she would have a good cry and feel sorry for herself. She deserved it, did she not? Bromby had said he'd be here, yet Christmas was over. Could he ever be trusted to tell the truth?

A few minutes later, the servants in the hall called out to one another, and there was a great deal of thumping. She cracked open the door and peered out. The housemaids rushed up and down the stairs.

"Jessie. What is happening?"

The girl turned briefly, her answer flung back at Isabella as though the reason had nothing to do with her. "Lord Bromby and Mr. Hobby are here, miss. We're all to make ready for them."

A flock of butterflies arose in the pit of Isabella's stomach and flew upwards into her chest and throat. Her heart fluttered as if spurred on by the beating of wings.

"Would you please send Clara to me?"

"I'm here." Clara seemingly materialized out of the shadows.

"Oh, good." Breathless, Isabella waved her inside. "Come help me dress, then."

"Yes, miss."

She sank back into her room followed by Clara, who helped her change out of her plain, muslin dress into a light green silk frock embellished with lace.

"This is a lovely dress, Miss Bankmill." Clara's eyes glowed. "It goes well with your hair. And look how it shimmers under the light of the candle."

"Yes, thank you. It was a Christmas gift from my parents." Isabella smoothed the fabric over her sides as she studied herself in the full-length mirror. "Clara, have you seen him yet? Lord Bromby?"

"No, miss. He was shown straight to his room."

"Well." Isabella touched her hand to her hair.

"Do you want me to do your hair, Miss Bankmill?"

"Yes, Clara, please."

Isabella breathed as though she'd been outside on a brisk walk or running with the dogs. She fidgeted with the hem on the sleeve of the dress.

As she re-pinned Isabella's hair, Clara prattled away about a friend of hers—a servant in another household—who had just been married. She elaborated on what the girl wore, what her husband was like, and who they worked for. Her words passed over Isabella like wind. What would she say to Lord Bromby? How should she act when she saw him?

She would be dignified, of course. She would extend her hand to him. She would welcome him and say that she was glad he had come. She would say nothing of the delay, her anxiety, or the fact that she'd feared a change of heart.

Her hand shakily caressed the banister as she made her way downstairs to the drawing room where she joined her parents. Her father sat in his usual chair by the fire and studied a leather-bound book. He looked up and stood when she entered. "Isabella. You look very well indeed. That dress suits you perfectly, wouldn't you say, dear?" He glanced in Lady Bankmill's direction.

Lady Bankmill looked as though she had eaten a lemon. Her mouth was pursed, pulled down at the sides with deeper, more pronounced creases. "Yes," she pronounced stiffly. "Very nice, Isabella."

Isabella positioned herself on a chair near the door. She straightened and re-straightened her dress. A door upstairs opened, and her heart jumped as footsteps made their way down to the landing. But she knew that must be Mr. Hobby. It was too smooth a gait to be Bromby's.

They all stood to receive him. "Mr. Hobby, it is so good to see you again," said Sir Ralph.

"Thank you, sir. I'm much obliged to you and Lady Bankmill for your hospitality." Mr. Hobby's pleasant, affable expression touched upon each one of them in the room, finally resting on Isabella. He bowed to her and she curtsied to him. "It is very good to see you again, Miss Bankmill."

"And you, Mr. Hobby."

"Lord Bromby should be down presently."

Just then, another door upstairs opened. The tell-tale shuffle of Lord Bromby's stride echoed in the hall. Oh, hang all notions of composure and decorum! Isabella rushed out of the room and up the stairs. Her foot caught on a step, tripping her, and she caught herself just before falling.

She looked up. Lord Bromby had stopped on the landing and was looking down at her, his forehead wrinkled and the corners of his mouth pulling up with amusement. Isabella flew at him. His eyes widened as she flung her arms about his neck and buried her head into his shoulder. The flood of tears came instantly.

"Bell, Bell," he said to her softly, his arms encircling her waist. "I'm here now."

She could not speak but gulped and sobbed as he helped her down the stairs—one arm around her waist, the other holding her elbow—and back into the drawing room where the others looked on.

"Everyone, please excuse me," Lady Bankmill mumbled and then quickly departed the room.

Isabella glanced behind her. Her mother climbed the stairs, most likely taking to her room. Isabella's tears surely had been the crowning blow to her mother's nerves.

Relief. No less than that of a person given a reprieve from death—or in this case, spinsterhood. Her right hand clutched the neckline of her dress as her chest heaved with an attempt at reeling in her emotion.

Bromby pulled a handkerchief from his pocket and handed it to Isabella. A little embarrassed, she dabbed at her eyes as polite greetings between her fiancé and father ensued.

Bromby said something about being held up at his sister's. A piece of news that struck at her heart. Had he not said in his letter that he'd intended to be in Seaham for Christmas? But what did it matter. He was here. Finally.

Twenty-Six

The night before the marriage, Bromby sat with John and Isabella in the drawing room. The fireplace blazed. He sipped his brandy calmly. Depressed resignation. His fate had finally come. Tomorrow he would be married. It was all done. Mightn't he have some time alone with his friend before the event the next morning? Could not his bride-to-be take herself off to bed?

"I confess that I'm not nearly the Biblical scholar that you are, Miss Bankmill, but I do know my Old Testament from my new," John Hobby said, regarding a discussion on Jonah and the whale and its relevance to Christ's resurrection.

"But you do believe in God, do you not, Mr. Hobby?"

"Oh, yes," he confirmed. "I am not like my friend here. I'm not an atheist."

Bromby looked at his friend. "I am not an atheist either, Hobby. I simply do not know that I can say for sure who or what God is. I don't know that any of us can."

Isabella sat forward in her chair. "But I am determined to change your friend's way of thinking, Mr. Hobby. I believe Lord Bromby really does believe in the God of the Bible, and upon closer study he will come to know the loving and forgiving nature of his Creator."

"The Brombys are a cursed lot." He spoke as he stared into the flames of the fireplace. "My grandfather committed suicide, and so did his sister. Insanity runs rampant through the family line. We are all doomed." He had said all of this before, but Isabella should really understand what she was getting into. Although from what he could tell, nothing he ever said seemed to bother her. Somehow, she seemed able to reconcile her faith and his philosophies.

Hobby endeavored to make light of his friend's claims. "Oh, come, Bromby. Do not be so melodramatic. You talk this rot all the time, yet you are as sound of mind as anyone I know. You are not tied to your family's fate."

"Generational curses, my dear Hobby," Bromby pronounced. "I am a Bromby, the Bromby line is cursed, therefore, I must partake of their fate. In Exodus, it says the sins of the father will be visited upon his children and his children's children unto the third and fourth generation."

Isabella slapped the arms of the chair, sitting forward again. "How is it that you believe that decree, but not the one in Galatians that says, 'Christ hath redeemed us from the curse of the law'?"

Bromby turned back to the fire. "As you can see, Hobby, my wife-to-be refuses to believe I am damned."

"I will *not* believe that," Isabella said promptly. "And I will pray that you will not believe that either."

"An eternal optimist." Bromby smiled.

Isabella's strength of determination that he would change his feelings on the matter of religion was amusing. And even though he was unsure how this marriage would play out, he did feel a sort of affection for her.

There was no doubt in his mind that Isabella Bankmill was in love with him. Her eyes said it all.

The following morning's events blurred together. One action led to another, and everything seemed to move at cataclysmic speed toward the eleventh hour.

I must not think too much. There was a great deal of activity in the house, but Bromby attempted to act as though everything was normal. There was no cause to hurry here or there. The imminent approach of his change in status was no reason for alarm.

John moved alongside him and slapped his shoulder. "How are you this morning, Bromby? How do you feel?"

"I feel quite well, Hobby. Thank you for asking."

Everything was fine. His mind was quite settled.

At eleven o'clock, Bromby, John, the Bankmills, and a couple of other relatives—cousins and such whose names Bromby quickly forgot—all stood in the drawing room before the vicar and awaited Isabella's entrance.

He ignored the sweat forming upon his brow even though the outside temperatures were freezing.

Isabella entered through the double doors wearing a plain, white muslin dress, and Bromby allowed a smile to stretch across his face. She looked quite pretty..

Isabella returned his smile, as she approached and stood beside him. Out of the corner of his eye, he glimpsed her turning to stare at him. Once he turned his head and met her gaze. As she spoke her vows, her voice was clear, solid, and certain in its tone.

When it came his turn, he consciously stared straight ahead, and when asked, he repeated his vows as though he recited poetry, faltering but a little over the vow to endow his worldly goods upon her. *What a fine joke. How very droll.* He arched an eyebrow and cast a glance toward Hobby. John shot back a scolding expression. Oh, and that reminded him—he still had not discovered the identity of the patron who had so generously covered his expenses for Broadwell Abbey's upholstery …

With any luck, this ceremony would soon be over. As he gazed over the room, he caught the stare of Sir Ralph and Lady Bankmill—her father red-faced and smiling, her mother serious and dour. But then, how else did that woman ever look?

It was as though someone else's wedding took place, and he was merely a spectator.

As soon as the pronouncement of their marital state was made, Hobby stepped forward and shook Isabella's hand. "Congratulations, Lady Bromby. I know you'll be very happy."

Were those tears in Isabella's eyes? Already? There was little time to confirm one way or the other, as she turned away and immediately left the room.

Strange. Oh well, she has managed the subjugation and now has only to ponder the consequences of her spoils. A compression pushed at his chest, an invisible hand grabbing hold of his lungs and squeezing. He turned as Hobby grasped him about the shoulders. "Congratulations, Bromby. I wish you both all the best."

Bromby smiled, nodded, and thanked his friend. He had spoken the vows. He had signed the documents. The ceremony was over.

He was a married man.

His mouth dried and his head ached. Even so, he went about all the niceties expected of him. Lady Bankmill came forward and kissed him, and he quickly fell into conversation with his new father-in-law as they awaited Isabella's return.

She returned some moments later, dressed in a satin cape with fur trimming. "I am ready," she said in a resolute tone.

In a slow procession, they made their way outside to the carriage.

Hobby handed Isabella a wedding gift. "I had it prepared for you in London."

Isabella tore off the brown wrapping and produced a leather-bound book.

"It contains all of Bromby's complete works."

"How lovely. Thank you." She smiled, the tears in her eyes like drops of rain. "I'm so glad you are Bromby's closest friend. We should be so happy to have you come and visit us in Piccadilly."

"Yes," Bromby said, his own voice sounding far away. "Do come, Hobby. Do come soon."

"I shall. I hope you will be very happy," Hobby repeated as he handed Isabella into the carriage.

She turned back to him, smiling. "If I am not happy, I will have only myself to blame."

Her words resounded with a clang in Bromby's mind and heart. A moment's guilt, perhaps? Had he done wrong in marrying her? If she took responsibility for all the happiness in their marriage, then that must mean she felt she could somehow control it. Did she think she could control him? A flash of anger ignited in his brain as he climbed into the carriage and settled beside her. *She'd better not think she can control me.*

Hobby closed the door. Instinctively, Bromby thrust his head out of the window, sharply inhaling the frigid air. He outstretched his arm to Hobby. How he wished he could stay with his friend.

"Safe travels." Hobby gripped Bromby's hand.

As the carriage began to move, Bromby grasped Hobby's hand ever tighter, forcing his friend to run alongside the carriage until he could no longer keep up. Finally, Bromby's fingers were wrenched away. He pushed himself further out of the window and looked back at the retreating road. John Hobby stood alone in the middle of the lot, watching them disappear into the snow-white afternoon.

The bells of the local church rang out, and he jolted upright at the sound of six booming musket shots fired in succession. A salute to their marriage. Bromby shivered.

Twenty-Seven

It was all too quiet in the carriage. Her nerves were on edge anyway, although she made every attempt at hiding it. No matter how her insides twisted and her temples pulsed, she would appear as decorous and self-possessed as possible.

As they made their way through Durham, more bells rang. She glanced over at Bromby and smiled. "They are ringing for us."

Bromby said nothing. He looked out the window, tapping his fingers upon the ledge. Isabella struggled for some conversational fodder that might draw him back into this moment, which should have been joyful and celebratory. She sensed that his mind and heart were elsewhere. His countenance suggested it in the tightness of his mouth and the lines around his narrowed eyes.

The bells continued as they passed through town. As the carriage moved away from the church and the peals faded, a low singing replaced the celebratory clangs. Isabella rocked her head to the side, attempting to discern what song Bromby sang, but suddenly his voice grew in volume, filling the carriage with a harsh sound—almost a bellow.

He sang a Scottish air, a tune she recognized, but he had replaced the lyrics with words of his own—vulgar, indecent words that filled her head with shock and dismay. Why would he behave in this manner? Did he mean this to be entertaining? Had he imbibed too much wine before their departure? His voice reverberated angrily against the walls of the coach, physically hurting her ears. Clenching her hands and teeth together, she pretended as though nothing was amiss.

Finally, he collapsed back against the seat, quiet and breathing hard.

She took deep, slow breaths and tried to pray silently. *Lord, help me to be a good wife to him. Please let him know how much I love him.*

"You'd better have married David Beringer," Bromby growled. "He would have made you a fine husband."

Her heart beat in her throat as a lump formed there. Aghast, she looked at him. "Why would you say such a thing?"

The frigid temperatures outside produced a bloodless effect in her hands, and his pale skin looked nearly translucent, although his expression was one of angst and heat. "Your parents should have known better than to marry you off to me—a blackguard, a fiend."

"What?" she gasped, her hand flying to her throat. "What are you talking about? This is nonsense."

He turned to her, his eyes dark. "Is it? Have you not heard that I come from a family of lunatics and heretics? We are all, all doomed. Why would you tie yourself to me—such a person? But then again, I blame you for some of my more recent actions. Had you agreed to marry me two years ago when I first asked, I would not have had the opportunity to commit some of my more atrocious sins." His voice grew in volume until all at once he was shouting. "So, you are to blame! You—the one so very interested in the nature of my soul."

Isabella shut her eyes and sat back against the seat, willing herself to breathe slow, calming breaths. Why was this happening? Why was he ranting so when they had just married? He had never acted in such a cruel way before. Was this some sort of nervous attack? She only wished they could travel faster and arrive at their destination, so she could be away from him.

"You know I only married you to stop all the gossips and to avoid more scandal. And I suppose I wanted to get at you as well—for refusing me as you did. No one refuses me."

Isabella's heart pounded with such pain. Was she suffering apoplexy? She gathered her pelisse around her, shielding out the cold as Bromby shifted against the far window—as far away from her as he could be.

"You came with a pathetic dowry. My mother always told me I would need to marry an heiress, but your inheritance is hardly worth my while. I should have known better than to marry into a family with a matriarch like yours. For years I've heard tales from Lady Melwood about how your mother rules over your father, how she belittles him and drives him to drink. There was evidence enough of this in the two brief times I spent with them. Your mother is a harpy, and your father puts up with it. Well, let me tell you that I shall never allow myself to be bandied about in that way."

She turned to him. "I would never—"

"I can only hope your uncle will die soon so you can inherit the money you are bequeathed. That is the only thing that will make this worth my while." He pressed his back against the window of the carriage, but his front was turned toward her—the words spewing from his mouth through curled lips.

Turning to the window, her fisted fingers pressing against her mouth and the base of her nose, Isabella fought tears. Her head was spinning. She swallowed again and again, willing the sobs to stay at bay. Tears would do her no good.

"You ought not to have married me," he repeated, concluding his tirade. "You ought to have married someone better. I am evil and wicked."

His words echoed in her mind as she fixed her stare out the window and watched the scenery pass. Snow began to fall. As they drew closer to the town of Darlington and Allanstone—one of her father's houses where they would stay the night—the snow fell faster, covering the ground with a deep, wet, smothering layer of white. As they turned down the path leading to the mansion, Isabella's heart was encased in ice.

Once the carriage came to a halt, she glimpsed the servants gathered outside of the house—a butler, housekeeper, and several maids and footmen. Without another word, Bromby opened the door and jumped from the carriage. She neither expected nor received any assistance from her husband in handing her down. Instead, an obliging servant opened her door and held her hand as she shakily disembarked. The footmen began to unpack the carriage at once, and she was received by the housekeeper, who curtsied to her, squinting against the falling snow, which stuck in her hair and on the shoulders of her habit.

"Milady." The housekeeper curtsied again. "We are so happy you are here. Everything is in order. We hope it will all be to your satisfaction."

Isabella looked beyond the woman. Bromby had already entered the house. "Thank you. I'm sure it will be."

Desiring to move quickly out of the snow, she threw a glance over her shoulder at the carriage containing their valet and lady's maid. Was Clara following her? She wanted her familiar face close by. Clara waved at her and bounded along, smiling, blissfully unaware of the conversation that had just taken place in the other carriage between her mistress and her mistress's new husband. With Clara at her side, Isabella made her way into the house.

Isabella was almost afraid to enter the rooms she was to share with her new husband. As she changed out of her traveling attire and into a dress she had packed for the evening of her wedding, she said nothing to Clara, who prattled away about how lovely everything was and asked her question after question about how she was feeling and had the journey been a pleasant one.

She would maintain the pretense of normality. "It went well enough, Clara. We are all here safely, and that is all that matters."

"Lord Bromby's man—Mr. Fletcher—is very kind, very polite. We talked in the carriage. He is a widower, but he has no children. His mother is from Sussex, just like mine."

"That's fine," Isabella said absently, her mind reeling and replaying Bromby's words to her in the carriage. "I'm glad you got on so well."

You ought not to have married me. I only married you to stop all the gossip and avoid more scandal. I am evil and wicked…

Her heart clenched.

"Are you nervous, milady?" Clara's question cut through her thoughts. "You seem a little out of sorts."

Isabella looked at herself in the full-length mirror. Her face was solemn and her eyes reflected horror. "Yes, Clara," she admitted readily. "I am nervous."

Isabella entered their rooms hesitantly. Bromby was on the sofa, reading and sipping from a glass of wine. He did not look up as she entered.

Perching on the edge of a chair opposite the sofa, she arranged and rearranged her skirts. She cleared her throat a little, and he glanced up from the book spread across his lap. It was the book of his own poetry—the wedding gift from Hobby.

"Will you read aloud to me?" Perhaps that would calm and center him—put a better mood on this afternoon, which had started so abominably.

His demeanor was calmer than it had been in the carriage just an hour before. With a sigh, he flipped through the pages, apparently seeking out a particular poem, finally stopping at one and smoothing his hand over the page. He began to read.

"These voracious trappings of my body feel not the love I should impart

For all my sorrows take to flapping like an owl to its perch

Yet in the deepest recesses of my own stone-bound heart

I am left to wonder at the image of love, so often in the lurch."

Isabella tensed. She knew this poem. In fact, she could recite it from memory, but now from his lips it sounded cold and unfeeling. It was not the romantic musing she had remembered.

"For one yet dwelleth in my inner eye whose beauty never fades

For her the depths of my heart doth cry but never shall we wed ..."

Isabella turned her face from him. This poem was not for her. No, it was a lament. A lament for someone he desired but could not have. Over and over, she had read this poem and crushed the words to her chest, certain that Lord Bromby was a man in search of Truth and the purest form of love. Something inside her sank. All along she had misinterpreted its meaning. Now she knew it was a call for an impossible life—or a woman he could not have.

As he finished reading the poem, their eyes met. Hers filled with tears, blurring his image.

"Shall we go down to dinner?" she asked softly. A good meal might offer a better outlook on things. She was hungry. That was part of the trouble.

"Yes." He stared at her like a wolf about to pounce upon its prey.

Her insides contracted, and her mouth went dry.

He rose from the sofa and approached her. Standing over her, he stripped his coat from his shoulders and then his gold, embroidered waistcoat, so that he wore only his shirt. "But first ... let's get this part over and done with."

———————◦≈≈◦———————

Later that night, Isabella dismissed Clara while she dressed for bed. *I must have some moments to myself, without questions or Clara's talking.* She sat at her dressing table and removed the pins from her hair. The brown curls fell heavily around her shoulders. Taking her brush from the table, she began to work her way through the thick tresses. Clara would usually do this for her, but tonight she welcomed the opportunity to brush her own hair and think.

She looked at her face in the mirror—placid but somber—some might even say expressionless. She was no longer what she had been just a few hours before. What had she done? Had she made a terrible mistake in marrying Lord Bromby? No. She couldn't allow herself to even think the words. She'd made her choice. She must press on. Make the best of things. Surely matters would improve.

Rising from the dressing table, she readjusted her gown and prepared to step into the bed chamber. After dinner, Bromby's mood seemed a little improved. He had said nothing cruel to her afterwards. In fact, he'd been quite congenial—talking of a new set of poems he meant to write during their "'moon" at Broadwell Abbey. She'd encouraged him, saying that she looked forward to reading what he would next write.

The door to the bedchamber creaked open as she slipped inside, clutching her candle for light. He was already in bed, a candle burning on the table to his left side, a book clutched in his hands as he lay back on the pillows.

She stood in place and looked at him, attempting to forget all that had come before. His dark hair contrasted with the white of the pillows and the white pallor of his skin. His eyes were downcast to the book he read. His lips full and bow-shaped. Yes, he was a beautiful man. And he was her husband. They were one flesh now.

His eyes snapped up to look at her standing at the foot of the bed. "What is it?"

She smiled and shook her head. "Nothing." Making her way over to the empty side of the bed, she pulled back the covers and prepared to crawl in.

"What are you doing?"

She stopped. "I'm getting into bed."

"What? You are planning to sleep here? With me?" His raised up a little, his eyes wide and dark with dilated pupils.

"Well, yes," she laughed a little. "I am your wife now. Where else would I sleep?"

His expression suggested that he hadn't considered the arrangement. "I … I never thought …" He broke off, shaking his head.

Her heart clattered to the bottom of her ribcage. She dropped the covers and stepped back from the bed. "But I am your wife. Where would you have me sleep?"

He sat back against the pillows and stared straight ahead as if the reality of the situation had just dawned on him. Then he turned back to his book. "Oh, please yourself. If you want to sleep in here, then so be it."

Isabella wavered. Should she find another room to sleep in? No. If she slept in another rom tonight, then that would set a precedent for all the nights to follow. She would sleep in here, in the bed beside her husband where she belonged. Without another word, she pulled back the covers and climbed in beside him.

"I guess it's all done now," he mumbled, not looking up from his book. "Nothing we can do about it now, can we?"

"What do you mean, Gregory?" Saying his name sounded strange to her. "Bromby" suited him better.

"I mean that you should have married another man. Someone better than I."

"Please don't say that again." She grasped at his arm, and he flinched. "I love you. I don't want to be married to anyone else."

With a groan and curled upper lip, he turned to her. "How could you love me? I am an evil, wicked man."

"Why do you keep saying that?"

"Because 'tis true."

"I do not believe it."

He laughed, a hollow sound. "Well, you can believe what you like, but I am telling you the truth. You simply don't want to believe it."

She sighed. It had been a long, emotionally trying day. She couldn't stand much more. "What have you done that you think is so evil?"

He looked at her, and the expression on his face changed. His brow furrowed, his mouth softened. Pity for her, perhaps? Or was it for himself?

"If I told you … you would run from this room screaming."

"Oh, that is silly. I would do no such thing."

He nodded. "I did things in Greece that would turn the tide of your love for me."

Now she was morbidly curious. "What did you do?"

He raised his book again and turned his eyes from hers. "Things I will never tell anyone. Except perhaps Agatha. She alone understands me."

Isabella breathed out. "Well, if she understands you so well, then perhaps I may come to understand you too."

"I doubt it."

His words pained her. He seemed determined to push her away as if she were a mere acquaintance, a distant cousin, or one of his hangers-on. He wouldn't confide in her as she so desperately wanted and needed him to do.

Finally, too tired and cold to keep prodding him, she settled under the covers and turned over and away from him. Perhaps she would write and ask Agatha to join them at Broadwell Abbey. Maybe having his stepsister there would make him happy and bring him some peace.

Sometime late that night, the wind began to rage, stirring Isabella with its pounding surges. She slept fitfully, caught between exhaustion and waking, with the winds roaring like an ocean tide rolling in. She dreamed she was home in Seaham, standing on the ocean shore and looking out over the white-capped waves. The ribbons on her bonnet flapped out in front of her—red ribbons. But she owned no red dresses. Why would she have a red ribbon on her bonnet?

The ground shook suddenly, and just as she wondered if it were an earthquake, she awakened to Bromby shooting up beside her, his silhouette illuminated against the red curtains around the bed. A candle still burned, glowing on the other side of the curtain.

"I must have died and gone to hell!" he bellowed.

She raised up beside him, placing her hand on his shoulder. "What is the matter? What is wrong?"

Slowly, he lowered himself back onto the pillows, groaning and sighing as he covered his eyes by slinging his arm over them.

"*Shh*," she soothed, running her fingers through the curls of his hair. "You were dreaming. You were just dreaming."

"Oh, but I am not," he moaned before dropping off to sleep once more.

Isabella lay back down but could not sleep. The wind continued to rage around Allanstone, and she felt its tumultuous blow in her heart.

Twenty-Eight

Over breakfast the next morning, Isabella ate very little. She sat at the table with Bromby as he ate a full breakfast of bread, jam, and tea, her mind full of the previous evening's events. All at once, she was terribly homesick, and her eyes filled with tears at the thoughts of her mother and father. As a girl she had spent time in this house, running up and down the corridors and playing in the gardens. A simpler, happier time.

Bromby stuffed a morsel of bread into his mouth and looked up at her as he chewed. She tried to blink back the tears before he saw them, but it was too late. "What on earth is the matter?"

"Nothing at all, I assure you."

He dropped his knife with a loud clatter, looking off to the side. "Oh dear. One day married, and my wife is already miserable."

"I am not miserable." The words sounded insincere, even to her.

"You are not miserable, yet your eyes are filled with tears."

She would not reveal the contents of her heart—that she missed her home and family, that she was desperate for him to bestow some kindness upon her.

He sat quietly for a moment, chewing, thinking. Finally, shaking his head a little, he resumed eating, stopping only to remark, "It is clear from day two that I will never make you happy."

She was more than tired of hearing these taunts. "I wish you would cease saying these ridiculous words. I do not regret my decision to marry you. I love you. Don't you understand that?"

He paused again, looked up at her, and sighed heavily. "How can you love me? A sinner. A flagrant heathen of the worst kind."

"God loves sinners. Who am I but a sinner myself?"

"You!" he laughed. "You a sinner? The prim and perfect Isabella Bankmill? Pray tell what mortal sin have you committed in your *twenty-two* years?"

His taunting tone picked at her heart. "I do not believe in mortal sins. There is only one sin that is unforgivable, and that is to reject God by rejecting his son as atonement for our sins. Any other sin is forgivable." She clung to these words more than ever now.

Again, Bromby's knife clattered against his plate, and he tossed his napkin on to the table. Still chewing his last bite of food, he thrust his chair back and stood. "Not when you are a Bromby, cursed from birth, deformed and degraded … destined for hell as surely as you are destined for heaven." He stormed from the room, throwing one last barb over his shoulder. "You should have married a better man. But it is too late now. It is all done."

The servants moved around the room, their heads down, pretending they had not heard. Isabella's face burned. In her father's house they had never had such antics, and even if a disagreement occurred, it was never performed so outrageously before the servants.

"May I serve you anything else, milady?" asked the butler, motioning toward her nearly untouched plate.

Isabella shook her head, unable to meet his eyes. "No, thank you. I am not very hungry this morning." She scooted out her chair and left the room.

———— ❧ ————

Later that morning they departed from Allanstone for Manchester. After a night's stay in the bustling city that did more to fray her nerves than calm them, they arrived a day later at Broadwell Abbey.

Isabella had heard so much about the place, and before their marriage, she'd been excited to see it, but now she could scarce feel anything but dread.

As she stepped out of the carriage, the Gothic structure stretched out before her. The house was situated alongside a lake, but all was covered with the blanket of white snow and the water was a great swath of ice.

I am evil. I am doomed. You'd better have married another. The words rang in her head until she wanted to scream. She'd heard them so often over the past three days, she started to believe them.

Isabella held her breath as she entered the house, as though she might breathe in some contagious evil from the place itself. Standing in the foyer, she looked around her. Tapestries of embroidered scenes hung from the high walls of the place, and ornate, gold trinkets decorated every table in sight. The floor looked as though it had been recently repaired. Large oriental rugs covered much of the boards.

A damp chill filled the place, no doubt due to the snow and gusts of wind that blew in behind her.

Clara's voice echoed when she spoke. "I cannot believe I'm actually here. I've heard so much about Broadwell Abbey, and now I actually get to see it."

"Yes," said Isabella, attempting to keep the despair from her voice. "It is a strange thing to finally be here, under this roof … as the wife of Lord Bromby."

"Is it how you expected it to be, milady?" Clara's eyes were wide as though she hoped to hear some tidbit that might give glimpse into her mistress's newly married life.

A long, shuddering sigh escaped Isabella's throat. "Not at all, Clara. Nothing about these past few days is as I expected it would be."

Bromby was nowhere to be found, and for the moment, Isabella was relieved. She walked up and down the damp corridors, pulling her shawl closely around her shoulders. The house was large, but there was little comfort in its high ceilings and drafty rooms.

She lifted a gold statue from a side table and inspected it—a centaur—half-man, half-goat, holding a harp. She replaced it and leaned forward to look more closely at a painting that hung on the wall just behind the table. It must have been Bromby's mother. There was a great likeness around the eyes and chin, although the plump woman's face was much rounder than her son's.

Isabella moved into the library, where she ran her fingers along the rows and rows of books and lowered herself into the chair by the desk.

Did Bromby ever perch there to write? Parchment paper and an inkwell sat atop the leather-topped desk, ready to be used. Yes, this must be where he wrote. It would be the perfect spot for inspiration, filled with natural light. She sat in the chair, drumming her fingers on the surface, feeling as removed as ever. She now bore the name of Lady Bromby yet still did not know the man to whom she was married.

She slid the drawer out of the desk, thinking quill pens must lie within. But there were no quill pens, only an ornate pistol.

Why would he have a pistol in his desk drawer? There were several more displayed upon the wall downstairs, but this appeared to be hidden for a reason. She quickly slid the drawer back into place, stood, and exited the library.

As she entered the study, she expected to come across Bromby reading or sitting by the fire, but the room was empty. She walked the perimeter, noting the repairs needed to the woodwork. One of the windows was ill-fitted to its opening, and when she placed her hand up to it, cold air puffed through the edges.

"You should have seen this place before, milady."

The voice startled Isabella, and she jumped a little. Bromby had told her there was a housekeeper—a Mrs. Thatcher. This thin, pale-faced figure standing in the doorway must be her. "The place was in very bad shape, indeed."

"Mrs. Thatcher?"

The woman nodded and moved into the room. "Yes, milady."

"How long have you been here?" Isabella stepped away from the cold of the window toward the warmth of the fireplace.

"I've been here about two months. Lord Bromby hired workers to come in and repair the place, and the staff arrived around the same time. Some left after swearing they heard strange noises in the attic. Even so, a few of us stayed."

"Noises in the attic?" Isabella smiled, amused.

Mrs. Thatcher smiled. "'Tis an old house, milady. People will imagine stories, hauntings, ghostly movements in the night. That sort of thing."

"You do not believe in that sort of thing, do you?"

The housekeeper's expression did not change at all. "I have served in a few houses. I confess that I have seen some strange things, but I have never seen a ghost or anything that claimed to be such."

"I do not believe in ghosts, Mrs. Thatcher. Only the Holy Ghost … and demons, I suppose."

Mrs. Thatcher nodded, her narrow, gray eyes inscrutable as to their emotion.

Isabella looked around her. "It must have been in very bad shape, indeed. Even now, I see a lot that needs doing before the place is sold."

Mrs. Thatcher appeared younger than Isabella had expected. Most housekeepers were round and red-faced. This woman looked to be in her thirties and elegant in stature and facial features. Even her manner of speech was more refined and fluid.

"You will let us know if you are in need of anything at all, milady?"

"Yes, Mrs. Thatcher, of course. Do you happen to know where Lord Bromby may be at the moment?"

"He is in the drawing room. By the fire. Fletcher just served him some brandy there."

"Brandy? It is but ten o'clock in the morning." Isabella immediately reproved herself for the outburst. The housekeeper was not in charge of her master's habits. She was there only to serve him. "Of course. I apologize, Mrs. Thatcher."

"Will there be anything else, milady?"

Isabella shook her head. "No, nothing at all. Thank you."

Isabella waited until noon before she sought Bromby in the drawing room. He sat in a red armchair, his right ankle propped upon his knee as he stared into the fireplace and bit his nails. He stopped only to move his glass to his lips. When he finally noticed her presence, he raised his glass in her direction.

"You've had quite a lot of those today," she said.

"I am celebrating our nuptials," he quipped. "Maybe you should have a few drinks, Isabella. It might improve your sense of humor. If, indeed, you have one. I'm beginning to wonder."

After only a few days in his company, Isabella expected his sharp words at every turn. "I find a great deal of humor in the world."

"Really?" He arched an eyebrow. "Tell me something you find funny."

She scrambled for something to relate. "I find my father's jokes quite amusing."

Bromby grimaced, his mouth twisting at the corner. "Yes, well, your father is easily laughed at to be sure." He looked back to the flames in the fire and resumed biting his nails.

Isabella held her tongue. *Do not goad him.*

"My stepsister, Agatha, is very funny. She mimics other people's voices. She always makes me laugh. No one can make me laugh like her."

She inhaled slowly. Again, there was Agatha.

"I only wish she were here now," he grumbled. "It might lighten the place up."

Isabella lowered herself into a chair across from him. "Why don't I write to her and ask her to join us here?"

He looked up, his eyes wide. "Join us? On our 'moon?"

She forced the words from her mouth. "Well, yes. If it would make you happy. The only thing I want is for you to be happy, B."

For a moment, something like a flash of compassion flittered over his face. His brow furrowed, and his lips compressed. "You are too good. You deserve—"

"Please do not say I deserve better. I do not think I can bear to hear those pitiable words again. I have grown tired of them."

His face collapsed into an expression of genuine amusement. A low chuckle gurgled in his throat and then erupted.

Isabella stared at him. What did he find so funny?

"There you are!" He coughed, choking on his own laughter. "You have made me laugh after all. There is some spark of fight in you, Bell. Well done."

Still perplexed as to what he had found so amusing and aching with exhaustion, Isabella ran a wan hand over her face. "Shall I write to Agatha, then?"

"Do," he said cheerfully. "Do write to her. Ask her if she will come. If she will, what a happy little trio we shall be."

Dear Agatha,

Gregory and I have been settled at Broadwell Abbey for a few days now. I am writing to invite you to join us here. I think he would be most happy if you would come. He talks about you all the time, and I know he would welcome your good humor and someone other than myself to keep him company.

Your sister,
Isabella

Dearest Isabella,

As much as I would love to see you and Gregory, at this time I cannot come as Georgiana has scarlet fever. Please remember her in your prayers.

However, I will extend the same invitation to you and my stepbrother on your return journey to London in a few weeks' time. I would so love to see you both, and I look forward to becoming more acquainted with my new sister.

Yours,
Agatha

"There is a separate letter for you as well," Isabella said, handing him the carefully folded parchment upon which his name was elaborately penned.

Bromby snatched the letter from Isabella's hand, suddenly more animated than she had seen him since they arrived at Broadwell Abbey. "Dear Agatha!" His voice rang like a bell as he tore open the seal.

"She writes ..." His eyes scanned the page. "She says I should be good to you ... treat you well. She writes that I should try to be happy." He continued to stare at the paper but grew silent.

"What else does she say?" she prompted.

Frowning, he folded the letter in his hand, stuffed it into the pocket of his coat, and left the room.

Isabella sat glumly and looked out the window. The glass was frosted all around the edges, resembling a snow-gilded frame. The snow was deep, but as the sun touched it, crystal-like glints glittered from its pristine surface. Where the servants had trudged through it or tried to clear it from the front of the house, the snow was muddy and brown. Only the snow that God alone had touched was perfect.

Did Bromby need to be told by his stepsister to try and be happy? Was it really that difficult?

Although the scene outside was picturesque, her heart weighed heavily with dark storm clouds. How could she enjoy this setting when her husband found her company so detestable? She longed to walk around the lake and in the surrounding fields to clear her head, but there was too much ice to safely manage. She might slip into the lake and drown or fall and break her leg. And who would help her? Not her husband. Most likely he would watch her in the icy waters until she flailed no more.

The thought chilled her. Was Bromby's disdain and repugnance for her so great that he wished her dead? She could not be sure. *The man I thought I married does not exist here.* She could not foresee a life stretching out before her in which she was treated so abominably, but she did not know where to turn for help. Agatha was the only help she could imagine.

Isabella sat at the leather writing desk in the library and penned another letter to Agatha.

I am certain we will stop off at Sevenoaks on our journey to London. B is eager to see you as am I. Your friendship is of the utmost importance to me, Agatha, as I know it is to my husband. She paused after writing the last word and stared at it. She felt it was important to write the word many times within the letter. Bromby was her husband now. They were man and wife. Forsaking all others.

That evening, instead of allowing Bromby to sit by himself in the drawing room after dinner, Isabella joined him. As he poured port in his glass and perched upon the sofa to stare into the fire or read his books, she took her book and sat next to him—as close as he would allow.

He did not ask her to leave, and for some time the two of them sat close and quietly read. After a while, she sensed his gaze upon her.

"You really do love me, don't you, Bell?"

Lowering her book onto her lap, Isabella looked into his face. His expression was a little sad and filled with what looked like pity. "Yes, B. I do love you. I have and always will love you."

"You just want to make me happy, don't you?" He reached his hand out to caress the side of her face. The clenching ice that had frozen her heart for days melted.

"Yes. That is all I want."

"Then ... for all of that, you *do* make me happy. I do love you, Bell."

Her spirits soared.

She only wished that the moment—and his feelings—would last.

Twenty-Nine

The snow finally ceased, and the thaw allowed them free movement around the grounds. Over the next couple of days, Isabella enjoyed the happiness she had expected all along. Bromby was kind to her. They walked together around the lake during the day, and he laughed at the muddy state of her petticoats after trudging through the slush of melted snow. She laughed too. It didn't matter. It only mattered that Bromby smiled, laughed, and appeared happy.

"Shall we race back to the house?" he asked as they stood in front of the lake.

Could he run? With his lame leg? What if she beat him? Would he be angry with her? "Through the mud?"

"Why not? Our shoes and clothes are already caked with it. What is a little more? We can strip them off as soon as we are inside." He arched an eyebrow at his suggestive comment.

Isabella straightened. "All right, then."

Without so much as a call to start, Bromby shot off in front of her, half dragging his left foot behind him.

Isabella soon caught up with him and even threatened to surpass him, but a deceptively deep puddle covered in snow caught her foot, and she went down hard, managing to catch herself with both hands.

Bromby looked over his shoulder at her, but he did not stop.

She pulled herself to her feet and looked down at her hands and the tops of her wrists, scuffed and scraped from the fall. Wiping them against her ruined skirts, she looked up to see that he had stopped and was coming back for her.

"Bell? Are you all right?" he called.

"Yes, I am well. Just scraped my hands."

"Let me look."

She flattened her hands out before him. He held them in his own, bent his head to kiss each one, and then dropped them. In an instant, he had spun around and started off again, limping along as fast as he could.

"You rat!" she called after him, laughing and running to catch up.

It wasn't hard to catch up with him, but she didn't dare allow herself to win. She held no desire to compete with him. She only wished to humor and amuse him, if possible.

That afternoon, the couple warmed themselves on the sofa in the drawing room before a roaring fire. Bromby sipped at his brandy, and Isabella drank her tea.

She stared at his foot. She had many questions about it, but broaching the subject would require caution and sensitivity.

"B," she began gently. "Does your foot ever bother you? I mean, does it give you pain?"

"Physical pain?"

"Yes."

"Not as such, no. When I was a child, my mother had me fitted for a brace in the hopes that it might restore some usefulness to the limb. All it did was cause me agony in the tendons and joints of my leg. In all probability, it did more harm than good. It was a great relief when I no longer had to wear it."

Even if the foot caused him no physical pain, it was clear that the mental anguish it caused was enough. She touched his hand, clasping it when he opened his fingers to receive hers.

"I was the subject of much ridicule as a boy. Especially in attendance at Eton."

"Children can be cruel."

"Yes. I have never liked children." He stared off. "Even when I was one, I abhorred them. Later, I witnessed their cruelty to other children and hated them for it."

"They do not know to do better."

"Monsters." His lips curled with disgust. "But then, I suppose I am a sort of monster with a foot that looks like a club."

Isabella squeezed his hand. "Not at all. You are too sensitive, my love. It does not affect my opinion of you in the least."

"Because you are too good," he said. "My foot is my mark of Cain. My symbolic reminder that I am doomed."

She dropped her hand from his, her heart heavy at his return to this tiresome topic. "Please. Let us not talk any more about that."

Reaching his arm around her, he pulled her against him. Thrilled that he had voluntarily pulled her into his arms, Isabella lay her head against his chest. She could hear the steady beat pounding underneath her ear.

"My heart is too hard to make you a pillow. You deserve something softer." He ran his hands over her hair, letting them rest in her loose tresses.

"My only concern is that our hearts do not break." She was resolved not to cry anymore. Now she only wanted to seek out ways to be close to him—to encourage intimacies between them. "I am glad you talked to me about your foot. I want you to confide in me about things. As you do my aunt—Lady Melwood. As you do Agatha."

His chest rose and fell heavily with an audible sigh. "I shall try." Clearing his throat and finishing off his brandy, he leaned forward to pour himself another glass. "I've been thinking. Tomorrow I shall begin working on a new cycle of poems. Since you know Greek and Latin, perhaps while I am working, you would like to translate some of my poems into Greek."

A wide smile spread across her lips and laughter bubbled up within her, spilling from her throat. "Of course! I should so love to translate your poetry. I will do whatever I can to help you."

That same expression swept across his face—as though he pitied her for her some reason, but a smile quickly replaced it and he squeezed her hand. "Dear Bell. You do love me, don't you?"

She exhaled a shaky sigh. "You know I love you, B. You know I do."

———⚬———

Isabella was unable to sleep. A noise from somewhere in the house rose above the roar of the wind. She sat up. Was that someone calling? Was it the voice of a child or a woman? She was suddenly reminded of her conversation with Mrs. Thatcher a couple of weeks before. Some of the servants had left because they feared the house was haunted. It was hard for her to understand, since she didn't believe in ghosts or hauntings or any of that.

She reached over to shake Bromby. Numerous glasses of brandy had left him in such a deep, snoring sleep that for all her shaking he would not rouse.

Slipping her shawl around her shoulders, Isabella made her way out into the hallway, the floorboards creaking beneath her feet.

The house was quiet, and other than the dim glow of moonlight and the illumination from the windows, the house was dark.

She took a candle from a nearby table and lit it to guide her steps. A clatter sounded from somewhere downstairs and she froze, her heart pounding so hard she could hear the thumping in her ears. Again, silence.

With one hand firmly grasping the candle, and one hand covering her mouth, she tiptoed down the staircase into the great hall. She instinctively moved toward the lower floor and the kitchen. Perhaps some remnants of a burning hearth might remain by which she could warm her feet.

In fact, in the kitchen hearth, a fire still flickered and flamed. She was surprised to see a figure seated there, her thin form wrapped in a shawl and seated in a rocking chair. Mrs. Thatcher's face glowed in the light of the fire as she stared into it, solemnly rocking back and forth.

"Mrs. Thatcher!" Isabella exclaimed. "I am very surprised to find you still awake."

The woman looked up and then quickly stood. "Milady."

"No, please. I do not wish to disturb you. I only wanted to come warm myself by the fire." Isabella sat in a chair beside Mrs. Thatcher and pulled her own shawl more tightly around her. "I could not sleep, and then I thought I heard noises, so—"

"Noises, milady?"

"Yes. As you mentioned a couple of weeks ago, this house seems to echo a great deal. I suppose some of the other servants must still be up and about."

"None that I know of. 'Tis past midnight. They've all gone to bed."

Isabella grimaced.

The two women sat quietly for a few moments and stared into the hearth.

"How long have you been in service, Mrs. Thatcher?"

"Twelve years. I was twenty-six when I accepted my first job as a lady's maid."

"Twenty-six? What did you do before then?"

"Mr. Elliot Thatcher is my husband. I used to live with him and my children in London."

"What happened? If you do not mind me asking."

"I do not mind. He … my husband made some bad choices. I had to find work to help pay our expenses. Now he lives in London. He works in a factory, and my children are cared for by distant relatives who may supply them with a better future."

"I'm so sorry. You must miss your children."

"Yes, ma'am. I do. But they are better off where they are. I am certain you do not want to hear the particulars."

"Only if you want to tell them." Isabella's curiosity was piqued. But she also did not want to winkle out details from a pained woman.

Mrs. Thatcher sat back in her rocker, her mouth compressed in a long, thin line. Her eyes moved to a faraway place. "My husband tries to be a good man, but he's not a smart one, Lady Bromby. We used to live quite well, until Mr. Thatcher began to play the tables. In a week's time, he gambled away everything we had. But I was not aware of this ... not until the bailiffs came to take all of our belongings."

Isabella shook her head. Her own father was known to play the tables now and again. He had lost some money and property in the same way. Never anything so extreme. "I am so sorry."

Mrs. Thatcher shook her head. "I blame myself. I did have some insight into his character before I agreed to be his wife ... but I was blinded by his charm."

Isabella tensed. This was a familiar story. "And your family? What did they say about the match?"

Tears gathered at the corners of the woman's eyes she swiped at them with the back of her hand. "My family disowned me when I married him."

Isabella gasped. "How tragic." Isabella experienced a sense of compassion she had not felt for anyone else in quite some time. "You poor, poor woman."

"It is perhaps why young ladies should choose wisely when they allow for attachments. I alone am to blame for my misfortune."

"You are not to blame!" Isabella protested. "He deceived you."

Mrs. Thatcher looked down at her hands. "I did not listen to those who warned me against his charms."

Isabella took a deep breath. She had little in common with the housekeeper, yet she felt as if she could somehow understand a small portion of her pain. "But to have no family ... and you could not return to your cousin's good graces?"

"There were none to be had by that time. I wrote to him and begged for mercy. He would not allow me to live with him again, but he and his wife agreed to take the children—give them a good education and so on. What were my choices? They were dismal at best."

Isabella's mind flashed to the women in the streets who sold their bodies out of desperation. It was too tragic to contemplate.

"And your children?"

Her eyes clouded, but her lips smiled. "My daughter is a proper young lady. I hear from her now and then. She has many suitors these days, I'm told. My son is married now—to a young lady with a great fortune." Her eyes lowered. "I don't hear from him anymore. Too much of an embarrassment to his wife's family."

"I am so terribly sorry for your pain, and I cannot imagine what you have been through."

"We all have our burdens to bear, milady."

"I suppose so." Like Mrs. Thatcher, she had made her choice. "Well. You are very welcome here, Mrs. Thatcher. You have performed amazing feats by cleaning up the mess of this house in such a short period of time."

"Thank you, milady. I hope I will continue to do everything to your satisfaction."

"I hope you will consider joining us in London once Broadwell Abbey is sold. Lord Bromby and I will make for Piccadilly shortly."

Mrs. Thatcher smiled a little and bowed her head. "May I fetch you some hot milk? To help you sleep?"

Isabella considered it, her thoughts returning to the sounds she had heard earlier. "No, thank you. I think I shall forego anything else tonight. I do wish I could have found the source of the noises, though."

Mrs. Thatcher breathed in deeply. "I do not mean to frighten you, Lady Bromby, but some of the servants, those who have lived in these parts all of their life, swear that something evil is here. Joseph, the gardener, is the oldest member of the staff. He was hired by the late Mrs. Bromby. He remembers the noises from when she was alive—even when Lord Bromby was a boy."

Isabella shivered, and her husband's words of "cursed" and "damned" and "doomed" and "evil" flapped through her mind like bats in an attic. She was suddenly eager to leave Broadwell Abbey, to pull her vulnerable husband from its clutches, and to have it sold off as quickly as possible.

"I see." She looked around her into the shadows that lurked in the corners of the room. Maybe if they left Broadwell Abbey, Bromby's moods would brighten and stabilize.

Standing with her arms wrapped around her, Isabella trembled. "Well. I should leave you."

Mrs. Thatcher stood. "I have enjoyed our talk, Lady Bromby. Thank you for your kindness."

Isabella made her way up the stairs. The house was quiet, so still that the darkness was tangible. Each gust of wind drafting through the cracks in the walls was like a hand touching her. When she reached the landing, she ran the rest of the way to the bedroom. Bromby's sleeping form was silhouetted against the moonlight streaming through the window. As he lay on his side, his face turned from the moon's beam, she could not make out his features.

"Bromby." She shook him again. Still there was no movement. "Bromby!" she said, shaking him harder.

"What is it?" he growled.

Leaning across him, she held her candle in front of his face. His eyes sprang open.

She sat back, sighing a little with relief. "I am sorry to wake you. I just wanted to ensure you were still ... here." She felt silly saying the words, but she didn't want to say what she was really doing—checking to make sure his face was not altered into some sort of demon.

It would all be better once they left Broadwell Abbey.

Thirty

A week later, the couple dined with Agatha Morley at Sevenoaks. Bromby regaled her with tales of their time away, even going so far as to say that he had grown accustomed to his new wife's constant presence and had a newfound appreciation for her.

"I was perhaps inebriated during much of our 'moon," he said. "But what man wouldn't be after altering his life so?"

Agatha smiled broadly, her eyes twinkling with affectionate teasing. "Dearest Isabella, you must take care to hide all of the brandy from him."

"Nonsense," said Bromby. "I shall continue to take my brandy whenever I like."

"Very fortunate that he has found such an understanding wife as you, Isabella." Agatha cast a glance in the younger woman's direction.

Isabella had seemed a little quiet—a little out of sorts and uncomfortable since their arrival—but Bromby couldn't be bothered to determine the particulars. Women were moody beasts anyway, and as long as he was meeting all of her necessaries and she was neither dying of hunger nor thirst, then he was doing his level best as a husband.

"It sounds like the honeymoon was a great success." Agatha's eyes darted back and forth between Bromby and Isabella.

"Our 'moon was cloyingly sweet," said Bromby. "Even sweeter than honey. Like a treacle."

Apparently ignoring his sarcastic barb, Agatha turned back to Isabella. "And in what state did you find Broadwell Abbey?"

"It is an impressive estate," Isabella said. "It still has some need of repairs, however."

"After all the money I spent on the place getting it ready for our arrival." Actually, the mystery of who had paid for it remained. When he returned to London, he would have to make more inquiries about that. "Anyway, she detested the place." The words tumbled from his mouth with such ease it surprised even him.

"Bromby!" Isabella exclaimed. "I did not detest the place. I thought it very beautiful, I only said—"

"She especially hated the orchards." Now that his tongue was loosened, he would pour out the venom building inside of him. Reminding his wife of the special place that had previously belonged only to his life with Agatha gave him a perverse pleasure.

"That is the most despicable lie, B," Isabella protested, her eyes wide. She even laughed a little following his claim. "I never even saw the orchards. It was too cold and then there was too much snow. We never walked there at all."

"I did." He leveled his gaze upon Agatha.

The smile slipped from her face.

Satisfied at the effect, he continued. "I walked in the orchards almost every day. Remember how we used to walk there as children, Ag?"

Her voice was thin and solemn as she replied. "Yes, Gregory. I remember."

"Our tree is still there. The one with our names carved upon it."

"Is it?"

"Yes."

Out of the corner of his eye, he caught a glimpse of Isabella's face. She looked back and forth between the two of them, her hands knitting an imaginary cloth.

"B acquainted me with many of the word games the two of you used to play." Isabella's voice cracked a little. "Since the weather was bad, we couldn't go out as much as we would have liked to."

Another urge rose within him to inflict a lash of his tongue. "That's right. We stayed in and acquainted ourselves with all sorts of games. Isabella seems to like the ones we played inside our private chamber the most."

A streak of pleasure coursed through him as the women's faces turned crimson. Agatha's shoulders rose with a slow intake of air. Her chiding gaze shifted from his. "Did you play *bouts-rimes*?"

"Yes," Isabella answered quickly. "Yes. I believe we wrote down and saved some of the more original verses we managed to create. Didn't we, B?"

"I recall a few of them which I committed to memory." Bromby was enjoying this. He liked seeing the women squirm with discomfort. It gave him a sense of power over them both. He began to quote some of the more vulgar and bawdy lines he and Isabella had used during their game. At the time, he had been excited by his wife's willingness to add a few colorful lines.

Now he garnered a great deal of pleasure watching her wilt with mortification. But it was Agatha's face that was most bewildering. She looked almost angry. Or was that jealousy?

"It seems, Gregory, that your wife may be able to rival you in poetic verse. At least a few of the lines you attribute to her sound every bit as good as yours. I think you have been extremely fortunate in matrimony." Her eyes were scolding.

He jutted out his chin, daring her to say more.

"I'm very tired," Isabella said suddenly.

Agatha reached over and patted her hand. "Oh, you poor dear. You must be. 'Tis late and growing colder. I want to offer you and Gregory my room for the duration of your stay. The bed in there is larger."

"Oh, no. We could not oust you from your own bed," Isabella said.

"Nonsense." Agatha waved her hand. "I can sleep anywhere—"

"She can," Bromby could not help adding.

Agatha rushed on. "And it is my wish that you both have a comfortable room during your stay. I shall be very happy in one of the guest rooms."

Isabella stood. "That is very kind of you, Agatha."

Agatha smiled warmly, pushing herself into a standing position.

Bromby had no intention of going to bed. "I am not tired." He planned to sit up with Agatha and talk. There was much to say and reprise.

"You are not coming?" Isabella's voice shook a little.

"No. I shall come to bed later."

Without another word, Isabella followed Agatha out of the room. Bromby drained his glass and poured himself more wine. The women's voices echoed in the hall, and the cry of a small child came from somewhere in the house. He was thankful for governesses and nannies to keep them from being underfoot, although the memory of his own childhood nurse gave him nothing but chills of anger and resentment.

Agatha returned and seated herself across from him. Her face was gentle ... she looked like an angel. Her hair was down and flowing about her shoulders. Her pale blue eyes pierced his with chastisement. "Why do you say such things, Gregory?"

He was amused. "I don't know what you mean."

She leaned forward, searching his eyes. "Oh, I think you do. That is a dear, sweet girl you have married. She is intelligent and capable ... and I might add, she loves you. Adores you. You could not have married better, I think."

He hated hearing these words from her, although he did not wish to fight with her. He sat back in his chair, sighing. "Come on, Ag. Let us return to our old selves. Say something to make me laugh. Do one of your voices. Mimic Demon Jack ... or how about Lady Catherine?"

Agatha was slow to respond. Several more moments elapsed of her prim-mouthed expression. Attempting to spur her on, he tried to mimic Lady Catherine's lisp. He couldn't do it like Agatha, but as he endeavored an authentic sound, her face softened and a smile spread over her lips. Her laugh rang out, and she rocked back and forth.

"You are ridiculous!" she cackled.

"Do it, then!" he called out to her, breaking into laughter himself.

And as Agatha mimicked Lady Catherine Lyon's voice and manner of speaking with spot-on accuracy, the pair burst into peals of uncontrollable laughter—the sound carrying up the corridor and echoing through the house. Isabella probably heard their laughter upstairs.

Two more hours passed as they talked and relived childhood memories from Broadwell Abbey.

"It looks better than it did," Bromby assured her.

"I am glad to hear it. Such a tragedy to let the old place go to rack and ruin. Someone will purchase it, surely."

"And soon, I hope." A heaviness moved into his heart. He had said nothing to Isabella about it, but he harbored great concerns about their financial situation. Relief flooded through him as he remembered that the refurbishments were paid. "Something strange occurred. Some person—I know not who—brought my account to right for Broadwell Abbey. I received a note from the creditor that I owed nothing."

Agatha's brow furrowed. "That is strange. And you have no idea who it could be?"

"None whatsoever."

"Isabella's father?"

"Perhaps. But if so, he said nothing about it." Bromby ran both hands through his hair, and left them there, grasping at the strands until his scalp hurt. "Bell and I shall be practically destitute until the place sells. Or perhaps her uncle will die soon and leave us the seven or eight thousand a year he's promised Bell."

"Are you really that badly off, Gregory?"

He didn't wish to trouble her with his worries about money. She suffered her own financial woes. "It will all come good. Proper living comes with a price."

Agatha looked down at her hands. "I wish I could help. But as you know the Colonel overspent as well, I'm afraid, and left me with a great muddle."

The room grew quiet. Only the clock clicked away. Yes. He might have been married to Agatha right now were things different in that respect …

"You should join your wife," Agatha said at last.

Bromby's heart dropped. He didn't want to go to bed. He wanted to remain there with her, talking until the sun came up. "My wife," he scoffed.

Agatha reached across the table to grasp his hand. "Gregory, you must do what you can to make a good marriage."

He stared at her, and a surge of anger arose within him. "You were the one who pushed me to marry. You and Lady Melwood."

"It was done for the best."

"It was done for the worst!" he shouted, the rage exploding within him. He shoved back from the table, stood, and began to pace. Confound them all! Why couldn't he have been left alone? Now he was trapped— like a wolf in a cage, a bear forced to dance and perform for the masses— just to seem respectable.

"Shh. If you would only try," she whispered. "You do her wrong to abuse her so."

He felt he might go mad. Grasping his hair, he sucked in air as if scorched by a hot iron. "I blame you for this, Agatha."

"Fine then. Blame me. But your wife is innocent in all of this."

His moment of rage passed, and he allowed his arms to drop to his side. He supposed no one was truly to blame but himself. "Oh, what a wonderful sight we shall make for the ton to shout and gossip about."

"The *ton* will always have something to talk about, Gregory."

He stared at her—her hair glowing gold in the light of the hearth, and her mouth plumped with warmth. He longed to kiss her. In fact, he *would* kiss her. There was nothing to stop him from doing so. Who would call him out? God? Hardly. Regardless of his wife's views on the Almighty's unfailing love, he had certainly never felt it. As far as he was concerned there was only this one life, and he might as well make the best of it.

As he moved toward Agatha, her facial expression changed. Was that fear he saw in her eyes? The chair legs squawked against the floorboards as she pushed away from the table. Once standing, she backed away from him, holding her hands in front of her. "No, Gregory. No."

Once she was in his arms again and remembered their kisses, she would succumb. He reached out, catching the edge of her shawl. The fabric came loose from around her shoulders, and he held only the square panel of wool in his hand.

"No!"

Bewildered by the sharp tone of her voice, he stopped. He had expected her to go along with his desires. Did she not still love him?

She looked at him, shaking her head, her eyes wide. "You cannot think … your wife is upstairs! I will not be a party to this anymore, Gregory. We are to be like brother and sister. Nothing more."

His head was spinning. Was she earnest in her refusal of him? He made another move toward her, and she immediately stepped back. "How can you expect me to—"

"I expect you to conduct yourself as a proper husband. And a proper gentleman. In my house if nowhere else."

Her usually pale eyes were dark with a serious gleam. She stood a good distance away from him now, her right hand still outstretched in a defensive stance.

Frustrated and defeated, he stepped toward her, extending his arm that held the shawl. He considered grabbing her wrist and pulling her to him when she reached out for the cover, but he stopped himself.

As if anticipating that he might try this, Agatha hung back. She reached her arm out for the shawl.

With fury bubbling in his chest, he flung it into her face. Turning on his heel, he exited the room as acid rose into this throat. Bitterness riddled his heart.

The next morning, he awoke early. Reaching for Isabella, he found that the space beside him was empty. He cursed under his breath. He had hoped to rise from the bed earlier than his wife.

He mulled over Agatha's rejection of him. Perhaps he had been wrong to pursue her. But he was a man, after all. And surely, Agatha still loved him.

As he limped down the stairs, a herd of children stormed behind him. "Uncle Gregory! Uncle Gregory!" The youngest girl, Rossalyn, a tow-headed four-year-old, clung to his right leg, nearly toppling him.

"Uncle Gregory?" Thomas, the oldest boy looked most like Agatha. "Will you tell us some stories today?"

"Yes, please do!" cried Georgiana, the middle child, quite recovered from her battle with scarlet fever. "I want to hear a ghost story like the one you told last time."

As much as Bromby detested children, he held a certain warmth toward Agatha's. Each of them bore some feature of hers, and he felt a tug at his heart when he stared into their pale eyes.

"I suppose I shall," he smiled. "But this evening. Once it grows dark. That is the best time for ghost stories."

"Aunt Isabella says she doesn't like ghost stories," said Thomas.

"She wouldn't," said Bromby glumly. "Your Aunt Isabella doesn't like anything fun."

They stared up at him, squinting and blinking. Peals of laughter emanated from the morning room. Agatha and Isabella.

"It sounds like she is having fun," said Rossalyn.

"So it does," Bromby muttered, limping the rest of the way down the stairs.

In the morning room, his wife and Isabella sat very close together on a sofa, sipping at cups of tea and laughing loudly. A strange sensation stabbed at his heart. He had not expected this sight.

"Good morning, Gregory!" Agatha called out. "We were just talking about you."

"Good morning, B." Isabella held her hand over her mouth, still snickering.

"Good morning, I suppose." He hobbled across the room to pour himself a cup of tea from the service on the table near the window. He peered out onto the frozen paddock. Grooms walked horses, moving them along the paths where snow still lined the embankments.

"You have some new horses, it would seem."

"They are not new, but they are for sale. The Colonel paid a pretty penny for them, but I can't afford to keep them. Racehorses, of course. Isabella, you ride, don't you?"

"Yes."

"Oh, splendid! Gregory, you must take her out riding today. There is a lovely mare—we call her Pip—that would make a perfect mount for you."

"I should so enjoy that." Isabella's face glowed.

How he resented her happy disposition.

"Thomas!" Agatha called out to her eldest son. "Run tell the groom that Lord and Lady Bromby will ride this morning. Ask him to prepare Pip and Chester. Chester will make a nice mount for you, Gregory. He is a calm, gentle thing."

Bromby rankled at her suggestion that he needed a calm, gentle horse. "Why should I have the insipid horse?"

"Insipid?" Agatha laughed, looking askance at Isabella. "I've never heard a horse termed insipid before." The two women laughed again at his choice of words. "I merely thought you might like a calm horse."

He tensed, insulted at her suggestion that he was not an adequately fit rider. "I am perfectly capable."

Her face flattened into a placid expression. "Fine, then." She turned back to her son. "Thomas, tell him to saddle Napoleon instead."

Now that sounded like the name of a horse he should like to ride. A strong, lead horse to be sure.

"You must join us, Agatha," Bromby said.

She shook her head, looking over at Isabella. "I shouldn't wish to intrude."

"Not at all!" Isabella said. "We insist that you join us."

She smiled. "Very well, then."

As the threesome mounted their horses and prepared to set off for their ride, Bromby hung back, allowing the two women to ride out ahead of him. Thick as thieves, they were. Tittering and laughing together, as if one or both of them had spoken the funniest words ever. They had practically ignored his presence all morning.

"I've always longed for a sister." Agatha's words carried back to him on the wind as he fell behind.

"I always wanted one too," said Isabella. "Alas, I am my parents' only child. No brothers or sisters."

"It seems all three of us are only children by birth." Agatha cast a glance back at him. "As you know, Gregory is the closest thing I have to a blood brother. And not even a blood brother at that."

"Well, then. We shall all have to be brothers and sisters to each other now," said Isabella. The two women reached out and clasped hands.

Bromby's stomach roiled, and he made a sound of disgust.

"What was that, Gregory?" Agatha called back to him.

"Nothing except that the two of you are giving me a stomachache."

"Did you hear that, sis?" Agatha reached out and knocked Isabella's elbow. "Our sweetness to one another is too much for Gregory."

Isabella laughed. "It does not surprise me. Sweets always give B a stomachache. He will touch none of them."

"What? No cakes?" Agatha asked.

"No, none."

"No, tartlets or puddings?"

"Won't even look at them."

The two women burst into laughter, and Bromby's blood boiled. Images of his wife taking a fall assailed his mind.

That was it! She might fall if they were to ride a little faster. She might be thrown from her horse, only to dash her head against a rock. It happened all the time, did it not?

"Shall we move at this snail's pace all day?" he called out. "Come on. Molasses pours faster!"

"Very well, then." Agatha nodded at Isabella. "Shall we?"

Surprising even him, Isabella called out with a sound that raised her horse's ears, and with a kick to the side-saddle, the two women were off. Bromby readied himself to press the speed of his own horse, but before he'd even had a chance to kick at Napoleon's sides, the horse bolted to keep up with the other two.

His balance was immediately compromised, and as the horse gained speed, Bromby's left foot, never completely fitted into the stirrup to begin with, slid out altogether. He slumped onto the horse's neck, grasping at clumps of black mane. He'd never ridden a horse going so fast, and he was immediately reminded that the Colonel's horses were of the racing sort—born and bred for speed.

The more he slumped over Napoleon's neck, the faster the horse advanced. "Stop! Stop you blasted beast!"

Napoleon blew past Agatha and Isabella's horses as they called after him. "Where are you going?"

Unable to maintain his balance, he began to slip off the right side of the saddle, and within moments he landed with a thud against cold, hard ground. His head was the last thing to slam against the earth. Pain shot through his temples.

Completely dazed, he sat up slowly. Had he broken anything?

Agatha and Isabella rode up before him. Isabella dropped from her horse and rushed to his side.

"B! B? Are you all right?" He winced as her hand pressed against his head.

"I'm fine!" he exclaimed. "Just ... do not touch me."

She straightened up and held her hand out to him. Begrudgingly, and with a loud groan, he stood and assessed the state of his limbs. All seemed to be in working order. Only his pride...

"He is a spirited one, is he not?" Agatha looked down at him from her mount.

Bromby breathed in slowly and shot her a glare. It was abundantly clear that she was no longer on his side.

—————⊷∞⊶—————·

They remained at Agatha's for the rest of the week. What had originally promised to be a week of bliss in Bromby's expectations, had turned into a nightmare. Any moment he might have had alone with Agatha was usurped by Isabella's presence. He was relegated to time spent with three rambunctious children who wouldn't leave him alone for a second.

"One more story, please Uncle Gregory!" Thomas demanded.

"Uncle Gregory, will you lead me around on my pony?" Rossalyn pleaded.

"I wrote ten poems last week, Uncle Gregory. Will you listen to them and tell me what you think?" Georgianna's voice began to grate on his nerves after hearing one pathetic and ill-phrased poem cycle after another.

When they went to bed in the evenings, he was never so happy and relieved. There was something about children that reminded him of his own childhood. And Nurse Green.

"Say it right! If ye do not say it right, I'll give ye a thumping you'll never forget!" He shuddered at the memory—the image of her reading her Bible in the daytime, quoting scripture and telling him to be a good boy or God wouldn't hear his prayers.

If there was any reason to be hostile toward God and religion, it was that woman. Her duality of angel and devil had seared his mind against the holy words she read, words that stood in complete opposition to her behavior toward a ten-year-old boy in her charge.

Shaking off the dreadful memories, he turned to watch his wife and Agatha, chatting and laughing. Agatha told Isabella tales about him as a child, and Isabella giggled. He pretended neither to hear them or care as he sat in a corner, scribbling letters to Lady Melwood and John Hobby.

There the two of them sit, snickering away at my expense. My new bride should be more concerned about where we will live once we arrive in London, since I have no money and no prospects of a house for us, he wrote to Lady Melwood, hoping that she might take pity on them and lend them assistance in this matter.

The woman knew everyone in London Society—she, of all people, should take an interest in her niece's living situation and have some means to secure it. For all he knew, Lady Melwood may have been the generous patron to settle his accounts with Crane.

Their last evening at Sevenoaks was spent in the same manner—the women teasing him and playing cards while he sat alone, alternating between scribbling and reading in the corner by the waning light.

"Come play with us, Gregory," said Agatha cheerfully. "We welcome your company at our little game of cribbage."

Looking up from his book, Bromby eyed the two women as they ate grapes from a bowl between them. "I am surprised that you welcome my company since you have not done so all week."

"Oh, come now, B," said Isabella. "We have repeatedly asked you to join us. It's our last night here. You must not deny us a game or two."

Bromby swilled down the rest of his port and stood, stalking close to where the women played. He circled the table and stared down at them. What biting comments could he make to show them how slighted, how ostracized they had made him feel?

"I have an idea." He stood over Agatha and met her eyes. "Let's play *Le Baisir a la Capucine*. We may all play at that."

The smiles dropped from both the ladies' faces. Agatha's gaze darted to Isabella.

Now he was beginning to enjoy himself again. "Come on. You know how to play it, don't you, Ag? Remember? We kneel on the ground back to back, and attempt to kiss one another. It's great fun."

Isabella stared down at her cards. "I daresay that's a most undignified game."

"'Tis the best game I know! And there should be no indignity about it. We've all kissed one another here—there should be no surprises."

"Sit down, Gregory. You've had too much wine." Agatha turned back to her cards, her face pale.

"I seem to remember a time when you liked to play it well enough, Ag. You were quite good at it, in fact."

She exhaled, and her eyes darted from side to side. "Please, stop," she said in a firm tone. "You are making all of us very uneasy."

"Oh, am I? Uneasy? Not half as uneasy as you've made me the last few days—hovering in corners, tittering and giggling like you were little girls telling secrets about me."

Agatha looked up from her cards. "You're being silly, Gregory. No one is telling secrets about you."

He circled the table again, his arms crossed over his chest. "Surprising. As you know Agatha, there are plenty of secrets to be had."

Isabella stood suddenly, dropping her cards to the table. "I am going to bed."

Relief filled him. It was toward Agatha that he wanted to vent his anger. Both of them froze until a door upstairs creaked and closed.

Then Agatha stood, her eyes blazing. "What are you playing at, Gregory?"

He laughed and began a slow pacing motion across the room and back again. "Oh, nothing. Just having a little fun."

"That's not fun for your wife, nor is it fun for me."

"Do you think any of this has been fun for me?"

"You are wrong to play Isabella and I against one another."

"Is that what I am doing?"

"Yes. Even a child can see what you are doing because your behavior is childish."

He stopped his pacing and faced her. In one swift movement, he reached out his hand and grabbed her wrist, yanking her towards him and mashing his mouth roughly against hers.

She pushed against him. Even though he attempted to hold her, she managed to wrest herself away from him and sent a stinging slap across his cheek. Her eyes flaring, she pointed a shaking finger at him. "You are never to touch me in that way again. Do you understand?"

His mind reeled. Why was she acting in this way? He'd never seen her so defiant and adamant before. Certainly, she'd never slapped him. In fact, he couldn't remember a time when Agatha had ever spoken harshly to him. The stance and defensive tone struck at his heart as if she had slashed him with a sword.

"Ag—"

"No," she spoke in a sharp whisper. "I am in earnest. Never. Or we can be brother and sister no more."

His shoulders drooped, and all the air was expelled from his lungs. He could not lose her. "Why did we ever call each other brother and sister? We are not, and we never were."

She shook her head, and he glimpsed the tears that seeped from the corners of her eyes. "It is too late for us to be anything else."

"Agatha…" His voice strained over the lump in his throat.

"You should not have come here." She turned and rushed up the stairs.

He approached the master bedroom—Agatha's room—where Isabella now slept. Was that the sound of a female sobbing? But he could not be sure whether the cries were those of Isabella's or Agatha's.

Part VI

Thirty-One

February 1815
Holly Bridge, Kent

"Help! Please, please help!"

The voice was shrill, panicked, obviously a woman's voice. Whenever riding, David avoided the woods, but the cries sounded as though she were in trouble.

Squeezing Thaddeus' sides, David pressed on through the opening of the trees, ducking his head to avoid low-hanging branches. "Hello, there!" He scanned the thick brambles and vines that tangled across the forest floor.

"Yes, hello! Over here. Please help."

He urged Thaddeus forward, but the horse was reluctant, backing away rather than moving toward the sound. "Whoa, boy. It's all right. Come on now." Finally, with a flick of the tail and a little bucking motion, the horse charged forth, leaping to avoid the thorny vines against its fetlocks.

A swath of pink became visible amongst the brambles. Another few steps brought him the full vision of a young woman. Her full-length gray pelisse, along with the skirts of her pink dress and her blond hair, were hopelessly entangled in the thorny vines. As David slid from Thaddeus' back, he glimpsed the girl's hands—scratched and bloodied where she'd removed her gloves and tried to extricate herself.

David tossed his reins over an obliging branch and stooped down to get a better look at the girl. Her pale face was scratched from the vines as well.

"Good heavens! What has happened here?" How would he ever disentangle her? It seemed she was gripped by forty vines all at once.

"I was riding," she replied. In the cold, her breath materialized like smoke. "Three boys came out of the woods and seized my horse and pulled us into the trees. I fell off and landed in these bushes. They took my horse."

"Are you hurt?" David tried to tear the fabric of her dress away from the spiky tendrils, thankful for heavy, leather gloves that protected against their sharp snares.

"I do not think so."

"Were they gypsies, the boys you speak of?"

"I do not know, sir. They appeared to be … wild children." Her refined manner of speaking suggested the woman was genteel, certainly not low-born.

David nodded. "There are some gangs of children who roam the countryside and steal. That is why a young lady should not be riding alone."

"Anyway, they have my horse. I want him back."

"All right. Well, allow me to first disentangle you from all of this." He finally freed her skirts, although the material was ripped beyond repair.

With a cry of frustration, the young woman jerked her head forward, attempting to release her hair from the branches.

"Here, allow me." David reached above her head to dislodge the captive tendrils.

A few strands pulled loose from her scalp. "Ow!"

"Oh, I do apologize. It's just that these thorns are so tenacious…" He glanced down into the girl's pained blue eyes. "My name is David Beringer, by the way. Of Holly Bridge."

She gasped with a sharp pain. "Rosaline Reese."

David successfully looped a strand of Rosaline's hair around the branch until her head was released. With a sigh, she sat upright. David stood and offered his hand to her. Grasping it, she stood.

"Are you quite all right?" he asked. Other than scratches and torn clothing, the girl seemed fit.

He held her arm as she moved forward.

"Ow," she cried out as she put pressure on her right leg. "I think my ankle is hurt."

"Can you walk upon it?"

Still clutching his arm, she took a few steps forward. "Yes. Yes. I can walk. Perhaps I only twisted it."

David led Miss Reese out of the forest and into the clearing. "Wait here." Then he went back for Thaddeus.

Within minutes, he returned to Miss Reese, who appeared to be assessing the state of her ruined skirts. She was very pretty, and standing under the midday light, her blonde, curly hair appeared silky and well cared for. "My mother and father will be furious with me."

"Why were you riding here alone?" he asked. "Do you not know these woods are dangerous."

"I wasn't riding in the woods, Mr. Beringer. The horse thieves pulled me in there. I was … well, I was being very naughty, I suppose. I had a disagreement with my parents. I was angry and … I often ride off when I'm angry."

"I see. Well, now that you are horseless, I shall escort you home."

"It is this way." She pointed north of their location.

He helped Miss Reese mount Thaddeus and, grasping the reins, he led the horse in the direction she'd indicated.

"Thank you for your assistance, sir."

"I only did what any decent man would do."

He looked up at her. Her features were small and delicate. She reminded him a little of…

David hearkened back to another time at Holly Bridge when he and Isabella had helped Miss Tickney after a spill. He could not help but wish things had gone differently that week, but that was some years ago, and he had worked hard to dispel Isabella from his mind. Even so, from time to time, thoughts of her resurfaced—like now when he had the privilege of rescuing a young lady.

"You are very kind, Mr. Beringer. But will Mrs. Beringer wonder at your absence?" Rosaline's eyes were wide, innocent.

"There is no Mrs. Beringer."

She bowed her head, and a smile graced her lips. "I believe my parents shall be pleased to make your acquaintance."

<hr/>

2 February 1815
London

Dear Bromby,

I believe I may have found the perfect house for you and Isabella. The property belongs to the Duchess of Devonshire. It is located in Piccadilly, very close to many of your friends and acquaintances. I have taken the liberty of speaking with Sir Ralph, and he is sending some of Isabella's clothes along to the place in question. I am a little nervous as to what you may think, however, as the rent amounts to £700 per annum. My hope is that this will impress your creditors, and possibly, they may allow you more time in the repayment of your existing debts.

I do hope you and Isabella enjoyed your honeymoon and visit with Mrs. Morley and that you will now settle into your new life and make the most of it with joie de vivre. I look forward to seeing you both as soon as you return to London.

Yours,

Lady M

---

25 February 1815
Sevenoaks

Dearest Isabella,

I miss you already and cannot wait to hear about your new home in London. Please give my dear brother all the attention and fussing over that he craves. Remember what I told you about how to govern him. He is best handled with tenderness and teasing. Do not let him take himself seriously, nor should you. He is full of bluff and bluster and nothing more.

Just after you and Gregory departed, I received an interesting piece of news. A letter arrived with word of an appointment to serve as lady-in-waiting to Queen Charlotte. Can you imagine? Silly old me a lady of the bedchamber? Oh, la! Although this is quite unexpected, I am considering it. This would allow me rooms in Flag Court and St. James's Palace, which must first be furnished. I will need to trespass on family or friends for a few days while I procure furnishings.

I hope you and Gregory enjoy safe journeys, and I will look forward to our next meeting.

All my sisterly affection,

Agatha

Isabella sat in the library alongside Bromby as he read a newspaper. She looked over at him. Was Bromby merely full of "bluff and bluster"? He had seemed perfectly miserable since they'd arrived in London. The brief joy they'd shared near the end of their honeymoon at Broadwell Abbey had all but ended once they'd arrived at Sevenoaks.

It was now perfectly clear. He'd wanted to marry Agatha, but she was unsuitable for him … and Isabella would be punished for not being her. She was in a city full of people, and she felt lonelier than ever.

Remembering Mrs. Thatcher from their time spent at Broadwell, Isabella asked Bromby if they might not send for her. "I liked her very much. I should like to have her here in Piccadilly as our housekeeper. And she'll be closer to her husband. They might meet more than twice a year that way."

Bromby didn't appear at all interested as she laid out her plan for Mrs. Thatcher. He didn't even look up from his paper as she spoke. "Perhaps Mrs. Thatcher does not wish to see her husband more than twice a year," he mumbled.

Isabella shook her head. "I do not believe that. No matter what he may have done, he is still her husband. I still believe she loves him."

Bromby rattled the paper. "Oh, look here. Napoleon has left Elba. He has returned to France in an attempt to conquer it once again. Oh, well done."

Isabella sighed and stood before him, unable to see his eyes. "Bromby, what do you think? May I write and ask Mrs. Thatcher to come?"

He peered over the top of his paper at her. "Yes, do whatever you like, Bell. One frosty housekeeper is as good as another, I suppose."

Isabella smiled, and she was filled with relief. She would write to her at once. Mrs. Thatcher would provide more company. She might prove to be a friend.

Bromby folded the newspaper in his lap. "Bell, you said you received a letter from Agatha … did she write one to me as well?"

"I read you the contents of her letter."

"Yes, but was there one just for me?" His eyes held the eager gleam of a child's.

"No. The letter was for me."

With more rattling, Bromby folded the paper in two and stood. "Well, she must stay with us," he said resolutely. "If she is to seek housing in London so as to be at Queen Charlotte's disposal, she must stay with us in the interim. I shall write to her at once and tell her that we will brook with no refusal."

Isabella cleared her throat. "Of course, B. I shall write to her as well, so that she may receive two invitations and be assured of my complicity in the invitation."

"Do as you like." He was already seated at his desk and brandishing a pen over paper.

In truth, a part of her welcomed Agatha's company. Since settling in to their new home in Piccadilly, Bromby stayed up most nights drinking until he passed out in a fitful and thrashing slumber that kept her awake. He did not imbibe as much in Agatha's presence.

But another part of her cried out that to invite Agatha to stay with them was to invite all kinds of trouble.

Thirty-Two

April 1815

At the end of April, Lady Melwood threw a dinner party, and Lord and Lady Bromby were the guests of honor.

Upon their arrival at Melwood House that evening, Isabella was overjoyed to see Rebecca Beringer, now Lady Meade, in attendance. The two women flew to one another, embracing. Isabella wanted to cry as she hugged her friend. It had only been a few months, but it felt much longer since they'd really spoken.

Rebecca's face shone with the happiness of a new marriage—her cheeks tinged with pink and her periwinkle eyes sparkling like sapphires. The red in her hair had darkened over the winter months and was fixed in the current style with short curls around her face and fine lace intertwined with the braided portions atop the crown of her head. "I can't believe this is the first I've seen of you since you've been in town," Rebecca said, clasping her friend's hands.

Isabella exhaled through pursed lips. "We've been in constant motion. Over the past fortnight, we've attended ever so many parties and balls. Dinners at the homes of members or parliament, receptions …"

Rebecca smiled. "Society is anxious to see what you've done to tame the wild poet and whether some of his charisma has been worn down into a comfortable amiability as the result of a felicitous marriage."

If that was what Society expected, they would be sorely disappointed. Isabella was anxious to change the subject. "Where did you spend your honeymoon?"

"In Kent. Near Dover. Sir Malcolm's family owns a house there. We were snowed in for days. Oh, it was wonderful, Izzy."

Envy stabbed at Isabella's heart. Sir Malcolm seemed a good sort of man, with strong principles, and a kind, gentle disposition. Isabella had no doubt her friend would enjoy a happy marriage. Self-pity besieged her heart.

"I am so happy for you, Rebecca." Isabella squeezed Rebecca's hands. "Truly, I am."

"And I you." Rebecca radiated one of her brightest smiles. "Now we shall have to call on one another for tea."

"Oh, please do. I am quite alone in Piccadilly and longing for company."

"Then I shall come to call next week," Rebecca promised.

Isabella hesitated to ask the question that burned in her mind, but she finally managed to force the words from her mouth. "How is your brother?"

Rebecca's hands dropped from Isabella's. "He is quite well. He's currently spending some time with my family in Kent. He'll be back in London by spring."

Rebecca's gaze lingered. Isabella turned away. She didn't want her friend to see the regret that lurked there.

Spotting Lady Melwood talking with Lady Torrington, Isabella moved closer, planning to enter the conversation. So well camouflaged was she amongst the other guests that it was obvious neither Lady Melwood nor Lady Torrington saw her approach—even once she was close enough to overhear their conversation.

"I see no change at all," said the dowager.

"Give them time," Lady Melwood replied. "I believe this marriage has great potential. They are still getting to know one another."

Oh dear. She and Bromby were the topic of this conversation. Isabella hung back and continued to listen.

"Yes," said Lady Torrington. "And he is still getting to know other ladies as well."

Isabella followed Lady Torrington's stare across the room where her husband stood close to one of Lady Melwood's protégés, a young woman named Miss Lucy Rowe. Earlier in the evening the young lady had been introduced to her.

Bromby brought the young woman a glass of punch as she sat at the wall's edge and fanned her face furiously.

"Well, at least there is no more of that business with Lady Catherine," said her aunt.

"But what about the other one—Mrs. Morley?"

Lady Melwood's shoulders raised and lowered with a great sigh. "We try not to talk about it."

"To be sure. But the word is that it still goes on—that the couple spent part of their honeymoon at the Morley's estate in Sevenoaks."

Mortified, Isabella sank back. Hopefully neither her aunt nor Lady Torrington saw her there. Was the gossip about Bromby and Agatha still so strong? Hadn't her marriage to Bromby assuaged all of that?

Isabella looked over at where Bromby had been standing with Miss Rowe. He was no longer there. Miss Rowe sat alone. Now where had he gone? Who was he with?

"Bell." She jumped at his voice, a whisper into her ear. She spun around, surprised to see his face smiling down upon her.

"Goodness!" Her hand flew to her throat as a nervous smile pushed its way across her lips. "Where have you been?"

"Just talking to people. I am here now." He clasped her hand and led her to a nearby chair. Dutifully, she sat. She was relieved to sit. She felt a little light-headed and hadn't been able to eat anything at dinner.

Bromby stood behind Isabella's chair, his hand on her shoulder. For the rest of the reception he stood close by her seat and engaged her in some of the politest and easiest conversation they'd had since before they were married.

Was this merely for appearances? An attempt to entertain and placate a rapt audience of admirers? Perhaps he had overheard similar conversations to the ones she'd witnessed and attempted to stem the tide of gossip.

———◦≈∞◦———

They left Lady Melwood's early. The contents of Isabella's sour stomach churned until it finally rose into her throat, and she'd barely made it outside where she'd vomited at the feet of the horses.

Once they were back at Piccadilly Terrace, she'd gone straight to bed. Several times during the night, Isabella awoke and rushed to the bedpan. Finally, not wishing to disturb Bromby each time she arose, she made her way downstairs where Mrs. Thatcher sat beside a waning hearth.

In the evenings after the housekeeper's day off, Isabella often joined her in fireside chats, where she would hear word of Mrs. Thatcher's visits with her husband. They had procured a small house in an unfashionable area of town, but it allowed for them to see each other more often.

Mrs. Thatcher prepared ginger tea for her and brought the cup to her by the fire. "Do you think it 'twas something you ate, milady?"

Swallowing back the nausea, Isabella dabbed at her forehead with a cold, wet rag. "I can't think what it would be. I ate next to nothing all afternoon."

Mrs. Thatcher grew silent for a few moments.

Perhaps a change of subject would get her mind off it. "Mrs. Thatcher, I am so thankful you have come to live with us."

The woman smiled. "I am grateful you sent for me. I enjoy being of service to you, milady."

"And are you enjoying the weekly visits with Mr. Thatcher?"

"Yes, milady. Although it will always be strained between us, I fear."

Another surge of illness assaulted Isabella. She grabbed the pot sitting at her feet, hung her head over it, and retched. Mrs. Thatcher rushed to the table to refresh Isabella's rag in cool water and brought it back to her. Then, she carried the soiled pot toward the door leading to the outside.

She soon returned and replaced the pan beside Isabella. "Do you think you might be in the family way, milady?"

Isabella was silent as her mind spun with the possibility. Of course. That was what was the matter with her. Why had it not occurred to her before now?

A fluttery excitement filled her. *Thank you, Lord. Thank you for giving me this gift. This may change Bromby's heart toward me. A baby! How wonderful...*

She could hardly wait to have the suspicion confirmed. She would see the doctor and then inform Bromby. *Please let this news of an heir please him, and perhaps change the course of our marriage.*

⸺⸺⸺

Isabella sat before Bromby in the library. Perched on the edge of her chair, her hands folded and placed neatly on her knees, she waited patiently for him to look up from his book.

His elbow anchored upon the armrest, Bromby braced his head as he bowed over a book on Greece. His left foot rested on a footstool.

"What is it?" He moved his eyes to glance up at her.

"I do not wish to disturb you while you are reading. I can wait."

With a sigh he raised his head. "How can I continue to read with you staring at me like that? Tell me what you want and be done with it, so that I may return to my solitude."

Her stomach roiled. Was she to expect anything more than gruff exchanges from him? Were his black moods ever to end?

"I have some good news, I think." A shy smile tugged at her lips. "I have seen the doctor today, and it would seem that I am with child. It is due in November."

She waited for a smile to eclipse the clouds blowing over his face. He stared at her, his eyes inscrutable.

"What do you think, B?" she pressed, tamping down her rising anxiety. No matter what, she would remain calm. "Is not this good news?"

After a long silence, Bromby turned his eyes to the ceiling and a long sigh escaped him. With a little shake of his head he replied, "I suppose," then turned back to his poetry.

Isabella's spirits plummeted. She had not expected him to jump up and whirl her around the room, but was there not to be some show of joy?

"Are you not happy? This child will be your heir." Her fingers clutched the fabric of her dress as though clasping the mane of a runaway horse.

"It will be another mouth to feed." He spoke to the pages of his book.

"Did you expect us to have no children?"

He looked up then. "No, I would have expected your uncle to have died by now and left you your inheritance."

Isabella flinched at his words.

He carried on. "I would not have expected creditors and moneylenders to stampede our door the very second we moved in, screaming for their principals and interest. I would not have expected to have to consider selling off our furniture to fulfill our debts …"

"It will not come to that. Surely."

"Oh, you think not?" He reached over and grabbed a stack of papers from the table beside him. "These are all bills from my creditors demanding I pay the sums I owe along with most exorbitant amounts of interest. How am I to do that? Where is the money to come from?"

"Perhaps you should consider taking money for your poetry. Other writers do it all the time."

"Gentlemen do not."

She nearly quipped that his status as a gentleman was questionable, but she caught her tongue before the words tumbled out.

"You are a spoiled, sheltered girl who knows nothing about the ways of the world, monetary hardships, or how debts are created or paid."

His words were painful, but she shook them off. She would not allow him to see how the verbal darts wounded her. "The economy has changed," she said, attempting to show that she knew a great deal more about money than he credited her. "Everyone is under a strain. I read in the paper yesterday that there is vast unemployment and banks are failing."

"We should not be in this situation. If only your uncle would be a good man and die."

Isabella stood. Tears pushed at the backs of her eyes and her stomach rolled. "Maybe when your sister arrives your mood will improve."

He turned back to his book. "That is the only event I can imagine which would give me any pleasure."

With those words, Isabella left him to his solitude.

Thirty-Three

May 1815

The ice had melted from the tree limbs in the park and buds sprouted on the branches. Green growth adorned the city, and it was more common to see people in the square—walking, rolling their babies, sitting on benches and reading.

But it had rained all morning as they awaited Agatha's arrival.

Passing through the foyer, Bromby's voice echoed through the upstairs as he castigated one of the maids. Isabella paused at the bottom of the stairwell.

"Why is Mrs. Morley's room so stuffy? Why would you not have the good sense to know that you should open the window and air out her room?"

"I'm sorry, sir." The maid's voice trembled, on the verge of breaking. "I opened it earlier, but since it were rainin' I thought—"

"Whatever you thought, it was wrong. Now, open a window and air out the room. And look at the tables, they are disgusting and dirty. Do you think Mrs. Morley should sleep in a room filled with dust and dirt?" he bellowed.

"No, sir."

He emerged on the landing, his eyes blazing as he yelled down the stairs to Isabella. "Where is Mrs. Thatcher? Why is she not looking after such things?"

"It is Mrs. Thatcher's day off. She is with her family today."

"See to it her *days off* are not affecting the state and cleanliness of this house!" He darted off again, this time to the left. *Clomp-drag, clomp-drag.* Isabella remained at the base of the staircase as he advanced to another room and there pronounced more which displeased him about the current state of the upstairs.

233

Accompanied by a cool wind, Agatha entered the foyer and removed her bonnet, laughing and making fun of the state of her hair. Fletcher and another servant carried her things inside. Her laughing ceased suddenly, and she stood beside Isabella, her face turned toward the upstairs where the shouting continued.

Then the two women turned and their eyes met. A retelling of events from the last three months—of Bromby's black moods, depression, and displeasure with everything—passed from Isabella to Agatha without a word being spoken. Grimacing, Agatha shook her head and swept up the stairs toward the voices above.

Within a few moments, Agatha's muted tones reverberated in the stairwell.

The maid's voice, broken with sobs, echoed much louder. "I'm sorry, ma'am. I'm sorry, sir."

"'Tis all right. There is no harm done," said Agatha in a smooth voice. "The room is lovely. I see no dust or dirt."

The maid passed on the landing, sniffing and snuffling and wiping at her eyes.

Frozen at the foot of the stairs, Isabella could not make out the words passing between Agatha and Bromby, but the tone of his voice was much different than it had been moments before.

Grasping the railing, she set her right foot on the first step and stopped. Sucking her upper lip under her bottom teeth, she hesitated. If she were to go up there now, would she witness something she did not wish to see? With her heart pounding and her blood beating hard in her temples, she waited and listened. Several more minutes passed, and when she heard the scuffling of their feet above, she went up.

After dinner and a game of cards, the trio sat together in the drawing room. Bromby and Agatha moved to the sofa, but Isabella remained seated at the table. She collected and stacked them, and then spread them out and restacked them all over again.

Bromby, suddenly cheerful and congenial after several glasses of port, relayed his recent London literary experiences with relish. "Sir Walter Scott and I are very much like brothers. He also carries a lame leg, and the two of us limp up and down the streets and in and out of taverns like two halves of a whole."

He stood and imitated how they shambled along, teetering this way and that.

Agatha laughed. "And didn't you say you are recently corresponding with that poet … oh, what's his name—Coleridge, wasn't it?"

"Oh, yes. Poor Coleridge. He's a victim of the public whims, poor fellow." Bromby seated himself by Agatha again. "Very talented, wonderful poet. But he's having trouble finding a publisher for his most recent work. You know how society's tastes move this way and that at any given time."

"Indeed," said Agatha. "But I thought you did not like him. Didn't you write a satirical poem about his *The Ancient Mariner?*"

Bromby waved his hand. "That is all forgotten. I am much more suited to helping other poets rather than hindering them. That was a shortcoming of my youth and pride, I suppose."

Isabella nearly laughed. Did he now suggest that his pride had been tamed? Perhaps in the literary sphere, but certainly she had not been the happy recipient of such change.

Bromby glanced over at her suddenly, as though he'd forgotten she still existed. "Darling, you look tired. Shouldn't you be in bed resting?"

Isabella bit her lip. She was tired. But she was always tired nowadays, and she didn't know whether to contribute it to her condition or the emotional strain.

"Do not linger on account of me, dear Bell," said Agatha. "I know all too well the fatigue that comes in the first few months. You will not vex me in the least if you choose to go to bed."

Tears prodded the backs of her eyes. *They wish me gone.* What could she do? Linger and incite Bromby's bad mood, or go and listen to them laughing and talking until late in the evening? Too tired to prolong the inevitability of either of these outcomes, Isabella sighed and stood. "I suppose I shall go to bed. Will you be long, B?" Perhaps the pleading expression upon her face sufficiently suggested he follow her.

"I am not tired yet." He looked back at Agatha with a smile. "I shall come up in a little while."

With a heavy heart, Isabella trudged up the stairs.

Once in bed, she whispered a prayer as she stared into the darkness. She could not feel God's presence around her anymore. It was as if, with the all-consuming emotions of her marriage, God had disappeared.

I will never leave you nor forsake you.

The words returned to her like a soft voice, but she was not sure she could believe them anymore. But perhaps it was she who had forsaken God …

Dear Lord, how I long to feel your presence. Just a little bit of comfort in my loneliness and misery.

More laughter floated through the boards of the floor.

Tears slid from the corner of her eyes and dampened the pillow around her head. She touched a hand to her stomach. She had to be strong now for the new life that grew within her. If for no other reason than to protect her child, she must not let him break her.

Sir Malcolm Meade greeted Isabella as she entered the drawing room and apologized that his wife was not yet downstairs.

"Rebecca was a little unwell this morning," he said.

Isabella removed her bonnet, scarf, and gloves and handed them to an obliging servant. "I am sorry to hear that. Should I not have come?"

"Oh, no. I think she is better now. We all bounce back remarkably well 'round here."

Several times a week, Isabella called upon Rebecca. Walking into Rebecca's home in Mayfair was like stepping into a springtime garden. There was nothing but happiness, laughter, and light in her friend's house. Quite the contrast from her own.

Although he often suffered bouts of illness, Sir Malcolm was always warm and affable. Isabella had always liked him, and each time she saw him she liked him more.

She noticed a scroll laid out on a table and motioned to it. "May I?"

"Oh yes, of course. That was sent to me by my cousin."

Isabella touched the scroll and rolled it out before her, revealing an elaborately painted map of the Americas. She ran her hand over it. "'Tis beautifully executed."

"Yes. I believe he bought it from a man in New York."

"I've read a great deal about America," said Isabella. "I'd always hoped to go there sometime within my life." She imagined what it would be like to board a boat and sail far away, leaving behind the travesty of her home, her marriage, her broken dreams. "But it appears I will not now."

"Oh, I don't know," said Sir Malcolm cheerfully. "It seems like exactly the sort of adventure Lord Bromby would go for."

Isabella looked up at him, releasing her hand from the parchment and allowing it to roll together once more. "My husband prefers to travel alone, Sir Malcolm. It is very possible that he would go there, but I doubt he would ever return to me if he did."

Sir Malcolm laughed a little, obviously uncomprehending of her meaning. Isabella was glad of that. She was simply being silly and self-pitying. She had spoken too much.

"Ah, here she is," Sir Malcolm said as a pale-faced Rebecca entered the room. "Well, I'll leave you ladies now."

As the two women settled into chairs across from one another, Rebecca's wan face suddenly brightened. "I have some news."

"Oh?"

"I think I am with child, Izzy."

Even underneath the pallor of her complexion, the glow of new motherhood shone through.

"Oh, that is wonderful. I am very happy for you."

"I can scarce believe it, but I am thrilled beyond words." Rebecca beamed. "I only hope the sickness subsides soon."

"It will. In a few weeks you will feel better." Although happy for her friend, a stab of envy prodded her heart. Rebecca's husband would share in her joy. He would no doubt look upon her pregnancy as something to be celebrated.

"I'm sure Sir Malcolm is overjoyed."

Rebecca smiled. "Oh, yes. He is so good. Although he treats me as though I were made of glass. I keep telling him that I will not break." She laughed, the familiar tinge of pink rushing into her cheeks. "And I'm sure Bromby is thrilled as well."

The flood of tears came at once and surprised even Isabella. There had been no warning before the emotion broke through, and she had even less control over the great, heaving sobs and dramatic hiccupping that followed.

The smile dropped from Rebecca's face as she rushed to Isabella's side. "Oh, my dear. What can I do for you? Do you need some cordial water, or … perhaps some tea?"

Isabella held out her hand. "No, truly, I am well. I am so sorry, Rebecca."

"Do not be silly. You are not well." Rebecca went to the door and called out to one of the servants. "Mrs. Moore! Mrs. Moore, would you please bring Lady Bromby some ginger tea?"

Desperate that no one else should see her in such a state, Isabella sniffed and dabbed at her eyes with her handkerchief. Some time passed before the servant rushed in with a tray of tea, cups and saucers, and it took every bit of that time for Isabella to slow her tears. Rebecca immediately poured some tea and handed it to her friend.

Isabella grasped the warm cup between both hands and brought it to her lips. The steam curled around her nose and mouth, diffusing the scent of ginger and spice. She breathed it in. "Thank you."

Rebecca settled herself back into her chair. "Now tell me. What is the matter?"

Isabella could not hold it in any longer. Rebecca was the best of confidants and would not gossip or share her news with anyone. Isabella relayed the nightmare that was 13 Piccadilly Terrace, holding back only on her suspicions regarding Agatha.

Rebecca listened intently. Completely incapable of concealing her emotions, all the shock and disbelief clearly shone in her eyes, in the hang of her mouth, and in the furrow of her brow.

"At first I thought his rash and violent behavior due to some sort of … influence within Broadwell Abbey itself. Surely, I thought, once we are away from there, he would revert to the sensitive, self-possessed man I knew previously." Her head dropped, and tears rolled off her chin into her lap. "But he has only grown worse, even after we departed."

"Do you feel you are in physical danger?" Rebecca breathed at last.

"No. I do not believe so. The violence is in his words and … well, in other ways I cannot mention."

Rebecca shook her head as though to dislodge any such thoughts.

"I believe," Isabella began again, "that his fury, his rage against everyone including himself, stems from a need for constant sensory stimulation. This is a failing of artistic temperaments, you know. He is easily bored, easily aggravated by the ordinary and mundane. He has a passion for pleasure. This, I believe, accounts for the constant drinking and gaming and …" She dropped her head again. Now unburdened of her pain, Isabella's face grew hot. "I had hoped that a child would bring us together in unity—that perhaps the thought of an heir would somehow make him want to be a good husband. But if anything, it has promoted the reverse."

Rebecca's expression was as desolate as her own. "My heart breaks for you, my friend. I wish I could help."

There is no help. There is no hope. "You can be my friend. You can pray for me."

Rebecca nodded. "I shall. Have you informed your parents?"

Isabella shook her head. "No. And I shan't. For what is to be done? I know there is nothing that can help me now."

"There is someone who can. And you know him. God can help you, Isabella."

Isabella tensed. "Oh, Rebecca. How can I approach a holy God when I have been brought so low? I would feel unworthy … I am ashamed and …"

Just then, the doors to the drawing room opened, and the butler appeared. "If you please, milady. Mr. Beringer."

A lash of horror struck at Isabella's heart and she shot to her feet. David Beringer appeared, his face stretched in a broad smile. The very idea that he should come at this inopportune moment when she was pouring out tears of regret and despair to Rebecca made her wish for a natural disaster to befall … and quickly.

"Lady Bromby! What a lovely surprise. I did not expect to find you here." The effervescent smile slipped from his face.

Isabella dabbed quickly at her cheeks and chin with her handkerchief.

His face paled as he stood awkwardly by the door. "Have I—shall I return later, Rebecca?"

Rebecca bit her lip as she stared at Isabella, apparently gauging whether he should go.

Not wanting to cause any dramatic hindrance to a brother and sister visitation, Isabella shook her head. "No, no, Mr. Beringer. Please. It is I who should return later."

In chorus, David and Rebecca begged her not to go.

"Please, Lady Bromby. If you are not unwell and do not need to leave this instant, I should very much like for you to stay." David's expression was as serious as she had ever seen it. "Or I could escort you home if you wish."

"Very well. I'll stay. I'll just take a moment, if you don't mind." Isabella moved to a corner of the room and allowed David and Rebecca conversation while she pulled a small mirror from her reticule. Oh, she was a sight indeed. Her face was a map of red blotches, running rivulets, and swollen mounds of flesh. If Mr. Beringer had ever found her attractive and worthy of a proposal, he would congratulate himself on escaping marriage to her now.

With her handkerchief, she swiped the tears from her chin where they had collected. She could do nothing for the blotches upon her cheeks or the swelling of her nose, but at least her face was free from tears.

Sniffing back any further emotion, Isabella forced a smile to her lips and turned to rejoin them in the center of the room. She took a sip from the ginger tea earlier provided as she seated herself across from David Beringer.

David appeared to attempt a congenial smile, but his eyes still reflected concern. "It is lovely to see you, Lady Bromby. Tell me, is Lord Bromby well?"

Isabella forced a smile in place. "Yes, I thank you, sir. He is quite well. Mrs. Morley is in town and staying with us. She has been commissioned as a lady-in-waiting to Queen Charlotte and is preparing for this honor."

David looked down at his hands momentarily. "Yes, well. That is indeed an honor, is it not, Rebecca?"

"Yes, an honor." Rebecca's eyes were sympathetic as they rested heavily upon Isabella.

Polite conversation ensued over the health of everyone's parents, the weather, and finally David's plans to remain in town for the foreseeable future. "I have some business interests in a local parish. For a number of orphans. Much is needed to feed, clothe, and educate them. It will keep me busy for many months, so I shall remain in London all of that time."

"Oh, my brother is too modest," Rebecca said. "David is providing much of the funding for them."

David's gaze fell and red blotches appeared on his cheeks. "Many of the parishes simply do not have proper funding to care for pauper children, and they are relegated to working for the mills instead. There, the children work long hours, and many of them are mistreated, maimed, or killed. My wish—and what I believe the Lord has called me to do—is to help prevent this."

"That is excellent. And what of your orphanage in the country?" Isabella asked. "Has anything come of that."

"Not as of yet. I'm still searching for the right location."

David Beringer may have been the best man she had ever known. Fresh tears flooded her eyes. "That is so good of you, Mr. Beringer."

His eyes darted quickly to meet hers before returning to his lap.

Rebecca smiled. "I, for one, shall be happy to see so much more of you, David."

David paused and took a deep breath. "I have come to apprise my sister of some news," he said with hesitation in his voice. "And Lady Bromby, it seems you will be one of the first to know as well."

"Oh!" Rebecca said with surprise. "What news have you, David?"

"I have …" he paused again and looked down at his hands, his face flushing with color. "I have convinced Miss Rosaline Reese to accept my proposal. We are to be married."

Rebecca clasped her hands together, and her face lit up. "Oh, this is wonderful news!"

"Congratulations, Mr. Beringer," Isabella managed. Even as she spoke the words, her chest compressed. She could barely breathe. "Who is the lucky young woman?"

"Well … I met her near Holly Bridge. She had taken a fall after some young ruffians stole her horse."

"Did she ever get the horse back?" Rebecca asked.

"Yes. I went searching for him the next day. I found him wandering near the woods. Still had the saddle strapped to his back."

"Were the horse thieves brought to justice?"

"The woods were searched, but they were not found. At any rate, following that incident, Miss Reese and I … formed an attachment."

"Naturally. I'm so happy for you." Rebecca sighed. "Finally."

Isabella's mind reeled with alternative endings to her own story. If only she had used her head before accepting Bromby. If only she had prayed more. If only she'd accepted David when he'd first asked …

But as Bromby daily reminded her, it was all too late now. It was done. There was no turning back. No way out. And now dear, good, kind-hearted Mr. Beringer would go off and marry another. *As he should…*

Parting ways that day, Isabella relished the few seconds her gloved hand rested in David Beringer's as he handed her into the carriage. It was wrong, of course, to have such emotions for him, but as they said their goodbyes that afternoon, she was full of regret. Did she see that same regret mirrored in David's eyes?

Through the window of the carriage, Isabella stretched out her hand toward Rebecca. Grasping her hand and squeezing, Rebecca whispered, "I will be praying for you."

But Isabella hardly received any comfort from her friend's words. It seemed a hopeless business. Only her unborn child deserved saving now.

Thirty-Four

David arrived at Sir Malcolm Meade's assembly of dinner and cards in the worst mood possible. All week he'd thought about his last encounter with Isabella—the way she'd looked when he'd happened upon her visiting his sister. That shattered expression ... her defeated, haunted eyes. Why could he not stop thinking of her? Anger filled his chest and flooded his mind. She was someone else's wife now, and her troubles were none of his business. He'd soon be a married man, himself. These leftover emotions must end.

At his sister's home, he arrived with Rosaline Reese on his arm, a forced smile on his face.

As he moved about the drawing room, his eye fell upon Lady Bromby and his heart plummeted. He had hoped, by some miracle of miracles, she would not attend. Not far from where she stood, Lord Bromby and Agatha Morley stood talking to Rosaline's mother.

David and Rosaline sat down to play a game of whist with Isabella's aunt, Lady Lydia Liddens and Lord Peterson. But he found it difficult to concentrate on the game or the conversations about corn laws or the severe weather of the past year.

His eyes continually trailed across the room to where Isabella stood alone, staring as though she were in a trance—her eyes downcast. Her face was placid as always, but her eyes held the same distress he'd seen a few days earlier. *God help her. It cannot be easy—married to such a man.*

David couldn't simply leave his fiancée to seek out another woman's company. He waited until the game was finished and then turned to Rosaline.

"Dearest, I would like to introduce you to Lady Bromby. Lord Bromby's wife and Rebecca's dear friend."

Rosaline smiled and rose to join him. "Oh, I've wanted to meet Lord Bromby for ever so long. Mamma once thought him a fine match for me, but Miss Bankmill was there before me."

David's stomach lurched. Was she in earnest? She laughed as though her words were humorous, but he was not amused. If only she knew the trouble that man had caused.

David's stride faltered as they made their way across the room toward Isabella.

"Are you quite all right?" Rosaline's brow furrowed. "Are you coming?"

He clenched and unclenched his teeth. "Yes." He must pull it together. His grievance with Bromby had nothing to do with Rosaline.

Suddenly, Rosaline was no longer looking at Lord Bromby but at something on the other side of the room. "Oh, look! There is the countess, Lady Rushton. Mamma is speaking with her. I will join you presently."

David released her arm and Rosaline glided off to join her mother in conversation with another illustrious member of Society.

In the last few weeks, David had seen a different side of his gentle, quiet fiancée who he'd rescued from the brambles. She was far more interested in the comings and goings of fashionable society than he'd first suspected. Anxiety nibbled at his brain. Would the life he offered her be enough? Would she grow tired of a the quiet, country world of Kent and Holly Bridge?

With a sigh, he turned his attentions back to Lady Bromby. He was within a few feet of her now, so it would be rude not greet her, ask after her family. Slowly, he approached her. "Hello, Lady Bromby."

She looked up, seemingly startled. "Mr. Beringer."

"Are you inspecting Sir Malcolm's rugs from Spain?" He meant the question in good humor. Hopefully, she wouldn't take offense.

Her mouth formed a tight smile that never quite met her eyes. "No, indeed. Although the rugs, I must admit, are very fine."

"I believe his father brought them back from Spain." He tensed and swallowed hard. This was a feeble attempt at making conversation.

The conversation halted, and his stomach began to churn.

"And when are you and Miss Reese to be wed?" Isabella asked.

He looked over his shoulder at his fiancée standing with her mother and the countess. A sigh welled up in him and expelled from his lungs. "In the next couple of months, I believe. We have not had the banns read yet, and there is much to be decided."

"She seems a dear, sweet, girl," Isabella smiled. "I am very happy for you."

"I fear the manner in which Rosaline and I were introduced set up grand expectations for her, which I cannot consistently meet."

"You rescued her."

"Yes, but I sometimes feel she still expects me to act ... heroically, somehow. And I am just a man. Not a hero."

Isabella's eyes glimmered with tears. "I see your meaning. Every young woman enters the marital state with expectations—some of them quite grand. Eventually she is forced to shed them—like tears." As though snapping out of a trance, Isabella looked at him and smiled. "I have no doubt you will meet Miss Reese's every expectation, Mr. Beringer."

David looked away, clearing his throat. "I should very much like for you to meet her. I hope you and Rosaline might be friends."

Isabella's sad little smile slipped away as a shadow slid over her face. David turned. Lord Bromby stood behind him, his mouth in a surly pout, his eyebrows knitted together. He nodded to Mr. Beringer. "Mrs. Morley is not feeling well. I think we should go at once."

David straightened. "May I be of assistance at all?"

"No," Bromby answered quickly. "None at all. I've asked to have the carriage brought 'round."

David turned back to Isabella. Her eyes met his, and somewhere deep within the dark blue pupils, a silent cry: *I am trapped.*

"Come." Bromby took hold of her elbow and led her across the room where they joined Mrs. Morley by the door. Isabella still looked over her shoulder at him.

David's heart wrenched.

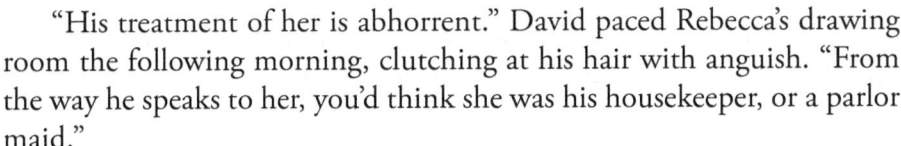

"His treatment of her is abhorrent." David paced Rebecca's drawing room the following morning, clutching at his hair with anguish. "From the way he speaks to her, you'd think she was his housekeeper, or a parlor maid."

Rebecca, paler than usual, sat sipping a cup of tea. "I know it all, David. She has confided some things I am not at liberty to relate."

David stopped pacing, his chest tightening with dread. "He has not hit her? If he has then—"

"David." Rebecca held up her hand to stop him. "Isabella is our friend. But you cannot involve yourself in this."

His shoulders sagged, and he slumped into a chair across from his sister. He was unused to emotion like this—unfettered anger.

Rebecca continued. "Bromby is deeply in debt. Broadwell Abbey has not sold. Isabella has had to write to the banks and his creditors in the hopes that they will extend a grace period."

David stared at her, recalling that evening in the winter when he had settled Bromby's refurbishment debts for Broadwell Abbey. "What an irresponsible, selfish libertine. Good heavens. What a debacle. What else has she told you?" Realizing the impropriety of his question, he turned away. "Never mind. I do not wish to know." Then turning again, "Does he abuse her?"

"And what would you do if he did, David? Beat down his door? Challenge him to a duel?"

David's heart sank. It was true. No matter what she suffered there was nothing to be done. "I could … write to her parents."

"Do not meddle in this." Rebecca's eyes held sharp reproof. "Isabella confided in me. She would not want me or you to upset her parents and embroil them in this mess. We must pray for her. It is all we can do." Rebecca took a long sip from her tea. "Perhaps you should pray for your own heart as well as hers. I can see that you still care for her."

David closed his eyes, attempting to shut out the truth of her accusation. "I have tried to shake her from my heart. God forgive me, I do still care for her. Even more now that I see her so abominably treated."

Rebecca smiled sadly. "You cannot rescue her, David. None of us can. Only God. You should marry Miss Reese and move forward with your life."

"Yes, I know."

A long silence passed between them. David rubbed his temples and scrubbed his fingers over his face. If he had only pursued her sooner, more fervently. Would that he had met her before Bromby …

Now she was a virtual prisoner.

"I hear they hardly ever have visitors," he said at last.

"That is true," said Rebecca. "Since Mrs. Morley arrived, there are few who enter their home. Lord Bromby says it is because of Isabella's condition. He prefers to keep her quietly resting."

Anger rose in him again. "What nonsense."

"He is now on the committee of Drury Lane Theatre. He's helping to run it. I do believe he is out quite a lot of the time."

David took his sister's words as an opening of sorts. If Bromby was away much of the time, then perhaps he might visit her, see what he could do. "Thereby leaving her alone."

"David—"

"Yes, I know, I know." He hung his head. His blood boiled again. Rebecca would surely tell him not to go to Piccadilly Terrace to pay a call. Leave well enough alone. "I just feel so helpless." If he could only make certain there really was nothing he could do.

"You must concentrate on Miss Reese. You will be married soon. She is your concern now, not Isabella."

David departed his sister's home with an ache in the center of his chest. Why God would have allowed such a terrible union as Bromby and Isabella to take place? And as for her part, Isabella should have known better than to marry him. But now that she had, what help could be offered her? Rebecca was right. He should think of Rosaline and be happy about his forthcoming nuptials, not concerning himself with another man's wife.

As the carriage came to a stop at the corner, he looked out on the street where drops of rain fell steadily. He breathed in the damp, cool air as he listened to the gentle, rhythmic fall of the drops puddling in the streets, within the crevices of the cobblestones.

David tapped on the edge of the window and poked his head out of it. He looked down the road at the line of waiting carriages.

"What is holding up the progress?"

"Sorry, sir. 'Tis a bit of flooded road. All the rain we've had."

One of the carriages in front of them turned off the main road and onto a side street to avoid the river of water creating treacherous passing.

"That driver seems to have the right notion," he called out.

"Yes, sir. I think I'll do the same," his driver responded. "'Tis the only way out, I fear."

Finally, they were moving again, the driver taking the same route as the carriage before him. David sat back, pulled a handkerchief from his pocket, and dried his wet face. As he did, a sudden thought occurred to him.

Perhaps Isabella had made a poor choice of marriage, but it did not follow that he should do the same. Perhaps love for Rosaline would grow with time, but what if it did not? Even so, how could he not marry Rosaline? If he were to cry off now, he would incur all sorts of scandal and public humiliation. His honor would be ruined. But at what price did he preserve his honor? Should he marry out of obligation and spend the rest of his life unhappy?

———————— ✧ ————————

14 June 1815

Dear Miss Reese,

I am in receipt of your letter dated the first of June.

I fully comprehend your decision to break off our engagement following your transfer of affection to Viscount Harper. I must assume some of the blame in this decision, and so I do. If I had not vacillated, circumstances might have been different.

I release you from our engagement and certainly bear you no ill will. I only desire your happiness.

May you be blessed, Miss Reese.

Yours,

David Beringer

Part VII

Thirty-Five

11 August 1815
Piccadilly Terrace

Dearest Mamma,

I thank you for your most gracious offer of the home in Darlington as a place of respite for my confinement, but I must decline. Bromby feels that a sudden displacement to such a removed locale would raise suspicions from his creditors. It would not be impossible for me to travel, but I would feel most anxious about going alone.

Broadwell Abbey did not meet the reserve at auction, and therefore did not sell. As for the creditors, I have done all I can to beg their patience, as they have threatened to confiscate the furniture and any other valuable possessions to offset the debt. Although I will not grieve over any other household possessions, I am most anxious that we do not lose the library. The monetary value of the books is perhaps £1,600, but the loss of such a literary inheritance to our children would be irreplaceable.

There are not enough words to show our gratitude for your efforts. I know poor Papa did not expect to sell off any farms in North Yorkshire, but the money will stave off several of the creditors eagerly awaiting their share. I know the bankers and lawyers will not be rushed, but as you know, we are facing a crisis of time.

I have written to several of Bromby's creditors begging for a stay of seizure. At least two of them have given me until November. I hope that will be enough time. If it will not, I shall ask for an additional time to repay.

In answer to your questions, Agatha still resides with us off and on. I waver daily as to whether her presence here is a help or a hindrance. She is very good to me, attends to my every need, and comes to my aid when Bromby is in one of his black moods—when nothing pleases him more than to find fault with my every word and action. In those moments,

Agatha does not delay in scolding and pressing him to apologize at once. He obeys her and I suppose I should be thankful, but it is distressing that I—his wife—have no such effect upon him.

As for Bromby's new employment at Drury Lane Theatre, it secures a creative venue for him. He hasn't composed poetry since Agatha's arrival. Or perhaps the creditors have caused this barren period.

When there is the most miniscule hope we shall recover, and all will be well, he is free from fits and tantrums. It is my sincerest resolution to maintain that hopeful lifeline.

Your loving daughter,

Isabella

Isabella nervously picked at her embroidery. Her mother was the mistress of screen embroidery, but Isabella showed no aptitude for the skill at all. She couldn't count how many times she'd pricked her finger today alone, and she was sure she had incorrectly executed many of the stitches. The flowers looked all wrong—as though they wilted rather than thrived.

Agatha, who now split her time between lodgings at St. James's Park in service to the Queen and their Piccadilly Terrace home, reclined on the divan and appeared to be reading a book. But every so often her eyes raised to look over at her stepbrother who sat close to the fire … silent, drinking his brandy, and cleaning his dueling pistols. Isabella had not seen his guns since discovering the one hidden in his desk drawer at Broadwell Abbey.

"Have I told you about the actresses at Drury Lane?"

The sound of his voice startled Isabella, and she looked up from her embroidery. Agatha glanced up from her book.

"There are many women—all charming, fetching, and talented— always circulating about the backstage of the theatre. I'm keeping my eyes open, as I'm sure one of them shall suit me."

Agatha narrowed her eyes and her mouth compressed.

How could she bear any more of this …this household in confusion? I'm not like Agatha. *I cannot cope with his incendiary words.* Putting aside her embroidery screen, Isabella stood and walked from the room.

Within seconds, Agatha's quick, light footsteps pattered behind her.

Isabella did not turn. Instead she marched up the stairs and straight to her bed, where she lay with her face turned away from the door.

The bed shook slightly as Agatha perched on the side of the bed. "Do not heed his words. You know he only talks. He says these things to rouse your temper. And mine, if truth be known."

Were his words mere prattle? He seemed sincere enough. "Why would he say such things? I would never think to say such things to him."

"You know how he is, Bell. He is just being silly and trying to taunt you."

Isabella turned onto her back and looked into Agatha's pale blue eyes. They creased at the corners and her eyebrows slanted. "He is naughty. He ought not to taunt you so, but I do think he cares for you."

Isabella's heart sank further. That Agatha *thought* he *cared for her* did nothing to relieve her fears. She wanted to hear that he loved her—absolutely and without reservation.

"Please leave me." A sob choked her. "I need to be alone for a while."

"Very well." Agatha left the room.

Isabella exhaled shakily.

Why am I even here? He would be happier if I were gone.

She could not trust Agatha. Agatha might tell Bromby things she said. She couldn't trust anyone in Society either. They were far too interested in the illustrious couple as a thing to behold, observe, scrutinize. They looked for cracks in the façade—anything that might offer them fodder for their whispered conversations in the corners of warm drawing rooms—a breath of scandal or the slightest exhalation of gossip.

Even Lady Melwood had backed away from soliciting their company. Her aunt's once-affectionate friendship with Bromby waned as her letters lessened and her invitations ceased. Isabella concluded that Bromby's debts, lack of decorum, his strange relationship with Agatha, and his unwillingness to fall in line with expectations had hurt his reputation—and by default, disgraced her as well.

———————⟡———————

Isabella was relieved when Agatha left the house the following day. She was even more relieved once Bromby finally left for the theatre.

She was alone with the servants when Rebecca paid a call, and the two women retreated to the drawing room where tea was served. In Rebecca's presence alone, she felt a sense of peace.

"He says he seeks refuge from marital bliss," Isabella told Rebecca as she breathed in the scent of the steaming tea. "I suppose that's why he often stays late at the theatre, not returning until well into the night. Agatha and I are left waiting, wondering, until he returns, staggering through the doors, singing some ridiculous song or other, drunk and smelling like the tavern …"

Rebecca's face fell.

"I am sorry to pain you with my truthfulness, Rebecca, but there it is."

"Would you like to hear my opinion on the matter, dear friend?" Rebecca's eyes were somber.

"You know I respect your opinion above anyone else's. It pains me to burden you with my brutal truths … but as you know, I look upon you as a sister, and I regret that you're my only confidante."

Rebecca scooted closer to Isabella on the sofa and her voice dropped to a whisper. "I think some of your misery may be quelled by the hasty and permanent removal of Mrs. Morley from your home. She isn't helping matters. In fact, it would seem she increases your anxiety and Bromby's cruelty toward you."

Tears pushed at the backs of Isabella's eyes. All she did these days was cry. Was there never to be any emotional peace in her heart again? *O Lord, I remember when I was at rest in your comfort and protection.*

"Agatha has been good to me. She has helped me a great deal. She often knows how to calm Bromby in ways that I cannot. He … listens to her."

Rebecca's hand fell upon hers. "Precisely why she should go. Why should she be the one to quiet him? He is your husband, not hers. It is as though you have turned over the reins to her, my dear Isabella. She should return to her own home, to her own children."

Isabella had felt as much since Agatha's arrival. But every time she mustered the courage to ask her to leave, Agatha thwarted a catastrophe and Isabella lost her nerve.

"You are right, Rebecca. I know you are. But I do not know how he will take it."

Rebecca squeezed her friend's hand. "He must. And you must strengthen your backbone."

A tear escaped Isabella's eye and rolled the length of her cheek and over her lip. She swatted at it and with a determined sniff, shook her head. "Enough of this dull talk."

She stood abruptly and moved across the room, smoothing her skirts. She looked into the glass of the mirror and saw a swollen face, scarcely looking like her own. Pregnancy had rendered her plump and round. Smoothing her hair and wiping all traces of tears from her blotchy cheeks, Isabella forced a smile to her lips and turned back to her friend.

A vision of David Beringer shifted into her mind's eye, and her heart dropped a little.

"Tell me about your brother. How does he do? Does he remain in Kent?"

"He does."

"I know we have not spoken of it, but I was very surprised when you told me of his cancelled engagement."

"I was surprised you had not already heard of it through Lady Melwood."

"Lady Melwood rarely communicates with us these days."

Rebecca nodded. "Then you may not have heard that Miss Reese is recently married to Viscount Harper."

Isabella resumed her seat beside Rebecca. *Poor Mr. Beringer. Another disappointment.*

Rebecca shook her head. "I, for one, was relieved. I did not think her right for David. My brother suffers from the most terrible need to rescue women from their plights. Finding her snared in the bushes, nearly freezing to death after losing her horse was the cause of all of this, no doubt. And as for Miss Reese ... well, her parents wished her to marry, and David was available and suitable. Otherwise, she was disinterested at best. But of course, he has taken all the blame upon himself."

"I am astonished."

"Rosaline's marriage to Viscount Harper will be a more advantageous match for her."

"Oh, I am sorry for your brother, though. I know well enough the horrors of being the subject of speculation and scorn." How much she hated to think of gentle, good-hearted David under such public condemnation.

Rebecca shook her head. "I believe it was harder on our parents. David was relieved and willing to risk the scandal to avoid a bad match. And after three thwarted loves ... well, I'm quite sure he will not be tempted to pursue another." A frown pulled at the corner of Rebecca's mouth. "I know I should not say it, Izzy. But I think he still regrets you."

Isabella stood again, agitated. She waved her hand in the air. "Oh, well, that is all in the past now. I look upon your brother much like my own." She had to force herself to believe it. Anything else was out of the question.

Rebecca's gaze dripped with remorse. "I know you do. And I know he cares for your well-being just as if you were his sister. He would visit you, but ... I have warned him that it would be best not to do so at this time."

A pang rippled in her stomach. She wondered if that was the kick of the child or her own lamentation. "Yes. I would not wish him to see me in such a state."

Later that evening, Isabella dined with Agatha and then retired late to a cold bed while awaiting the familiar stomp and shuffle of her husband's footsteps.

At length, the front door thumped closed and voices sounded in the hall. He was home from the theater.

She lay as still as possible, her eyes wide against the darkness, listening for his footsteps on the stairs. Instead, Agatha's voice echoed in the foyer followed by Bromby's. Their somber vocal echoes faded. They must have drifted into either the library or the study.

The house grew eerily still, and a sudden chill swept over her. She stiffened. An ill notion, one that propelled her up and out of the bed, beat at her brain like a battering moth. Why was it so quiet? What were they doing down there?

Wrapping her robe about her, she lit a candle and made her way through the corridor of shadows. As she reached the stairway, she grasped the banister, straining her ears against the silence below. Taking one step at a time, the wood creaking beneath her feet, Isabella descended into the darkness.

She reached the landing and moved first toward the drawing room, its doors open and its interior dark. With her heart pounding, she continued down the hall toward the library. The doors were shut, and a flickering light shone like a beacon, streaming from the bottom of the door and swathing the floor in an orange glow.

A floorboard creaked beneath her feet and Isabella stopped, reaching her hand toward the door knob. From within, Agatha's voice. In one swift movement, Isabella grasped the door knob and wrenched the door open, flinging it wide.

Even though the sight was not unexpected, a gasp—like a groan— caught, then expelled from her throat.

Bromby's back was to her, but his arms were around Agatha.

They immediately pulled apart. Agatha staggered a few steps away, her eyes downcast, her face flushed as she stood with her hand over her mouth.

Bromby turned toward his wife. His eyes widened and then narrowed in a glare. No shame lingered there.

Dozens of scenes flashed through Isabella's mind, ones she had chosen not to heed. Now they all came together like puzzle pieces, forming the sight before her.

"Isabella, I…" Agatha fumbled for her composure, but her words were lost in a swallowed sob.

Isabella straightened, strengthened. She allowed her dry gaze to swing from her flustered, fidgeting houseguest, to her unabashed husband, who now sat on the edge of the couch, swilling from a flagon.

"Good evening, Bell," he rasped. "Come join our party, since you are awake."

Rage ignited somewhere in her midsection and burned up through her chest, filling her throat, her mouth, stinging her eyes.

She turned to Agatha. "I want you out of this house. First thing in the morning."

Her head down and hands braced against her mouth, Agatha hurried out of the room.

Isabella's gaze remained locked with Bromby's. His eyes blazed with defiance. For the first time in her married life, Isabella understood that her husband despised her.

Thirty-Six

Early the next morning, the servants helped pile Agatha's trunks and cases upon the carriage. Agatha would return to her rooms at St. James's Park ... or home to her children. Isabella wasn't really sure, nor did she care.

Agatha's skirts rustled as she turned briefly in the doorway. Then a servant accompanied her outside and the click of the door sounded behind them.

Isabella sighed. Relief.

But the pain soon followed. She had lost a friend, a sister, a confidante of sorts—no matter how little she had trusted her.

Now she knew all of her suspicions had been true. She hadn't been conjuring insane visions in her mind. She had seen it with her own eyes.

Oh, how she wished she had never met Lord Gregory Gordon Bromby. But what could she do now? She'd handed her life over to a man—a monster—a self-professed heathen who cared for neither God nor man. Perhaps she deserved her fate. *Oh, God. How can I bear it? How will my child bear it? The shame ... the scandal. The torture and loneliness of remaining with a man who loves neither of us.*

The voice came out of the shadows, audible, as though a human had produced the sound. "My grace is sufficient ... I have not left you. I will not leave you."

Isabella turned in the foyer, eager to find the source. The foyer was empty, save for the shadows that moved like waves to and fro as the wind blew in gusts, rattling the walls until the frames of the paintings vibrated against the plaster. A chill ran over her. God. She must cling to him. He was all she had.

She clutched the curve of the stairwell railing until Bromby returned from seeing off Agatha's carriage. He moved through the doorway, his coattails billowing out behind him, his hair wild—rising from his scalp like little black snakes turning in the wind. But it was his eyes that most disconcerted her. Narrowed, dark. His dark brows sat over them like black smoke settling over long-burning flames. Isabella stood her ground.

Bromby kicked the door shut, leaving the servants outside just as the morning rain swept in.

She should be fearful of what she saw in his face, but the voice that had spoken to her moments before gave her strength.

She straightened her back and raised her chin, resolved to face him. He had no reason to be angry with her. It was she who should be angry with him.

As he advanced upon her, his face maintained the menacing expression, the jutting chin. She tried to make herself as tall as she could, lifted her shoulders, expanded her rib cage, even as her arms wrapped protectively over her protruding midsection. He paused in front of her only a few seconds before sweeping past, his shoulder roughly bumping against hers, jarring her from her stance.

Only when she heard his limping gait grow faint and the door slam at the other end of the corridor did she relax her bearing. Three servants emerged through the front entrance, their eyes questioning as they busied themselves with daily household chores. Mrs. Thatcher stood in the corner, a smile raising the corners of her lips. She caught Isabella's gaze, nodded to her, and mouthed the words "Well done."

With every ligament straining and every muscle trembling, Isabella turned and made her way to the morning room. A strange calm settled over her, and she suspected it was one of a supernatural nature.

———————— ⟋⟍⟍⟋ ————————

She was gone. Once again, he was without his Agatha. As Bromby sank into his leather arm chair and swilled from the dark brown bottle of laudanum clutched in his fist, a cloud of despair and fury settled over him.

He stared at his library collection. The books lined the shelves—their leather bindings with their gold and black letterings were exposed to the room and looked as vulnerable as a spine stripped of its skin. The bailiffs would soon take them. They had already removed much of the furniture and other valuables. Even his leather chair was on loan from Hobby. They couldn't take that away. As long as he had Hobby's friendship, he would have the chair.

As if to assure himself, Bromby squeezed the arms of the chair and the topaz-colored hide bent beneath his fingers. All he held dear had been taken from him piece by piece. His father, his mother, Agatha, his possessions … his sanity.

"What God would do this to me?" he cried aloud, springing from his chair so violently that he nearly spilled the contents of the bottle. "I *am* doomed!" he called to the ceiling. "You made sure of that. You never cared that I wanted to know you. From the time that my perverse old nurse spouted scripture to me, I wanted to believe in you. I wanted to think you were for me—just as your word said. I wanted to believe there was some good to be had from the abuse I endured from her by day and by night. I wanted to believe that someone cared for me when it was so obvious that my own father did not. But you never showed up! You never showed me love … only its counterfeit." He sank back into his chair and tears coursed from his eyes like the mouth of a river.

It disturbed him to hear his own sobs bouncing between the floor and the ceiling of his room. He hadn't cried like this since he was a little boy—that same nine-year-old boy who fell victim to the hands of his nurse.

"The only person who has ever truly loved me is Agatha—and her love is now denied me. Will you take everything and everyone from me?"

That was it. Isabella was a different form of Nurse May Green, even though he knew Isabella to be kind and good. With every Bible verse she quoted, he heard the voice of his nurse forcing him to repeat the scriptures with letter-perfect accuracy.

"That's not right, Gregory. Say it again!"

If May Green told him it was not right, then he must desperately attempt to remember what word he'd missed. "I'm sorry, Nurse. I'll get it right. Just allow me a moment."

"Oh, you'll get it right, all right. And if you do not, I'll beat the devil out of ye until ye do." He closed his eyes against the memory of her Scottish accent.

"Blessed are the meek, for they shall be called the children of God." His voice trembled as he spoke, his tongue adhering to the roof of his mouth as he glimpsed the switch she held over her head, ready to bring it down upon his back if he missed a word.

"No!" she shrieked. "Tha's wrong!" *Thwack!*

The piercing shrill of her voice was worse than the sting of the stick, and the ugly way her face reddened and blue veins stood out on her forehead made him want to turn from her in disgust.

"Tha's the peacemakers, ye idiot child!"

He gasped, the delayed, radiating sting of the thrash momentarily stunning him. He bit his lip. Right. It was the peacemakers that would be called the children of God. What happened to the meek? *Oh, God. Help me.* "Bl-blessed are the meek, for they will be … I mean, they will inherit the earth."

Thwack! "Say it right! Say it all together, else it's wrong!"

His mind scrambled. That was right, he knew it. But she wanted him to say it without stuttering. Clenching his hands, he straightened, squared his shoulders and stared straight into her muddy brown eyes. Jutting out his chin, he spoke slowly, resolutely. "Blessed are the meek, for they shall inherit the earth."

Her arm was still poised to thrash him, but as he spoke the verse looking straight into her eyes and she realized he'd recited with complete accuracy, the red drained from her face and her arm lowered. "Tha's correct."

He'd breathed out—a shaky, shuddering sound.

"Took ye long enough. Next time do na stutter along like ye did tonight. I'll thrash ye harder!"

He shook his head to dislodge the memory, poured himself a glass of brandy, and downed it in one swallow. Such an injustice—oh, how he hated the control of women, of marriage, of God! Why should he ever be at the mercy of any of these things?

A rush of fury shot through his limbs, and he looked at the glass in his hands. Wrenching his arm back, he pelted it at the wall of books with a force that impressed even him. The glass shattered, and tiny, damp shards clattered to the floor.

His blood still rushing like the Aegean Sea, he went for a chair, and grasping the back of it, he smashed it against the wall, relishing the sound of wood splintering and breaking. One less item for the bailiffs. A tripod table served the same purpose, it's gold-flecked chips floating through the air like fairy dust. Porcelain statues of Cupid, hand-painted vases from the Orient, and decorative crystal bowls all met the same fate.

None of this! They would have none of this. And what did any of it matter now anyway? His life was over.

The sound of feet on the floor above him, rushing here and there. No doubt the servants were distraught. And his wife? Well, she had been the one to send Agatha away, so what cared he for her state of mind?

From the drawer of his desk, he removed his pistol. Its black, carved handle fit nicely in his hand. He turned it, the barrel pointed at his forehead. He lowered it and stared down the barrel. What would it feel like? Pulling the trigger would be easy, but what happened after? He turned the gun away from himself, pointed it at the window, and fired.

The glass pane exploded with a most satisfying shatter. The voices were louder now, many of them calling out to one another. Servants.

Placing the smoking pistol on the desk, he rose.

Breathing heavily and coughing as he moved through a cloud of gunpowder, he opened the doors of the library. As he stepped into the corridor, several servants stopped their rushing around. Annoyed by the crunching of the tiny shards of glass attaching themselves to the soles of his shoes, he scanned the collection of frightened eyes.

His gaze finally rested on Mrs. Thatcher. Her eyes showed no fear at all, only disgust and accusation. Of course. She was always on his wife's side. He wished Isabella had never brought her here. He knew all about her husband and his criminal past—his gambling, debtor's prison. He had a mind to throw her out of the house. Certainly, that would hurt Isabella in the same way she'd hurt him by expelling Agatha. But then he'd be without a housekeeper. And it was too much trouble to find another one.

Instead, he tightened his jaw and tersely gave instruction. "Mrs. Thatcher, please send someone into the library to clean up the mess."

———— ❧ ————

Later, when the house had grown quiet, Isabella crept downstairs.

He was in the library, and she hated the thought of returning to the library—the room in which she had discovered the scene she'd not been able to shake from her mind. She replayed it over and over again. Agatha's head turning, Bromby's hateful glare.

All morning she'd listened to Bromby destroying the room, and now she knew she must see about him. With a deep breath, she made her way inside. Bromby was facedown at his desk, his forehead flat against the surface, his arms splayed across it—as if he had been shot down in battle and there had fallen.

"B," she said softly.

No response.

The room was quiet except for the mechanical clicking of the gilded clock high upon one of the bookshelves. One item that hadn't been destroyed. She moved closer, her mind churning. Was he drunk? It was only three o'clock in the afternoon, but considering the stress they'd experienced that morning, she wouldn't have been at all surprised if he'd taken to early drinking. She focused on his shoulder blades. Were they moving? Was he breathing?

To the left of one of his outstretched hands, a dark brown bottle rested. The sight of it had become all-too-familiar in the last few weeks. Laudanum—to calm his state of agitation over the money worries. But he carried it around like a pocket watch.

"Bromby." She reached out a hand to touch his back.

He was warm.

He was breathing.

Slowly, his fingers began to move, and he pushed himself into an upright position. Squinting against the light streaming through the windows, he seemed disoriented, glancing at her and looking around him. His face was childlike, devoid of all bitterness and anger. Her heart yielded a little.

"How long have you been sleeping?" It was simply something to say, not that it mattered. The redness of his forehead suggested his face had been pressed against the leather of the desk for some time.

"What time is it?" he croaked.

"'Tis just after three." She straightened a little and crossed her arms.

"I thought I heard you go out."

"I went for a walk midday."

He stretched his arms out before him, cracking his neck from side to side. Recollection settled over his face along with the old bitterness. "Where did you walk?"

"Just around the square."

"Alone?"

"Yes."

"That should have all of Mayfair talking."

Indignant righteousness rose up in her. What did he think? That she had been as faithless as he? "I doubt my brief walk will give them any more to talk about than what you have given them. I seem to recall it was you smashing up the place. Shooting out a window." She looked around her. Whatever had been broken, the servants had lately swept away. Where the window had been, jagged shards of glass hung. A chair was missing. The glass vase from the mantel.

She didn't want to fight with him. That wasn't why she'd come. She moved around the side of the desk and pulled a nearby chair close to him. His eyes remained fixed upon the desktop as she hesitantly laid her hand upon his shoulder.

"I do not understand what is happening to you. What is happening to us? What have I done that has displeased you so?" Even as she asked the question, she knew the answer. She was not her. His poems were rife with the theme. It would always, always be Agatha.

"I do not think marriage agrees with me."

He did have a way with words—they were perfectly formed to devastate her. She flattened her mouth, refusing to cry. "You've fought nearly every moment of this marriage to make certain you're not happy. The glimpses of happiness and love we had on our honeymoon were completely stamped out once we arrived at Sevenoaks. Agatha—"

"Do not bring Agatha into this," he snapped.

"Oh, would you stop!" Isabella sprang from the chair. "You are not to be reasoned with, and I'll not sit beside and coddle you if you insist on clinging to your sin. Have you forgotten that just last night I walked in and saw the two of you…" Isabella broke off, the lump in her throat overwhelming her.

Bromby met her gaze. "Yes. So why do you stay? I told you when I married you that I was wicked—that you ought not to have married me."

"So why *did* you marry me, then?" her voice shrilled. "You waited to tell me after we were married. You left me no choice but to forge ahead. If ever you have perpetrated evil, it was in doing that. I loved you. I love you still." Again, she broke off, incapable of fighting back the tears. They spilled from her eyes, choking out her voice.

Bromby was silent for a few moments. "Perhaps I should go abroad."

He fidgeted with some paper, spreading it out before him and then stacking it again. "When Hobby was by this week, I told him I was thinking about it. Returning to Greece …"

"And you would leave me here with the baby—all alone?"

"No. You would return to Durham with your parents. You could have the baby there. You asked about traveling to Allanstone for your confinement anyway." He said the words as though they made perfect sense.

"Is that really what you want?"

He sighed. "I do not know what I want."

She returned to his side. She must plead her case, make him see sense, else everything would be lost forever. "B, please try. Things do not have to be so bad. I know we are waiting for Broadwell Abbey to sell, but it will. And then our finances will be better. You'll see. And think about the baby. Once he is here, you'll have your heir. And you'll love him. And then … things will be different."

He stared at her as though she spoke a foreign language. "Different? I just want these blasted bailiffs to be gone before you give birth." He stood and moved with an unsteady gate to the door of the library. "Fletcher!" he called out. "Bring me some soda water and biscuits."

Isabella sank down on the divan—one of the few pieces of functional furniture left in the room. Her head throbbed with exhaustion as if she had walked to Camden and back.

Bromby turned and looked at her. "You appear tired, Bell. Perhaps you should lie down." Returning to his desk, he restacked his parchment and dipped his pen into the inkwell.

Thirty-Seven

November 1815

The birth pains started early, waking Isabella from a fitful slumber. She shook Bromby's arm, and when that elicited no response, she sat up in bed and pushed at him. He drank so much brandy and laudanum nowadays that he slept like the dead.

"B, wake up. Wake up. It's time. We'll need to fetch the doctor."

Over the next hour, a dizzying stir of activity ensued—the noise and rattle of preparations. Servants carried in fresh sheets and laid them upon the bed. Bowls of hot water and a multitude of towels soon followed.

When one of the pangs was especially sharp, Isabella cried out. She had promised herself she wouldn't be like the women who screamed and shrieked so loudly the neighbors could hear. But she couldn't help it. She'd never felt pain like that.

From across the room, her maid Clara turned and met her mistress' eyes.

Isabella reached out to her. "You'll stay near me at all times, won't you Clara?" A terrible fear swept over her. Too many women had died in childbirth. They simply went unconscious or bled out, never to awaken.

"Don't you worry," Clara said, clutching Isabella's hand. "I won't leave your side. And I heard from one of the other maids that Lady Meade has just arrived."

"Rebecca," Isabella breathed, closing her eyes. "Send her up as soon as possible."

"I am here already," Rebecca's voice rang from the threshold as she rushed toward her. Clasping Isabella's hand, she leaned forward and kissed her sweating forehead. "How are you? Is the pain very bad?"

"Off and on it is."

The maids brought a chair for Rebecca and positioned it close to the bed.

"You are too good to come. Especially as you are soon to be delivered as well."

Rebecca's eyes sparkled, and her cheeks were flushed from the cold outside. "I still have a while, my dear friend. Barring a natural disaster, forced confinement, or a very early delivery of my own, I would not have missed being here for you."

Piercing agony shot through Isabella's lower back, and she arched herself against it. She clutched hard at Rebecca's hand, while Clara smoothed a damp washcloth over her brow. Within minutes the pain subsided, and she breathed hard to recover. "What time is it?"

Clara looked behind her at the clock on the table. "'Tis half past ten, milady."

"Where is the doctor?"

"He's been sent for. Should be here anytime."

Time seemed to crawl as the pain intensified, came with more regularity, and the moments of relief grew shorter. Isabella's head whirled with recurring images—Bromby, Agatha, her parents, David Beringer ... Rebecca's eyes were so like his ...

The doctor arrived just as the intervals of relief ended. Isabella barely noticed his arrival. She no longer cared about holding in her screams as they echoed against the high ceilings of the bedroom. The sounds of her own pain intensified her fear.

From downstairs, the sound of breaking glass rippled through the house.

Not again!

Isabella shot a questioning gaze toward Clara, who finally slipped out of the room. More voices mingled in the hallway.

Rebecca squeezed Isabella's hand and murmured, "Almost there. The baby will be here in no time at all now."

Was that Agatha's voice outside the door? No, it couldn't be. Yet it sounded just like her voice echoing through the halls.

As the doctor instructed Isabella to push, Clara reentered the room.

Rebecca beckoned Clara to her side, asking softly, "What is happening down there?"

"Fletcher is hiding Lord Bromby's pistols, and the other maids are cleaning up brandy from the smashed decanters. He has been knocking off the heads of the bottles with a poker stick," Clara rasped.

"What?" Rebecca's eyes widened. Shaking her head, she turned back to Isabella. "You're doing so well, Izzy. It will all be over soon."

Isabella could not think about what went on downstairs. She had to concentrate on delivering the baby.

God forgive me for marrying a man who does not worship you. Please do not hold it against our child. Our poor child ...

A cry other than her own pierced the room, bringing her back to her senses.

"It is one o'clock," pronounced the doctor, "and a little girl is born to you."

Isabella lay panting against the pillows as Clara continued to wipe her brow. The squalling child was washed and wrapped, and within minutes laid in Isabella's arms.

"She is beautiful," Rebecca sighed. "Oh, and she is perfect."

For the moment, Isabella forgot all about her husband, pistols, and smashed decanters. She gazed into the eyes of her little girl, and love like she'd never known coursed through her, flooding her body with an intensity that surpassed all other feelings and fears. This was what mattered now. Only this.

Several minutes later, Lord Bromby was called into the room. He paused in the doorway, his face pale, his eyes glassy.

"You have a daughter, Lord Bromby," crowed Rebecca. "A beautiful baby girl."

As he approached, Isabella hoped that the grim expression on his face might soften when he saw his daughter. He lifted the child from Isabella's arms and stared into her mewling face before placing her on the bed and unwrapping her blankets to reveal her kicking feet. The room grew quiet as he inspected both feet, counting her toes.

"Her feet are fine. She has no deformities." His shoulders relaxed.

"No, of course she does not," said Isabella. "She is perfect. What shall we name her, B?"

He turned his eyes to the ceiling and seemed to ponder this. Everyone in the room appeared to hold their breath, waiting for his pronouncement. Would he suggest his mother's name? Or perhaps even Ophelia—after Lady Melwood.

Tapping his finger against his chin, he said finally: "What if we name her ... Agatha?"

Thirty-Eight

January 1816

Sitting across the desk from Dr. Francis Ballard in Doughty Street, Isabella fidgeted with the reticule in her lap. She could not sit still. Was she doing the right thing?

"I remember you once treated him for his lame leg," she explained to Dr. Ballard. "I thought ... well, I have no one else to turn to." She slid a book over the desktop surface toward him. "It is the *Medical Journal*. You will see I have marked some pages."

Dr. Ballard received the book and opened it to the portion marked with a red piece of silk. His mouth twitched as his bespectacled gaze wandered across the pages upon which she had drawn arrows, underlined passages, circled words, and written notes in the margins. "What are his symptoms?" he asked in a deep, sonorous voice.

She was almost too embarrassed to say the words. "He returns again and again to this idea that he is doomed—predestined for damnation. Declared so from birth. I have heard the same words for an entire year." She shook her head, looking down at her hands as she twisted a damp handkerchief.

He nodded. "Obsessive notions. What else?" He stared at the annotated pages.

Isabella took a deep breath. "He says that he has done evil by marrying me. That he was a fool for going through with it. Based upon things done in his past—behaviors to which I am not privy, nor do I wish to be—he has determined that he can never be anything but a villain."

"Interesting," breathed Dr. Ballard, turning the page to look at more scribblings and underlines. "Is he ever ... violent?"

Isabella's face burned. "Yes. More often now than before. He ... breaks things ... rants, raves ... wakes in the night with dreams in which he says he is tormented."

"How much liquor does he consume?"

"Ever so much brandy … and laudanum, as of late. There are bottles of it all around."

"Laudanum?" Dr. Ballard looked up and pushed the book aside. "Laudanum is very dangerous if not used properly."

"He says he takes it for his nerves."

He leaned forward, placing his forearms upon the desk and touching his fingertips together. "Lady Bromby, could you speak to the level of your fear?"

She sniffed. "I am fearful for my child, Dr. Ballard. But I confess I am just as fearful for Lord Bromby's sanity. He appears to be going mad. And now he wishes to travel abroad—which he did once before several years ago. It is my understanding that some of the evil he speaks of took place abroad, and I wonder—should I tolerate, allow him to indulge his whims and fancies? Are we to stay behind knowing that he is there and doing … whatever it is he wishes to do?"

Dr. Ballard nodded. "No, you are quite right. You are right to come and see me. I am concerned about his laudanum use. We must be discreet, of course. But we must watch him. I will come to the house and examine him. Are you willing to concoct a reason for my visit? Perhaps that he has been looking pale or some such thing?"

"Yes, of course, Doctor. Anything. My marriage depends upon it."

As Dr. Ballard prepared to depart 13 Piccadilly Terrace that afternoon, Isabella knew they had not fooled anyone.

Before leaving, Dr. Ballard expressed his concerns regarding Bromby's health. "You are consuming too much alcohol, Lord Bromby. I suspect your liver is bad, and that is why your coloring is poor. Combining brandy with laudanum is a bad combination. It's sure to addle your brain at the very least."

"And what is your recommendation, Doctor?" Bromby asked with a wry expression. "Perhaps I should take a respite in the country? Fresh sea air? Wholesome company? Clean thoughts?" Bromby turned his head to glare at Isabella—his eyes dark with knowing and accusation. *You called him here. You think you can control me.*

Isabella's heart clenched with dread.

"Yes," said Doctor Ballard. "With your wife accompanying you, I'd say that would be a fine idea."

"Yes," Bromby sneered. "I am sure my wife would say so as well." His mordant gaze chilled her. She had only made things worse.

———————— ⌖ ————————

That night, Isabella startled awake. She immediately sat up. What was happening?

Bromby's voice echoed down the corridor. "I shall end it all!"

Isabella pushed herself from the bed, disentangling her foot from the bedsheets, and emerged from the bedchamber into the cold darkness of the hall.

Bromby stood a few feet away—his back to her. Without an illuminating candle, she could only make out the outline of his form illuminated against the window at the other end. He was more like a shadow than a man.

As her eyes adjusted, her heart jolted at the distinct outline of a steely pistol—two, in fact—each of his hands holding one aloft.

"B!" she called out to him instinctively.

He turned, leveling one of the pistols in her direction. She gasped and sank back into the bedroom, expecting to hear the gun fire and feel the blast through her chest at any moment. Instead, Fletcher's voice eclipsed her sounds of shock.

"I think you may be sleepwalking, Lord Bromby." Fletcher stepped out of the shadows.

"What?"

"Sleepwalking. Dangerous practice to stalk the halls with your dueling pistols. Let's get you back to bed, shall we?"

"I'm going to end it all tonight, Fletcher. All of this wretched life of torture!" Bromby's words were slurred.

Fletcher's voice was placating. "Not a good night for it, milord. Nasty weather. Maybe another night. Travels to the next life are always done best in good weather. Let us put the pistols away, shall we?"

Fletcher moved slowly. His eyes grazed Isabella's as he placed his hand over Bromby's wrists and pushed them down, forcing him to lower the pistols. Fletcher walked Bromby down the hallway as though he were an invalid. They moved away from her, their feet shuffling. Fletcher spoke calmly, making light of the madness.

Without warning, a fit of sobbing overcame her. She covered her face with her hands. A plaintive cry echoed through the halls. The baby.

Hurrying toward the sound, she darted down the corridor and into the room where the French nurse, Mathilde, held the little girl in her arms.

"Let me take her." Isabella lifted the warm bundle and held her tightly against her chest. Moving to the window, Isabella swayed and patted the baby while staring out the frosty panes. The wind whipped the trees from side to side, and a cold rain puddled in the street.

This was the last thread. She could hold out no longer. No matter what, she had to protect her daughter. She would go to her parents. At least until Bromby's sanity could be recovered, she could no longer risk their safety.

Undeserving as she was, God had given her this child, Ada Agatha—the second name given to appease Bromby—and she would raise this little girl in a home of love and prayer.

If Ada couldn't know her earthly father, she would certainly know her heavenly one.

The next morning, Isabella wrote to her parents at Halford Hall, their home in Kent, for the month of January. They had prepared to pay a visit to her and the new child in London, and she would intercept them before they traveled to her.

Do not come to London as you originally planned. Ada and I shall join you at Halford Hall instead. We will depart for Kent on 14 January. I have no idea that B will accompany us, but you shall see your granddaughter, Ada Agatha. She is beautiful with bright blue eyes and a full head of black curls. Clara will travel with us, as well as our newly acquired nurse, Mathilde. I am ever so anxious to see you both.

"I'll miss you ever so much, ma'am." Mrs. Thatcher said, dabbing at her eyes. "I don't know how this house will continue on while you're in Kent."

Standing at the window, Isabella turned to look out over the garden. She suddenly had a strange notion that she might never see it again.

"I will leave the maintenance of this house in your capable hands, Mrs. Thatcher. Lord Bromby will need the assurance of a regular schedule here. The house should run exactly as it has all along." Guilt washed over her. She feared she was leaving the servants to his tirades now—replacing her own endangered state with theirs. "See to it that you water the brandy down as much as possible, you and Fletcher. The less of it he drinks full strength, the better."

"Yes, ma'am. I know the method."

Over the past year, the housekeeper had been invaluable to her. She'd been a companion and confidant to Isabella. She was good at her job, but she was also discreet and didn't gossip as the other servants did. If society heard about the goings-on at 13 Piccadilly Terrace, it would not be because of Mrs. Thatcher's flapping tongue.

"I owe you a great deal of gratitude, milady," she sniffed. "If not for you …"

"Shh." Isabella grasped her hand. "Let us speak no more about it. And Ada and I shall see you … well, I don't know how long we shall stay with my parents, but I hope to return … sometime in the near future."

Mrs. Thatcher nodded, but her eyes drooped. "I have doubts you will ever return. May I speak plainly, milady?"

"Of course. I always value your good opinion."

"It pains me to see you in such a state. I remember when I first saw you at Broadwell Abbey. You looked so young, so hopeful. But even then, I recognized in you what I once knew in myself."

Isabella swallowed, bracing herself. "What was that, Mrs. Thatcher?"

"Idolatry."

The word touched something deep inside of her. The pronouncement rang true. Even so, she was loath to confess it. "I'm sure I don't know what you mean."

"Forgive me, milady. But I mean idolatry for Lord Bromby. Just like I had for my Elliot Thatcher. I worshipped him in a way that no human man should ever be worshipped."

Isabella felt a pinch in her throat as tears sprang to her eyes. Mrs. Thatcher was right. Her love for Bromby had been all consuming, eclipsing even her relationship with the Almighty. And if she'd taken the time to listen for his still, small voice, she might never have succumbed.

Isabella swiped an escaping tear from her cheek.

"I mean no offense, milady. I, too, had to learn that my husband was just a man. I'd lifted him up to a place where he was higher than God. Until I found out that he was just a mortal. And a sinner. And not worthy to be praised."

Isabella nodded, and she fought the sob that threatened to escape from her throat. "You are right, Mrs. Thatcher. I am guilty of idolatry. And now I must pay for my sins."

Mrs. Thatcher met her gaze. "I don't know how many times I've heard you say to Lord Bromby that our Savior is faithful and just to forgive sins. Do you not believe that for yourself?"

Isabella swallowed. "Of course, I do." But did she really? She couldn't be sure. With her heart so heavy and punctured by all that had occurred, it was hard to believe in redemption.

Fletcher appeared in the doorway. "Lady Bromby, the bailiffs are here again."

She nodded. The bailiffs came regularly. She'd grown accustomed to them, even knew a few of their names. They barely had anything left to give them.. "I'll see to them."

"And there's a Lady Beringer and Mr. Beringer here to see you, ma'am."

Isabella shot up out of her chair, whirling in surprise. "What?" Her heart sank. How mortifying that the Beringers should arrive just in time to witness their disgrace and degradation.

"Yes. Shall I show them in?"

Isabella's heart pounded. What did it matter now? "Yes, I suppose so, Fletcher. Thank you."

She glanced at Mrs. Thatcher. The housekeeper's eyebrow arched. "Bad timing, milady."

Isabella dropped her head. "Yes, indeed."

With leaden feet, Isabella made her way toward the drawing room. Voices from the foyer stopped her on the landing, and she listened from above.

"...here for the books—the library collection."

Lady Beringer's voice trilled. "Oh, do you hear, David? They are here to take the Brombys' library."

"Yes, Mother. I do hear."

More mumblings and low voices ensued. Isabella wished for a sudden, natural disaster—anything to assuage the humiliation. Dizziness threatened her, and she stood back from the stairs. How could she face the Beringers in the light of such shame?

Lady Beringer's voice crested again. "David, is there nothing we can do to help?"

"Yes," David said. "Please. Allow me to offer payment for the value of the books. I am only too happy to oblige."

Was it possible for one to die from mortification? Isabella thought it might be. Her heart, brain, and limbs all seemed to shut down simultaneously. She wasn't even sure she could manage the rest of the walk to the drawing room.

Nevertheless, a few moments later, Isabella stood before Lady Beringer and David. Her face burned, but her hands perspired. She could barely meet either of their gazes.

"My gratitude is only overshadowed by my complete humiliation," she finally managed.

"Nonsense," said Lady Beringer. "No one need know anything about this."

Isabella forced herself to look at the older woman's face.

A few strands of gray appeared at the sides of Lady Beringer's hair as she removed her bonnet and ran her hands over the lace cap underneath. "Everybody needs help from time to time."

Yes, but this was above and beyond.

David cleared his throat. "I'm only glad we were here to help. It would have been a terrible loss."

As she looked at David, a burning began at the backs of Isabella's eyes. She tried to remember the lightness and ease of his face when she'd first met him. In the past four years, his eyes had gained a soulfulness, a sadness—the type borne of living life and seeing its unhappiness and strife brought to others. Even so, the kindness had not left them. His smile may have tempered in its exuberance, but it still offered warmth and sincerity.

"I do not know how we can repay you." Her voice trembled. "Once Broadwell Abbey sells, I will reimburse you. With interest, of course."

"Absolutely not. I won't hear of it," David said. "I would prefer you say nothing of this to your husband, Lady Bromby. It is sometimes difficult for gentlemen to accept help when it's needed."

"Oh, but I must, Mr. Beringer. I cannot allow you to …" She broke off, the lump in her throat rendering speech nearly impossible.

Lady Beringer waved her hand. "Let us speak no more about it." She grasped Isabella's hands in a manner reminiscent of Rebecca's. In Lady Beringer's eyes, Isabella glimpsed the same compassion that graced David's.

She swallowed. "Won't you both please sit down?"

Lady Beringer sat on the sofa next to Isabella.

David continued to stand. "Lady Bromby, we do not wish to interrupt your preparations for departure. My sister informs us that you're to make your way to Kent tomorrow, and as we are on our way there ourselves, we should like to accompany you—to escort you."

"The roads this time of year can be treacherous, and with a newborn … well, it is not safe for you to travel alone," said Lady Beringer.

Isabella struggled to maintain control over her emotions. It touched her that they cared for her safety and thought to offer protection.

"Thank you so much. But you have already done far too much for me. I couldn't ask you to go to so much trouble. I shall have my maid and Ada's nurse traveling with me."

"We will have our own carriage, of course," David added quickly. "We ask only that we may stay close behind and ensure your safe delivery to Halford Hall."

Staring up into David's troubled eyes, the solemn set of his chin and mouth, tears threatened to beat down the door of her resolve. She fought them back and dropped her gaze.

"I am humbled by your generosity. I fear, though, I should not accept—"

"Nonsense," said Lady Beringer. "We would do the same for Rebecca if she were traveling alone." Her voice softened. "And we look on you quite as our own daughter. And David sees you like a sister. Do you not, David?"

He nodded silently. His Adam's apple bobbed with a swallow. "Quite like a sister."

Isabella wrenched her gaze from his. "Very well. For Ada's sake, I accept your offer."

A half an hour later, Isabella and Mrs. Thatcher saw the Beringers off. Both women stared out the foyer windows as the carriage departed.

Once the Beringers had pulled away, Mrs. Thatcher turned to Isabella. "If you did not believe that the Lord cares for your troubles before, milady, you must believe it now."

Thirty-Nine

There had been nights during their honeymoon when quiet, snow-laden evenings had been quite wonderful. But now, the wind howled around Piccadilly Terrace, and a cacophony of ice pellets assaulted the roof. Isabella chose not to tell Bromby about the bailiffs or the Beringers' generosity. His state of mind was precarious enough as it was. He sat and stared into the fire, slumped so far down in his chair that his chin tucked into the collar of his shirt.

"They say the weather is to be especially bad this year. Something to do with Mt. Tambora's eruption in the East Indies last year." Isabella hoped for some conversation to spring up between them—words that might rekindle what once was. "They say no eruption like that has taken place in that part of the world for over a thousand years.

"I have seen her again." Bromby spoke suddenly, his voice low and clouded.

"Who?"

"Agatha."

Her heart faltered. "When?"

"The night you gave birth to Ada."

Isabella closed her eyes. All the air seemed to leave her body with one long exhale. So it had been Agatha's voice she'd heard that afternoon.

"When I heard your screams, I sent for her."

"Why?"

He turned his head slowly to look at her. The dilated state of his eyes suggested he'd already taken laudanum this evening. "Because I couldn't bear the screaming. Your pain. I was the cause of it. And what if you'd died? I needed her."

Isabella clenched her jaw and swallowed. "And, how was she?"

"She did nothing but talk of you. She's far more concerned for your welfare than for mine. She seeks nothing other than your forgiveness … and your happiness."

"I do forgive her."

A silence consumed the room. Bromby turned back to the fire, and Isabella moved toward him, lowering herself to sit on the floor beside his footrest. Looking up at him, she placed her hands on his lame leg propped up beside her. He flinched, and his face changed—his eyebrows knitting together as his forehead compressed.

This may be the last time I ever touch him.

"I wonder when we three shall ever meet again." His voice cracked.

Isabella exhaled a long, shaky breath. "I hope we shall all meet again in heaven."

He rolled his head against the back of the chair and closed his eyes. For a moment she wondered if he had fallen asleep, but then his lips moved. "You depart for Kent tomorrow."

"Yes. Early in the morning."

He nodded. "That is for the best. You should leave as soon as possible."

His words were darts in her soul. He longed for her to be gone. He was burdened by her very presence. There may have been some part of him that loved her, but it was too much for him to feel it. Loving her required him to love God's presence within her, and he could not do it. In fact, he'd tried to kill that part of her, but he couldn't do that either.

He'd challenged God and lost.

But her heart still ached with every throb.

"I wish you would ask me to stay." Her gaze wandered from Bromby's face illuminated in the firelight to a mat on the floor where his Irish wolfhound lay at his feet by the fireplace. The pelting ice outside had frightened the dog into a hiding place in some other part of the house. A strange notion overtook her—one in which she thought to curl up on that mat like his faithful dog.

Perhaps they couldn't live together now, but she'd wait for him to realize the folly of his ways and return to her. But then she thought of Ada and recovered her senses. No, she would never degrade herself so.

"Why would I do that?" he asked. "You have said you must go, and I agree. Time apart will do us good. It will no doubt be a welcome change for you."

"Would it change anything if I told you that I do not wish to go?" The words sounded pathetic even to her, but it was her last attempt to change this ship's course.

He didn't open his eyes but rolled his head slowly from side to side. "No. I would still tell you to go."

———————— ❧ ————————

The following morning, David and Lady Beringer traveled with Isabella into Kent. Despite her heaviness of heart, Isabella was relieved to know their carriage was behind hers. It was God's protection and provision to have another party so interested in her safe passage.

Upon the party's arrival in Kent, Sir Ralph and Lady Bankmill were equally thankful for the escort their daughter had been afforded.

"Won't you stay the night, or at least stay for dinner," Sir Ralph offered.

"We thank you, Sir Ralph, but we cannot." David smiled. "We have yet another hour's worth of travel before we reach Holly Bridge. We should carry on."

"As you wish, as you wish." Sir Ralph patted David on the shoulder.

When they all returned outside to see the Beringers off again, Isabella glimpsed her mother and Lady Beringer standing a few feet off from the others. Their faces were serious as they whispered to one another. Isabella could guess what they were talking about.

David moved toward her, his eyes lowered. "Lady Bromby, if you or Ada need anything—anything at all—you will send for me, will you not?"

A shiver ran through her as she looked up at him. "You've done too much for us, Mr. Beringer. You've been far too kind. I couldn't trespass on your generosity again."

He stepped closer with lined forehead and furrowed brow. "I insist that you promise, Lady Bromby. If you need anything at all …"

She nodded. "Yes, of course, I will. Thank you."

"My desire to be of assistance to you isn't exhaustive. I would do anything to help you."

Blinking, Isabella fought tears and a lump welled into her throat. "Thank you. I shall either have to return to London in a few weeks, else I'll travel on to Durham with my parents."

David's eyebrows compressed, and his forehead lined. "You're shivering. You should return inside at once. You'll catch cold." He bowed to her and moved quickly to the carriage where he handed his mother inside before climbing in himself.

Isabella and her parents stood and waved as the carriage moved down the length of the drive.

"Come, dear," her mother said, putting her arm around her daughter's shoulders. "Let us go inside."

It was difficult to tear her eyes away from the departing carriage. A crushing pain seized her heart, filling her chest with a dull ache and an acidic taste in her mouth. How had she come to this end? As the realization sank in that she was now in the safe harbor of her parents' home, the tears she'd fought exploded. She nearly dropped to the ground with the simultaneous force of her grief and liberation.

She had left Bromby.

Forty

February 1816
Kent

"I understand he has an army of people staying in the house with him." Sir Ralph held a letter over his empty breakfast plate, scanning its contents.

"Who is it from?" asked Lady Bankmill.

"Oh, from Charles Kirkby. One of Bromby's creditors we paid off in November. He went by the house to settle up with some remaining balance or other and says that Bromby has a house full of guards, so to speak. Young George Bromby, his cousin and next in line for the barony, has installed himself in the place to watch over him, make sure he doesn't off himself or anything like that. And apparently, a Dr. Ballard is paying daily visits. There is some concern he might have suffered a slight stroke."

Isabella dropped her knife. "A stroke?"

"Oh, we could only hope," Lady Bankmill mumbled just before depositing a bite of bread into her mouth.

"Mamma!" Isabella scolded before turning to her father "He said nothing of this to me in his last letter."

Now it was Lady Bankmill's knife that clattered to her plate. "He is still writing you letters? Whatever for? Do not write him, Isabella.."

"He is still my husband, Mamma. Whatever you may think of him, we are still married. And we shall remain so … whether I ever live with him again or not."

Sir Ralph shot her a bespectacled glance over the top of the letter. "It says here that Agatha Morley and her oldest daughter are also lodging at 13 Piccadilly Terrace."

An acidic brewing in her stomach caused Isabella to hold her hand over her mouth, forcing a hiccupping sound.

"Perhaps," continued Sir Ralph, "that would account for the fact that my first letter to Lord Bromby requesting a formal separation was returned. Would you say that's her handwriting, Isabella?"

With bile rising in her throat, Isabella glimpsed the writing on the front of the envelope. She nodded. Yes, that was Agatha's writing.

Sir Ralph rose from the table holding both letters in his hand. "No matter. I am to travel to London next week. I shall simply deliver it myself."

"When are we to leave for Durham?" Lady Bankmill asked. "I am more than ready to go."

"As soon as I return from London." Sir Ralph glanced at Isabella. "And you shall come with us, my dear. You and Ada. We will take you home."

Isabella fought the urge to scream. She did not want this. Oh, how she wished things could return to what they once were. Either that or her heart could become disengaged from Bromby, and when they returned to Durham and Seacrest Hall she could live there happily with her parents as she once had, or that she could live with Bromby again—not as they had been, but as they *could have been.*

Lady Bankmill's hand covered hers as Isabella's gaze followed her father's retreating back. "You know this is all for the best, dear. Think of Ada."

"I am thinking of Ada, Mamma. And the fact that she shan't know her father."

"Her father is a madman," Lady Bankmill retorted. "And a philanderer, and … well, who knows what else. A fiend! That's what he is. And I knew it all along."

If only she hadn't told her parents so much, given them ammunition against Bromby and Agatha Morley. Now their names and reputations would both be ruined, and she would be tainted by association. No one in society would ever solicit her company again. A scandal was a scandal no matter who was to blame.

She hardly minded for herself. She could hide out in Durham for the rest of her days, but for Ada … she didn't want her daughter to be looked at as an untouchable.

On her knees by her bedside, she prayed for mercy upon her daughter. And she prayed for Bromby—that God might yet save him.

On the day her father was to travel to London, Isabella received a letter from Rebecca. She was overjoyed when she saw the writing and the Meade seal on the back. She tore it open, anxious to read her friend's words. The letter was mainly an announcement that Rebecca had given birth to twin boys: Nash Malcolm Meade and Gabriel David Meade.

Rebecca's letter didn't mention society's reaction to Isabella's current living situation, and for this she was thankful. Once this news reached the ears of Lady Melwood and Lady Catherine, it would spread with ferocity. Especially after her father delivered the letter to Piccadilly Terrace. Everyone would be talking and speculating about the separation.

Rebecca's letter ended with a paragraph completely unrelated to all her other news.

Finally, dear Izzy, I write on behalf of my brother, who will be paying a visit to my aunt in Scotland at the end of April. He wishes to ascertain your willingness for a visit from an old friend. If you are amenable to the idea, he will break his journey in Seaham where he will stay at the inn. If you or your family is indisposed, then he will stop in York instead.

David Beringer was coming to Seaham? Her heart soared at the possibility. She longed to see an old friend. She already felt lonely and isolated, and each day required every ounce of resistance to keep her from returning to Piccadilly Terrace.

She returned Rebecca's letter with the resounding message: *Please tell your brother to break his journey in Seaham. We would love to receive him.*

The very same day, she received a letter from Mrs. Thatcher. From the second paragraph of the missive, Isabella's heart fell.

Things are very bad here. I am writing to give you notice, milady, which I have already given Lord Bromby. I do not believe it safe to stay. I do not need to detail all that we endure under Lord Bromby's tantrums and tirades, but his behavior has become reckless. One night he returned from the theater at three o'clock in the morning and left the front door wide open. We were all fortunate not to have been murdered in our beds!

Fletcher and I have attempted to add water to both the laudanum and the brandy, but Lord Bromby now locks them up.

I shall return to my husband's house by the end of the week. He has troubles of his own, and I should be with him.

Isabella laid the letter aside and wiped a tear from her eye. She was not surprised, and she'd worried about this very outcome when she left

London. But Mrs. Thatcher's letter reassured her she'd done the right thing in leaving. If his behavior was increasingly erratic, and there was no sign of any positive change, then she must continue with her present course of action. As much as it broke her heart.

Forty-One

Bromby flung the letter across the room. "What is this?" John Hobby retrieved it from the floor. "It is a letter from your father-in-law."

"Yes, I know what it is, Hobby. I'm not an imbecile. 'Tis a letter requesting a formal separation, is it not?"

John picked up the letter and perused the words on the page as though he hadn't read it already. "The Bankmills are seeking *divortium a mensa et thoro*, thereby you will continue to be legally married, but you will not live together. He asks that you send any of Lady Bromby's remaining belongings to Seacrest Hall, where she will reside for the foreseeable future."

With a cry Bromby barely recognized as his own voice, he grasped at his hair and turned to pace a circle around the study. How could this have happened? Why on earth would she want a formal separation? He'd been expecting her imminent return any day now. He'd even thought to write to her today and ask when she would return. She'd been gone a month. It was time.

"On what grounds do they seek this … *separation?*" He spat the word as though he'd bitten into a rotten apple and now wished to expel the morsel.

John's voice was calm as he explained. "Sir Ralph writes that you dismissed Lady Bromby from your house—"

"Dismissed her? I did no such thing. I didn't dismiss her. She left of her own volition. She left upon medical advice. She left on very good terms. Nothing but harmonious." Bromby couldn't imagine why his father-in-law would make such an accusation. He'd never have done such a thing. At least, not that he could remember.

Hobby eyed him with a look that suggested his skepticism and cleared his throat. "The letter also states that you treated her very ill."

"What? Treated her ill? When did I ever treat her ill?" He tried to remember a specific incident that would have counted as such. She'd seen him in bad moods, and perhaps she'd seen him in a temper time and again, but he had no recollection of ever treating her badly. Not really. Had he?

He paused, gnawing upon his thumbnail. "This simply cannot happen. Two of my poems are being published this week. Rumors of this sort will materially damage their reception."

Hobby stared at Bromby with a slack mouth, his eyes drooping. "Bromby, is that really your concern in all of this? How it will affect your literary following? What of your wife? What of your daughter?"

Bromby shook his head. Their absence had relegated Isabella and Ada to a nearly nonexistent status, but he had to admit there was something in him that missed them. Especially Isabella. She'd always been kind to him. She'd always loved him no matter what. And now, he'd lost her. Perhaps there was something to the accusation of poor treatment after all. He hadn't been the best husband to her …

Hobby continued to read. "And he also says there is a strong suspicion of … of marital infidelity."

Bromby collapsed into a chair, running both hands through his tangled hair. He clenched his eyes shut. He would definitely need laudanum—and quite a lot of it—to get through the rest of this afternoon,. "She means to destroy me."

John looked at his friend over the top of the paper. "There is no proof of this. It will not hold up in court. Her word alone cannot prove adultery."

Bromby pulled his fingers from his hair and dragged them down the front of his face, painfully pulling several strands from his head in the process. "Her word alone can destroy my standing in all good society." He knew his friend couldn't argue with this, nor did he. "We should take this to court. I will clear my name and prove she was wrong in her allegations."

"I would not advise it," Hobby said. "If a trial stretches out for long enough, with enough … eh, witnesses … something could be proven against you." His friend was speaking of Lady Catherine, of course. No doubt she would flock to such a spectacle with all her minions in place, ready to spout all sorts of nonsense about him.

John Hobby cleared his throat. "I would recommend Agatha and her daughter move back into the lodgings at St. James's Place as soon as may be."

"Yes," Bromby said absently.

Funny. Now that there was absolutely nothing between him and Agatha other than friendship, he was being accused of infidelity.

His mind whirred with what to do. How long could the news of this separation be repressed? Not long, he suspected. No doubt rumors already flew from the lips of that traitorous housekeeper, Mrs. Thatcher. And who knew what Lady Catherine circulated these days? With the release of her blasted novel, people were already speculating that he was the fiendish vampire character—Lord Bellevue, or whatever the name.

And how far did his wife plan to take this separation from a legal standpoint? His name would be ruined—he would become *persona non-grata*.

In one swift movement, Bromby propelled himself from his chair and moved across the room to the small leather chest upon a table. Removing a set of keys from his pocket, he unlocked the case, opened the lid, and pulled the clear bottle from between the brandy decanters. He popped off the cork and drank a large swallow of the laudanum. He knew what he would do. He would have to. It was the only thing he could do.

"I shall go abroad, Hobby. At once."

"Italy?"

"Yes. Italy. Or perhaps Greece. England is not for me. Best to leave before things become too uncomfortable. If she wishes to live apart, then I shall have to abide by that. But in this way, we may avoid the legal complications."

He swilled from the bottle again and paced across the room. Yes. Immediate exile was his only solution. No one in Italy would care what he'd done. They would accept him there.

He stopped pacing momentarily, the gravity of his condition resting heavily upon him. He turned to face John Hobby. "You see, Hobby? I've been telling you all along. I'm a Bromby, and I'm doomed. Cursed from birth."

Hobby stood slowly, still holding the letter in his hand. He shook his head sadly and looked up at his friend. "Bromby, you know I love you dearly. But many of the situations you face are of your own doing. I would venture to say that as you are exiling yourself now, you have cursed yourself all your life. Speaking doom and gloom over all your days. Nothing good can come of that."

Bromby laughed a little. Perhaps Hobby was right. But perhaps it was just as his mother had told him all those years ago … just as the fortune teller had told him … just as Nurse Green had told him…

Forty-Two

David Beringer moved along the busy streets of London. He had just left a business meeting with Mr. Shackleford, his banker. David had decided upon the future sight of his long-held notion for an orphanage in the country, and now he only hoped the seller would be amenable.

Usually, this was the day of the week he attended the Alfred Club, but he'd stopped going as of late. He understood that Bromby was no longer attending either. Therefore, to speak with the man, he'd have to go to Bromby's house. As much as he didn't wish to do so.

As he approached 13 Piccadilly Terrace, a young woman strolled along the street in front of him, pushing a perambulator. From the back of her blue bonnet, wisps of brown hair trailed. From behind, the woman could have been Isabella. She must have felt his stare, as she whipped her gaze to the right in time to meet his. He looked quickly away and hung back, allowing her to move in front of him.

Of course, it was not her. Isabella was in Durham, where he would soon be visiting her.

Why wouldn't God remove her from his heart?

Thinking of her does me no good. Even if she no longer lives with him, she's still a married woman.

But this was not about him. His decision to purchase Broadwell Abbey was for the good of the orphans. It would help Bromby pay off his remaining debts, thereby helping Isabella. It was what he was supposed to do.

Just as he arrived, the door opened. Servants emerged, carrying trunks and cases.

"I beg your pardon." He stepped out of the way, allowing them to pass. He recognized Fletcher, Bromby's manservant, carrying a box to an awaiting carriage. He caught his eye.

"I should like to see Lord Bromby." He extended his card.

Fletcher put down the box and took his card. "I'll see if he's at home, Mr. Beringer."

David readjusted his top hat and waited as Fletcher disappeared inside.

Although he had no desire to meet with Lord Bromby in person, the matter was too important simply to ask his attorney to send a letter.

Some time passed, and more trunks were carried to awaiting carriages. Was Bromby going on a journey? Perhaps he was moving out of Piccadilly Terrace.

A few moments later Fletcher returned, and David followed him inside. From the state of the foyer, it was clear that Bromby was moving out. Maids and servants rushed here and there, carrying boxes and trunks, and any remaining furniture was covered.

Bailiffs scribbled upon paper as objects were removed from the house. "Take the parrot, too. Oh, and that trunk of things."

"Those things belong to Mr. Fletcher!" exclaimed one of the maids.

"Don't care," said the bailiff. "It'll serve for the monies owed in arrears."

Fletcher seemed unfazed by the activities. He led David down the corridor to a room he assumed had been the library. Nothing remained inside except for a leather chair in which Bromby sat, dressed for travel in a long, black coat and heavy scarf.

"Lord Bromby." David removed his hat and nodded.

Bromby looked up. "Mr. Beringer." His eyes appeared wider than usual, more dilated. "I would ask you to sit, but as you see…" He motioned with his hand to the emptiness of the room. "The bailiffs have taken everything."

This was uncomfortable … and it must have been for Bromby too … a humiliating spectacle. "Are you going on a journey, sir?"

"In a few hours, I will be en route to Italy."

This was news. "Italy? What on earth do you do in Italy?"

Bromby's jaw set as he stared past David. "I'm sure you know of my troubles, Mr. Beringer. The rest of the country does. My present situation makes it impossible for me to remain in England any longer. I must go where I will not be under the constant scrutiny of others."

"I see." David wondered if Isabella knew of this. "Well, sir, I won't take any more of your time than necessary. I have come because I'd like to purchase Broadwell Abbey."

Bromby turned his head slowly. "What? Purchase Broadwell Abbey? Whatever for?"

"For some time now, I have searched for the right place to secure an orphanage and foundling hospital—a large one in the country. Broadwell Abbey seems the perfect location."

Bromby appeared to mentally debate the seriousness of David's offer. "A foundling hospital? At Broadwell Abbey? Are you joking?"

"I am perfectly serious. And I've just come from my banker and am prepared to pay your asking price of £94,500."

Bromby stood. With his hand over his mouth, he walked in a circle, looking at the ground. His limp seemed more pronounced. Finally, he stopped and stared at David. "I still don't understand. Why Broadwell Abbey?"

David exhaled. He daren't assault Bromby's pride by hinting that he knew of his money woes. "I believe it is the right thing to do, Lord Bromby. The purchase will help many people."

"Are you aware that the place is haunted? Nothing good has ever come of that property."

David shrugged, undaunted. "Well. Perhaps now something shall."

More circular pacing. Bromby stopped again. "Orphans? At Broadwell Abbey. I would never have imagined." A small smile pulled at the corners of his mouth.

"May we agree upon the sale, then?"

Lord Bromby sat once more, his eyes wide and staring straight ahead. "I have proved to be a terrible husband and father, Mr. Beringer. The most basic of God's roles for man, and I have failed." He looked up at David.

David thought to politely protest, but he stopped himself. He couldn't deny the truth of Bromby's statement. "I am sorry for your pains, sir."

Bromby shook his head, his gaze scanning the floor. "I did love her, you know. In my way. I still love her, I suppose. It is as though her absence has made my feelings for her stronger. That's a strange thing. Don't you think, Mr. Beringer?"

David nodded. "Yes, it is strange." He suddenly felt sorry for him. How terrible to be unable to show love. Bromby had been given gifts of immeasurable worth, yet he was unable—too damaged, perhaps—to appreciate the blessing.

"It's just that … oh, never mind. I have only myself to blame." Lord Bromby looked up at David again, his forehead lined. "Isabella always told me that God would forgive me my sins. Do you think that's true, Mr. Beringer?"

David nodded, encouraged by Bromby's words. "Yes, I believe that absolutely."

"Even for someone as wretched as I?" Bromby's eyes appeared tired, older than his years.

"We're all wretched, Lord Bromby. We all fall short of God's glory." Were they really having this conversation? Could it be that God had carefully orchestrated this moment for such a purpose? "We are told that is why we need a savior."

"And you believe that too?"

David nodded. "I do, sir."

Bromby raised to his feet, sighed, and shook his head. "Maybe one day, I will as well, Mr. Beringer." He reached inside his coat and produced a sealed letter. He held it in his hand, staring at it. "I've been debating whether to send this letter to my wife. After much consideration, I think I shall."

"If you like, I can hand deliver it. I shall see Lady Bromby in a few days' time. I'm on my way up to Scotland to visit with my aunt who will provide some of the means by which this orphanage shall be procured. I mean to break my journey in Seaham."

Lord Bromby met David's eyes. "You would deliver it to her?"

David smiled. "Of course."

Bromby nodded, and with one swift motion he handed over the letter. "Here."

David took the letter and glanced at the front of it briefly. The address was already penned on the front. He slid it into his coat pocket.

"Thank you," said Bromby. "You are a good man, Mr. Beringer." He lifted a cane that rested against the back of his chair. "When you see her, tell Lady Bromby … well, tell her—"

"I beg your pardon, milord." Fletcher appeared in the doorway suddenly. "We should depart soon. Your carriage awaits."

"Thank you, Fletcher."

David walked with Lord Bromby through the corridor. Just as they reached the foyer, Bromby turned to him. "Oh, and Mr. Beringer, Broadwell Abbey is yours. I'll have Mr. Hobby draw up the papers." He paused by the door. "My daughter may never live in our ancestral home, but at least she may visit it from time to time."

David nodded and followed Lord Bromby outside to his awaiting carriage.

A great sense of fulfillment surged in his chest. Despite everything, he experienced great happiness in the knowledge that this business transaction, so simple and common in its nature, would help so many. He thought of the face of the orphans—their desperation and need—and an excitement he hadn't felt in some time filled him. They would be fed and clothed and educated. Somehow God would bring good from bad.

Lord Bromby waved to him before the carriage pulled away, and David stood and watched until it had reached the end of Piccadilly Terrace. Then it turned and disappeared.

Forty-Three

April 1816
Dover

Bromby was late. The ship was about to sail, yet he was still striding down the street from the hotel in a desperate attempt to make this voyage.

He fairly ran across the street to the pier where he could just make out John Hobby's form, waiting with crossed arms and a tapping foot. "Bromby!" he called out to him. "We'd nearly despaired of you. Everyone is aboard. The captain is ready to leave without you."

"I overslept," Bromby panted as he caught up to his friend. Together they walked down the quay.

"Good heavens," said Hobby. "I had to beg them to wait."

As they stepped aboard the ship, Bromby's balance was compromised and he caught Hobby's arm to right himself. Nearly the moment Bromby's foot touched the ship's deck, the vessel began to move away from the dock.

"I had your coach put aboard early this morning," said Hobby, "in case the bailiffs thought to travel to Dover to claim it."

"You did well in this," said Bromby, still trying to catch his breath. He stood along the railing and watched the land move away.

Hobby smiled over at him. "This is a bit like days of old, is it not? You and I traveling together once more?"

Bromby nodded. "Yes. Those were some of the best times of my life."

Workers walked along the dock, coiling ropes, and shuttling crates. The English world would soon disappear from his sights—the white cliffs would turn to blue, and choppy British seas would transform to placid Mediterranean waters.

Despite the already rough waters that soured his stomach, he relished the sun on his face and the salty sea air in his nostrils.

"We have a long journey before us," said Hobby.

"I shall enjoy it." Bromby looked out at the sea. The solitude would give him time to think—something he hadn't been able to do in some time. As he glimpsed the white cliffs of the coastline, a sudden nostalgia overtook him—a funny little pain in the pit of his stomach for the loss of his home.

"Perhaps I will return next spring," he said.

Hobby's eyebrows raised. "That is the first I've heard you mention coming back to England."

Bromby glanced at Hobby and smiled. "Yes, that will be my plan. A year in Italy—or even in Switzerland—will do the trick."

"And Isabella and Ada?" Hobby spoke their names gently, almost reverently.

Bromby inhaled sharply as his stomach rolled with a sudden wave of seasickness. "A year's separation might change Isabella's heart toward me. Perhaps a reconciliation at that time would not be out of the question."

Hobby nodded but said nothing.

"Farewell." Bromby spoke the word aloud and into the winds, but it occurred to him that the word might form the foundation of a new poem. Later that night he would write it. Perhaps he would publish it.

Farewell, hearts pulled asunder,
And if the separation last,
Then I shall never wonder
At the pain that holds me fast.
My loss is that of home and heart
But never shall I blame thee, love,
Would that I yet remained a part
Of life and blessings from above.
Farewell.

Forty-Four

Isabella was overjoyed to see David again.

He entered Seacrest Hall with a reserved manner, but his sky-blue eyes reflected genuine happiness at seeing her again.

Lady Bankmill fussed over him, making certain tea was served and insisting he join the family for dinner.

Isabella, Lady Bankmill, and David settled in the drawing room. Mathilde sat nearby with Ada upon her lap.

The dimples in David's cheeks creased as he gazed at the little girl, and something inside Isabella twisted. David's terrible misfortune with young ladies had left him undeservedly alone.

"What a bonny lass she is." David adopted a Scottish accent for the sentiment. "She has your eyes, Lady Bromby."

Ada gurgled and made high-pitched noises as Mathilde held her in the air, then returned the little girl to her lap and bounced her up and down. Isabella motioned to Mathilde to bring Ada to her, and Mathilde rose from her chair and placed the baby in Isabella's arms. She snuggled her close. "She is the most wonderful gift I've ever received, Mr. Beringer."

Lady Bankmill rose, moved toward Isabella, and stooped to take Ada out of her daughter's arms. "Come little Ada. You and I will take a turn about the house. What do you say to that?"

As Lady Bankmill carried Ada from the room, Mathilde gathered her embroidery and bent over it, working furiously with needle and thread.

Isabella was almost afraid to ask David any questions, although he probably carried news of Bromby, as well as what everyone in town was saying.

David finally broke the silence. "Are you happy to be back in Durham, Lady Bromby? Will you ever return to London, do you think?"

Isabella inhaled sharply. She didn't know how to answer. Seaham was beautiful, but it was also lonely and remote, and she couldn't imagine her days stretching out with nothing beyond walks by the sea and an occasional benevolent visit with a sick friend or a bed-bound elderly villager. "I do not know, Mr. Beringer. Perhaps for the immediate future, Ada and I shall stay here. But I hope to one day return to London."

He nodded. "I understand."

Isabella smiled. "I have been thinking ... perhaps there is some bit of good I could do in the world."

"I have no doubt there is much good you can do in the world, Lady Bromby." David averted his gaze and shifted in his seat. "I have a bit of news. I hope you will think it is good news."

Isabella sat forward in her chair. "Indeed? I long for good news."

"I have purchased Broadwell Abbey."

A band of memories pulsed through her brain at the mention of the place—some favorable, some regretful. For so long she'd waited to hear that the place had sold, that Bromby was finally free of the place and it's hold over his family. And now David had purchased it? What was she to feel about this news? "What? But why?"

"Broadwell Abbey will be the location of the foundling hospital. As you know, I have been searching for some time for the right location, and as the property was sizable and available, I purchased it."

Isabella glimpsed David's face, his eyes filled with eagerness, hopefulness. Finally, she smiled. "I must confess I'm surprised. I'd no idea you considered Broadwell Abbey for such a purpose."

"The decision was quite sudden. I ... er ... visited Piccadilly Terrace just last week and spoke to Lord Bromby about it."

Her heart pinched a little. She almost feared hearing news of him. "Oh? And, how was he?"

"He is going abroad. To Italy. He claims public sentiment is so hostile toward him that he finds the proposition of staying in England impossible."

Isabella had suspected that Bromby might leave England. He had threatened to do so for such a long time. "He will stay indefinitely, I have no doubt. He always preferred the exotic spoils of the Mediterranean region."

David reached into his coat pocket. He pulled out a sealed letter and extended it toward her. "He asked me to give you this."

Isabella's hand shook as she took it. She had received correspondence from him since their separation, but that had all stopped after her father's letter. She looked down at Bromby's handwriting on the parchment. "Was Mrs. Morley traveling with him?"

"No. He was quite alone. Only Fletcher, I believe."

Relief flooded her.

"I know I'm bold to tell you this, but Lord Bromby did suggest that he regretted his conduct toward you."

Isabella looked up. "That is surprising." It was hard to believe that he would acknowledge any wrongdoing, much less regret it.

"And may I say that we had a most interesting conversation before his departure. Lord Bromby may not be as eternally lost as we all feared. I believe there is some hope for him … in the future, perhaps."

Isabella laid the letter on the table next to her. For now, she would enjoy David's company. "I shall read it later."

He stood suddenly. "It is a beautiful day. Shall we walk in the garden with Ada?"

Isabella turned to the young Frenchwoman sitting quietly in the corner. "Mathilde? Would you fetch Ada from Mamma and then favor us with your company?"

She smiled. "*Mais oui,* madame."

David, Isabella, Mathilde, and Ada made their way out into the afternoon spring sunshine. There was only a hint of coolness left over from a harsh and stormy winter, but no rain marred its beauty. They walked along the grounds. Flowers of purple and pink were in bloom, and the foliage was especially green from a large amount of recent rain.

"I am happy you have purchased Broadwell Abbey. Now I may visit it knowing that it is in your hands. One who is doing good in the world." She smiled at him.

"I will do my best." Their walking slowed until it stopped. He turned to look at her. "Just before I left Lord Bromby's company, he said something that struck me as strange."

Isabella could only imagine.

David continued. "He said that although his daughter would never live at Broadwell Abbey, at least she would visit from time to time. That made him glad. Since he has no idea of that happening, I thought the assumption odd."

"Perhaps he is aware of our close friendship, and from that he assumes Ada will enjoy the benefit of seeing your good deed put into place."

David's gaze dropped. "You will always be welcome there, and I hope you shall both visit often."

She breathed in. "Perhaps we shall. Perhaps I will join your cause, Mr. Beringer, and bring some hope from the word of God to an orphan in need. Whatever I do from here on out, it will be in the service of the Lord."

"That is admirable."

A sense of hope filled her. "I'm not exactly sure what he wishes me to do yet, but I feel it will involve those who are hurting in some way. I don't believe my life is yet over."

"Of course, it's not. You are a young woman with many more years before you. I daresay there is much for you to do. You are an important person to your parents, to Ada, and I know how much Rebecca values your friendship."

"And I hers. And…" she paused. Should she say more? She didn't want to seem too forward or indecorous. "And I value your friendship, Mr. Beringer. It was good of you to come here to see me … especially when my name is under a veil of scrutiny."

His eyes leveled. "I don't believe you are the member of this union most scrutinized, Lady Bromby. Those who are so fortunate as to claim an acquaintance with you know you are not to blame."

She cringed at the compliment. The last few weeks in Durham had given her time to reflect upon this very matter. "Oh, but I am, Mr. Beringer. I am to blame for not listening when my friends and family warned me. When God whispered in my ear that I should not marry Lord Bromby. I wanted what I wanted. At any cost. And as you see, the price was high."

David's gaze lowered. "You will always have my friendship. I can promise you that. And if there is ever anything that you or Ada need, you shall have it."

"Thank you. But you've already done too much."

For a moment that familiar, sad droop returned to his eyes and his face flushed. "I would do more … if I could."

She continued quickly. "I don't know why you chose to bestow your generosity on my husband, but I'm sure he has never shown you his gratitude. For my part, at least, I wish to do so now. Thank you, Mr. Beringer."

"It is my greatest pleasure to help you, Lady Bromby—and if it helps Lord Bromby as well, then all the better. May Broadwell Abbey be a place of optimism and light for the children whose lives have been so dark."

May light emerge from darkness.

They walked on in silence.

That evening, after calling for his carriage, Isabella and David stood in the foyer, draped in shadows cast by the lit candles.

She swallowed hard against the lump in her throat. "Will you leave early tomorrow morning for Scotland?" Her voice faltered.

David looked down at her. "Yes, as early as may be."

He did not touch her, but the sincerity in his gaze reassured her as though he had taken her hand. "Lady Bromby, my only desire is to see you and Ada happy and safe."

The sounds of the approaching horses' feet broke the moment. David donned his hat and with one more glance into her eyes, he bowed. The servant opened the door, revealing the sight of an awaiting carriage and footman holding lanterns. David stepped into the doorway and turned. "We shall see each other again very soon."

She nodded. "Yes."

Once David had departed, Isabella returned to the table in the drawing room where she had left the letter. Sinking onto a chair, she broke the familiar seal and stared at the elegant hand. She looked away again, fearful of reading the words. Then, with a deep breath, she steeled herself and read.

April 1816
Piccadilly Terrace

Dearest Isabella,

Tomorrow I will leave England—possibly forever. Tonight, I sit in this empty house and lament your absence.

What have I to say in defense of my miserable conduct which you do not already know? I could fabricate excuses and reasons, but you would see through them.

Dearest Bell, you knew all too well the deplorable nature of my heart and my soul, yet you loved me despite it. How could I have expected that you would stay within a house so wretched with the vexations I brought upon it? I have only myself to blame for your absence now.

I bear you no ill will for your decision to quit my house and my company. I did wrong to you and Ada, and it pains me that my daughter shan't know me. Will you tell her of me? I would beg that you tell her of my good qualities, few as they may be. Or perhaps, at least spare her my worst ones.

Perhaps, by some miracle of God, we shall one day be reunited. What was once so hard for me to convey in your presence now seems so easy in your absence. I shall always love you, Bell. As I once told your excellent aunt, Lady Melwood, you were too perfect for me. I still consider you the kindest, most forbearing soul I have ever known. To say I am sorry to have caused you grief would never be enough.

May God richly bless you and Ada.

Yours always,

B

When Isabella finished reading the letter, she folded it carefully and carried it upstairs to her room. Should she burn it? No, she would not. Instead, she placed it at the bottom of a coffer underneath her childhood Bible and locked the chest. In not burning the letter, she forgave him, and one day, she would show it to Ada as proof that he had loved them both.

Symbolically, placing the letter at the bottom of a coffer underneath her Bible represented much more. She no longer worshipped Bromby. Never again would her regard for him be higher than that of her Lord. Her emotions were secured and managed by someone much stronger and infinitely more worthy.

As she placed the coffer at the bottom of her drawer, she sat back on the bed and sighed. For the first time in four long years there was peace in her heart. And freedom.

Author's Note

It took me nearly twenty years to write this novel.

In 1998, while in graduate school, I took a class on the Romantic poets as part of my degree requirements. Although the poetry itself was beautiful, I was much more interested in the lives of the poets. When the professor lectured on Lord George Gordon Byron, I got cold chills. I remember thinking, "I want to write a novel based on that guy." I tried a few times over the years, but a completed novel never materialized.

I'm glad I waited so long. The novel I would've written in 1998 would've been very different from this one.

I was always drawn to tortured souls and could easily have married one myself (I dated far too many of them), but fortunately, God saved me from the pain of the unequal yoke.

Lady Caroline Lamb (the person upon whom the character Lady Catherine Lyons is based) said that Byron was "mad, bad, and dangerous to know." Indisputably, Byron was a celebrity who enjoyed rock-star fame after the publication of his narrative poem, Childe Harold. During 1812-1815, he was in constant demand throughout London Society, and women fell madly in love with him. Various historical accounts claim ladies fainted when he walked into a room.

When reading any of the many biographies written about him, it's easy to label Byron a rake and a cad. In actuality, he was a complicated individual. Highly intelligent, talented, and sensitive, but also tormented by his own sin nature. A troubled childhood contributed to many of his indulgences, vices, and destructive tendencies.

His marriage to Annabella Milbanke was a disaster. They may have been equal in status, but their spiritual life was vastly dissimilar. She was prim, proper, and devout in her Christian faith, whereas Byron was a mixture of agnosticism and Calvinism. His childhood governess, Nurse Gray, was physically and sexually abusive and used religion as a weapon against her young charge. Byron never found comfort in Christianity and professed to be inherently cursed, insisting all Byrons were doomed.

Although this novel is heavily influenced by the relationship between Byron and Annabella, and many of the incidents depicted therein actually occurred, I have tempered some of the circumstances for literary palatability. I knew I would be taking the story in a different—more redeeming direction—from the historical Lord and Lady Byron marriage. Obviously, the character's names are different, and some characters are fabricated. David and Rebecca are creations, but John Hobby is a form of John Cam Hobhouse, Byron's closest friend; Lady Melwood is a version of the meddling, but highly esteemed Lady Melbourne.

The main purpose for writing this novel (and this series) is to explore the dilemma of what happens when hero-worship of a mortal man dangerously overpowers love for God. God's decree that Christians should not be unequally yoked is as true today as it was in 1815, and women were as ensnared by physical beauty and charm then as they are now. In the case of London Society, a man's financial state was often more important than his spiritual state. Many tragic and unhappy marriages were made in this way.

Additionally, I wanted to show that although choices have consequences, God is faithful and just to forgive. All things work for good for those who love the Lord.

My heart goes out to those young women in love with the Byrons and Brombys of the modern day. May God preserve them from marriages that will break their hearts.

About the Author

Megan Whitson Lee is passionate about tough, relevant topics and the redemptive power of God. She is the author of the contemporary novel, *Suburban Dangers*, which addresses sex-trafficking. Her self-published novel, *Captives*, was the winner of the 2016 Blue Ridge Mountain Christian Writers Conference Director's Choice Award. It was also a 2016 Selah Award finalist.

Megan has a Master of Fine Arts in Creative Writing from George Mason University. She is an editor for Pelican Book Group and teaches high school English in Virginia where she lives with her husband and two greyhounds.

www.ingramcontent.com/pod-product-compliance
Lightning Source LLC
Chambersburg PA
CBHW072110020726
47501CB00003B/790